Praise for *New York Times* bestselling author Jeaniene Frost, and The Night Huntress Series

'With compelling writing and a new twist on the classic vampire mythos, *Halfway to the Grave* swept me in from the first page. Sympathetic characters, a foreboding and moody world, kick-butt action, and deliciously dark and forbidden romance abound. *Halfway to the Grave* is sure to please fans of Kim Harrison and Kelly Armstrong. Jeaniene Frost has a winner on her hands. I loved it'
New York Times bestselling author Yasmine Galnorn

'*Halfway to the Grave* has breathless action, a roller-coaster plot, flashes of dark humor, and a love story that will leave you screaming for more. I devoured it in a single sitting and I can't wait for the sequel. Sign me up for Jeaniene Frost's fan list'
New York Times bestselling author Ilona Andrews

'Jeaniene Frost is dynamite. *Halfway to the Grave* is dark, sexy, and supernatural, blended with a touch of humor. I dare you to disagree – Cat will have you staked in five seconds flat'
USA Today bestselling author Cheyenne McCray

'Ms Frost's undead world is fascinating, populated by unique and spooky characters, and led by one of the most entertainingly kick-ass heroines in the paranormal genre'
Fresh Fiction

'Take one half-human/half-vampire female with serious anger and parental issues, add in a sexy ancient vampire with his own agenda, and you have the makings for a truly combustible series'
Romantic Times

Also by Jeaniene Frost

The Night Huntress Series

Halfway to the Grave

One Foot in the Grave

At Grave's End

Destined for an Early Grave

AT GRAVE'S END

Jeaniene Frost

The right of Jeaniene Frost to be identified as the author of this
work has been asserted by her in accordance with the
Copyright, Designs and Patents Act 1988.

First published in Great Britain in 2010 by
Gollancz
An imprint of the Orion Publishing Group
Orion House, 5 Upper St Martin's Lane, London WC2H 9EA
An Hachette UK Company

1 3 5 7 9 10 8 6 4 2

A CIP catalogue record for this book is available
from the British Library

ISBN 978 0 575 09380 5

Printed in Great Britain by
Clays Ltd, St Ives plc

www.jeanienefrost.com

www.orionbooks.co.uk

The Orion Publishing Group's policy is to use papers that are
natural, renewable and recyclable products and made from wood
grown in sustainable forests. The logging and manufacturing
processes are expected to conform to the environmental regulations
of the country of origin.

To my husband,
for accepting without judging,
loving without conditions,
laughing instead of getting angry,
and thinking of others before yourself.
I'm the lucky one.

Oπe

The man smiled and I let my gaze linger over his face. His eyes were a lovely shade of pale blue. Their color reminded me of a Siberian husky, except the person sitting next to me was no animal. Of course, he wasn't human, either.

"I have to leave now, Nick," I said. "Thanks for the drinks."

He stroked my arm. "Have another one. Let me enjoy your beautiful face a little longer."

I stifled a snort. Wasn't he flattering? But if he liked my face so much, then his eyes wouldn't have been glued to my cleavage.

"All right. Bartender . . ."

"Let me guess." The loud voice came from across the bar. An unfamiliar face grinned at me. "A gin and tonic, right, Reaper?"

Shit.

Nick froze. Then he did what I was afraid he'd do—he ran.

"Code Red!" I barked, vaulting after the fleeing figure. Heavily armed men in black clothes sprinted into the bar, shoving the patrons aside.

Nick threw people at me as I went after him. Screaming, flailing bodies hit me, making my attempts to catch them and fling a silver knife through Nick's heart even more difficult. One of my blades landed in Nick's chest, but too far center to have hit his heart. Still, I couldn't just let those people splatter to the floor like so much garbage. Nick might think of people that way. I didn't.

My team fanned out, guarding all the exits and attempting to herd the remaining patrons out of the way.

Nick reached the far end of the bar and glanced around frantically. There was me, advancing with my silver knives, and my men with their Desert Eagle handguns pointed at him.

"You're surrounded," I stated the obvious. "Don't make me angry, you won't think I'm pretty anymore when I'm angry. Drop the girls."

He had two of them in his grip, one hand on each vulnerable throat. Seeing the terror in those girls' eyes made anger flare through me. Only cowards hid behind hostages. Or murderers, like Nick.

"I leave, they live, Reaper," Nick hissed, no romance in his tone any longer. "I should have known. Your skin's too perfect to be human, even if your heart beats and your eyes aren't gray."

"Colored contacts. Modern science's a bitch."

Nick's icy blue eyes bled to glowing vampire green and his fangs slid out.

"It was an accident," he yelled. "I didn't mean to kill her, I just took too much."

An accident? Oh, he *had* to be kidding me. "Her heartbeat slowing down would have warned you," I replied. "Don't try that accident crap on me, I live with a vampire, and he hasn't had an 'oops' moment once."

If possible, Nick looked even more ashen. "And if you're here . . ."

"That's right, mate."

The accent was English, and the tone was lethal. Invisible waves of power rolled over my back as my men parted to let Bones, the vampire I most trusted—and loved—through.

Nick's gaze didn't shift, which I'd been hoping for. No, his eyes didn't leave me as he suddenly yanked my blade from himself and then stabbed one of the girls in the chest.

I gasped, catching her instinctively when Nick threw her at me.

"Help her!" I yelled to Bones, who'd lunged at Nick instead. With that wound, unless Bones healed her, she had only seconds to live.

I had time to hear Bones mutter a curse before he spun around, abandoning his pursuit of Nick to drop to his knees beside the girl. I vaulted after Nick, doing some cursing myself. Gunshots went off, but only a few. With the rest of the bar patrons still scrambling for the doors, plus Nick holding the other girl like a shield, my team couldn't just open fire. Nick knew that, and so did I.

Nick leapt across the heads of the crowd in a gravity-defying burst, flinging the girl at a member of my team as if she were a weapon. Helpless, the nearby soldier fell back with the girl on top of him, just in time for Nick to swoop down and yank his gun away.

I flung three more of my knives, but with all the jostling from the people around me, my aim was off. Nick let out a yell as they pieced his back, missing his heart. Then he turned and fired at me.

I had a fraction of a second to realize that if I ducked, those bullets would hit the people around me instead. They weren't half vampire like I was; it would likely kill them. So I braced myself . . . and was spun around in a blur in the next heartbeat, my head jammed into Bones's chest while three hard vibrations shook him. The bullets meant for me.

Bones let me go, whirling around and flying across the room to Nick, who tried to snatch another hostage. Nick didn't make it. Bones plowed into him hard enough for both of them to smash through the wall. I ran, hopping over people, in time to see Bones twist his knife in Nick's chest.

I relaxed. Silver twisted through the heart meant curtains for Nick—and any vampire.

Bones gave one last twist for good measure and then drew his blade out, his eyes flickering over me.

"You're bleeding," he said, concern creasing his face.

I touched my cheek, where someone's belt or shoe or whatever had scored me when Nick was using people like human speed bumps to slow me down.

"You've been shot, and you're worried about a scratch on *me*?"

Bones came over, touching my face. "I heal instantly, luv. You don't."

Even though I knew what he said was true, I couldn't help but feel his back to reassure myself that his skin was smooth, no more shredded flesh from the bullets.

"Speaking of, there are dozens of injured people here you need to heal. You can get to my scratch later."

Bones ignored that, drawing his thumb across a fang and touching the cut it made first to my cheek, then to my mouth.

"You always come first for me, Kitten."

No one else called me that. To my mother, I was Catherine. My team called me Cat. To the undead world, I was the Red Reaper.

I licked the blood off, knowing that arguing with him was useless. Besides, I couldn't help but feel the same way when it came to Bones.

"All right," I said, the burning now gone from my cheek. "Let's wrap this up."

The girl Nick had thrown at one of my men was lying a short distance away. Bones gave her a sweep of the eyes, saw she wasn't physically hurt, and moved on.

"That's a . . . he's not . . ." she started to babble, seeing his fangs and glowing green eyes.

I patted her shoulder. "Don't worry. You won't remember any of this in ten minutes."

"B-but what . . . ?"

I ignored the rest of her stammering and started checking on the other people. No one seemed to have gotten killed, thank God, aside from Nick. Bones had healed the other girl who'd been taken hostage. Now the only thing on her chest was a blood smear and a tear in her shirt where my knife had been. We'd gotten lucky.

"Damage report?" I asked Cooper, who was kneeling over one of the patrons who'd been chucked at me.

"Not too bad, Commander. Multiple fractures, abrasions, contusions, the usual."

I watched as Bones picked his way through the injured to force the ones in serious condition to swallow a few drops of his blood. Nothing worked like vampire blood for healing.

"Another Code Red, *querida*," one of my captains, Juan, observed. He pointed to the loudmouthed vampire across the room being restrained by Dave, our other team captain. Dave was a ghoul, which meant he could hold the wriggling vamp. None of the humans on my team could have managed to.

I nodded. "Unfortunately."

Juan sighed. "That's three times in a row. You're not easily camouflaged, even with a different eye and hair color."

He wasn't saying anything I didn't know. I caught Bones's look, and his face nearly screamed, *I told you so*.

Things *had* gotten more dangerous in recent months. Too many people in the undead world now knew there was a half-vampire human who hunted them, and they knew what to look for.

I glared at the captive vampire. "Thanks for blowing my cover."

"I only wanted to buy you a drink," the vampire sputtered. "I wasn't even sure it was you, but your skin . . . it looked too perfect to be human, no matter that you breathe. And you're a redhead, I saw that when you raised your arm. The shadow of hair there wasn't blond."

Incredulous, I hefted my arm and inspected its shaved crease. Now I'd heard everything.

Dave studied my armpit, too. "He's right. Of course,

who'd think people would be checking out your armpit?"

Who indeed? I ran a frustrated hand through my dyed blond hair. There were no more colors left for me. I'd done black and brunette, too, to try and throw off my targets, plus wearing multiple-colored contacts, but lately it hadn't helped.

"Juan, hold these," I said, handing him my knives. After blinking several times, I got the brown contacts out. Ah, relief! They had been annoying me all night.

"Let me see them," the vampire suddenly asked. "I've heard, but can you show me?"

Dave tightened his grip. "She's not a carnival freak."

"No?" I sighed, and then let my eyes blaze forth.

Their new glow shone like twin emerald headlights, exactly as all vampire eyes could. Indisputable evidence of my mixed heritage.

"All right, start talking. Tell me why I shouldn't kill you."

"My name's Ernie. I'm from Two-Chain's line. Two-Chain is a friend of Bones's, so you can't just kill me."

"With friends like you, who needs enemies?" Bones said scathingly, gliding over to me once he'd finished healing the injured humans and instilling their new memories with vampire mind control.

"Bloody hung a target around her neck by screeching her name out," Bones continued. "Just for that, I should rip off your stones and feed them to you."

For some people, that would just be a figure of speech. Not Bones. He never bluffed. Apparently Ernie had heard of his reputation. He crossed his legs.

"Please don't." Now he went from negotiating to

pleading. "I didn't mean her any harm, I swear to Cain."

"Right." Coldly. "But you'll need more than the maker of all vampires to help you if you're lying. Kitten, I'd like to box him and take him back to the compound, until I can verify that he really is one of Two-Chain's people."

Bones was deferring to me, since in work matters, I was in charge. In matters of personal vampire affairs, however, Bones outranked me by more than two centuries.

"Sure. He'll hate the capsule, though."

Bones laughed a trifle grimly. He knew from firsthand experience how unpleasant our vampire transportation was.

"If he's lying, that'll be the least of his concerns."

Cooper came up to us. "Commander, the capsule's prepped and ready."

"Strap him in. Let's get this scene contained as quickly as possible."

My second-in-command, Tate Bradley, walked into the club. His indigo gaze swept over the room, seeking me out.

"Cat, this is the third time you've been recognized."

As if I didn't know. "We'll just have to come up with a better disguise. Fast, before the job next week."

Tate didn't let my tone dissuade him. "All this risk is going to get you killed. One of these days, someone's going to recognize you and just pull a fucking gun instead of offering to buy you a drink. This is getting too dangerous, even for your standards."

"Don't tell me what to do, Tate. I'm in charge, so you don't get to play all Papa Bear with me."

"You know my feelings for you aren't *paternal*."

Before I could blink, Bones had Tate by the throat with his feet dangling several feet in the air. I was so annoyed by Tate's comment, it took me a moment to tell Bones to let him down.

If I hadn't known Tate for several years, I'd throttle him myself for how he continued to bait Bones over me.

Instead of kicking or fighting, Tate managed a grimace that resembled a smile.

"Whatcha gonna do, Crypt Keeper?" he garbled. "Kill me?"

"Put him down, Bones. There are bigger problems than his attitude," I went on. "We have to finish up here, check on Ernie's lineage, give our report to Don, and then get home. Come on, moonlight's burning."

"One day, you're going to push me too far," Bones growled, letting Tate drop to the ground.

I gave Tate a warning look. That's what I was worried about, too. Tate was my friend and I cared for him, but his feelings for me ran along very different lines. It didn't help that lately Tate seemed determined to show those feelings, especially around Bones.

Which was like waving a red flag at a bull. Vampires weren't known for their gracious sharing tendencies. So far, I'd been able to prevent a real fight from breaking out between them, but I knew if Tate ever made Bones truly lose his temper, he wouldn't live long enough to regret it.

"Senator Thompson will be pleased that his daughter's murderer was punished," my uncle and boss, Don Williams, said later when all of us were seated in his office. "Cat, I heard you were recognized again. This is the third time."

"I have an idea," I suggested. "Maybe you, Tate, and Juan can line up and all shout it from the rooftops. I know it's the third fucking time, Don!"

My language didn't ruffle him. Don hadn't been around for the first twenty-two years of my life, but he'd been front row and center for the last five. I hadn't even known I was related to him until a few months ago. Don hid our family connection from me, since he didn't want me knowing that the vampire who—allegedly—raped my mother was his brother.

"We're going to need to get another female to play bait," Don stated. "You can still lead the team, Cat, but there's too much liability to have you dangling on the hook any longer. I know Bones agrees."

That made me give a sharp bark of laughter. Bones liked me risking my life on a regular basis about as much as I liked my father.

"Of course he does. Hell, Bones would dance on your grave if I quit my job."

Bones arched an unperturbed brow, not disputing that.

"You'd just have him pull Don out from under the dirt, Cat," Dave said with a wry smile.

I smiled back. That's what Bones had done to Dave after Dave had been killed on a job. I'd known vampire blood was a powerful healing elixir, but I hadn't known that if a mortally wounded person swallowed some before dying, he or she could be brought back later as a ghoul.

Don coughed. "Be that as it may, everyone agrees it's become too dangerous for you to continue on as bait. Think of the bystanders, Cat. Whenever there's a Code Red, more of them stand a chance of getting killed."

He was right. Tonight was a prime example. Vampires and ghouls got pretty desperate when they were cornered. Add in the fact that I didn't have a reputation for taking prisoners, and what did they have to lose by taking as many humans down with them as they could?

"Shit." It was an acknowledgment of defeat. "But we don't have any females on our team, thanks to your sexist rules, Don, and we have another job next week. That's not enough time to round up a qualified female soldier, break the bad news to her about vampires and ghouls, train her to defend herself, and then have her dolled up and ready for action."

There was silence after this pronouncement. Don tugged at his eyebrow, Juan whistled, and Dave cracked his neck.

"What about Belinda?" Tate suggested.

I gaped at him. "But she's a murderer."

Tate grunted. "Yeah, but she's performed well as a training toy with the men. Based on her good behavior, we've promised to let her go in ten years. Maybe taking her out on jobs will be a good indicator of whether she's turned over a new leaf like she's claimed."

Bones gave a slight shrug. "It's risky, but Belinda's a vampire, so she's strong enough for the work. Plus she's fetching enough to pose as bait, and she'd require no training."

I didn't like Belinda, and that wasn't just because she'd once tried to kill me. She also had a history with Bones that involved his birthday party, another vampire named Annette, two other girls, and very little talking.

"Don?" I asked.

"We'll try Belinda next week," he said at last. "If she can't handle it, then we'll find a suitable replacement."

Using a vampire as bait to trap and kill other vampires. It was almost as crazy as what we'd been doing, which was using me, a half vampire, for the same thing.

"There's one more thing to discuss," Don said. "When Bones joined us over three months ago, it was with conditions. His most significant contribution to our operation hasn't been requested . . . until today."

I tensed, because I knew what that meant. To my left, Bones lifted a bored brow.

"I won't welsh on our agreement, so name the man you want me to change into a vampire."

"Me."

The single word came from Tate. My gaze swung to him.

"You hate vampires!" I burst out. "Why would you want to turn into one?"

"I hate *him*," was Tate's immediate agreement. "But you're the one who said it's the person who makes the character of a vampire, not the other way around. Which means I would have hated Bones when he was human, too."

Nice, I thought, still shocked by Tate's intention. *Good to know he was keeping an open mind about the undead. Yeah, right.*

Bones raked Don with a look. "I'll need time to prepare him for the transition, and let's get one thing clear straightaway." He turned his attention back to Tate. "It won't make her love you."

I glanced away. Bones had said out loud what I'd

been worried about, too. God, I hoped I had nothing to do with Tate's decision to be the first person on the team to turn into a vampire. *Please let him not do something that drastic because of me.*

"I love you as a friend, Tate." My voice was soft. I hated to say this in front of a group, but they all knew how Tate felt. He hadn't been very shy about it recently. "You're one of my best friends, in fact. But a friend is the only way I see you."

Don cleared his throat. "Unless you or Bones have a legitimate concern, Tate's personal feelings are irrelevant."

"Motivation is my concern," Bones said at once. "What if bitterness overwhelms him when he can't pry her from my side, and let me assure you, mate, you won't. So the question remains—is he choosing this for himself, or for her? If he does it for the wrong reason, he'll have plenty of time to regret it."

At last Tate spoke. "My reasons are my own, and my commitment to my job won't suffer for them."

Bones gave him a thin smile. "In a hundred years this job and your boss will be long gone, but you'll still be my creation. You'll owe me your fealty unless I permit you your own line or you challenge me and take it. Sure you want to sign on for that?"

"I can handle it," was all Tate said.

Bones shrugged. "Then it's settled. If all goes well, soon you'll have your vampire, Don. Like I promised."

Don had an expression that was both grim and satisfied. "I hope I won't regret it."

So did I.

two

I WOKE UP ALONE IN OUR BED LATER. A SLEEPY glance around showed that Bones wasn't in the bedroom. Curious, I went downstairs and found him on the couch in our family room.

Bones was staring out the window at the mountain ridge in the distance. Vampires had the ability to sit with utter stillness, as immobile as statues. Certainly, Bones was beautiful enough to be a work of art. Moonlight made his hair look lighter than its deep brown shade. He'd changed it from blond back to its natural color to be less noticeable when we were on jobs. Those faint silvery rays also caressed the dips and hollows of Bones's crystal skin, highlighting his lean, rippled physique. His darker brows almost matched the color of his eyes when they weren't lit up by vampire green. Shadows made his high cheekbones look even more perfectly etched when he turned his head and saw me standing there.

"Hey." I tightened the robe I'd thrown on, feeling his tension in the air. "Is something wrong?"

"Nothing's wrong, luv. I'm just a touch nervous, actually."

That got my attention. I sat next to him. "You never get nervous."

Bones smiled. "I have something for you. But I don't know if you'll want it."

"Why wouldn't I want it?"

Bones slid off the couch to kneel in front of me. I still didn't get it. Only when I saw the small black velvet box in his other hand did it hit me.

"Catherine." If I hadn't already guessed, his one and only use of my real name would have clued me in. "Catherine Kathleen Crawfield, will you marry me?"

It didn't hit me until right then how much I'd wanted Bones to ask me that. Sure, we were married under vampire law, but having Bones cut his hand, slap it over mine, and declare me to be his wife didn't feel quite like the white wedding fantasies I'd had as a little girl. Plus, Bones had done it to prevent an all-out brawl between his people and his sire Ian's people over the issue of who had dibs on me.

Looking at Bones now made all my childish imaginings pale into nothingness, however. True, Bones was a former-human-gigolo-turned-vampire-hitman instead of a charming prince, but no fairy tale heroine could have felt the way I did, with the man I was insanely in love with asking me on bended knee to be his wife. My throat closed off with emotion. How had I ever gotten so lucky?

Bones made a noise of amused exasperation. "Of all the times for you to be speechless. If you don't mind, choose one response or the other. The suspense is torturing me."

"Yes."

Tears came to my eyes even as I started to laugh at the sheer joy bubbling up inside me.

Something cool and hard slid on my finger. I could barely see it, since my vision was blurred, but I caught a flash of red.

"I had this cut and fashioned into a ring almost five years ago," Bones said. "I know you think I was pressured into binding myself with you before, but that's not true. I'd always intended to marry you, Kitten."

For about the thousandth time, I regretted leaving Bones the way I had years ago. I thought I'd been protecting him. Turned out I was just hurting both of us needlessly.

"How could you be nervous about asking me to marry you, Bones? I'd die for you. Why wouldn't I want to live for you as well?"

He gave me a long, deep kiss, whispering onto my lips only when I pulled away out of breathlessness.

"I know it's what I intend to do."

Later, I was stretched out in his arms, waiting for dawn, which wasn't far off.

"Do you want to elope, or do you want to do the whole big wedding thing?" I asked sleepily.

Bones smiled. "You know vampires, pet. Always like a fancy show, we do. Also, I know our vampire binding didn't feel like a real wedding to you, so I want you to have something that does."

I gave an amused grunt. "Wow, a big wedding. We'll have a hell of a time explaining the menu to a potential caterer. Choice of entrée: beef or seafood for the humans, raw meat and body parts for the ghouls . . . and a keg of hot fresh blood at the bar for the vampires. God, I can just picture my mother's face."

Bones's smile turned devilish and he leapt up. I watched him, curious, as he went to the other side of the room and dialed his cell phone.

"Justina."

I vaulted after him as soon as I heard my mother's name. Bones sprinted away from me, fighting back his laughter and continuing to speak.

"Yes, it's Bones. Now really, that's such a foul name to call me . . . um hmm, same to you, I'm sure . . ."

"Give me that phone," I demanded.

He ignored me, darting out of my reach. Ever since my father, my mother hated vampires with a pathological passion. She'd even tried to have Bones killed before—twice—which was why he was taking such delight in giving her a little payback now.

"Actually, Justina, I didn't just ring you to chat about what an undead murderer I was . . . right, degenerate whore as well. Did I ever tell you my mum was one? No? Oh, blimey, I come from a long line of whores, in fact . . ."

I sucked in a breath as Bones divulged yet another tidbit about his past to my mother, who must be frothing at the mouth by now.

". . . called to give you the good news. I asked your daughter to marry me and she accepted. Congratulations, I will officially be your son-in-law. Now, do you want me to call you Mum straightaway, or wait until after the wedding?"

I flew through the air in a dive that finally tackled him, wrenching the phone away. Bones was laughing so hard, he had to breathe to get it all out.

"Mom? Are you there? Mom . . . ?"

"You might want to give her a moment, Kitten. I believe she fainted."

*   *   *

There were some days when I felt a pang of wistful regret that I'd never be a mother. Sure, my father had been newly undead enough that he'd managed to impregnate my mother, but as a rule, vampires couldn't reproduce. And I'd never risk passing on my genetic abnormalities to a child by means of artificial insemination, let alone my dangerous lifestyle by adopting one.

Right now, however, I was glad I wasn't a mother. I'd faced some scary sights hunting vampires and ghouls, but hordes of children hyped-up on sugar, squealing as they ran from one video game to the next, while I knew there was no escape for me? Truly frightening.

Bones was outside the Chuck E. Cheese, lucky bastard. It was because of his power level. Other vampires felt him when he was near, like inside, so Bones usually watched the premises until the gig was up and our target knew he or she was being hunted. I lacked the typical undead aura that felt like anything from static electricity to full-blown electrocution, depending on the strength of the vampire. No, I had a beating heart and I breathed, which made me look harmless—to those who didn't know what else to look for, anyway.

Toward that end, I had almost all my skin covered up. Hey, I wasn't playing bait, so I didn't need to wear my usual slut gear. Belinda was the one in a low-cut top with hip-hugging jeans that revealed several inches of her belly. She'd curled her hair and wore makeup, which was a rarity, since as Don's captive, she didn't get out much.

Looking at Belinda, with her blond hair, pouty smile, and eye-popping curves, people would never guess she was a vampire, especially since it was daylight. Even those who *might* believe in vampires still bought the myth that vampires could only come out at night, which, along with the whole sleeping in coffins, being repelled by religious symbols, or being killed by a wooden stake, was wrong.

The little boy next to me tugged my arm. "I'm hungry," he announced.

I was confused. "But you just ate."

He rolled his eyes. "Lady, that was an hour ago."

"Call me Mom, Ethan," I reminded him, fixing a bright smile on my face while I fished out more money. This had to be the strangest job ever. Where Don had gotten a ten-year-old boy to act as a prop, I'll never know. But he had arranged for Ethan to come with us, saying if we spent hours lurking at a Chuck E. Cheese without a child, we'd be suspected of either being pedophiles or—duh—being vampire hunters by our target.

Ethan snatched at my handful of money without waiting for me to peel the bills off.

"Thanks!" he said, and scampered off toward the pizza counter.

Okay, *that* looked authentic—I'd seen kids do the same thing to their parents all day today, plus all day yesterday. Good God, between the food and the endless tokens for games, I'd gone through more money in two days here than I normally did at a week's worth of bar jobs downing multiple gin and tonics. At least this was on Uncle Sam's dime, not mine.

There was only one floor at Chuck E. Cheese's, so that made it easier to keep Belinda in sight without resorting to looming over her. She was in the section to the left of the front door, playing Skee-Ball. She landed yet another perfect throw into the center of the circles. Lights went off while more tickets spat out of the side of the machine. Belinda had a pile of them near her feet, and more than a few admiring fathers as well as kids clustered around her.

But no other vampire was here, even though this Chuck E. Cheese had been linked to the disappearance of a family three weeks ago. Not that any of the patrons here knew that. It was only because a security camera had caught a pair of glowing green eyes in the parking lot that Don even suspected vampires were involved in the family's odd disappearance.

Undead killers liked to hit the same hunting grounds more than once. Which confounded the hell out of me. If vampires or ghouls never went back to the same crime scene, my uncle's special department of Homeland Security would be out of business. Some of them didn't have enough sense to be like lightning, never striking the same place twice.

My cell vibrated. I took it off my belt, glanced at it—and smiled. The number flashing was 911, which meant a vampire had just been seen in the parking lot. I kept my eye on Ethan as I sidled over to where Belinda was. She gave me an irritated glance when I laid a hand on her arm.

"Showtime," I murmured.

"Get your hand off me," she replied without losing her sweet smile.

I squeezed instead. "If you try anything, I'll kill you. And that's only if Bones doesn't beat me to it first."

Belinda's eyes flashed green for a second, but then she shrugged. "Ten more years, then I don't have to deal with you anymore."

I let her go. "That's right. So don't fuck up a better deal than you deserve."

"Don't you need to get away from me, *Reaper*?" she hissed, so low even I could barely hear her. "You don't want to scare the fish away, do you?"

I gave Belinda a cool, evaluating stare before I turned my back and walked away. I'd meant what I said. If Belinda pulled any tricks during this job and endangered one of the many kids here, I'd kill her. But, as the saying went, we were giving her enough rope to hang herself. Now we had to wait and see if she swung from it.

On my way over to Ethan, my cell vibrated again. I glanced at it and mentally groaned. Another 911. That meant there were two vampires. Not good.

I reached Ethan, wanting to keep a sharp eye on him as well as the door. It wasn't long before I saw two men walk in with the distinctive skin and purposeful movements that marked the difference between a regular person and a vampire.

I gave the interior of Chuck E. Cheese's another frustrated glance. With all the children here, this was the worst kind of place to have a showdown with the undead. If I were playing bait, I'd try to maneuver the vamps into the parking lot to minimize the danger to bystanders. But Belinda probably wouldn't care enough to do that. Well, I'd just have to try and help her out.

I grasped Ethan's hand. "It's time," I told him.

His blue-green eyes widened. "The bad people are here?" he whispered.

I doubted Don had explained to Ethan—or his parents, whoever those crazy folks were to let their son do this—what sort of "bad people" we were after. I wasn't about to elaborate, either.

"You don't leave my sight, remember?" I said, soft but stern. "It'll be okay."

He nodded, visibly mustering up his courage. "Okay."

What a good boy.

My cell phone vibrated again, with another series of numbers flashing across the screen.

911–911

"Oh, f— crap," I caught myself just in time.

Ethan blinked up at me. "What's wrong?"

I got a tighter grip on his hand. "Nothing."

That was a lie, of course. I looked up in time to see a third vampire walking in the door. Then a fourth. I saw Belinda pause in her next Skee-Ball toss, look at them, and smile. Widely.

This was going to be a hell of an afternoon.

†HREE

†HE VAMPİRES DİDΠ'† †AKE LOΠG †O ΠO†İCE
Belinda. Maybe they even smelled her before
they saw her, because they weren't inside the place for
a minute before they sidled over to her. I kept a good
grip on Ethan's hand as I heard Belinda exchange
hellos, straining my hearing to make sure she wasn't
saying anything else. Like, *trap* or *Reaper.* So far, so
good. Belinda was just being flirty—with a homicidal
edge to it, inquiring if they were up for eating anyone
here.

"Why do you think we're here?" one of them said
with a smirk. "It ain't for the big fake mouse."

The others laughed. My jaw clenched. Bastards.

"You here with anyone?" another asked, giving Belinda an up-and-down leer.

"Some chick I met and her son," Belinda said dis-
missively. "One of you can eat her, but I call dibs on
the kid."

"Point them out," the dark-haired vampire said.

I glanced away right as Belinda's hand arced up, putting a false smile on my face as I looked at Ethan. *Don't worry. Nothing's going to happen to you.*

"The blonde wearing the black turtleneck sweater and jeans, holding the little boy's hand. That's them."

"Pretty," the brunette drawled, then added quickly, "but not as pretty as you, of course."

"Thanks." Belinda's voice said his backpedaling wasn't sufficient, but she'd let it go. "So, how do you all normally do this? Just snatch a kid and run?"

"See that guy over there?" The tall, scrawny vampire pointed to someone wearing an employee badge. "After a few flashes of my eyes, I'm going to steal his outfit from him."

"Why would you want to take some guy's *clothes*?" Belinda asked in disbelief. I glanced back over to them casually. I'd just been wondering that myself.

"Not his clothes, the Chuck E. Cheese costume," the vampire replied with a grin. "It's easy to get kids to follow you outside without arousing suspicion when you're wearing that. Even if their parents notice, one of us just gives 'em the gaze and they go home thinking everything's fine. Takes them a day or so to even realize their kids are gone, and they don't remember where they lost 'em from."

"We take them out one at a time and store them in the trunk," another added. "It's cool enough this time of year, so they don't die and go stale, and with a flash of the eyes, they stay quiet while they're there."

My hand tightened on Ethan's until he let out a yelp. I loosened my grip, fighting to keep my eyes from glowing out of pure rage. I couldn't kill these guys soon enough.

Belinda smiled. "A vampire in a Chuck E. Cheese costume? That I have to see."

The vampire returned her grin. "Wait right here, honey. You'll love the show."

As if on cue, the robotic figures in the theater came to synthetic life. The kids squealed in delight. I watched as one of the vampires followed the employee they'd pointed out behind the stage. My intention to follow as well was cut short by what I heard next.

". . . hungry now, I'm getting someone to eat," the russet-haired vampire said, sauntering away from Belinda and the others.

I let go of Ethan's hand. Belinda had pointed him out as hers; he was the safest kid in the place at the moment. I knelt down until I was eye-level with him.

"See that game?" I asked, pointing to the one closest to us. "You play that and you don't move from it until me or one of the other guys you met earlier comes to get you. Promise me."

Ethan nodded. "Promise."

"Good boy," I murmured. Ethan went over to the game and set all his tokens down by it. Cold fury seized me as I watched the other vampire hunt for his prey.

"All units, stand by," I whispered into my cell phone. This could get ugly real fast.

I discreetly kept him in sight as the vampire wandered through the room, his sharp eyes picking out which kids were being supervised and which weren't. There was a young boy by the change machine, gathering up his tokens. The vampire watched him, sidling up behind him as the boy started to browse the games. Then he waited until they were near a corner, and put his hand on the boy's shoulder.

The boy looked up—and that was all it took. The vampire's eyes flashed green for a moment and he murmured something, too low for me to catch. No one else noticed. The boy followed him into the next room without a pause, disappearing behind one of the partial walls.

I went after them, noticing the vampire had picked the least busy place, where all the out-of-order games were kept. He was kneeling, the little boy in front of him. I could see the green light of the vampire's gaze reflecting off the skin of the boy as he stood there, making no attempt to run or scream.

He's going to bite him right now. Right here, and he could have his body stuffed behind one of those broken machines in less than a minute. His parents will never even know he's in danger until he's already dead . . .

The russet-haired vampire leaned down, no fear of parents or God or anyone else stopping him. I pulled out a silver knife from my sleeve and crept forward. *Say hello to my little friend, asshole!*

"What the—?"

I whirled, feeling the inhuman power at my back even as I heard the voice. The vampire wearing the Chuck E. Cheese costume stood behind me, his big fake mouse head tilted questioningly to the side. The other vampire dropped his hands from the little boy, and his gaze narrowed on my knife.

"Silver," he muttered.

The gig was up. "Deploy!" I screamed, knowing Bones would hear me, and flung the knife.

It buried into his chest to the hilt. I leapt on him in almost the same movement, knocking him over to give a few rough twists of the blade. At the same time, something heavy landed on me. And cushy. It was the vampire in the Chuck E. Cheese getup.

I rolled over, crunching my legs up and then kicking the vampire off me. He hit a video game hard enough to make it crash through the window. I heard Tate shout, "Homeland Security, nobody move!" as I palmed more knives and then flung them with perfect accuracy into vamp Chuck E.'s chest. He staggered back, but didn't go down. Damn costume must be too thick.

I grabbed more knives from under my clothes and tackled him. He fought as hard as he could—while being encased in a large mouse suit. Our struggles had us rolling, me attempting to stab deep enough to penetrate that costume, and him trying to beat me while seriously hampered in his movements.

"Leave Chucky *alone!*" I heard a child wail. Several more screamed.

Jesus, Mary, and Joseph, talk about emotionally scarring these kids, watching what must appear to be a crazy woman trying to stab their beloved icon to death. They'd have nightmares for years unless Bones wiped their memories.

I didn't focus on that, however. I kept hammering away with my knives, hearing another fight break out. The other vampires. I finally got a deep enough slant on the knife under me to have the vampire go limp, and I gave the blade a final twist.

I got up to the horrified gaze of children and parents alike, but there was no time to explain that Chucky wasn't Chucky, but his evil twin instead. The blond vampire came roaring across the room to me, almost kicking people big and small out of his way. I reached for another knife, found I had only a few left, and went toward him as well. I couldn't risk throwing my knives at him—if he ducked, whoever was behind him would get hit. No, this would have to be a brawl. My eyes blazed green. *Come on, Blondie, let's see what you've got.*

Seeing my eyes glow made him falter, but only for a moment. In my peripheral vision, I could see Belinda wrestling with the dark-haired vampire. We hadn't given her any weapons, for obvious reasons, but it was a relief to see her fighting for us instead of against us.

Behind the blond vampire, the last one appeared. He snarled and started toward me, too. Then his gaze flickered to the door.

"Oh shit," I heard him say right before he turned and ran behind the stage.

I didn't have to turn to know what had scared him; I could feel Bones enter the place. But the other vampire hit me at the same time, so I couldn't enjoy the view of that one tucking tail and running.

"You take him, I've got Blondie," I called out, avoiding a set of fangs aimed for my throat.

"I'll get the sod," Bones growled, disappearing behind the large, fuzzy, robotic figures that still sang and joked among themselves on the stage.

"Let's move it outside, people!" I ordered in between receiving and giving brutal blows. Fast, before any parents or kids became hostages.

A quick glance showed Belinda roughly handling the dark-haired vampire, moving him outside by almost bear-hugging him. She seemed to be speaking to him, too, but with all this racket, damned if I knew what she was saying.

A hard swipe brought my attention back to the blond

vampire in front of me. *Just a little farther*, I chanted in my mind. *I don't want to kill you, too, in front of dozens of children. They'll have nightmares as it is.*

When he was in front of the hole in the window left by the video game, I charged him, ducking low to avoid his mouth. We spilled out the window into the parking lot, pounding each other on the asphalt. I only had a couple knives left on me, not expecting losing so many of them to Chucky's thick hide. I had to make sure I chose my moment.

"Mommy, make them *stop*," a child wailed, and I cursed inwardly. This was the *worst* setting for a vampire takedown. From the sounds of it, the guys were having a hard enough time keeping the parents and kids from fleeing to the parking lot in a panic, which would compound the problem even more. Dave barked out orders to have the dark-haired vampire Belinda had wrestled out secured in the capsule. Smart. He'd be no threat there, and we could cart him off and stake him at our leisure later.

I was ducking to avoid a roundhouse punch that would have snapped my neck when I saw Belinda, no longer restraining the other vampire, suddenly seize Zachary, a newer recruit, and bury her fangs into his throat.

"Tate, stop her!" I screamed, helpless to do anything as Belinda gave a jerk and Zachary fell back, clutching his neck with red streaming between his fingers. Then Belinda ran.

I heard gunshots, cursing, and the scrambling of feet as several of the team rushed over.

"Hostile on the loose, secure the perimeter!" Cooper shouted.

I gave the vampire in front of me a grimly cold

stare. "I don't have time for this," I growled, and charged him, knocking both of us over. His fists pummeled me, but I didn't defend myself. I took the battering, holding his mouth away from my throat with one hand and ramming my knife into his heart with the other. Three rough scissors of that blade and he was dead the permanent way.

I crawled off him. My ribs hurt tremendously, but I didn't cradle my aching sides like I wanted to. A scuffle to my left made me whip my head around, just in time to see the dark-haired vampire who had been about to be pronged in the capsule fling the two soldiers nearest him to the ground. Most of the team who weren't guarding the exits had gone after Belinda, except for the ones kneeling by Zachary. This vampire had taken full advantage of their distraction.

Dave leapt for him, but the vampire ducked under, slid like a macabre penguin on his belly, and then took off at a flat run.

I sprinted forward, following the sounds from Tate and Cooper as they chased after Belinda. But being human, there was no way they could catch her.

I made my decision in a split second and went after Belinda instead. She was the bigger threat. Belinda knew the names of my team. She knew intimate details about the workings of Don's organization, and she'd had enough experience being trapped by the security system in the compound to give detailed descriptions to anyone who might be crazy enough to try to breach it. There was no way I could let her repeat any of that.

I ran as fast as I could, quickly catching up to Tate and Juan. Up ahead, I couldn't see Belinda, but I could hear where she'd been by squealing brakes and exclamations from people as she crossed what must have been a busy intersection.

"Get the car," I gasped out to Tate, darting past him. "Track me!"

I had a transmitter in my beeper, and by car, they could follow faster. Plus handle any police, if it came to that. There were more tires screeching and I headed in that direction, bursting through an intersection and catching a glimpse of Belinda right before she darted down a side street. *Oh no you don't*, I thought.

I put more effort into it, wishing my ribs didn't feel like they were breaking with every step. Inside I was praying that Belinda didn't dash into someone's home and try to get a hostage, but maybe she'd seen and heard enough about me and the team to know that wouldn't work in her favor. No, she just ran like hell, and I was cursing her even as I kept up.

Belinda leapt over a fence without even a pause in her stride. At least she wasn't a Master vampire who could fly; I'd be screwed then. I took the fence almost as quickly as she had, but the gash it gave me when a jagged edge of metal scored my leg didn't heal instantly, as it did for her. There were days when I envied undead healing abilities. Just not enough to turn myself fully into a vampire to get them.

When I gained on her enough to take the chance, I threw my knives. I only had two of them left, so these had to count. The blades landed in the right area in Belinda's back, making her stagger, but she didn't go down. Dammit, I missed her heart! My accuracy while running full-out over uneven ground with a weaving target wasn't nearly what it was if we'd been in close quarters while I was stationary. *Note to self: Work on knife-throwing skills while in a chase.*

But the blades began to slow her. All that jostling must be driving the one dangerously near to her heart, and Belinda couldn't stop to get a good enough grab on the handles to pull them out. She tried swiping at her back while maintaining her breakneck speed, but all she succeeded in doing with her flailing was to slant a knife deeper in her back instead of pulling it out. Belinda staggered again, and I willed myself to go faster. *Almost there . . . hit the gas, Cat, you can't let her get away!*

I gathered my strength and sprang, managing to grasp Belinda's ankles and knock her over. She whipped around, her fangs snapping at any piece of my flesh they could find. I ignored that and flung myself on top of her, bearing all my weight into her torso.

Belinda stilled at once. Her wide, cornflower-blue eyes met mine for a second, and then her lids dipped even as she let out a scream that was cut off in the next moment. Those blades, still in her back, had been driven through her heart.

I wasn't about to take any chances. I flipped Belinda over and gave both knives a hard twist, feeling her go completely limp under me. *You should have taken the ten-year deal*, I thought coldly. *Instead you brought it to this.*

A scream alerted me to my surroundings. Belinda and I were on the edge of someone's lawn, it looked like. The homeowner, an older woman, was clearly upset at seeing two women fight to the death in her backyard.

I sat back with a sigh. "Go ahead, call 911. It'll make you feel better." Even though the police would never get their hands on me. No, not with Don's credentials.

Besides, Tate and the guys would be here soon, and so would Bones, I'd bet. He didn't need my transmitter to track me; he could do it by scent.

She babbled something that sounded like, "Murderer," and went inside, slamming her door. Moments later, there was the sound of her calling the police.

I stayed on the grass near Belinda, nodding politely at the few nearby neighbors who came out to gawk at me before running inside and placing their own emergency calls. I'd been there less than three minutes before Bones came streaking into view. He slowed when he saw me, walking the last several yards to where I sat.

"All right, luv?"

I nodded. "Scratches and bruises, nothing serious. The vampire you were after?"

He knelt next to me. "Exchanging hallos with Belinda in hell by now, I should think."

Good. One might have gotten away, but three didn't, and the most dangerous of those three was starting to shrivel in the late afternoon sun.

"Zachary?"

Bones shook his head. I took in a deep breath, wishing I could stab Belinda again and somehow make her feel it.

The squealing of tires announced the guys' arrival as, moments later, Juan and Tate jumped out of the car that skidded to a stop by us.

I stood up, brushing some of the grass and dirt off me.

"As you can see, guys, Belinda has been fired."

FOUR

THE OTHER VAMPIRE GOT AWAY. DAVE BLAMED himself for not being the one to strap him in the capsule, but he'd been so distracted after Belinda attacked Zachary, which was what she'd intended, of course. Zachary bled to death before Bones finished with the last vampire, so he hadn't gotten to him in time to heal him. Zachary had had the team's version of a living will, too. One that stated he didn't want to be brought back as anything inhuman if he were killed on a job. So, all of us somber, we honored his wishes and buried him.

Ethan turned out to be an orphan, which explained why his parents hadn't strongly opposed the part he'd played as my son. I made Don promise never to use him or any other child again for something so dangerous, and to find him a good foster home. If Don could run a secret branch of the government to fight the undead, finding a foster home for an orphan shouldn't be too hard.

At last, V-day for Tate arrived. Everyone was at the

compound. We were only short one person, and that's because her flight had been delayed due to mechanical difficulties. Annette, the first vampire Bones ever created, was coming in to help with Tate.

That had been my idea. Bones had barely spoken to Annette since her attempt to scare me off with sordid details of his past, but I knew their estrangement bothered him. So I suggested Annette could trade off shifts in the cell Tate would be locked in after his change. It could take up to a week before Tate would be able to control his hunger without ripping open the first vein he saw, so no one with a pulse could help Tate those first several days. Dave had already volunteered, but with a third person, it would free up some of Bones's time. And give Annette a chance to mend fences. Wasn't I just the little peacemaker?

Now, however, I was nervous. In half an hour, Bones would kill Tate, only to bring him back again. The time from bite to rebirth could last one hour, or several. We'd scheduled this for eight P.M., right after sundown, when Bones would be at his strongest. It took a lot out of a vampire to change someone over, or so I'd been told. This was my first experience with it.

True to form, Don had videos set up. He even had electrodes stuck to Tate's chest and head to monitor the exact moment of death as well as brainwave activity. Bones shook his head upon seeing all the high-tech setup, acidly inquiring if it was being broadcast over the Internet as well. Don didn't care. He intended to glean all available information he could for study. In that, he was shameless.

Tate was in a room reinforced with a series of titanium locks. Hell, they even had a macabre-looking operating table outfitted with clamps made of the same metal. Bones told Don all these precautions were overkill, pun intended, but Don was worried about Tate busting out and running amok. Tate was strapped to that table now, wearing only a pair of shorts to allow for easier electrode access. I slipped in to see him as a human one last time.

Numerous bags of blood sat in a cooler nearby for Tate's first few meals. My gaze met his indigo one as I stood next to the inclined slab, maneuvering it until he was upright.

"God, Tate." My voice wavered. "Are you sure about this?"

He attempted a smile, but it lacked its usual depth. "Don't look so spooked, Cat. You'd think you were the one about to die, not me."

I laid my hand on his cheek. His skin felt as warm as mine. This was the last time it would be that way. Tate sighed and inclined his head closer.

"It's been a strange ride, hasn't it?" he murmured. "I remember when I didn't believe in vampires. Now I'm about to join their ranks, led by a son of a bitch I despise. Ironic, huh?"

"You don't have to do this, Tate. You can change your mind and we'll call the whole thing off."

He took another deep breath. "As a vampire, I'll be stronger, faster, and harder to kill. The team needs that . . . and so do you."

"Don't you dare do this for me, Tate." My voice trembled with vehemence. "If this is for me, then get off that table right now."

"I'm doing this," he repeated, his tone equally vehement. "You can't talk me out of it, Cat."

Bones saved me from a response by coming up behind me. "It's time, Kitten."

I went to the small observatory one level up, where the video from that room fed into. My uncle was already seated, watching the screen. Juan, Cooper, and Dave came into our room. I couldn't look away as on the screen, Bones walked over to Tate with the slow grace of a true predator. Tate's breathing and heartbeat began to accelerate.

Bones studied him without emotion. "You won't gain what you're hoping for, mate, but you will have to live with this decision the rest of your days. So, one last time, do you want this?"

Tate took a long breath. "You've wanted to kill me for months. Here's your chance. Just do it."

In the next second, Bones's fangs were sunk deep into Tate's neck. The machines picked up Tate's skyrocketing pulse as he gasped, stiffening. Dave gripped my hand and I clenched back, watching as Bones drank the life from my friend with deep, long pulls of his mouth. That pale throat worked over and over as he swallowed. The sounds from the EKG monitor slowed, decreased, and then made only intermittent, brief bleeps when Bones lifted his head.

He licked the spare drops of blood around his mouth before pulling out a blade and making a gouge in his own neck. Then Bones pressed Tate's lolling head to the wound, keeping the tip of the knife in his neck so it didn't close.

Tate's mouth moved, at first feebly lapping at the blood, and then sucking with more vigor. The EEG monitor began to make alarming noises. Bones dropped the knife as Tate, eyes closed, clamped his teeth around his neck and tore at it. Bones held Tate's head, not flinching as he chomped at him for more. Tate gnashed and sucked as the minutes ticked on, his heartbeat skipping longer and longer in between blips until at last there was . . . silence.

Bones tore Tate's mouth free, wrenching it loose and staggering back. The EEG went haywire while the EKG showed a straight flat line on its monitor. A great tremor wracked Tate's body, rattling the clamps holding him. Then he slumped in his restraints, motionless. Dead, but waiting to rise.

The hours dragged by with painful slowness. Bones sat on the floor of the cell, looking like he was resting, but I knew he wasn't asleep. Every so often, his gaze would flick over to Tate's still form. I wondered if he could feel changes in the energy around Tate. Lord knew the EEG could. It hadn't shut up the whole time. Bones must have wanted to smash it more than once by now, with all the bleeps and squawks it made.

Bones had helped himself to two of the blood bags after Tate—died? Passed out? What was the term for the state Tate was in now, anyway?—even though Bones hated bagged plasma. He'd likened the taste to rotten milk, for an analogy I'd understand when I'd once asked him why he didn't just eat that instead of biting people. But with what he'd drained into Tate, Bones needed a refill, taste preferences notwithstanding.

Juan yawned. It was after midnight, and so far, we'd done nothing but watch Tate lie there. Still, no one seemed to want to tear their eyes from the screen.

"You can all get some sleep, I'll buzz you when there's any change," I suggested. I was used to being awake late. Being half vampire had its quirks.

Don gave me a tired but firm look. "I think I speak for everyone when I say hell no, I'm staying."

There were grunts of agreement. I shrugged, defeated, and turned my attention back to the screen.

The only warning I had was Bones standing up. Then, suddenly, Tate's supine body was a seething mass of motion. His eyes were open, every muscle strained against the clamps, and a howl so unearthly feral it rocked me back in my seat came from the speakers.

"Jesus Christ," Don muttered, his former slump gone.

Tate's scream grew impossibly louder. Through the blur from the frenzied scissoring of Tate's head as he fought against his restraints, I saw his mouth was open . . . and fangs were clearly visible as he continued to howl like he'd just come straight from hell.

Bones had said new vampires woke up with a burning, mindless thirst. That reality was playing out before my eyes. Tate didn't seem to be aware of where he was, or even *who* he was. There was nothing left of him in the gaze that scoured the small room he was trapped in.

Bones had none of my inner panic at seeing my friend in such a condition. He went over to the cooler, drew out a few blood bags, and walked over to Tate.

I couldn't hear what he said, because Tate's screams drowned it out, but I saw Bones's lips move as he dropped one of the bags right onto Tate's gaping mouth. *Nummy, nummy?* my frozen mind supplied. Or, *Bottoms up?*

It didn't matter. Tate didn't drink from the bag—he tore at it until his face was covered in red and his snapping jaws made him look more like a great white shark than a man. Bones, unperturbed, plucked the plastic remains from Tate's face, nimbly avoiding his fingers getting chomped, and then dropped another bag onto Tate's mouth. It met the same garbage-disposal fate as the first one.

I glanced away, disturbed. That made no sense, because I'd known what to expect, but hearing it and seeing it were two different things. To my right, I also noticed Juan looking away from the screen. He rubbed his temple.

"It's still him."

Dave's voice seemed very soft in the sudden break from Tate's screams as he slurped. Dave nodded once at the monitor.

"I know it's hard to believe from what you're looking at, but Tate's still in there. This is only temporary. He'll be himself soon."

God, I wanted to believe that. I knew there was no reason I shouldn't, except that now, Tate looked more frightening than the most homicidal vampire I'd ever come across. I guess I truly hadn't been prepared to see my friend this way, even though I'd thought I was.

It took five bags before the demented gleam left Tate's eyes. Of course, most of the first two had spilled around his face and shoulders, not in his mouth, since he'd sawed at them so crazily. Now, covered in blood, he finally looked at Bones and seemed to recognize him.

"It hurts," were Tate's first words.

Tears came to my eyes at the bleak rawness of his voice. There was so much despair leaking out of that short sentence.

Bones nodded. "It gets better, mate. You'll have to trust me on that."

Tate looked down at himself, licking at the blood he

could get. Then he stopped—and stared straight into the camera.

"Cat."

I leaned forward, pressing the button on the monitor that allowed them to hear me.

"I'm here, Tate. We all are."

Tate closed his eyes. "Don't want you to see me like this," he mumbled.

Shame over my initial reaction made my voice raspy. "It's okay, Tate. You're—"

"I don't want you *seeing me like this!*" he snarled, jerking against his clamps once again.

"Kitten." Bones glanced up at the screen. "It's upsetting him. That'll make it harder for him to control the blood craze. Best do as he wants."

My guilt deepened. Was this a coincidence, or could Tate somehow tell that I'd been repelled by watching him before? What a crappy leader I was, let alone a bad friend.

"I'm going," I said, managing to keep my voice steady. "I'll . . . I'll see you when you're better, Tate."

Then I walked out of the room, not looking back as I heard Tate's screams start up once again.

I was sitting at my desk, staring off into space, when my cell phone rang. A glance at it showed my mother's number, and I hesitated. I so wasn't in the mood to deal with her. But it was unusual for her to be up this late, so I answered.

"Hi Mom."

"Catherine." She paused. I waited, tapping my finger on my desk. Then she spoke words that had me almost falling out of my chair. "I've decided to come to your wedding."

I actually glanced at my phone again to see if I'd been mistaken and it was someone else who'd called me.

"Are you drunk?" I got out when I could speak.

She sighed. "I wish you wouldn't marry that vampire, but I'm tired of him coming between us."

Aliens replaced her with a pod person, I found myself thinking. *That's the only explanation.*

"So . . . you're coming to my wedding?" I couldn't help but repeat.

"That's what I said, isn't it?" she replied with some of her usual annoyance.

"Um. Great." Hell if I knew what to say. I was floored.

"I don't suppose you'd want any of my help planning it?" my mother asked, sounding both defiant and uncertain.

If my jaw hung any lower, it would fall off. "I'd love some," I managed.

"Good. Can you make it for dinner later?"

I was about to say, *Sorry, there was no way*, when I paused. Tate didn't even want me watching the video of him dealing with his bloodlust. Bones was leaving this afternoon to pick Annette up from the airport. I could swing by my mom's when he went to get Annette, and then meet him back here afterward.

"How about a late lunch instead of dinner? Say, around four o'clock?"

"That's fine, Catherine." She paused again, seeming to want to say something more. I half expected her to yell, *April Fool's!* but it was November, so that would be way early. "I'll see you at four."

When Bones came into my office at dawn, since Dave was taking the next twelve-hour shift with Tate,

I was still dumbfounded. First Tate turning into a vampire, then my mother softening over my marrying one. Today really was a day to remember.

Bones offered to drop me off on his way to the airport, then pick me up on his way back to the compound, but I declined. I didn't want to be without a car if my mother's mood turned foul—always a possibility—or risk ruining our first decent mother-daughter chat by Bones showing up with a strange vampire. There were only so many sets of fangs I thought my mother could handle at the same time, and Annette got on my nerves even on the best of days.

Besides, I could just see me explaining who Annette was to my mother. *Mom, this is Annette. Back in the seventeen hundreds when Bones was a gigolo, she used to pay him to fuck her, but after more than two hundred years of banging him, now they're just good friends.*

Yeah, I'd introduce Annette to my mother—right after I performed a lobotomy on myself.

"I still can't believe she wants to talk about the wedding," I marveled to Bones as I climbed into my car.

He gave me a serious look. "She'll never abandon her relationship with you. You could marry Satan himself and that still wouldn't get rid of her. She loves you, Kitten, though she does a right poor job of showing it most days." Then he gave me a wicked grin. "Shall I ring your cell in an hour, so you can pretend there's an emergency if she gets natty with you?"

"What if there *is* an emergency with Tate?" I wondered. "Maybe I shouldn't leave."

"Your bloke's fine. Nothing can harm him now short of a silver stake through the heart. Go see your mum. Ring me if you need me to come bite her."

There really was nothing for me to do at the compound. Tate would be a few more days at least in lockdown, and we didn't have any jobs scheduled, for obvious reasons. This was as good a time as any to see if my mom meant what she said about wanting to end our estrangement.

"Keep your cell handy," I joked to Bones. Then I pulled away.

My mother lived thirty minutes from the compound. She was still in Richmond, but in a more rural area. Her quaint neighborhood was reminiscent of where we grew up in Ohio, without being too far away from Don if things got hairy. I pulled up to her house, parked, and noticed that her shutters needed a fresh coat of paint. Did they look like that the last time I was here? God, how long *had* it been since I'd come to see her?

As soon as I got out of the car, however, I froze. Shock crept up my spine, and it had nothing to do with the realization that I hadn't been here since Bones came back into my life months ago.

From the feel of the energy leaking off the house, my mother wasn't alone inside, but whoever was with her didn't have a heartbeat. I started to slide my hand toward my purse, where I always had some silver knives tucked away, when a cold laugh made me stop.

"I wouldn't do that if I were you, little girl," a voice I hated said from behind me.

My mother's front door opened. She was framed in it, with a dark-haired vampire who looked vaguely familiar cradling her neck almost lovingly in his hands.

And I didn't need to turn around to know the vampire at my back was my father.

FIVE

MAX, MY FATHER, STOOD ABOUT THIRTY yards away between some trees. His red hair blew in the breeze and those identical gray eyes bore into mine. But what really held my attention was the rocket launcher Max had balanced on his shoulder. He also had a gun in his other hand. The disparity between the two weapons almost made me laugh out of sheer hysteria.

"I *was* going to blow up your car before you even pulled into the driveway," Max said in a genial tone, nodding at the rocket launcher, "but then I saw you were alone. And how could any dad pass up the chance to spend some time with his little girl?"

If at first you don't succeed, try, try again. That was what Max had spat at me months ago after he'd been busted for hiring two hitmen to put me out of my misery. I hadn't thought he would try more brazen attempts to kill me since Bones married me vampire-style, but it looked like I was wrong.

"Where's your sire, Max?" I asked, my voice even. "Is Ian running late? Is he still that pissed at me for getting away from him months ago?"

"Ian?" Max laughed. "Fuck my sire, I don't need him. I've got new benefactors, little girl, and they want you dead as much as I do."

I debated going for my knives again. An icy smile stretched across Max's face, which looked enough like mine for anyone to tell we were father and daughter.

"Think you can get to your weapons before I shoot you? Maybe you can. But not before this rocket plows right through your mother, and wouldn't that be a shame."

My jaw clenched. Max and the other vampire were in the exact opposite direction from each other. Even if I was fast enough to take out one of them, the other would still have time to kill my mom.

"Why don't we go inside? I think a family chat's long overdue," Max said, gesturing with the gun.

There was no way I could do anything with the two of them this far apart. I started toward the house, but his laugh stopped me. "Drop your purse first, little girl, and kick it over my way. Slowly."

A dozen different attack scenarios skipped through my mind, but fear for my mother made me reject all of them. *If only it was just Max here. If only I'd strapped some weapons on me before heading over. If only I had another damn watch with a panic button in it, so Bones could realize my mother and I were in deep shit.*

I dropped my purse and gave it a sideways kick over to Max. He grunted and came closer, his aim not wavering with either weapon.

"Let's make you a little more respectful," he said, and pulled the trigger.

The bullet hit me low in the stomach, doubling me over. It took a few seconds for the pain to hit, but when it did, it was merciless.

Behind me, I heard the other vampire giggle. It wasn't much louder than the sound of the shot. Max's gun had a silencer.

"Inside," he directed me with another wave of the gun. "Or the next round goes in your leg."

With my fists covering the rapidly bleeding hole in my gut, I staggered into the house. As soon as Max closed the door behind us, he fired again, striking me in the thigh.

I'd screamed at the second shot, which knocked me off my feet and sent me sprawling onto the floor.

"It was too much fun to resist," Max smirked, then waved the gun, this time at my mother. "You make one more sound and she gets the next slug."

Max would love to shoot my mother. It hadn't escaped my notice that she had a dull, glazed look on her face. Max had green-eyed her into compliance. The thought of how terrified she must have been to open her door and see my father there almost made my rage match the pain in pure intensity.

But that was short-lived. Waves of pain, nausea, and dizziness assailed me. Max might have missed arteries or vital organs, but in my current condition, I wouldn't be able to fight off him and the other vampire, plus rescue her. It was only because of being half vampire that I was even still conscious at all.

Bones. I'd often teased him about being paranoid over my safety, but it looked like the joke was on me. Sure, if I didn't show up at the compound later, he would be worried. Probably enough to come straight here, but from Max's expression, he'd arrive too late.

"You should have killed me when you had the chance," Max said, staring down at me. "Bet now you wish you'd done that instead of marrying Bones back at Ian's that night."

Even if this was it for me—and I wasn't ready to concede that by a long shot—I couldn't bring myself to agree.

"Have I ever mentioned how much I hate you, Max?" I managed to grit out. Maybe I could stall him. Get him pissed enough to want to take his time killing me.

The other vampire laughed. "She has such spirit," he said, eyeing me even as he stroked my mother's hair. "What a waste."

Recognition dawned about where I'd seen the black-haired vampire before. He was the one who'd gotten away from Chuck E. Cheese's that day!

"You," I said.

He smiled. "Nice to see you again, too."

Max set the rocket launcher down, but that didn't do me nearly as much good now as it would have a few minutes ago.

"Calibos," he said, "if my daughter moves, kill her mother."

With that grim directive, Max disappeared into the kitchen. I kept applying pressure to the hole in my gut, since it was bleeding worse than my leg. *God-damn you, Max,* I thought through the pain. *I'll see you dead even if it's the last thing I do.*

And from the looks of it, it probably would be.

My mother still stared sightlessly ahead. Aside from that, to my relief, she didn't look hurt. Calibos, as Max called the other vampire, let his hand wander down the front of her shirt to squeeze her breast. A low growl came from me that made him grin.

"Temper, temper," he purred, letting his hand creep lower.

Max came out of the kitchen and glared at Calibos. "Not her," he said curtly. "If there's time, you can have Cat, but Justina's mine."

Oh dear God. Renewed determination surged through me. I couldn't let Max live, even if I ended up killing me and my mother in the process of taking him down. I knew my mother. She'd rather be dead than raped by a vampire, especially Max.

"I think it's time to wake her up, don't you?" my father asked me in that same chipper tone. He handed his gun to Calibos with directions to shoot me if I twitched, then went over to my mother. Max cut his thumb on one of the four knives he'd returned from the kitchen with and held it to her mouth.

"Rise and shine, Justina," he said, rubbing the blood on her lips.

My mother licked it, blinked once—and then screamed.

Max's hand clamped over her mouth. I tried to push the pain back enough to concentrate on a plan. *Come on, Cat, think! There's got to be a way out of this.*

"Hello, beautiful," Max said, putting his face right next to my mother's. "I'm going to take my hand away, but for every time you scream, I'm going to cut something off our daughter. Understand?"

My mother's gaze flicked to me, widened, and then she nodded. Max dropped his hand.

"That's better. Now, to make sure kitty here doesn't spoil the fun . . ."

Max walked over to me, still holding those knives. I braced myself, wanting to grab for those blades like I'd wanted nothing before it. But Calibos had the gun pointed at me and my mother within biting distance. I'd make my stand, but this wasn't the time.

Max smiled, kneeling to grab my wrist. "You're going to die," he said, low enough that only I could hear him, "but I'll let your mother live just so she can remember that she watched it happen. But if you fight me, little girl, I'll rape her and kill her in front of you before I finish you. How much do you want to save her from that?"

I'd never felt such hatred for anyone as I did for my father. There was a chance that Max would kill us both anyway, but I had three choices. Hope I came up with a brilliant plan and managed to rescue both of us, hope Max took long enough torturing me that Bones showed up in time . . . or go for those knives and risk watching Max make good on his threat about my mother. I knew he was capable of it. There wasn't much I thought was beneath him.

"Let her go when it's over," I said very softly, opting for Plan A or B.

Max smiled. "Smart girl." His fingers stroked my wrist. "Why did you come here alone? Where's Bones?"

Lying always sounded more authentic when it was mixed with the truth. "He's at the compound. He changed one of my team last night into a vampire, so he's staying with him until he's over the blood craze."

Max's smile widened. "Tate."

I couldn't hide my shock. My father laughed. "How do I know about that? Belinda gave Calibos the information. Once I found your mother, all I had to do was compel her to invite you over. I owe Belinda a huge thank-you."

Belinda. Son of a bitch, I'd underestimated that blue-eyed bimbo. Now I knew what she'd been whispering to Calibos as she led him out of Chuck E. Cheese's. What was the one thing Belinda knew that no one else outside my unit did? The date and time we were changing Tate. Belinda must have figured with me dead, no one would piece together how Max had done this. But she hadn't figured on dying herself.

Another wave of light-headedness swept over me. I must have been bleeding internally, since what was leaking out onto the floor didn't account for how I felt.

"You'll have to save the thanks, Max, because she's dead."

He shrugged. "That's a shame. Nice girl."

"Max."

Both of us turned. My mother was still standing where she'd been. Slow tears trickled down her face. I'd never seen her cry before.

"It's me you want," she said in a raspy voice. "I raised Catherine, and I taught her to hate every vampire she met. Let her go. This is between you and me."

This, not being shot twice, was what brought tears to my eyes. All the times I'd thought she didn't love me, and here my mother was trying to use herself to barter with the vampire she feared the most.

Max lasered a green glare her way. "Oh, I have unfinished business with you, Justina. Do you know what a pain in the ass it's been, being the vampire who fathered the half-breed? I've had strangers beat me on sight! But I get no protection if I just kill you, whereas taking *her* out garners me new friends. They wanted Bones dead, too, but I'll take what I can get."

I was about to ask who these new friends were, when Max took one those knives and speared it straight through my wrist, hard enough to pin it to the floor. I gave a harsh gasp, but it was my mother who screamed.

"Stop it!"

Max grinned, keeping the other knives well away from my reach. "Thanks, Justina. Now I get to do a little slicing, courtesy of you."

Calibos let out an annoyed sigh I could hear even above my own labored breathing.

"This is boring. Am I going to get to do anything fun today?"

Max took another knife, giving a meaningful glance at my mother before touching its tip to my skin. "Go on, fight me. Give me a reason to make you watch your mother suffer before she dies," he whispered.

I set my teeth and didn't fight as he drove this blade slowly through my other wrist. It hurt even more than the first one had. My mother let out a moan that sounded like she was in pain, too.

"Please." It was barely audible, and she held her hand out to Max. "Please, no more. This is my fault, leave her alone!"

"What time is your playboy vampire expecting you back?" Max asked, ignoring her.

It would take Bones twenty minutes to get to the airport from the compound, maybe less with the way he drove. Then another fifteen or so minutes to load up Annette's ridiculous amount of bags and head back. Would Bones call me once he'd gotten back to the compound? I had my phone set to vibrate, so I wouldn't be able to hear it if he did, since it was outside in my purse. God, would it take him hours before he even wondered why I wasn't back yet?

"Three hours," I said, keeping my face as blank as possible.

Max let a nasty smile curl his lips. "I'm going to assume that really means one hour. But don't worry. I'll make it count. Oh, and I'll take this."

Max yanked my engagement ring off my finger. He held it up to the light and grinned.

"Must be five carats," he said admiringly. "This'll net me a couple million, easy."

"It's a ruby," I snapped, hating the sight of my engagement ring in his hands.

Max laughed. "Stupid little girl, that's a *diamond*. Red diamonds are the rarest in the world, and Bones has had this stone for over a century. Ian's wanted to buy it from him for decades. But you won't be needing it anymore."

Max sliced up the front of my shirt, remarking that this was for Calibos's benefit, not his. The throbbing from my wrists, combined with the searing pain in my legs and gut, made it so easy for me to pass out. I kept fighting the blackness that crouched temptingly near.

My mother darted forward. Calibos caught her, giving her a hard shake.

"You're nothing but animals," she hissed at them.

"Insults count as screaming," Max replied, laughing as she gaped in disbelief. "My game, so I get to make up the rules. That's two things I get to cut off Cat now. Want to make it three?"

I met my mother's gaze over Max's shoulder. Her eyes were wide and overflowing. I gave the barest shake of my head. *Please don't. You can't make it better. Just run when you have the chance.*

She couldn't hear my silent urgings, of course. Max

let the tip of his knife dip to my jeans, and he slit them down the side.

"Here's where I'll start," he remarked, then grabbed a handful of my hip and gave a hard upward swipe with the third knife.

I bit my lip so hard to keep from screaming that I tasted blood. Calibos snickered. Max held up my severed piece of skin like it was a trophy.

"Nice tattoo," he said, flinging it to the side. "Maybe I'll have that shipped to Bones, so he can have a spare."

My hip flamed where there was now a bleeding open wound instead of the crossbones tattoo I'd gotten to match the one on Bones's arm. My mother didn't cry out this time, but she drew in a deep, shuddering breath.

"I love you, Catherine," she whispered.

I had to look away, because I didn't want to give Max the satisfaction of seeing me cry. I couldn't remember the last time she'd said that to me. She must believe we were both doomed to die.

"I'm sick of holding her, I'm putting her under," Calibos said, turning green eyes to my mother.

"Stop it." Max's voice was a whip. "She's going to see this. She's going to *know*."

Calibos made an exasperated noise, then dragged my mother over to the drapes by the window. He yanked one off, ripped it down the center, and then tied the end of it around her neck.

"Max," I said warningly.

He swatted me in the head, hard. "Shh, I want to see what he's got in mind."

Calibos threw the other end over one of the railings in the banister on the second floor. My mother was struggling, but she was no match for the vampire. I began to strain against the knives pinning me down. Max shoved another one through my wrist almost like it was an afterthought, then punched me in the gut where I'd been shot.

The blast of agony must have knocked me out for a minute, because when my eyes focused again, my mother was standing on a chair, one end of the drapes wrapped around her neck, and the other tied to the banister upstairs. There was hardly any slack in the line, and one of the chair's legs was missing.

"Now she can watch, and I can join the fun," Calibos smirked.

Max gave him an approving grin, then turned his attention to me.

"Do you want to know what I'm going to do to you, little girl?" he asked in a conversational tone. "After I torture the hell out of you, I'm going to chop you into pieces. Can't risk Bones getting someone to raise you into a ghoul, now can I?"

Vicious prick wasn't stupid. With my half-vampire bloodline, it was entirely possible I could be raised as a ghoul, if Max were just to murder me. But if I was dismembered, that option was out.

"Same rules apply. Let's see how long you last before you scream and I get to cut something off Justina," he taunted.

Max's fist began knocking my head back and forth like a toy on a spring. Blood filled my mouth and my lip split, but I bit my tongue and didn't make a noise. After a few minutes, the ringing in my ears dulled the thwacking sounds of him beating me. Then he stopped.

"Stubborn bitch. Hmm, let's see if you can keep quiet through this . . ."

He pulled a lighter out of his pocket, flicked it, dialed the flame up as high as it could go, then held it to my arm. My whole body shuddered and I twisted futilely, gasps and grunts coming from me. After a few minutes of unimaginable agony, I couldn't hold back my scream any longer.

Max laughed, delighted. Vaguely I was aware of throwing up.

"I think that's going to cost Justina a finger," he remarked. "What else will you make her lose?"

"Even if you kill me, Bones will find you," I panted. Sweat was pouring off me and my arm hurt in ways I didn't know were possible. "Believe me, you'll be sorry when he does."

Calibos and Max chuckled like I'd told a joke. "That vampire won't start a war over you." Max grinned. "Hell, the only reason Bones married you was to spite our sire."

That's why Max felt secure enough to risk pulling this? Because he thought he had enough protection from his new "friends" and Bones had only married me to piss off Ian?

"Oh, Bones *will* find you. Count on it."

They glanced around, uneasy at the vehemence of my tone.

"Pathetic," Max said at last. "You're trying to scare me into letting you live, but it won't work. Still, Calibos, go outside and keep watch. Just in case her playboy decides to drop by early."

"But I haven't gotten to play with her yet," Calibos protested, with a look my way that made me recoil.

"You'll get your chance," Max snapped. "But I set this up, so I go first."

Calibos smirked at me as he headed out the door. "I'll see you soon, sweetie."

Max got up and sauntered over to my mother next. She was almost on her tiptoes to keep the drape around her neck slack enough to breathe. Underneath her, the chair wobbled ominously on its three legs. Her hands were tied together with another piece of drapery, and Max grinned as he contemplated her fingers.

"Which one will you lose, Justina? Let's see, this little finger went to market," he started to singsong, tapping one of them. "This little finger stayed home. This little finger had roast beef . . ."

I tried to mentally prepare myself for my chance. Now that one of them was outside, this was my best opportunity. It was hard for me to focus, however. I'd had years of experience getting knocked around, but with all of my injuries, I kept feeling myself wandering closer to unconsciousness.

My mother met my eyes . . . and then kicked the chair out from under her.

"Goddammit," Max snapped, holding her up with one hand. "Why'd you do that?"

In the second that he was distracted, I yanked against the knives on my wrists with all my strength, feeling my flesh shred. I'd gotten one of my hands free when Max turned around.

"What the hell?"

He let my mother go. She dangled by the neck, her feet well above the floor, while I wrenched my other arm free, ignoring the white-hot burst of pain that caused. I tried to grab one of the knives, but my wrists were too damaged for me to hold anything. I kicked them away and then lunged at Max instead, head-butting him hard enough to knock him over. *All*

I need is a little of your blood, I thought, biting at him savagely, *and I'll be healed enough to fight.*

A burst of noise jerked my head toward the window. The last thing I saw was glass smashing—and then there was a burning in my neck and my vision went black. I thought I heard screams, but all at once, everything seemed farther away. I couldn't feel anything, either. It was a relief to be free from the pain.

Awareness came back with something wet being poured down my throat. I tried to cough it out but couldn't. The flow wouldn't stop, forcing me to swallow. Again. And again.

". . . don't you let her die!" I thought I heard my mother scream, then there was Bones's voice, very close.

". . . come on, luv, drink! No, you have to have more . . ."

I gagged, the liquid overflowing my mouth, when shapes around me formed into clarity. I had my mouth plastered to a blood-slicked neck, and I pushed away even as I coughed and swallowed once more.

"Stop it," I managed to say.

Hands set me back. It was Bones's throat I'd been pressed against. His neck wasn't the only thing smeared red, either. So was the entire front of him.

"Christ Almighty, Kitten," Bones breathed, stroking my throat.

"Catherine," my mother cried. I jerked my head around in time to see her slip in something as she staggered toward me. That drape was still tied around her neck, but the other end was no longer attached to the banister. In the far corner of the room, I heard Max's muttered cursing and a feminine English reply.

"Don't you move, you little shite."

"You've got him?" Bones asked in a truly chilling voice.

Annette sounded as fierce as I'd ever heard her. "I've got him, Crispin."

My mother reached me. She was hugging me and trying to pull me from Bones's arms even as she kept feeling my neck.

"Did he fix it? Are you all right, Catherine?"

That's when I noticed the rest of the blood. It wasn't only splattered on Bones, but all over me, around me, even on the nearby wall.

"What happened?" I asked, torn between dizziness, numbing gratitude that we were alive, and being aghast at all the blood surrounding us.

"Max ripped your throat out," Bones replied. There was the weirdest mixture of relief and rage in his blazing green gaze. "And he's going to dearly wish I'd kill him before I'm through with him."

Six

DON ARRIVED AT MY MOTHER'S WITH THE full team less than fifteen minutes after I called him. They must have broken every traffic law known to man, not that any local cops could give them speeding tickets.

Bones and Annette strapped Max into the capsule. Don was taking him—for now. Bones curtly said he'd send someone by later to collect Max, and the tone he used made me glad my uncle didn't argue. Of course, I didn't think Don wanted Max on his hands very long. The look the brothers had exchanged while Max was being strapped into that capsule was filled with so much history, Don glanced away even before Max started to curse him.

I had to be given several pints of blood to replace what I'd lost. Bones's blood had healed my multiple injuries, but my pulse had been dangerously weak.

"That was close," I said to Bones with a shaky smile after my final transfusion. I was sitting in his car. He'd used a towel to wipe off as much blood from me as possible. We were leaving soon. Bones didn't want to stay longer than necessary here, since we couldn't be sure who else Max and Calibos might have told about their ambush plans.

Bones met my eyes with an unfathomable look. "I'd have brought you back one way or another, Kitten. Either as a vampire or a ghoul, even if you hated me for it afterward."

"Not if Max had his way," I muttered. "He was going to cut me into pieces."

Bones let out a hiss that made the hairs on the back of my neck stand on end. Then he seemed to get himself under control.

"I'll remember that," he said, each word bitten off.

So many emotions were surging in me. Relief, delayed panic, anger, exhilaration, and the urge to clutch Bones and babble about how thrilled I was to even *see* him again. But there wasn't time for a meltdown, so I stuffed those feelings back. *Get it together, Cat. Can't have you turn into a mass of psychological goo, there's too much to do.*

My mother was in the backseat. She'd refused to go to the compound, even though she wouldn't have been there long. Don was moving everyone out. Max had found my mother's house, so it was an easy guess to make that he knew where the compound was, too. Don wasn't taking any chances that Max had told other vampires where to find it. Don's operation had killed enough of them that some might decide to pay it a visit.

So my mother was leaving with Bones and me now, and Don would get her set up with another place to live later. Once he finished relocating our entire team.

"I'm sorry, Catherine," she mumbled, not meeting my eyes. "I didn't want to call you. I heard myself saying the words, but I couldn't seem to stop."

I sighed. "It's not your fault. Max used mind control. You couldn't help what you were saying."

"Demon power," she whispered.

"No," Bones said firmly. "Max is the one who told you all vampires were demons, right? You think he's capable of telling the truth, even after this?"

"Whatever Max told you back then," I added, "you would have been compelled to believe, just like you were compelled to call me before. Vampires are another species, Mom, but they're not demons. If they are, why are you still alive? You've tried twice to get Bones killed, but today he saved you instead of letting you hang."

Her face was twisted with emotion. Being confronted with the reality that what she'd fervently believed for twenty-eight years might be wrong was a hard thing for anyone to swallow.

"I lied to you about your father," she said at last, so soft I could barely hear her. "That night, he didn't . . . but I didn't want to believe I *could* have let him, not after I saw he wasn't human . . ."

My eyes closed for a moment at her admittance. I'd suspected that the night I was conceived wasn't rape, but here was confirmation at last. Then I met her gaze.

"You were eighteen. Max had you believing you were giving birth to a modern-day version of Rosemary's baby, just because he thought it was funny to tell you all vampires were demons. Doesn't make him any less of an asshole. Speaking of that . . ." I pulled the IV out of my arm, then put on the jacket

Cooper had kindly left for me, since my own shirt had been cut open and was sopping with blood. When I was covered, I hopped out of the car. No more horizon-tilting dizziness. It was amazing the difference vampire blood and three bags of plasma could make. I didn't even have a mark on me anymore, whereas by rights, I should be in a body bag.

"What are you doing?" Bones asked, lightly holding my arm.

"Saying goodbye to my father," I replied, walking over to where the capsule sat like a huge silver egg in the driveway.

"Open it," I said to Cooper, who was standing guard until it could be loaded into our specialized van.

Cooper unsealed the outer locks. He didn't look away when the capsule's door slid open and Max was revealed, so I figured he'd swigged some vampire blood on the way here. That was the only thing that could inoculate a human from falling victim to nosferatu mind control, even if it did have other side effects.

My father was pronged in several places with silver. The hooked end of those spikes made it impossible for him to pull himself free without shredding his heart, not to mention several other choice pieces of him. Once the door closed, he couldn't even wiggle, because the inner structure prevented movement while the spikes continued to drain the blood and strength out of him. I knew all this, because I designed it.

Bones's gaze sizzled into Max. "Go on, mate, say one word, see what it gets you," he urged him in a voice smooth as silk—and frightening as the grave.

"Right now, Daddy dearest, 'I told you so' doesn't even begin to cover it," I said grimly to Max. "So I'll repeat what you said to me earlier: You should have killed me when you had the chance."

Then I turned to Bones. "Why are we taking him anywhere? I'd just as soon kill him now and not have to worry about him again."

"You *don't* need to fret about him," Bones said in that same icy, neck-ruffling tone. "Ever. But he doesn't get off that easily."

Bones reached out and touched Max's face. It was a light stroke, but Max flinched as if Bones had sliced his cheek open with a knife.

"I'll be seeing you soon, mate. I can't wait."

Annette came over. Her champagne-colored eyes considered Max from a face lightly lined with age. Annette had been thirty-six when Bones changed her. Times were different in the seventeen hundreds, so she looked around forty-five, but she made it look good. Unlike her normal impeccable appearance, her strawberry-blond hair had half-fallen out of her chignon, and her navy tailored suit looked a lot worse for wear.

"I say, it's been quite the day already," she remarked.

I stifled a snort. How like Annette to describe an afternoon of torture as calmly as "quite the day."

"Seal him back up," I said to Cooper, not wanting to look at my father anymore. Or ever again.

Cooper complied, and the capsule's door slid into place with a series of locks clicking back together. Even as it did, a frightening thought occurred to me.

"What happened to Calibos? There was another vampire here besides Max."

"His head's over there," Bones said, nodding by the trees, "but the rest of him's farther back."

I felt a cold satisfaction at that. "How'd you know to come here?"

"The airline lost Annette's luggage." Bones sounded almost bemused. "I rang you twice to tell you we'd be late, that we were stopping off to fetch her some new togs. You didn't answer. You always answer, so I drove straight here. About a mile away, I heard you scream. I pulled off, and Annette and I circled round the house on foot. We found the one bloke. Didn't know how many more might be inside, so we smashed through the windows at the same time."

A bark of laughter escaped me. My mother and I owed our lives to Annette's *luggage* being lost? How ironic.

"Bet you wish you'd carried on," I couldn't help but quip to Annette.

A ghost of a smile flitted across her lips. "Not quite, darling. I just rang Ian," she continued, more to Bones than me now. "He was furious to hear what Max did. He's formally cutting Max off from his line."

That was the worst punishment a vampire could inflict on a member of their line. It meant no vampire would challenge whatever happened to Max in the future, and right now, my father's future looked pretty grim.

"Max said Ian didn't know about this," I added, even though I was no fan of Ian's. "He said he had new friends who wanted me dead as much as he did."

Bones gave a short nod. "We're going home, luv. To find out who helped Max orchestrate this, so we can kill every last one of them."

Our house was a large cabin at the top of a hill, with sweeping views of the Blue Ridge Mountains out of bulletproof-glass windows. It was remote enough that we'd never met our neighbors, so the helicopter pad and hangar on the side of our house hadn't been cause for any awkward conversations.

Annette went back with Don to help with Tate, as was the original plan, although Bones refused to go with her. He told my uncle his priorities had changed, not that Don had any trouble understanding why. Tate would be okay with two undead people taking care of him. It was my safety that seemed to be in a more tenuous position than Tate's, according to what Max had said.

When I walked into my house, my cat jumped out to twine around my legs. We hadn't figured on being back for a week, so I'd set up the automatic feeder and litter-box cleaner. Now my kitty would get some of my leftovers instead of just his dry food. No wonder he was glad to see me.

My mother had never been to Bones's and my house, but I was too anxious to wash the blood off me to give her a proper tour.

"Here's the guest room," I said, directing her to the downstairs bedroom. "I've got some clothes in it, too, so help yourself to whatever's there. I'm taking a shower."

Bones followed me upstairs. I stripped off the jacket Cooper had given me, plus my bloodied bra and pants. If I never saw those clothes again, it would be too soon. Bones also peeled off his crimson-spattered shirt and pants, kicking them into a corner before joining me in the shower.

At first, the water was icy. It took a couple minutes to heat up this time of year. I shivered as the frigid spray landed on me. Bones folded me in his arms and moved to where the majority of it splashed on him. Even when it turned warm, however, and Bones turned to let the heated water rinse my blood away, I was still shivering.

"I didn't think I'd make it today."

My voice was low. Bones's arms tightened around me.

"You're safe now, Kitten. And nothing like this shall ever happen again, I promise you."

I didn't reply, but I was thinking this was one promise Bones might not be able to keep. Who knew what could happen in the future? This wasn't just about the revenge my father had wanted on me—and my mother—for my existence. Max had done this with promises of rewards and help. Now the question was, from whom?

But I didn't say any of that. Bones was correct—I was safe now. And he was here. Right now was all I'd concentrate on.

For the moment, anyway.

We weren't home for more than an hour before people started showing up. First it was Juan and Cooper, who Don sent as added protection for me. Both of them were carrying enough silver knives and guns with silver bullet clips to take on a dozen vampires.

Then Bones's brand of added security arrived in the form of three vampires I hadn't met before. The one named Rattler reminded me of a young Samuel Elliott, Zero looked albino with his long blond hair and glacier eyes, and Tick Tock was pitch dark with black skin, black hair, and black eyes. Mentally I referred to them as Cowboy, Salt, and Pepper.

Then came Spade, or Charles, as Bones called him.

Spade preferred everyone else to call him by the tool he was assigned when he was a lowly penal colonies convict. Something about never forgetting how helpless he'd once been. Bones had picked his name after rising as a vampire in Aborigine burial grounds. Vampires sure made it complicated to remember what name to call them by.

Rodney the ghoul was next. He endeared himself to Juan on the spot by starting to cook up a storm. I didn't eat, I went to bed, but to no one's surprise, I didn't get a very restful sleep. My dreams were filled with seeing my mother dangle by the neck from a banister and my father's sneering face as he shot me.

Don showed up a little after noon. I was seated at the kitchen table with Juan, Cooper, my mother, and Bones. We'd been talking about anything but the obvious when my uncle came in. I was surprised to see him, actually. I thought he'd be busy directing the transfer from one base to another.

"Does your boss know you're playing hooky?" I asked.

Don gave me a dry smile. "I can't stay long, but I wanted to go over a few things and . . . just see how you were doing."

He could have gone over any pertinent work-related items on the phone, so I was guessing his presence had more to do with the latter part of his statement.

"I'm glad you're here," I said, meaning it. We might have had a rough start—okay, a *very* rough start—but aside from my mother, Don was the only family I had.

"Have some breakfast," I offered, gesturing to the multiple covered dishes near the stove. "Rodney's cooked more food than I even knew I had."

Don gave the items a wary flick of his eyes that made Rodney laugh.

"It's a ghoul's version of vegetarian," he assured Don. "Nothing in there you wouldn't find in a grocery store."

Don, still looking hesitant, filled a plate and sat down. I watched him take a tiny bite, swallow . . . and then spear a bigger portion. Yeah, Rodney was a superb cook.

Bones's cell rang. He excused himself to answer it, speaking in a low tone. I could only make out a few words, since Juan and Cooper began talking to Don about the new compound we were moving to. Getting everything up and running on no notice was going to be challenging.

Bones came back in the room and snapped his cell shut. There was something tense in his shoulders that hadn't been there before.

"What?" I asked.

"I have to leave for a while tonight, Kitten, but it's nothing to fret about."

"Who was on the phone? And what's going on later?"

Bones seemed to choose his words. "That was my grandsire, Mencheres. He was confirming he'll be at the showing."

I sighed. "You're being deliberately vague, Bones. What showing? What's this about?"

The other vampires all pretended to be fascinated by the decor around them. Bones's expression closed off into unreadable planes.

"I'm calling together members of my line, Ian's, and other pertinent vampire Masters to witness Max's torture."

I blinked. "You're holding a rally just to beat on my father in public?"

"Whoever aided Max and Calibos didn't fret over my reaction to you being tortured, murdered, and mutilated. It's obvious some people believe I don't care, or that I've gone soft. But soon everyone will see what happens to those involved in a scheme to harm you."

"There's a certain sense to it," Don said. "Making an example of one keeps the rest in line. But killing Max tonight, Bones, even if you hurt the literal hell out of him first, will only postpone another attack. You'll still have to find out who else is involved to prevent this from happening again."

"Quite right, old chap," Bones agreed. "But I'm not going to kill Max. I'm going to keep him alive to demonstrate a new meaning of the term *cruel and unusual punishment*. Only when Max is completely broken in spirit will I kill him. I expect it will take years of daily suffering before that happens. Personally, I'm hoping it takes decades."

Don looked ashen at this pitiless pronouncement. Rodney, Spade, and the three other vampires showed no surprise.

My mother stared at Bones. Then she smiled. "Now *that* I have to see."

"You have got to be—" I began when Bones held up a hand.

"Wait, Kitten, this is between me and your mum. If you go, Justina, you understand you'll be the only human there. You'd have to keep your insults directed only at the vampire on display. Can you handle that?"

My mother tossed her hair. "I've waited a *long* time for this. I'll be fine. We'll shake on it."

Bones took her hand in the first time she'd ever willingly touched a vampire. To her credit, she didn't wipe it on her clothes when he let go.

"Then we have an accord. Juan or Cooper, I want one of you to come, too. You can carry back what you see to her team as a warning of what awaits them should one of them be tempted to ever betray her. Don, you are not going. You don't need to see what will happen to your brother."

My mother stood up even as I thought, *Uh oh*. "Max is your *brother*?" she asked Don in a scathing voice.

He didn't flinch from her anger. "Yes. He's the reason why I founded my department. I wanted to kill my brother and all of his kind. I even used my niece to help me do it, and I never told her who I was. Bones did, when he found out. So if you're angry at anyone, let it be me, not Cat."

Brave words in a room full of pulseless creatures. Spade gave Don a disgusted glance while Rodney just licked his lips. No doubt he was mentally salting and peppering Don.

"You knew she was your niece when you found Catherine?" my mother asked in disbelief.

Don let out a sigh. "I read the assault report you filed that night you met Max. I knew it was him from your description, and then you gave birth to a child with an unusual genetic anomaly. Yes, I knew all along that Cat was part vampire—and my niece."

My mother let out a bitter laugh. "So both of us used her for our own selfish reasons. That vampire over there has treated her better than her own family."

Bones's brows went up. "Justina, I believe that's the nicest thing you've ever said to me."

I was taken aback, too, but we'd gotten off the subject.

"I'm coming with you tonight," I said, noticing Bones hadn't included me in his list.

His face hardened. "No, Kitten. You're not."

Disbelief flared through me. "I'm the one who was beaten, shot, knifed, sliced, and burned, remember? Hell yeah, I am."

"No you're not," Bones repeated, his voice sharpening. "If you want to give Max some comeuppance yourself, grand, but you'll do it another time. Not tonight."

The reason hit me. Bones thought I couldn't handle what he'd dish out to Max. I'd been up to my ears in blood and guts since I was sixteen, but all of a sudden, I had to be sheltered from the ugly side of the undead?

"Bones, I'm not some delicate flower. I won't be seeing anything I can't handle."

"Yes you will," Bones replied. "If you go, you *will* be horrified, because I'm going to make damn sure it's horrifying, else it doesn't serve its purpose. No, Kitten. Your compassion is one of the things I love most about you, but in this case, it will drive us apart. You're not going, and that's the end of it."

I couldn't believe what I was hearing. Hurt and anger competed inside me. How could Bones just take it upon himself to decide what I could and couldn't handle? This was supposed to be a relationship, not a dictatorship.

"Want to know one of the things I've loved most about *you*?" I asked, a feeling of betrayal welling up in me. "That you never lorded your age over me. Yeah, there's nothing I've seen or done that isn't old news to you, but you'd always treated me like an equal. Well, now you're treating me like the pathetic little girl Max accused me of being. You want to have your nasty event without me? Fine. But whatever I would have seen later wouldn't have come between us as much as what you just pulled did."

"Kitten . . ." Bones said, reaching out to me.

I brushed past him and went upstairs. Below, Juan cleared his throat. Rattler whispered something about giving me time to cool off. Don coughed and muttered that he had to make more calls. Bones didn't say anything else, and he didn't come after me.

SEVEN

MY HURT LASTED THE REST OF THE DAY. I stayed in my room, not wanting to talk to anyone, especially Bones. He'd left me alone, too, not even attempting to come upstairs.

But as the sky darkened, I decided I couldn't just keep sulking. I showered again and went downstairs. Rodney had made dinner. God only knew where he'd gotten the steaks from; he must have sent someone to the store.

Don, seated at the table with my mother, gave me a wintry smile. "We were just discussing hiring Rodney to cook for the team. I think it would improve productivity by thirty percent."

I snorted, noticing Bones was outside on the porch. "Probably more. Speaking of the team, where's the new base?"

"Tennessee, that former bomb shelter the CIA used to occupy. With some basic renovations, we should be up and running again within a week or two. The underground reinforcements make this facility the safest choice."

"I agree. When are you going there?"

"Later tonight." Don nodded at my mother. "You'll have a place to stay there as well. We've also relocated your friends Denise and Randy on the off chance that Max discovered their home as well as yours."

"God, I hadn't even thought of that!" I exclaimed, lashing myself for being an idiot. How could I have forgotten to consider the safety of my best friend and her husband?

Don sighed. "You had other things on your mind. Being tortured and almost killed will do that to a person."

Rodney set a plate in front of me, and one in front of my mother. I almost fainted when she began to eat instead of hurling it at him. Had one of the vampires gotten tired of her bitching and bitten her into a better mood?

She caught my flabbergasted look. "I watched what he put in it," she said defensively.

Rodney, instead of being insulted, just laughed. "You're welcome, Justina."

I dragged my attention away from the unbelievable sight of my mother eating food a ghoul had prepared. "If you're going to the new compound later, Don, I'm going with you."

Bones had been pacing on the porch while talking on his cell. At that, his booted stride stopped.

Don cast a pointed glance out the window before meeting my gaze. "Are you sure that's wise?"

"Unless you fire me, I am going there today to check on my team," I interrupted him. "That's where I'm needed." Since I clearly wasn't wanted with Bones later.

I ignored the muttered curse outside. Don spread out his hands. "Of course I'm not going to fire you. I'm sure the men will be glad to see you."

"Zero, Tick Tock, Rattler, you will be accompanying her," Bones said. He didn't bother to come inside or raise his voice. With their hearing, it wasn't necessary.

"How did you move Tate to the new location, anyway?" I asked without comment on my assigned guard. Transporting a blood-crazed new vampire must have been tricky.

Don coughed. "The only way we could. In the capsule."

My jaw dropped. "He could have been killed."

Don's expression clouded. "It was Tate's idea. He knew how dangerous he was to the team any other way. He arrived safe and is now confined with Annette and Dave again. She's said Tate's already making strides in controlling his hunger."

It was less than a day since Tate had been turned. "Wow."

Bones came back inside. I didn't look up, but concentrated on my food. When I was done, I rinsed my plate, put it in the dishwasher, and started back toward my room.

"Just a moment, Kitten," Bones said. I paused, half up the stairs. He held out something that flashed in the light. "Did you want this back?"

I glanced down at my left hand and felt a sting of shame. I'd forgotten about my ring. Good God, I had to get my head out of my ass. First not thinking of Denise and Randy's safety, then not even remembering Max had stolen my engagement ring. That whole tortured-and-almost-killed thing wouldn't cover every screwup I was making. No wonder Bones was treating me like a stupid little girl—I was acting like one.

"Thank you," I said, looking him in the eye. "I do want it back, of course."

No matter how upset I was over him leaving me behind tonight, my anger wasn't going to be permanent. I'd fight Bones to see the error of his ways over treating me like a damsel in distress, but I wasn't giving up on us. Not now, not ever.

Bones almost smiled. "I'm glad to hear it."

He came up the stairs. I stretched out my hand, but instead of handing me the ring, Bones slid it on my finger. The cool touch of his skin on mine, that familiar tingle of his power . . . all of it made me want to do nothing more than fling myself in his arms and forget about the world around us.

But there was so much more going on than just the two of us, and how we felt. Who would have ever guessed that my falling in love with a vampire was turning out to be the easiest part of our relationship? I remembered when I thought him being undead was the biggest obstacle to our having a life together. Now I knew the stakes were much higher.

"I'm leaving now, Kitten. Don will give me the location where you'll be. I'll pick you up afterward."

I let my hand slide from his. "What time?"

"Before dawn, but not by much."

It wasn't even eight. Bones had a *long* party planned for Max. "Uh huh," was all I said.

He inhaled with a slow breath. Maybe he was gauging my emotions by my scent. "I love you," he said at last, and then left without waiting to see if I said it back.

He was already down the stairs by the time I murmured my reply.

"I love you, too."

I gave the interior of the new building a once-over. "Cozy. For a bomb shelter."

"It will be much more difficult for anyone to monitor," Don pointed out. "The exterior looks like a private airport, and the underground levels are extensive. We'll add upgrades each day until it's completed."

"Oh, I like it."

Rattler, Zero, and Tick Tock looked around with curiosity as well. Don hadn't been wild about three strange vampires accompanying me, but he must have known better than to argue with Bones. Rodney, Cooper, and my mother had gone with Bones on his grisly field trip. Juan didn't, so he was perusing the facility as well.

"Where's the team?" I asked.

"On the fourth sub-level. They're busy moving the pieces of the obstacle course into the new training room."

I swallowed. It would be a huge undertaking to get everything up to speed, and it was all my fault. I was the one with the homicidal father who'd found out where our last facility was, after all.

"I'm going down there. You coming?"

Don shook his head. "No. I'm going to check on some of the online transfers, make sure everything's being routed correctly."

I left him to go to the elevators, following the signs. Juan and my three undead watchers trailed me.

I did a couple hours of lifting and moving with the

guys to try and get things into somewhat of an order. This was where having those three undead body-guards came in handy, since they could hoist cars on their shoulders if they wanted to. We made the most of them with the really heavy items, but they didn't complain, although I was sure this wasn't they had in mind when they were told to watch my back. I was just about to get the rappelling platform in place when Don walked in. He waved me over, an odd expression on his face.

"What's wrong?" I asked at once, checking my cell to make sure I hadn't missed any calls.

"Nothing. Come to my office for a minute. There's . . . something you should see."

"Why does everyone think being cryptic is cool?" I wondered. Don didn't answer. He just headed back up and left me to follow. My watchdogs quit what they were doing and followed as well. If only my team were so obedient.

I was still grumbling as we got to Don's office. His door was closed, and I yanked it open—and then stopped in my tracks.

Tate stood on the other side of it. Indigo eyes ringed with green gazed at me with suppressed heartbreak. I glanced at my watch. It was just a few minutes after midnight, only a day since he'd been changed.

"He's mastered his hunger enough to be let out for a short while," Annette said. She was standing a little off to the side behind him. "Remarkable, really."

Pink tears slid out of Tate's eyes as he stared at me.

"I'll never forgive myself, Cat. I'm the one who sug-gested using Belinda as bait on jobs, and it almost got you killed. I'm so fucking sorry."

I touched his face, wiping away those pink streaks. "It's not your fault, Tate. No one saw this coming."

He grasped my hand. "I heard Max had gotten to you. I had to see for myself that you were all right."

Tate grabbed me, hugging me so hard, I knew I'd have bruises. He was probably unaware of it, not having had much time to get used to his new strength.

I pushed at him. "Tate . . . you're squeezing me too hard."

He let me go so fast I almost staggered. "Oh Christ, I can't do anything right!"

It hadn't escaped my notice that my three vampire guards were very close by. Their energies coiled in the air, as if the snow, coal, and Western-themed vampires were just about to strike.

"Ease down, guys," I told them.

"You shouldn't be so close to a new vampire," Rattler said. "It's not safe."

Tate's eyes went green. "Who the fuck are they?"

"Bones's way of being overprotective. They're my shadow until he gets here sometime later."

Annette cocked her head. "Is Crispin dealing with Max tonight?"

"Yep. And he thinks I wouldn't be able to stomach seeing him at his vampy worst. But he had Cooper and my mother go along. He must figure they're tougher than I am."

"Or more accurately, he doesn't care what they think of him," Annette replied.

"Figures you'd take his side," I scoffed.

The icily blond Zero moved closer to Tate. I saw it and let out an annoyed sigh.

"For crying out loud, he's not going to bite me, so back down."

"Your temper and scent are exciting him," Zero responded in a flat tone. "He's too newly turned to restrain his hunger from such triggers for long."

I cast a glance back at Tate. His eyes were blistering emerald, and if I could see his aura, it would probably be sparking. Oh. Maybe Whitey had a point.

Tate snarled, "I'd never hurt her."

Don, who hadn't said anything the last several minutes, spoke. "Then go back to the chamber and prove it."

Tate rounded on him before he seemed to catch himself. He took in a long scent of air and blew it out through his nose.

"You're right. Everyone in this room with a pulse is starting to smell really good. Okay. Back in the box, better safe than sorry."

He brushed by me as he went, taking in another long, lingering breath. "You smell like honey and cream, Cat. I'm going to make myself breathe the rest of the night, just to catch another whiff of you on my skin."

Oh shit. Why did he have to say things like that?

Tick Tock's hand went to the knife at his belt. Zero moved in front of me, almost stepping on my toes to do it. Rattler just shook his head.

"You'll be dying twice, boy, if you keep talkin' that way."

Tate gave him a cold look. "That gets scarier every time I hear it." Then he was gone, heading toward the elevators and the lowest level where his holding cell was.

I cleared my throat. "Well. At least that wasn't awkward."

Annette's mouth quirked. "Before I join Tate, might I have a word with you?"

I shrugged. "Sure. What's up?"

She glanced around. "In private."

"Fine, whatever. Come into my new office."

The three Fangsters didn't try to follow us. Guess they didn't feel Annette was a threat. Little did they know she and I were more likely to brawl than anyone else here.

I shut my door more for the illusion of privacy than thinking it would prevent undead eavesdropping. "Okay, what's up?"

Annette sat in one of the two chairs in the room. "Crispin's right to keep you away from this, Cat. Even though you're clearly sore with him about it."

I rolled my eyes. "Don't *you* start."

She stared at me. "I was fourteen when I was forced into an arranged marriage with the meanest, most revolting man I'd ever met . . . at the time. On the third night, Abbot called one of the chambermaids to join us in bed. I refused, and he beat me. After that, whenever he brought a woman into our bedchamber, I didn't argue. A few years later, a married duchess named Lady Genevieve invited Abbot and me to her estate when her husband was away at court. She drugged Abbot, and when he slumbered, she told me she had a surprise for me. There was a rap at her door and then a young man walked in. You can guess who it was."

"Do I need to hear this?" I interrupted. "Although on an objective level it's fascinating, I don't want to hear you reminisce about having sex with Bones."

She waved a hand. "There's a point. Crispin and I were both trapped by our circumstances, you see. Divorce only existed for kings then, and a woman was nothing more than a flesh machine for reproduction. I did conceive, whose child I don't know, since I'd been shagging both Crispin and Abbot, but at the time of delivery, Abbot refused to summon a midwife. The baby was breech, I almost bled to death, and my infant son strangled on his cord."

That took away my irritation. Even well over two hundred years later, there was no mistaking the pain in Annette's voice. "I'm sorry," I said sincerely.

She nodded once. "The stillbirth rendered me sterile and I was ill for months. Crispin snuck to care for me as I convalesced. Then soon after, he was arrested for thievery. Lady Genevieve arranged for me to have a private session with the magistrate. I convinced him not to hang Crispin, but to transport him to the South Wales colonies instead. It was the only thing I could do to repay Crispin for his many kindnesses."

"Thank you."

I'd never said that to Annette before, but over this topic, it was more than due. Yeah, Annette and I had our problems, but without her—and Ian, come to think—Bones wouldn't have lived beyond the eighteenth century.

"Nineteen miserable years passed. One night there was a knock on our bedchamber door. Abbot opened it, and then was thrown backward through the air. The hood fell back on the intruder and there was Crispin, looking not a day older than when I'd last seen him.

"Crispin told me he hadn't forgotten me or the misery I'd endured. Then he broke every bone in Abbot's body. After he'd killed him, Crispin showed me what he'd become, and he gave me a choice. With Abbot dead, I would inherit everything and could live out the rest of my life at court. But to me, that was only exchanging one cage for another, so I chose the other option Crispin offered. He turned me, and he has sheltered me ever since."

She paused to wipe away a tear. "And now to my point. You're strong, Cat, but you're not cruel. Nor is Crispin unless he is enraged or forced, and he is both in this instance. You'd be stricken by what you saw, but he would do no less than what was necessary. Crispin blames himself, and in part he's correct. Vampires respect what they fear. Mercy is considered a weakness. So love him enough to give him this, even if it's at the price of your pride."

She stood. Despite being confined in a room with Tate all day, she still looked as perfect as if she'd stepped from the salon.

"You confuse me," I said at last. "Why would you care about smoothing things over with me and Bones? It wasn't too long ago you did your best to split us up."

She paused on her way to the door. "Because I love him. Even though I can't have him anymore, I still want him to be happy."

She left, but it took me several minutes before I did. Things were much easier when I just hated Annette, not when I felt she had a point I needed to listen to.

Eight

BONES ARRIVED AT TEN AFTER MIDNIGHT.
I went outside to watch the helicopter land,
Cooper at the controls. Bones was the first one off.
Then came my mother, Rodney, and Cooper. Cooper
looked downright ghostly, but my mother seemed
almost blasé.

"Now *that* was informative," were her first words.
"Catherine, you never told me that no matter how
many times you sliced something off a vampire, it
grew back."

Charming. "Guess I don't have to ask if you had a
nice time," I muttered. "I suppose it'll make you easy
to shop for this Christmas, though."

She frowned. "Must you always wisecrack? Never
mind, I'm tired and I just want to get some sleep."

I swept out an arm. "The barracks are right this
way."

She gave a disparaging glance around. "I remember
barracks all too well from when you first started with

Don. It's like sleeping in a coffin and since I'm not a vampire, I'll pass on that."

"Mom." My teeth ground together. "It's only temporary. We'll get you another place soon. I would say you could stay with Bones and me, but then there's the whole vampire thing again."

"I can get a hotel," she insisted.

"Registered under the same name Max found you at?" I shot back. "No. Don's going to get you a new ID and another house, but until then—"

"She can stay with me."

The offer didn't come from Cooper. No, he'd been studying the ground in a rapt way during this exchange. Bones lifted his brows in surprise.

Rodney shrugged. "I have a house about two hours from here. I'm not there much, since I travel a lot, and it would be safe until your uncle found her something else, Cat."

I sighed. "Rodney, thanks for offering, but—"

"You don't have body parts there, do you?" my mother interrupted. "I don't want to open the refrigerator and find a head on the shelf."

Rodney laughed. "No, Justina, it doesn't look like Jeffrey Dahmer's hideaway."

She gave a measuring look toward the exterior of the building and then back at Rodney. "If my choices are staying in a barrack with a bloodsucking new vampire on the premises, or at the home of a ghoul, I'll take the ghoul. Catherine, I'm sure one of your soldiers can give us a ride?"

She swept away toward the barracks, Rodney following after her. *Dead Man Walking*, I thought, and it had nothing to do with him being a ghoul.

Bones watched them go and then turned to me. "That woman is frightening."

I snorted. "I've felt that way my entire life."

Bones stared at me, his expression guarded. No doubt he was wondering if I was going to start bitching at him again over how he'd kiddie-tabled me, but I wasn't. I still disagreed with his reasons, but Annette's admonition struck a chord in me. My relationship with Bones was worth a hell of a lot more than my wounded pride over what he'd done. I had to work through this issue with him, and avoidance or whining wasn't the way to do it.

Still, I felt awkward, not knowing what to do with myself. I hadn't given him a real greeting. My normal routine would have been to kiss him, but that didn't feel appropriate, either. I settled on stuffing my hands into my pockets and shifting uneasily on my feet.

"So . . ."

I let the single word trail off. Bones gave me an ironic smile.

"Better than 'rack off,' as it were."

"I understand why you did it, but we need to find a way to get past this sort of thing," I said in a rush. "Protecting the other person from what we assume he or she can't handle, I mean. I didn't think you could handle Don and my mother years ago, so I left, but I should have trusted you to make that decision for yourself. Just like you should have trusted me to decide about this."

Bones snorted in disbelief. "You're comparing my leaving you for one night to you disappearing on me for over four years?"

I felt a flush rise in my face. "Well, no . . . er, I mean, the principle's the same," I stammered. "What I did was wrong and stupid and I can honestly say I regret it more than anything in my life. But tonight you didn't give me a choice, Bones."

I paused, taking a deep breath and trying to let my eyes convey what I was having a hard time articulating.

"If you would have *asked* me not to go, for the same reasons you *ordered* me not to, I would have been okay with it. I would have still thought you were being paranoid, but it wouldn't have made me feel like you were pulling a 'me big bad vampire, you silly little girl' routine."

Bones shot me a frustrated look. "Of course I don't think you're a silly little girl."

He began to pace. I watched him, saying nothing.

"I'm very weary of being the reason you need to be strong," he said, his eyes edging with green. "Because of me, you dangled yourself out as bait to a group of murdering white slavers years ago. You had to drive a car through a house to rescue your mum—while covered in your grandparents' blood. You took a job with Don that's nearly gotten you killed countless times. All because of me."

He stopped pacing to come over to me, grasping my shoulders.

"I am well sick of seeing you forced to prove your strength on my behalf, so I didn't want you to do it yet again with Max. Can't you understand that?"

I covered his hands with mine. "Yes. But you didn't make me do any of those things, Bones. Even if I'd never met you, I'd still be going after vampires, and I would *still* have to handle the consequences of that."

He was silent for a long moment, staring into my eyes with that hard, penetrating gaze of his. Then at last, he gave a short nod.

"All right, luv. Next time I'll give you the choice, not make the decision for you."

I gave his hands a squeeze. "I promise not to decide things for you again, either."

His mouth twisted. "Turns out I'll be the first to make good on my word over this new accord. There have been some developments. Max gave us the name of the chap who sold him the missile he was going to use on your car."

"Do you know where he is now?"

"Yes."

I felt cold anticipation at the thought of confronting that person.

"I'm going with you."

Bones's expression said he hadn't expected any other response.

"Tomorrow."

This was my third trip to Canada. I'd traveled there on missions for Don, but maybe one day I'd get to just visit Niagara Falls as a tourist and not kill anything.

I sat in a van with my companions. Dave was half a mile away, negotiating the sale of three hundred surface-to-air missiles, five hundred grenades, and three high-powered explosives. He was acting as the front man, since Bones was much more recognizable. With Dave's extensive military background, he could talk shop with the best of the black market arms dealers. Even now they were quarreling over the grade of plastique for the potential car bombs.

No one spoke in the van. We could hear every word ourselves, so that meant any undead ears trained in our direction could as well. Cooper and Juan rechecked their machine guns, which were equipped with silver bullets. That modified ammunition wouldn't kill any ghouls, but it would make a vampire's day very unpleasant. Our numbers were low for a reason. Less chance of getting noticed that way.

Spade was there, picking at his fingernails as the time ticked by. He wasn't carrying a gun. Master vampires like him and Bones didn't need to, since they were weapons themselves. Deadly ones.

The modified bulletproof bodysuit I wore chafed underneath my clothes. It was the newest thing, a thin, flexible piece that covered all the major organs and looked like a medieval teddy. Of course, if my head got blown off, it wouldn't do me any good, but the rest of me was protected. Cooper and Juan were also outfitted with the same material. Range of motion was greatly increased with this versus the old bulky vests.

". . . not going to give you a fucking dime, this is not the product we agreed on," Dave was saying. "I'm supposed to go back to my client and tell them maybe the trigger mechanism will work or maybe it won't, praise Allah and it will. You stupid amateurs. There is so much shit for sale now, I don't need to pussy around with this Blue Light Special quality at Rembrandt prices, so fuck off and have a nice day."

He must have started to walk away, because there was a scurry of footsteps behind him.

"Wait a moment. Perhaps we could discuss—" the agitated bargainer began before he was cut off by a laugh. Bones stiffened beside me, and Spade perked up. This must be our target.

"Harrison, I'll take it from here," a cool voice interrupted.

We slid the van door open and crept out. Spade and Bones went first, their lack of heartbeats being an advantage. The rest of us would follow after the attack started. The element of surprise was priceless.

"Who are you?" Dave asked, sounding annoyed. "Another lackey?"

"I'm Domino, and yes, I am the boss," was the icy reply. "You must excuse this sample of material. It was a test. Occasionally we get undercover officers posing as buyers, but they can't tell the difference between a bomb or a basket. You clearly know your merchandise, however. Even if I've never heard of you."

This last part was colder than the first, and with open suspicion. Dave grunted.

"How many undercover agents have you had poking around your business that lost their pulses? Last I checked, the police academy hasn't called for undead admissions."

"Ah, but there is always a first time, isn't there? Now then, I have other business to attend to. Logan, bring out the other crates. We need to finish this up—"

Domino stopped speaking just before the explosion. He must have felt them coming before the two bombs that had been thrown into the warehouse detonated. The staccato burst of gunfire that erupted along with screams let me know there were more inside than we'd figured.

Juan, Cooper, and I sprinted toward the structure where flames were now leaping into the night. Keeping our heads down, we returned fire. In the blackness, I saw human and undead defenders trying to locate the cause of the bodies on the ground. Our machine guns crackling in the dark had two advantages. They kept the guards' attention on us while Spade and Bones slaughtered, and we took out several targets more at the same time. Dave had two primary goals in the melee of violence around him—keep Domino from getting killed, or getting away.

Juan grinned wolfishly and chanted unknown taunts in Spanish as we breached the perimeter. Cooper was cooler, methodical even as he sighted down his marks with admirable accuracy. He had a slight curl to his lips. For him, that was the equivalent of cackling glee.

Once close enough, I threw the gun away in favor of my knives, which were my favorite weapon. Almost as fast as I'd fired the bullets, I threw off silver blades at the remaining two dozen fighters. The humans were easy to drop, clawing at chests as the knives sank home.

Someone jumped me from behind, knocking me down. I wrestled him, holding his snapping fangs at bay. The vampire had a look of disbelief, then his features began to shrivel as I jammed a dagger through his heart. Chucking him off, I whirled to face the next one.

It was a human about to fire point-blank in my direction. I spun in a midair cartwheel to avoid the bullets, savagely amused by the dumbfounded expression he wore as none of them hit me. I wrenched the gun out of the man's hands and turned it on him. A few short bursts later and he was dead on the ground.

The next three vampires were all of lesser ages and powers. I dispatched them with my knives as Juan and Cooper unloaded round after round into the remaining forces that had lost their formation. Domino's men were firing at anything, including one another, as our attack continued. Inside the warehouse I heard more sounds of death being dealt. Choked curses and fruitless scrambling to get away. Out of the corner of my eye I saw Dave, Domino trapped underneath him, a silver blade near the vampire's heart.

For a moment, his disbelieving green gaze met mine before it widened in comprehension, and Domino began to struggle harder.

Dave cracked his head against the pavement hard enough to fracture his skull. It wouldn't kill him. It would just take him time to heal it.

Everything began to get quiet soon after. Intermittent shouts were cut off before they could be completed. A glance around showed minimal resistance now, as those who were left alive began to surrender. Strapped to my leg, along with the myriad of weapons, was a cell phone. I dialed Don and let him know to hold off any police that would have been alerted by the explosions. Several members of my team were ten miles away, waiting for this call. They would keep the Canadian authorities at bay while we finished up here.

There was a sudden whoosh of air above me. The knives I'd been ready to fling stayed in my hand as Bones dropped from the sky. He looked me over, assuring himself that I wasn't hurt, no doubt, and then swung his gaze around to the vampire Dave was restraining.

"Why hallo, Domino. Do you know who I am?"

Bones gestured for Dave to let Domino up. Spade appeared, red stains splattering him, and held Domino with an unyielding grip. Juan and Dave rounded up the few remaining survivors.

Domino glared at Bones. "No. What's the meaning of this?"

It was an outright lie. Domino did know. His eyes kept flicking to me.

Bones smiled. "Oh, grand. Going to make me beat the truth out of you? My favorite way to work."

Even I blinked at the suddenness of his movement. One moment Domino's legs were kicking, the next they were ripped off and in Bones's hands. Ew.

New body parts hurt when they grew back. So I'd been told, anyway. Domino screamed like that was true.

"Still don't know me, mate? Come on, lie to me again, see what it gets you."

"Stop," Domino shouted. "I know you, but I didn't know what the missile was for. I swear to Cain I didn't know!"

A dark brow arched. "Max didn't pay you himself, so who did?"

Domino stared with fascinated revulsion at his own limbs on the ground in front of him. "Promise you won't kill me, then I'll tell you everything."

"You don't want me to do that," Bones said softly. He leaned closer until he was mere inches from Domino's face. "Because if I let you live, you'll wish I hadn't. Or I can kill you here. Much easier that way. See, I believe you when you say you didn't know what that missile was for. That's why you get a choice, but either way, you *will* tell what I want to know."

I watched as denial, hope, despair, and bitter acceptance flashed on Domino's face.

"The money was wired, I don't know who from," came his flat reply at last. "Max was given an account number to transfer it into, but he didn't handle it himself. I know this because he kept calling me to see if the money had arrived. It took a few days, and he got impatient and said something about a deadline."

"Back to the bank wire," Bones said. "You're going to give me all of your account numbers, and then the locations of where you store your other merchandise. Make it quick. Don't want to stand here all bloody night."

Domino began to strain against Spade, but the other vampire was too strong. "Why do you need all of them? You can take the account it was sent to, but leave the rest alone!"

Bones chuckled, but it wasn't pleasant. "Why I want them is because I'm taking every last cent you have, along with your life. It'll be a lesson to others about what will happen to them if they cross me. Now, do you need more incentive to talk?"

Domino swore as he began to spout off numbers, locations, banks, stocks, investments, safety deposit boxes, all but what was hidden underneath his proverbial mattress. Bones took notes, pausing to question in more detail certain nuances. When Domino was finished, he just stared blankly ahead.

Bones rested his hands on either side of Domino's head, a light touch that belied his intention.

"Now, mate, if you've left anything out, or lied to me, you won't be around when I find out. But you have a son. Drug runner, isn't he? He won't be past my reach, and I'll have no qualms about taking all of my anger out on him, so the next bugger doesn't try to deceive me when I offer him a fair deal. One last time, have you left anything out?"

"I'd always heard you were a vicious bastard,"

Domino said in a dull voice. "All I've worked for, gone. My son will have nothing."

Those pale hands tightened. "He'll have his life. Unless he was involved in this or tries to collect vengeance on me later, I'll leave him alone. Last chance."

Domino must have believed the warning, because three more bank account numbers were revealed in a monotone of resignation. Being an arms dealer paid well. Between the money and the illegal merchandise, Bones was getting millions. No wonder he laughed at my salary.

"Wise choice," he commented when Domino finished. "If you've been truthful, your son is safe from me and mine. Any last words?"

"You're an asshole."

Bones just shrugged. "I already knew that."

Two hard turns later and it was over. I looked away from the head that dropped to the ground next to the rest of Domino's body.

Nine

In spite of the feverish tracking of Domino's accounts to try and pinpoint who supplied the money, we'd come up empty-handed. Whoever it was, he or she was clever. There were ghost companies, fake names, and canceled bank accounts, to name a few of the obstacles we encountered.

Two weeks later, Bones's cell phone rang. The crescendo should have sounded like a warning, but I'd been concentrating on the papers in front of me.

"Hallo . . . ah, didn't recognize the number, Mencheres . . ."

The name snapped me to attention. What did Bones's version of a vampire granddaddy want?

Bones's relaxed features hardened into unreadable planes as he listened. Then he said, "Right. We'll see you shortly," and hung up.

"Well?" I prodded.

"Mencheres is summoning me to his house to discuss a proposition he has for me."

I frowned. "Why couldn't he just tell you whatever it is over the phone?"

"It must be important, pet," Bones snorted. "My grandsire isn't much for dramatics, so whatever he wants to propose, it's not whether I'll water his plants for him for a small fee when he goes out of town."

Even though I was bundled under a thick sweater, I felt a chill go up my spine. What could Mencheres want to discuss with Bones that was so important, he was having him drop everything to meet him in person?

There was only one way to find out.

Mencheres answered the door himself, and I couldn't help but shiver as I felt his aura wash over me. The waves of energy coming from him were like a mini lightning storm. Mencheres's features announced him as Egyptian, and he had that whole wannabe pharaoh thing going on with his regal bearing and waist-length black hair. I guessed Mencheres to be well over two thousand, though from his appearance, you wouldn't think he was a day over twenty-five.

"Nice place you have here," I remarked, looking over the ornate mansion as we entered. "I can see why you'd need the space, what with all your houseguests."

If I'd thought we'd be surrounded by Mencheres's usual underlings, I was wrong. It sounded like we were the only three people in this mansion aside from some dogs. Mastiffs. Noble animals. I was a cat person myself.

Bones gave me a glance that made Mencheres smile. "Don't worry, she can say what she pleases. I like her directness. It's very similar to yours, albeit less diplomatic at times."

"My wife makes a good point, although tactless," Bones said. "Normally you have several of your people on hand. Should I assume their absence means you wish to keep our business private?"

"It's what I thought you would want," was his reply. "Before I go any further, can I offer either of you something? The house is fully stocked."

I bet it was. This place was three times the size of our home, and with huge grounds to boot. Bones had said Mencheres kept a vampire and ghoul staff with him, plus some members of his line, and then their live-in snacks as well. Being as old as he was, he had a large entourage.

Bones accepted an aged whiskey. I declined anything, wanting to get right to the point. Mencheres led us to a lovely drawing room done in masculine tones. Leather couches with buttery textures. A stone fireplace. Hardwood floors and hand-stitched rugs. One of the dogs came to sit at Mencheres's feet when he settled himself on the couch opposite us. Bones had one hand around his glass and the other was holding mine.

"Do you like the whiskey?" Mencheres asked.

"For the love of God, just say what your proposal is already," I burst out, since with Mencheres's ability to read minds, he would have heard my internal, impatient wonderings anyway.

Cool fingers tightened around mine. "I can't help it," I went on, more to Bones than Mencheres. "Look, I'm good at flirting with things and then killing them, or just killing them. Not beating around the bush. Mencheres had us fly all the way here for something, and it wasn't to ask if the whiskey was good."

Bones sighed. "Grandsire, if you would be so kind . . ."

He waved a hand to indicate what the rest of the sentence dangled. *Let's have it.*

Mencheres leaned forward, his steel eyes meeting Bones's dark brown ones. "I propose a permanent alliance between your line and mine, Bones. If you agree to this alliance, I will give you the same gift of power that was once given to me."

Wow. Sure didn't see *that* coming.

Bones tapped his chin while I shifted on my seat. Vampire politics made me edgy as a rule, and the thought of a permanent alliance with this particular mega-spooky vampire didn't make me happy at all. There had to be something behind this. I didn't see Mencheres throwing it out there solely to be magnanimous.

Bones seemed to agree. "You want to merge lines and give me a power upgrade? Why do I feel like there's more than you're telling me, Grandsire?"

Mencheres's face was impassive. "War is coming, I've seen it. With your new strength and our combined lines, we'll have a better chance to win."

"You've seen it?" I asked. "Or you've *seen* it?"

In addition to being able to mind-read anyone with a pulse, Mencheres was also known for his visions. Little glimpses of the future and all that. I wasn't sure whether I believed it—why wouldn't Mencheres be playing the lottery all the time?—but Bones believed Mencheres had that ability, and he'd known him for centuries.

"It's certain," Mencheres replied, no emotion in his tone.

Bones mulled this over. I kept silent. This was his call. He was the one who'd known Mencheres all of his undead life. Far be it for me to start voicing my disapproval just because Mencheres gave me the heebie-jeebies.

Bones nodded after a long moment. "I'll do it."

And I knew Mencheres could hear it when I thought, *Aw, shit*. He didn't comment, though. He just rose, all long black hair and sharp granite eyes, and then embraced Bones.

"We will seal our new alliance next week. Until then, speak of it to no one but those you trust the most."

Then Mencheres released Bones and gave me a wintry smile.

"*Now* you can leave, Cat."

The house Mencheres used to host the gathering in honor of his and Bones's forthcoming alliance had sentimental value for me, in a way. It was the same mansion where I'd met Ian when he'd tried to blackmail me into joining him, but I'd ended up binding myself to Bones instead. Apparently it belonged to Mencheres, and Ian had been just using it for that night.

Speaking of Ian, as Bones's sire, he'd earned himself an invite for tonight's festivities. Bones also had all of the direct members of his line here, well over two hundred vampires, and that didn't count the ghouls he'd had a hand in siring, which was roughly another hundred.

Mencheres couldn't fit all of his direct descendants without renting a football stadium, so power level and preference had decided the cut on who was invited. To showcase their new alliance, several prominent Master vampires of other lineages were present, and not all of them friendly.

Many of the ornate couches that had lined the area around the arena months ago were absent as well. There were too many people here now to have that much space taken up. It was practically standing room only, with chairs and couches reserved only for the very elite who dared to sit in them. At the arenalike center of the room, there were no such trappings. We would all stand.

This was the largest number of undead people I'd ever been around. My skin practically danced from all the vibrations coming off them. Our troupe of elite guards consisted of Spade, Tick Tock, Rattler, Zero, and about a dozen more somewhat familiar vampires. Their names might escape me, but their power levels didn't. Even in a room filled with more than half of Bones and Mencheres's people, our escorts were crackling with unspoken warning. I was glad I was on the inside of this group, not facing them in battle. I'd be roadkill against them.

When we entered the square elevated platform, I had the sensation of being in a boxing arena. There was Mencheres's side and Bones's on either corner, no one talking. Even the spectators were hushed. Then Mencheres strode to the center and addressed the faces fixed on him.

He'd dressed in an Egyptian tunic, all white, with a belt around his waist that I'd bet my ass was pure gold. Around his upper arms he had more gold bands, and his pale skin had a faint yellow sparkle. He must have dusted himself in it. With his long dark hair loose, held back only on his forehead by a thin lapis lazuli crown, he looked like he'd stepped out of an ancient fresco from a pharaoh's tomb. Hell, for all I knew, there *was* a fresco of him somewhere in a pharaoh's tomb.

"All of you are here to witness me declare my loyalty in an alliance that will only be broken by death. From this night forward, I promise that every person who belongs to Bones is also mine, as all of mine are now his. As proof of my word, I offer my blood to seal this alliance. If I betray it in any way, it will also be my penalty. Crispin, you who have renamed yourself Bones, do you accept my offer to merge our lines?"

Bones squeezed my hand once and went to stand next to the other vampire. "I do."

Mencheres paused, maybe for dramatic effect. "And what do you offer as proof of your word?"

Bones's voice was strong. "My blood is proof of my word. If I betray our alliance, let it be my penalty."

Normally they would have each sliced their hands, clasped them in a formal handshake, and called it a day. Kind of similar to a vampire marriage ceremony, in fact. But there was more going on tonight than our guests were aware of. Everyone here knew that Bones and Mencheres were merging their lines, but what they didn't know about was the bonus activity. The transference of power. Only those of us on the platform showed no surprise as Mencheres eschewed the traditional hand cutting and bent his head to Bones's neck instead.

There was a flurry of exclamations from the observers. Guess they'd caught on to what else this was about. Three rows up, I heard Ian spit out a foul curse, and I smiled. *Uh oh, did someone feel slighted?*

Ian wasn't the only one. There were several more unhappy voices from Mencheres's side of the huge room. People who'd obviously thought one day to be the lucky recipient of this gift themselves. That was the other reason why we had the guards with us. In case someone, or a group of someones, got more than vocal with their dissatisfaction.

Mencheres ignored all that and didn't stop drinking from Bones's neck. When at last he lifted his mouth, I saw Bones sway a tad on his feet. Draining a vampire made him weaker, and from the looks of Bones, Mencheres had cleaned his plate.

"My word, sealed in blood," Bones rasped. "Freely given and accepted."

Mencheres tilted his head in invitation next, and Bones sank his fangs into the other vampire's exposed throat.

It was different than when Mencheres drank. Something changed in the air. An invisible current in the room grew. Static electricity seemed to jump off the two figures in the center of the platform, and I blinked, rubbing my arms like I'd been zapped. Here it was, the transference of power. Bones told me that Mencheres had to will it out with his blood; it wasn't something that could be stolen just by anyone drinking him. Even as I watched, the Egyptian vampire's skin started to glow with an eerie inner light, as if a million stars were trying to break out of his flesh.

Above us, there was the sound of abrupt movement and scuffling. Someone was either trying to start a brawl or trying to make a break for it. Spade barked out a command, and unseen vampires descended from the roof like lethal spiders. They dropped onto the small melee, and then the noise stopped with equal speed.

Still Bones drank, ignoring everything around him, his legs solidifying underneath him. I knew he wasn't getting nourishment from Mencheres's blood, but was ingesting raw power with every pull of his mouth. Those sparkling stars of light on Mencheres's skin merged into Bones's flesh with the same ease that sand absorbed seawater. It was lovely to watch—and frightening.

A hum began to grow in the air, then it rose to a piercing, thunderous crescendo in a split second. Instinctively I clapped my hands over my ears even as Bones staggered backward, going limp all at once. I jumped forward and caught him, lowering him to the ground. Mencheres fared better but not by much. Two of his men grasped him as his head drooped and he swayed, looking barely conscious.

I held Bones on my lap. Our guard formed a protective circle around us with a barked warning that anyone who approached would be killed. It wasn't an exaggeration. They were all armed with silver. So was I. It lined my legs underneath my red dress.

Mencheres regained himself enough to mumble, "My blood, freely given and accepted as proof of my word," before biting the neck of a human brought to him for that purpose. I looked away, stroking Bones's face and waiting for him to wake up.

Several minutes later, he did. I sensed it in the rush of energy that made me twitch before his eyelids even fluttered. All of a sudden, Bones felt unfamiliar to me. The vibrating power that normally exuded from him didn't just increase—it kept growing and growing, until he felt like he was going to explode right in my arms.

His hand closed over mine in the next instant, and I jerked back. It felt like I'd just shoved my fist in a light socket.

"Bloody hell, luv, this feels quite different," were his first words.

I laid a tentative hand back on him. "Are you okay?"

It was almost stupid to ask with that crackling energy nearly shooting sparks up my arm, but I couldn't help myself.

He nodded and opened his eyes. "Very much so. In fact, I've never felt better. At least not unless we were alone."

Pig. Now I knew it was the same man I'd fallen in love with. Bones might have changed in power, but not in any other way. It was almost a relief to find his mind still in the gutter.

"Let's get you off me, then, your elbow is jabbing me in the kidney—"

Something on his face made me stop in midsentence. "What?" I asked.

"Did you just call me a pig?"

I froze. Had I said that out loud?

"Bloody hell, no you didn't!" he answered for me, springing to his feet in a lithe motion.

Good God, *he* could read minds now? There was something neither of us had thought would happen.

Bones pulled me up and kissed me. There was so much raw energy permeating from him that his tongue almost hurt when it slid into my mouth, but then it felt good. Very, very good.

"Shh," he whispered into my ear when his mouth trailed from mine.

I could guess why the secrecy, of course. We were in mixed company, and if Bones's enemies didn't know he had the new ability to read minds, then they wouldn't worry about it being used against them.

I won't say anything. But you and I will have to talk about this, because you can't just invade my mind whenever you want to be nosy.

"Ahh!"

It came out of me in a gasp when he bit my neck in the next moment. Mother of God, my knees went weak. Bones supported me when they lost strength entirely in the next second.

We'd planned on him taking some of my blood afterward. Even though he was now hyped full of vamp juice, it wouldn't nourish him. Only human blood could, and mine still half qualified. Thus it wasn't the shock of him biting my neck that buckled me. No, it was the fierce erotic waves pouring over me with each pull of his mouth. Holy shit, it had never felt like this before. He'd gone down on me with similar effect.

Bones raised his mouth from my throat but didn't let go of me, which was good, because I might have toppled over. Thank God he'd stopped biting me when he did—I would have been mortified to have an orgasm in front of a thousand people. It was bad enough that they could all sense just how much I'd liked having my neck turned into a straw, but at least I wasn't about to ask for a cigarette.

"Don't be embarrassed," Bones said low. "I feel the same way every time I drink from you. We'll finish up here soon, Kitten, now that the formalities are over."

He still had his arm around me when he turned to Mencheres. The other vampire was refreshed as well from his blood donor, albeit less sensuously, I'd bet. They clasped hands once before facing the crowd.

"Our alliance has been sealed," Mencheres said formally.

Bones was more casual about it. "Then this is a party, mates. Let's have at it."

ҭєṅ

BónᴇS, ᴇVᴇR PARAṅOíD ҭHAҭ oṅᴇ oF ҭHᴇSᴇ guests could be Max's mysterious benefactor, was plastered to my side. I didn't mind for two reasons. First, he could be right. There was a shitload of pulseless people here, and who knew how many of them were really allies? The other reason was simple. That new throb of his power felt like a caress along my skin.

But when the naked human men and women came out to mingle among the guests, I stopped in my tracks.

Bones chuckled, hearing the question in my mind, or guessing from the look of my face.

"These are the hors d'oeuvres, Kitten. See that glitter they're covered in? It's a very special mixture, edible as well. Note the ones with the extra arms? They don't have birth defects, those arms are food delicacies shaped like limbs and glued onto them. Ghouls have to eat also."

I stared in disbelief as one of the walking treats sat on the lap of a vampire, offering her neck. Meanwhile, a ghoul sedately gnawed on what appeared to be a fake fourth arm protruding from her torso. Yuck!

I found my voice. "That is the sickest version of a snack plate I've ever seen. How did you get these people to agree to this? Mind-fuck them?"

He snorted. "Not nearly. They're willing volunteers, pet. Some are humans who belong to Mencheres or me, and others are groupies, for lack of a better word. People who know about vampires and ghouls and are hoping some nice undead bloke will choose them to change over. It happens, of course. Else they wouldn't flock to us in droves. Some of them offer more than a bite or a beverage, but that's their choice. I don't require it."

Oh, so they were dinner and entertainment. How my life had changed. Here I was, one of the hosts of a bang-and-bite soirée honoring Bones's alliance with a mega-Master vampire. What next, presiding over a massive orgy?

Bones caught my hand. "We're sneaking away for a moment," he whispered, backing me into a nearby study. Once past the floor-to-ceiling bookshelves, he pressed a lever, and then we were in a narrow dark passageway before I'd ever seen where it was.

"Secret tunnel?" I teased. "How very cloak-and-dagger."

He smiled. "Ah, here we are. Alone at last."

"Here" was a small room, unfurnished, no windows. Only a hatch in the ceiling about three feet square in size.

"Leads to the roof by way of the attic," he supplied. "Quick way to make a dash for it, if one needed to. Also, this room has thick concrete walls, so less sound travels."

So that meant we could talk without being overheard. "You can read my mind now," I breathed. "God, Bones, that kind of freaks me out."

"I'd tell you I won't listen to your thoughts, but that would be a lie. You're too close to me for me to block them out completely, and I can't say I would even if I could. I want to know all of you, Kitten. What you show me, and what you try not to."

There was no use arguing over it. If I'd been endowed with the same power, I'd be just as guilty of using it. Mencheres had said Bones's strength would grow, but he hadn't mentioned that he might get new abilities altogether. I wondered what else was going to be different.

"My vision and hearing are clearer," Bones answered for me. "And of course I feel significantly stronger. As for what else is different, we'll have to wait and see."

"I still don't know about this," I muttered. It was weird having him pull the questions out of my mind before I could even ask them.

Bones studied my face. "I haven't changed, luv. Just my abilities. Can you believe that?"

He would have heard the answer before I said it out loud, but I did it anyway.

"Yes."

Bones gave me a few drops of his blood to replenish what he'd drunk before we returned to the questionable festivities. I felt like I'd downed a bottle of NoDoz, I was so wired. *Don will be doing backflips when he gets his sample for his weekly collection,* I thought irrelevantly.

Tate was across the room. He caught my eye and rubbed his nose, twice. I tensed. That was an old signal that there was trouble. He turned around in the next moment, so it wouldn't have been obvious to anyone that a message had just been exchanged.

This was a time when Bones's new telepathic eavesdropping would come in handy. *Something's up, Tate's freaked. If you have a lockdown mode for this place, now would be the time to implement it.*

Bones made his way over to Mencheres, keeping me close to his side as we passed by other people. They didn't exchange words. Maybe Mencheres had also heard my mental warning, because he nodded once and then gestured to a nearby guard.

That's when all hell broke loose.

A vampire walking toward us blew up. Just blew into pieces of scorched body parts. Then three more rushed in our direction at kamikaze speeds.

Bones threw me across the room like a Hail Mary football to Tate, who darted forward. It wasn't a moment too soon. The explosion from the charging vampires momentarily deafened me. Tate caught me, using his body as a shield from the sudden attack of human and inhuman bombs that seemed to be all around us. Two more of our breathing treats went off like Roman candles, splattering gore on whoever was lucky enough not to be killed by their close contact. I craned over Tate's shoulder and kicked as he barreled us away from the crowd.

"Goddammit, let me go!"

"You don't understand," Tate ground out, giving

me a rough elbow to the head that briefly stunned me into limpness. Then I started to wrestle with him as he sped through the throngs of people. Each exit was guarded by vampires who belonged to Bones or Mencheres, but they let us pass after a shouted command from Bones. Hearing his voice made me weak with relief. At least he was still alive.

Tate clamped his hand over my mouth, not letting go, even when I bit him. It was the most damage I could inflict in the position he had me in, flung over his back like a sack. Only after we were outside on the lawn did he stop running.

"Let go of my hand, I have to go back inside," he almost snarled, dropping me.

I released my bite and began to yell. "What the fuck, Tate! You think I'm just going to stay out here while people are exploding—"

"There's a bomb, Cat. This place is going to blow."

That shocked me into silence for a second, then I started toward the house again.

Tate punched me, hard, rocking me back.

"I don't have time to explain," he spat. "But I am going to get everyone out, even your vampire lover. If you see Talisman, grab him. He's involved. Guard the perimeter, Cat."

He sprinted back inside, and I wrestled with the choice whether or not to follow him. Everything inside me screamed to go back in and tell Bones about the bomb. What if Tate didn't get to him in time? Mentally I kept shouting the warning at him, but with all the chaos, I didn't know if he'd hear me.

My decision was made when I saw three forms streaking stealthily across the roof. Oh, we had rats trying to abandon ship, did we?

I got them in midair as they jumped to the ground, throwing them into the walls from the velocity of my leap. There was only a split second to identify them before I crashed into their bodies, and in that instant, I knew which ones to skewer. The two lesser vampires each got a chestful of daggers while I split Talisman's skull on the stone walls, not killing him, but dazing him.

He came to awareness with a frenzy of snapping teeth. Talisman was a Master vampire and he wasn't willing to go down gently. We rolled around on the grass, both of us tearing at each other. Soon I was covered in messy bite marks where his teeth sliced me but hadn't locked on. Only when I jabbed a knife through his heart did he freeze. With a malicious smile I moved it a fraction.

"One twitch and you're beef jerky, asshole. I'd stay real still if I were you."

But he wasn't me. "I won't be held like your father," he said, and proved his statement by thrashing on top of me, shredding his own heart with his actions and going limp.

"Shit!" I exclaimed, and shoved him off.

There wasn't time to ponder Talisman's suicide. The doors to the house opened and groups of vampires and ghouls came out, led by the guards. There were so many of them, it looked like an anthill evacuating. None of the faces belonged to Bones, however.

I saw Annette amid the throng and grabbed her. "Where's Bones? Why isn't he out here? He knows, doesn't he?"

I didn't say *bomb*, not wanting to cause a panic if people didn't know yet. Annette looked rather frazzled herself, her usual cool composure absent.

"He's still inside. He won't leave until all his people are out and he finds the others who are involved."

"Oh no he doesn't," I growled.

Annette yanked on my arm and didn't let go. "Crispin said to keep you out here," she insisted, holding me back.

Everything else aside, I enjoyed what I did next. Shallow of me, but true. I whirled and hit her so hard, she dropped to the ground with a dent in her skull. On the practical side, it also kept her from restraining me. See? It wasn't all for fun.

As I rushed toward the house, I almost barreled into Spade.

"Don't even think about stopping me," I warned him, palming some knives to punctuate my threat.

He barely looked at them. "You have to come with me, we need to get Crispin out. Tate is still inside as well. At a guess, we have less than four minutes."

Four minutes! Vampires could survive many things, but having their entire body blown to bits wasn't one of them. Fear made me reckless, and I dashed forward into the house at a dead run, Spade keeping pace.

We were in the deserted hallway when he sprung. I'd been searching the corners for danger and hadn't expected it from the man at my side. His fist shot at my head, but I never even saw it coming. All I knew was one moment, I'd been peering around a corridor, and in the next, I was seeing stars before everything went black.

When I opened my eyes, we were sprawled on the lawn a hundred yards from the house. Spade still held me in an unrelenting grip. Even his legs were tangled around mine.

"You backstabbing son of a bitch," I managed, struggling without success.

Spade gave me a grim smile even as he tightened his grip.

"Sorry, angel, but Crispin would kill me if I'd let anything happen to you."

Something moved on the roof. With Spade half on top of me, I couldn't see what, or who, it was.

"Is that him?" I asked desperately.

Spade craned his neck. "I'm not—"

An explosion cut him off and lit the sky, as bright as if God himself flipped on a switch. I screamed, struggling even as Spade flipped me over with his body covering mine. My face was pressed in the grass while heavy thunks landed everywhere. It had to be pieces of the house raining down on the lawn like pro-verbial brimstone. The smoke was choking even with my face in the dirt.

Spade didn't move for a few minutes, ignoring the threats I gasped out. Not until the sounds of falling objects ceased did he allow me to sit up, but he kept his rigid grip.

The vampires and ghouls milling around hadn't screamed at the sight of the house exploding in the night. They looked discomfited, but not traumatized.

"Charles, give me a hand with these."

Bones appeared above us in the swirling smoke. I was so relieved to see him, I almost cried. He was covered in soot, mostly unclothed from where his shirt and pants had been burned off, and his hair was in singed patches. He also had three vampires in his arms. When he landed, he dumped them to the ground.

"Hold those two. Bloody sods," he grumbled, kicking one. The third sat up and shook his head as if to clear it.

It was Tate. Thank God, he'd made it out alive as well. Spade released me as Bones knelt next to me, and I threw my arms around him.

"I'm so glad you're okay . . . and don't you ever tell your friends to hold me back again, dammit!"

Bones chuckled. "Can we fight about that later, Kitten? We still have business to sort out, after all."

Then he set me back to look at me. "What happened to you? You look chewed."

He took one of my knives and sliced his palm. I took his blood, feeling the pain in my head ebb.

"Are Juan and Cooper okay?" I asked, trying to spot them among the throngs of people.

"I can hear them," Tate answered. "They're all right."

Bones gave Tate a sharp look. "How did you know what was about to happen?"

Green flashed in Tate's eyes. "That scumbag Talisman approached me while you and Cat were off somewhere. He said he'd heard I was in love with Cat, and offered me a chance to get her all to myself. All I had to do was make sure you stayed inside the house after the bodies started to firecracker. Talisman guessed you'd want Cat as far away from any walking grenades as possible, so I was supposed to take her outside, then I just had to save my own ass in time. Presto, you dead, one Reaper looking for comfort. I gotta say, it was pretty tempting."

"I would have known you'd never do that, Tate," I said at once. "You're too good a man."

He laughed with more than a trace of irony. "Don't be so sure. I'll probably regret it later."

Bones stared at Tate for a long moment. I didn't say what else was obvious—that despite how much Bones didn't care for him, either, he could have left Tate in that house to die. But he'd grabbed him and saved his life instead. Without Bones flying them away, Tate would have burned. Both of them were more alike in their honor than I thought either would ever acknowledge.

But as Bones had said, there was more pressing business at hand right now. Like the two very unhappy vampires fifteen feet away. My eyes narrowed as I glared at them. Try to blow up the man I loved, would they? We'd just see about that.

Eleven

WE WERE ON THE FAR SIDE OF THE LAWN OF the still-smoldering house. The fire department had come. So had the police, but this time, Juan and Tate didn't even need to bother with their credentials. Not with so many vampires able to green-eye the emergency crews into putting out the flames first and asking questions . . . never.

Which was why no police had wandered over despite some very loud yelling by the six perpetrators of tonight's bonfire. The other four had been rounded up when the original two outed them under extreme duress. None of the guests had been allowed to leave while this went on, for obvious reasons, despite some protests. After two hours of "questioning," the main architect of the attack was finally revealed to be a vampire named Patra.

And wouldn't you know it, this Patra was also Max's mysterious benefactor, though I had no idea who she was, let alone why she'd wanted me dead.

As soon as Bones heard the name, his head whipped up and he stared at Mencheres. The Egyptian vampire closed his eyes with a look I might have called pain.

"Let me guess," I said, noting their reactions with alarm. "We're talking about a really old, powerful vampire?"

Bones turned his gaze back to me. "Yes. Over two thousand years old and a Master. Mencheres, you know what this means."

The other vampire's tunic wasn't all sparkly white now, and that pretty gold dust on his skin had been replaced by ashes. Right about now, I was thinking it matched his expression.

His steel eyes opened, and whatever emotions he might have been feeling were slammed behind an impenetrable mask.

"Yes. It means war."

"Those of you who are not of our lines," Bones said in a clear voice, "make your choice now. Stay here and align yourself with us, or choose Patra and walk away. You get free passage tonight only. Should I ever see you or yours again without invitation, I'll kill you."

Mencheres glided over next to him. "Decide," he said simply.

Some of those who walked over to us were a given. Spade had moved before the words finished being uttered. Rodney did, too, and several other notable members of the pulseless community. Vampires and ghouls I didn't recognize were taking our side, either out of loyalty to Bones or Mencheres, or out of fear of them.

Then there were the holdouts.

Several glided off into the night, their absences wordless but pointed. Then there were the undecided ones, waiting to see how many stayed and how many left before they chose a side. The person who surprised me most by leading his people over with a curt nod to Bones was Ian. I'd been sure he'd take that long walk into the night, what with how he'd been upstaged by Bones twice in the last few months. I glanced at Bones and thought a single sentence: *I don't trust him.*

A half shrug was his only response.

When it was finished, roughly seventy percent of the independent Masters had cast their lot with us. The other thirty were only an indication of the opposition. Who knew how many really meant it by standing at our side tonight? Only time would tell.

Pledges made, everyone left the ruins of the house. I hoped Mencheres had insurance, because he'd just lost a shitload of valuables in that detonation. Then again, I didn't think "undead vendetta" would look like a plausible reason on his homeowner's policy claim form.

Mencheres, Rattler, Tick Tock, and Zero accompanied Bones and me in our specially equipped SUV. It had bulletproof glass, among other things, and before we turned it on, Zero checked it over for any explosive devices. Fool us once and all that. Spade and Rodney were in charge of our four party spoilers. I was betting they were going to have a long day in front of them.

Once we'd driven off far enough that I wasn't worried about other undead ears listening, I asked the questions I hadn't wanted to utter before.

"How did this woman get those vampires to Krispy Kreme themselves? Obviously the humans had to be tranced into becoming walking bombs, but the vampires? It doesn't seem like their style."

Tick Tock was driving. Mencheres rode shotgun,

and Bones and I were in the backseat. Good thing this vehicular monstrosity had a third row so that the other three vampires weren't perched on our laps.

"Likely by holding whomever they love hostage and then threatening wretched torment on them if they refused," Bones replied. "Not much else would make a vampire give up their own lives in that way, but we'll find out for certain when we question the others more fully."

I winced. "God, then I can't really blame them for what they did. Maybe you shouldn't be so rough on them—"

"Did they come to me with the plot?" Bones interrupted. "No. I would have tried to assist them and their family if they had, but they didn't, so they knew the consequences."

I didn't argue further. Vampires played by a whole different set of rules, and for nearly killing Bones . . . yeah, they deserved what they got.

"Will she really let their families go?"

Bones shrugged. "It's in her favor to. Else the threat doesn't work as well next time."

"I hate this shit," I grumbled. "Backstabbing. Hostages. Suicide bombings. Family and friends hurt just because they love someone on the wrong side of the fang border. It's only going to get worse now, isn't it?"

"Yes."

Most of the time Bones's honesty was what I loved about him. Then there were the times when I wished he would just fucking lie to me.

I let out a deep sigh. "This puts our wedding on hold. There's no way we could expect to pull off a shindig like that with everything going on now. Instead of 'Here Comes the Bride,' I'd probably be walking down the aisle to a bunch of ticking noises before a big *boom*."

"I'm sorry, luv," Bones said. "It wouldn't be safe, not at this time."

Not unless we drive straight to a post office and do the honors there, I thought bleakly, then lashed myself for being childish. So we'd have our wedding another time, big deal. Considering how tonight had almost turned out, a canceled wedding should be the least of my concerns.

"So who is this Patra chick, anyway?" I asked. "Doesn't make sense that she'd go to such extremes to help my father murder me . . . and then let her lackey Talisman offer Tate a deal to get me out of the house before it blew."

In the front seat, I saw Mencheres tense even as Bones said, "No, it doesn't, does it, Grandsire? In fact, while I can think of several reasons why Patra would want you dead, and me as well now that I've merged lines with you, I don't have the slightest idea why she'd come after my wife."

Something in his tone made me look sharply at him . . . and then at the silent vampire in the front seat. There was more going on here than met the eye. The tension grew until you could almost see it like a haze.

"It was never about Cat," Mencheres said at last.

"Excuse me?" Now I was pissed. "When someone tries to see you dead, then it *is* about you in my book."

Mencheres didn't turn around, but kept staring ahead at the highway. "Then your book would be wrong, because there is another reason to kill you.

Max and Calibos believed that Bones didn't care about you, so they thought they could get away with what they did. But Patra knew Bones loved you. Enough that your death would be a crippling blow to him, which would make him easier to kill later. That's the only reason she aided Max, because she has no interest in you, Cat. Killing you was just a means to get to Bones."

Bones muttered a curse even as I burst out, "But why? What did *Bones* do to her?"

Bones's face was grim. With the soot and ash smeared all over him, he looked very dangerous.

"I think it's time you explain, Grandsire."

"Everyone envies me my visions," Mencheres said with bitterness. "You don't know what it's like to be asked why, why, *why* didn't I see the earthquake coming, or the tsunami, or the volcano, or the plane crash, or whatever tragic event that claims the lives of those around me. I don't know what makes some things come to me with diamond-sharp clarity, while others are murky, and some are never glimpsed at all. I can only warn what I am sure of . . . and then wait to see if I'm ignored."

I blinked. This was as upset as I'd ever seen Mencheres. His slick-as-ice exterior was seriously cracked, and he looked like he wanted to put his fist through the windshield. Tick Tock cast him an appraising look out of the corner of his eye, no doubt deciding whether or not to pull over.

"No one is blaming you for what happened tonight," Bones said in an even tone. "But you still haven't answered my question."

No, he hadn't, but he'd done a good job at clouding the issue. Hell, I could barely remember what the question was myself after that outburst. Oh, right, why the really old bitch wanted Bones dead. *Focus, Cat!*

"I warned Patra many years ago what would happen if she went down a certain path." Mencheres's voice was so low, I had to strain to hear him. "Centuries ago, I saw a vision of a man marrying a woman who was neither human, vampire, nor ghoul, and then the same man wielded the knife that killed Patra. So you see, Bones . . . as soon as Cat was revealed to be a half-breed and you wed her at Ian's, Patra knew what I'd told her all those years ago had come to pass. So the only way she can avoid that fate is to kill you."

"You son of a *bitch*." My voice was a furious growl. "You knew Patra would come after Bones with all she had, but you didn't warn him. You didn't do *any*thing!"

"Kitten, infighting won't solve anything," Bones said, but he didn't sound pleased, either. "We have to stick together, else we'll be doing Patra's work for her."

The logic penetrated that red part of my brain that was thinking, *Kill! Kill!* toward the vampire in the front seat.

Mencheres shook his head. "I've had guards watching Bones since that night at Ian's. The only time I didn't was when you both were carrying out your missions with your uncle. Furthermore, I . . . I'd hoped when Patra realized I'd been right, that she'd cease her plots against me. But after what happened to you, I knew she was set on her course. And that is why soon afterward, I made my offer of an alliance with Bones. Without it, do you think either of you would have a chance?"

Hard words. Bones gave Mencheres that same flat stare. "You're very right I'm going to kill Patra for what she's done to my wife. No matter if you plead with me not to."

"Why the hell would he?" I wondered irritably. "Seems to me she wants him dead, too, or she wouldn't have just barbecued his home hoping he'd be in it along with you. In fact, oh powerful one, why haven't you taken her out yourself? Can't you handle her on your own?"

Mencheres closed his eyes. It was Bones who answered my question.

"There's more about Patra you don't know. She chose her vampire name in honor of her mother, one of Egypt's most famous rulers, and merely shortened it when she changed over. Patra is the daughter of Cleopatra, and Mencheres refuses to kill her . . . because she's his wife."

Twelve

MARQUIS WAS A SWINGERS' BAR WHERE S&M was in vogue and humans were the minority. To blend in with their anything-goes style, I was posing as the third in a trio with Tate and Dave. Bones was here somewhere, but I hadn't seen him. It was hard enough for me to disguise who I was without walking in arm-in-arm together.

Not that we were here for kinky fun and games. Even though we were at war with the undead—the very *famous* undead, to be precise—I still had a job to do. After the deadly fiasco with Belinda, Don hadn't found another woman to be a replacement for me as bait yet, and this club was reported to be a place several people had disappeared from. Even though it was getting very difficult trying to juggle my job with all the upheaval in my personal life, work waited for no one. Not even the two-millennia-old daughter of Cleopatra.

I still had a hard time coming to grips with that, but Bones reminded me that people who were remembered hundreds or even thousands of years after their time were bound to make a lasting impression on their contemporaries. Put like that, I guess it wasn't such a surprise that some of history's notables—or their offspring, like Patra—had been changed over by a vampire or ghoul. But Mencheres hadn't just changed Patra, he'd also married her a mere few years after turning her. Practically a whirlwind courtship, as far as pulseless couples went. And even worse for him was that while he couldn't bring himself to kill his estranged wife, she sure didn't seem to have that same hesitation with him.

To blend in with the Marquis crowd, I'd had a drastic makeover. My hair was streaked with wide black highlights, and my outfit, if it could be called that, looked like a combination of *Last Tango in Paris* and *American Chopper.*

Two black leather circles attached to my breasts by thin metal chains were all that covered me from the waist up. Black leather thong panties were the bottom half, with more chains dangling from my waist in an absurd version of a skirt. Leather-topped thigh-high stockings embedded with spikes doubled as my hosiery, and I wore solid silver high-heeled shoes. All the better to kick the hell out of someone with. I'd gone heavy on the black eye makeup until raccoons and I could pass for cousins. Add numerous chains crisscrossing my arms, and this evening couldn't end fast enough.

Dave and Tate were dressed with equal heinousness. More black leather, chains, and whips. Either Don's staff truly had costumes for all possible occasions on hand, or someone at wardrobe had a lot of explaining to do.

We were checked for weapons at the door, all our chains notwithstanding. As usual, my silver shoes went overlooked. Hiding a weapon in plain sight had proven to be very effective. I was ushered in with Tate and Dave without anyone guessing a thing. Let the free-for-all begin.

The three of us surveyed the interior of the club. Even I, who'd seen a lot, blinked at the spectacle around me.

Couples led each other around by collars, dog-walking style. Every other person had a whip. I almost felt left out. In front of us a domestic dispute was going on. A man backhanded his date so hard, blood pearled at her mouth. My abrupt step forward was put on hold when she moaned in pleasure, asking for another blow.

Ew. Well, what did I expect? *S&M* didn't stand for *soft and mushy.*

What almost gave me away as a quasi-normal person was my reaction when I got a look at the dance floor. Random beatings aside, which seemed to be the norm, some humans and their undead companions were giving dirty dancing a whole new name.

"Wow," Tate whispered. "They're fucking *right on the dance floor.*"

"I see that." There was an edge to my words.

Dave gave me a sideways grin. "Juan will cry at being stuck in the van. If he were here, he'd be screaming, *Authenticity's imperative!* and taking his pants down."

That relaxed me enough to laugh. "You're so right. Well, let's boogey, boys, but keep your pencils in your pockets. We have a job to do."

For the next half hour, we grooved while managing to do a sweep of the area at the same time. So far, nothing looked murderous, even if it was nasty and rough.

I felt a hum of power nearby. Bones had gotten to be so familiar to me that I knew him by aura alone. As casually as I could manage, I glanced over Dave's shoulder, seeking him out. My eyes widened when I found him.

Bones was shirtless, those luscious muscles moving under his crystal flesh as he danced. And holy hell, when had he found the time to pierce his nipples? Those rings must be silver; that was the only thing a vampire's body wouldn't naturally dispel, but would need to be forced out by willpower instead, which Bones obviously wasn't doing. Those shiny silver circles drew the eye to his sculpted chest. It took me a minute to even notice his pants, and then I did freeze.

"Keep moving, Cat," Dave whispered.

I picked up where I'd left off, staring over Dave's shoulder as I danced. Bones's pants were made entirely of thin metal chains linked together. Skin peeked through the gaps whenever he moved, and anyone could tell he wasn't wearing anything under them. He caught my eye and grinned, running his tongue over his lip slow enough for me to notice that his nipples weren't the only thing he'd pierced.

I was just starting to get warm all over at the thought of how that spike in his tongue would feel, when a brunette jostled around other people to peer up at Bones, her expression one of delighted shock.

"I don't believe it, it's you! Do you remember me? Think Fresno, late eighties. Of course, I was human then. I almost didn't recognize you with the dark hair, you used to be blond . . ."

Bones was giving her a glare that would have frozen steel, but she went on, heedless.

". . . come here before? I'm here all the time, and I can show you the *private* party area."

Bones lost his annoyed look at once and beamed at her. "Priscilla, wasn't it? Of course I remember you, my lovely. Private area, you say? Show me."

Bones let her drag him off to the side. Tate watched, a faintly disgusted curl to his lips.

"Don't you get sick of it? How half the women he runs into have had a piece of him?"

I ignored that and focused on Bones and Priscilla. Bones was telling her I was on the menu for tonight, if that private area was discreet enough for dining.

"It is," Priscilla was saying as she ran her hands over him. "I can't wait to fuck you now that I'm a vampire. You were so amazing before, and it'll only be better . . ."

My teeth ground together. Tate just let out a knowing snort.

Priscilla pulled Bones's mouth down to hers next. I knew I should look away, but I couldn't. Nor could I leap across the dance floor and pummel her into a mass of goo, which is what I really wanted to do. But if I did, I might as well grab a bullhorn and announce myself. So I watched Bones kiss her with a thoroughness that had my nails ripping into my palms. *It's not real, just like it's not real when you have to romance targets on a job,* I reminded myself.

But it hurt like it was real, making me wonder how Bones stood it when the situation was reversed and it was me French-kissing and getting feely with other men. At least he grabbed Priscilla's hand to stop her when the tramp reached for the front of his pants.

"Soon, sweet, after I've eaten," Bones told her in a sensual purr. "Wouldn't want to be distracted, would I?"

Bones propelled her back toward our little group.

"This is William," he said with a nod to Dave, still in my arms. "The rest aren't worthy of names," he finished, indicating me and Tate.

Priscilla ran a finger over his chest. "What's yours? You never did tell me."

He brought her hand to his lips. "I'll tell you afterward."

My teeth ground again, but I didn't say anything.

"Follow me," Priscilla said. "This way."

His former promiscuity is finally coming in handy, I thought darkly as we approached the entryway into the hidden room. This would have taken time to find on our own.

It was concealed underneath the unused bar in the far corner. You stepped behind a half wall and lifted the false cabinet to reveal stairs. They traveled down, the noise from the revelers and music masking the sounds below. Something thumped in the room beyond the narrow passage, rising and falling with increasing volume as we approached.

"Welcome." Priscilla smiled as she opened the door. "To the real Marquis."

The room wasn't large, but it was filled from top to bottom with unnatural devices of every kind. Manacles hung from the walls, the cuffs attached to them stained with blood. We stepped past benches of a variety I never wanted to know about, straps and buckles worn from repeated use. A wheel? I didn't even want to guess what that was for.

The thumping noise we'd heard turned out to be the flogging of a couple tied to one of the welded poles. They were faced away from their tormentor, foreheads smacking into the pole with every blow, and from the looks of them, they weren't enjoying their punishment.

The whip master paused in his measured staccato to glance up at us. He was a vampire, roughly two hundred from the feel of his aura.

"What have you brought me, Priscilla?"

Another vampire lounged on the nearby couch, drinking from the neck of an unconscious woman on his lap.

"Guests, Anré," she said.

He rested his sherry-colored eyes over me. "I'll take her. It will be a pleasure to mark her flawless skin." Next he considered Bones. "You look familiar, have we met?"

Bones gave him a cold smile. "Not formally, but we did run into each other in London, round 1890, when I was looking for a bloke named Renard. Recall me now? I took his head but left you the rest of him."

Anré lowered his whip. Realization bloomed on his features, and then he shot Priscilla a truly evil glare.

"You idiot, do you know who this is?"

Priscilla gave Bones a confused look. Her distraction gave me the chance—and the great satisfaction—to knock her down and then ram my silver-heeled shoe right through her heart.

"She pissed me off for the last time," I said to no one in particular.

The vampire on the couch, watching this exchange with alarm, froze over his victim's neck. I lunged at him next. The girl was snatched from his hands and thrown to Dave while I head-butted the vamp with brutal force. He was stunned for a moment. Just long enough for me to jab the heel of my shoe into his heart and straight out through his back.

Anré began to back away, although there was nowhere for him to go. Tate and Dave were behind him, Bones and me in front of him.

"Please don't kill me, I have done nothing to you," he whimpered.

"Bloody hell, show some dignity. You're an embarrassment to the race," Bones chided him.

"Tate, get the unhappy couple," I directed him.

Tate went over to them, slashed his palm, and clapped it across each of their mouths. Soon their welts disappeared. Then he untied them from the pole, herding them well out of the way of the other bodies.

Anré held out a hand to Bones. "You have no cause to harm me. You want the humans? They're yours."

I shook my head. Wasn't it always the bullies who feared retaliation the most?

"You're afraid of him, but it's me you need to worry about."

I retrieved one of his fallen whips and cracked it for punctuation. Bones had thought I couldn't handle seeing what he dished out to Max, but I could prove that I wasn't too squeamish when it came to doing necessary dirty work.

"Give me the names of your other playmates, Anré. Refuse and, well . . . you have a lot of mean-looking toys here. Tried any of them out on yourself lately?"

An hour later I was in possession of a name—Slash. He was here somewhere, scouting out his potential dinner. With all the noise from above, I doubted he even knew what had happened to Anré.

I made my way through the dancers, seeking a man with the tattoo of a silver dragon along his jaw. Along the way, I was bumped, jostled, and even slapped by an overzealous woman whose partner turned away at the last moment. She didn't even apologize, either. Just glared at me and snapped, "That wasn't your gift!"

"I'll give it back, then," I responded, and whacked her a good one. Honestly, whatever happened to saying, *Excuse me*?

Someone grabbed me from behind. Cool hands moved over my breasts in a rough caress. I stiffened but didn't slam my elbow into their rib cage. Not yet.

"I'm better from the front," I purred in my best bondage-tramp imitation.

My head was jerked back next, so hard there would be strands of it in his grip. I gritted my teeth. This better be Slash, or I was going to stomp the shit out of the unknown asshole.

That cool hand made its way from my breast down my stomach—and didn't stop. Okay, enough being Little Miss Submissive!

I whirled around, losing more hair, and smashed my knee up at the same time. Tall, Dark, and Depraved, who did *not* have a silver dragon tattoo on his jaw, doubled over. Then I shoved him into the gyrating mass of revelers surrounding us.

"I *said* I'm better from the *front*."

There was laughter by the other dancers close enough to witness this. I gave Tall, Dark, and Depraved another nasty glare before scouting around again for Slash. He had to be here. I didn't want to come back tomorrow if I couldn't find him. In fact, I'd be pretty happy if I never set foot in this place again.

Two more cool hands slid along my waist, pulling me back against a hard chest. I clenched my fist, about to let loose a roundhouse punch, when something out of the corner of my eye stopped me. Were those scales etched on the side of my new Romeo's face?

I turned around . . . and smiled. "You look good enough to eat, handsome."

The man grinned, stretching the dragon's tail that curled from his jaw to the side of his mouth. "Funny you should say that. I was thinking the same thing about you."

We began to dance. Slash was about my height, and he used the alignment of our bodies to his greatest advantage. I let it go on for a few minutes. Right up until he unzipped his leather pants and pulled out Mr. One Eye.

"Whoa," I said, twisting away as he attempted to find a home for his stiff friend. "Isn't there somewhere we can be . . . alone?"

Slash glanced at his cock, as if expecting it to voice an objection. Then he tugged my arm.

"Come with me. I know just the place."

I saw with relief that I was being pulled toward the fake bar. If he'd gone in the opposite direction, all hell would have broken loose. Slash never bothered to tuck his dick back in his drawers, either. That thing stuck out the whole time like it was pointing the way.

"Oohh, how exciting," I said as he lifted the faux counter to reveal that hidden staircase.

Slash took my hand, almost yanking me beside him. The narrowness made for a very uncomfortable walk as we went down. *Mental note: Shower as soon as possible.*

"I think you'll be surprised," he said as he opened the door. Then he stopped short. "What the—?"

I shoved him in with all my strength. Slash went sprawling. He skidded to a halt at that awful pole, which now had the very bloody form of Anré shackled to it.

I closed the door behind me. Bones went over to Slash, raised a brow at his rapidly deflating erection, and then gave him an icy smile.

"No, mate, I expect *you're* the one who's surprised."

"If we can leave quietly, I think we won't have to call in the team," Tate said as he piled Slash's body on top of Anre's. Priscilla and the other nameless vampire were stacked next to them.

"Skulk out the back with our tails between our legs?" Bones snorted. "Fear's a valuable motivator. If we sneak away, then there's nothing to give someone pause who might consider setting up shop in this place again, is there?"

I considered that. In most of our operations, we had a smash-and-grab approach. Smash the bad guys (or girls!), grab the evidence (meaning bodies) and then leave. Maybe that strategy needed rethinking. Bones was right about fear being an excellent motivator. Patra was using that tactic against us now. Maybe we needed to highlight that we played for keeps, too.

I glanced at Dave. He gave me an almost imperceptible nod. Tate, however, was incensed.

"Brilliant plan, Crypt Keeper. You want us to bring up those heads like souvenirs, then shake our fingers at them and say, 'They were naughty' at all the freaks out there? You're out of your mind!"

"Foolish. Coward."

Bones bit out both words precisely. Tate snarled, and I tripped him as he stalked toward Bones.

"You must have slipped, because I *know* you weren't about to do anything, were you?"

Tate glared up at me, and then must have seen the consequences of following through with that intention in my gaze, because he lost his angry posture.

"Your call, Cat. What's it gonna be?"

Oddly enough, it's what happened when I'd pushed off Tall, Dark, and Depraved that made my decision. The people around us, human and otherwise, had just laughed. Not jumped in and helped him beat me into submission.

"We give a warning and show the proof. Like you said, Tate—I'll use those heads as props."

"All units, stand by," Tate said into his radio. It didn't escape me that he sounded both pissed and re-signed.

We made our way single file back up the stairs. Bones went first, followed by me, Tate, Dave, and our rescued couple, who hadn't said much all night. When we were all out, Bones lifted me up onto the counter of the fake bar, since my hands were full, and let out a whistle that pierced even over the loud music.

"Shut that noise off," he barked, giving a menacing green glare to the puzzled vampire in what I assumed was the DJ box.

The pumping techno beat was silenced. There were sounds of protest that cut off when people saw me. You could say I stood out, what with being perched on a bar holding four severed heads by their hair.

"I'll make this quick so you can get back to your fun. I'm the Red Reaper, and these four"—I held the heads up for better viewing—"took their games too far by killing my kind. If it happens again here, I'll come back."

Two hundred pairs of eyes stared at us, and most of them didn't come with heartbeats. Inside I tensed. Who knew how this would go? Things could get very unpleasant very fast.

Bones held out his hand to help me down, and I dropped my grisly trophies and took it.

Maybe some of them recognized who he was, or could guess. Or maybe it was simple apathy. Either way, one by one, the humans and nonhumans pulled back until there was a clear path from our position to the door. Bones set me down from the bar, and all of us walked uninterrupted to the exit.

"Un-fucking-real," Tate muttered when we reached the parking lot.

"Which just shows you how much you have to learn," Bones replied.

Thirteen

Bones and I drove to Denise's the next day. I hadn't seen my best friend in a while, what with gearing up for Tate's change and then the whole aftermath of my kidnapping. So just to hang out with her and relax was nice. Denise also knew everything about me, Bones, vampires, ghouls, and even the war we were in. I had to call her and explain the reason behind her abrupt relocation, after all. Don probably just told her and her husband, Randy, to pack without giving any reason why.

Their new house was on the outskirts of Memphis. It was a good thing Randy was a private computer consultant and could work wherever, because I would have hated to be the cause of him losing his job. Denise had quit her job shortly after they got married, so again, I was spared some guilt. They hadn't said anything, but I thought they were trying for a baby. It would explain her sudden interest in things she'd never bothered with before. Case in point, she made dinner for us instead of ordering out. Definitely a new trait.

"This is really good," I enthused, helping myself to more pot roast. "We'll have to come here for the holidays. As you know, I burn water."

Denise grinned. "Or you could have your own party and let Rodney cook. Didn't you tell me he was amazing in the kitchen?"

"Oh, he is," I answered, mouth still full. Then I cocked my head. "Bones, how dangerous would it be for us to have a Christmas party?"

He considered the question. "Have to only invite a few people, but I don't think it would be cause for any real alarm."

I swallowed as the idea grew in my mind. "I've never done that kind of thing before. My grandparents weren't social butterflies and I didn't much feel like entertaining during the years we were apart. Our guesthouse is finished, so we'd have plenty of room. We can't have our wedding right now, but we can have a small holiday party. It'll be our first Christmas together, Bones."

He smiled at me. "That's an excellent reason to celebrate, and I know Rodney would be delighted to come and cook. It's his favorite pastime."

Denise clapped her hands. "Oh, it'll be so cool. I've never celebrated a holiday with dead people before!"

Randy rolled his eyes, but Bones just laughed. "Yes, that usually does make for a more interesting time than a midnight Mass at church, I suspect."

"We'll have to invite my mother, too," I said. "In fact, she's not that far from here. Rodney's place is what? About an hour away?"

Bones nodded. "Yes. Want to visit her next?"

I considered my options. If she knew I'd been this close to her and hadn't stopped by, I'd never hear the end of it. Okay, so that was settled.

"We'll drop by. God knows she'll be there. The woman never goes out."

"When's her new place going to be ready?" Denise asked.

"Next week. I think Don deliberately took a while relocating her out of Rodney's to pay her back for some of the grief she's heaped over him in the past. There's no reason it should have taken so long to get her a safe place, not that I'll tell her that."

Denise got up, rummaged in her pantry for a minute, and then came out with an unopened bottle of gin.

"Here. If you're going to your mother's, you'll need this."

We said our goodbyes to Denise and Randy an hour later and headed off to my mother's temporary residence. It had been a pleasant drive through the country, very relaxing—until suddenly Bones cocked his head to the side as if concentrating, and then stomped on the gas pedal.

"What's wrong?"

He'd said moments ago that we were almost there. Alarmed, I strained my ears, but my range wasn't as far as his. All I could hear were the sounds from various families as we whizzed by their homes.

"Don't bleedin' believe it," Bones chuckled.

"What!"

He continued to streak through the streets at a high rate of speed. "Oh, you'll see. And you'll need that bottle Denise gave you."

I figured there wasn't a bloodbath going on, because

he still grinned with maniacal humor. Hopefully the sound of my mother being axed to death wouldn't make him so gleeful. When we pulled up in the driveway of what I assumed had to be Rodney's house, all I heard was her fumbling around and muttering curses. What was unusual about that?

Bones darted out of the car without even turning the engine off and pounded on the door hard enough to rattle the windows.

"Open up, Justina, or I'll break down this door!"

The front door flung open as I approached at a slower rate than Bones had. Someone had to turn the car off, after all.

Bones went right past my mother, ignoring her demands to stay out. He gave her a wicked rake of the eyes, and his lips twitched uncontrollably.

"Well. As I don't live and breathe. Justina, hair's a bit disheveled, luv, been cleaning house? No? And your face . . . if I didn't know better, I'd say it was flushed. Back when I was a degenerate whore, as you like to say, I'd see women look like you do all the time. After they were *shagging*."

My mouth dropped and I took in her appearance. She was wearing only a robe, her brown hair was indeed going every which way, her face was distinctly colored, and holy shit, was that a *hickey* on her neck?

"You filthy animal, get out of here," she commanded Bones.

He laughed so hard it bent him double. "Really, that's a bit of the pot calling the kettle black now, isn't it? And to think how Kitten used to be terrified about you finding out she was shagging a vampire. You can't say much about that anymore, can you? Come on down, mate, take a bow! I stand in abject awe."

"Bones," Rodney's voice called out gratingly from upstairs. "Just get out of here."

I staggered. "Mom? You and *Rodney*?"

A scarlet blush graced my mother's features. "He was making me dinner," she sputtered.

I found my voice amid the astonishment. "And dessert, too, apparently! I don't believe you. All those years, you crucified me for sleeping with a vampire, and look at you. Rodney's a ghoul, you hypocrite!"

"He doesn't kill people, they're dead when he gets to them!" she thundered back with questionable logic. "And I am forty-five years old and don't need to be explaining myself to my daughter."

I stared at her like I'd never seen her before. "Did Rodney like them?" I asked.

She huffed. "Did he like what, Catherine?"

"The balls on you, that's what!"

Bones laughed again and wiped his eyes with his sleeve. "Let's go, Kitten. Just had to rub it in, I couldn't resist. Justina, good on you, and Rodney"—another decadent chuckle—"*admirable* courage."

Bones propelled me, still bitching, from the house. The door slammed behind us.

Bones still couldn't contain his laughter as we drove away at safer speeds. "I'm delighted you didn't ring her in advance, luv. That was priceless."

I didn't answer, just settled back in my chair and broke the seal on the gin.

My dress was silver. It hung to my feet in a clinging line from the waist, two ties forming a halter at the neck. The back was bare, and the front had a deep V that made a bra impossible. Those stick-on ones didn't do the trick, either.

I frowned at my reflection. "You'll be able to tell right off if I get cold. I'm the hostess, I'm not supposed to look cheap."

Bones appeared behind me in the mirror. "You don't look cheap, you're stunning."

A brush of his lips on my back punctuated his compliment, and as if on cue, both my nipples puckered. Yeah, it looked indecent, all right.

"Ravishing," he whispered into my skin.

He should like the dress, he picked it out. Bones always chose more revealing outfits than I did. At least I had on underwear, minuscule though it was. Some things I insisted on despite his limitless powers of persuasion.

Bones tilted his head to the side for a second. "Your mum's here."

I went downstairs to greet her, since Bones wasn't dressed yet. I hadn't seen her since that unbelievable night at Rodney's, and I didn't even want to know if they were now, um, dating. Rodney, being a gentleman, hadn't mentioned the incident when he showed up this morning to prep for the evening's meal, but I'd heard Bones greet him with an "All hail the dragon slayer!" salute.

I opened the door . . . and my smile froze. This *couldn't* be my mother.

Her brown hair was free of gray and had new lighter highlights. Whether it was makeup or a chemical peel that seemed to have taken ten years off her in less than three weeks was anyone's guess. Her dark amethyst velvet dress was tighter than mine, and cut high on one leg before draping down to her ankle on the other side. One shoulder was bared in Grecian style, and her hair was swept half up with stray pieces trailing. Her blue eyes were the only thing familiar about her.

"Catherine." She swept by me without a hug. Okay, *that* was familiar, too. "You really should wear something warmer, it's freezing out."

Hello to you, too, Mom. Or whoever the hell you are, because you sure don't look like the woman who raised me.

"You should talk," I managed. "I can see all the way up to your thigh. My God, if Grandma saw you now, she'd come right out of her grave!"

My mother opened her mouth, paused, and then smiled. "I won't tell if you won't."

I was going directly to the kitchen to fall to my knees in awe before Rodney. Lo and behold, he'd managed to give her a sense of humor, and here I'd figured that would take voodoo, several headless chickens, and a lot of gris-gris.

"Let's get you some eggnog, Mom," I said, recovering from my shock enough to steer her into the living room. "It's spiked."

Fourteen

OUR LIST OF GUESTS WAS SMALL DUE TO THE unfestive circumstances of being at war. There were Rodney, Spade, Rattler, Tick Tock, Ian, Zero, and another vampire Annette brought as her date named Doc. Mencheres wasn't here, and that was fine by me. My guests consisted of Denise, Randy, my mother, Don, Cooper, Dave, Juan, and Tate.

Bones had invited Ian at the last minute. He hadn't been on my original list of people I wanted to spend time with, but since he'd thrown in his side with ours, Bones felt he'd deserved the nod. I'd been hoping he wouldn't show, but that was in vain. In fact, I wondered if the reason Ian came was because he knew he was here against my preference—and got a kick out of that.

We were sitting in the dining room. Ian had arrived late and as soon as he crossed the threshold, my mother and Don had gotten up from the table. They were lingering near the porch with Dave, Cooper, and

Juan, who also had reason not to like the chestnut-haired vampire across from me.

"Why, Cat, you seem edgy," Ian baited me after my silence at the table grew pointed. "You're not still cross at me over kidnapping your ex-boyfriend last summer, are you?"

I resisted the urge to hurl my plate at him. "Of course not, Ian. It's just that normally at this hour, Bones and I are fucking like rabbits, so I get twitchy when I have to wait for him to climb aboard."

Ian wasn't amused. "Do you let her insult me when I have come in goodwill, Crispin?" he demanded.

Bones lifted a brow. "You're not insulted in the least, and bringing up reference to how you attempted to force Cat into your line was extremely ill-mannered. Let it be the last time you speak of it."

The words were mild—his eyes weren't. They were swimming with green.

Ian leaned back in his chair. "Well, mate, look at you. Claws come shooting out straightaway, and here I was barely even being rude. At first I thought you snatched her away from me out of spite, but that's not it, is it? You of all people to fall prey to love."

They had over two hundred and twenty years of history between them, both good and bad. The air seemed to thicken around the table.

"You didn't come here just to discuss my wife, did you?"

Ian leaned forward. "It was Max's treatment of her that prompted you to declare violent retribution to any who had a part in it. Why wouldn't I want to see how committed you were before I stuck my own neck out farther than I already have? If you were merely angry out of a sense of pride, well . . ." Ian dangled the sentence with a careless flick of his hand. "Why endanger me and mine over ruffled feathers?"

"Do you remember the time I jammed a silver knife into your heart, Ian?" I asked brightly. "You can't count how many times I've wished I'd twisted it. Ruffled feathers over my kidnapping, torture, and attempted murder? Fuck you!"

"I'm not downplaying what happened to you, Cat," Ian said at once. "Only stating my interest in Crispin's reaction to it. What he's done to Max is deserved, but that could have been the smart response of a leader showing his mettle, nothing more. You do appreciate the difference?"

Ian's piercing turquoise eyes met mine. He was a cold bastard, I knew that from experience, but there must be more to him than I saw. Or Bones would have killed him decades ago.

Bones inclined his head. "You have your answer, Ian. My response is entirely personal when it comes to her."

"Lucky for you that Mencheres merged lines with you and gave you more power. And speaking of your new alliance, I can't imagine why Mencheres chose you over me, considering of the two of us, I'm not the one who shagged his wife."

I froze even as Bones let out a vicious curse. Ian, catching my expression, began to laugh.

"What, didn't Crispin tell you about that? Don't know why, happened before your parents were even born."

I got up from the table. Discussing this in front of Ian was not going to happen. Bones followed me as I went outside on the porch. Once we were alone, I rounded on him.

"Why? I know you didn't think much of screwing around before me, but Patra was your grandsire's wife!"

His jaw clenched. "I didn't know who she was when it happened. Mencheres and Patra hadn't been on good terms since before I became a vampire. A few decades ago, I met a woman, spent the night, and then a week later I found out she was Mencheres's wife. Patra knew who *I* was. She did it to hurt Mencheres, bloody hell, who do you think told him about it? I didn't understand why he didn't kill me back then, but after what's happened recently, I suppose he knew one day he'd need me around."

By having sex with another vampire's wife, Bones would be under a death sentence—if the wronged spouse chose to claim it.

"Is there anything else I don't know? Because I better not find out there was something more you decided to keep from me."

"There's nothing else. I promise."

I stopped my pacing to look at Bones. He was gorgeous, and the longer I was with him, the more I was reminded that many women had shared that opinion. I was sure there'd be a lot more ex-flings of his popping up, but here's hoping they wouldn't be powerful, homicidal ones like Patra.

"All right. Let's go back in. I'm sure Ian misses us."

Bones ignored my sarcasm and pulled me into his arms. "Do you know it's nearly midnight?" he whispered. "Only two more days until Christmas Eve."

So much had happened since last Christmas. What would the next year bring?

"Better things," Bones answered low. "I promise."

He kissed me, his lips cooler than usual, but who needed ninety-eight degrees when he made me feel this way? In fact, I began to feel warmer as his hands slid lower on my back.

A branch snapping nearby doused my mood and put me on instant alert. Bones straightened, breaking the kiss.

"Well, mate. I wondered how long you'd spy on us."

His sardonic tone confirmed what my belated senses finally picked up on. God, Bones distracted me to a dangerous level when we kissed. Good thing he could still pay attention, even though I suppose that wasn't an endorsement of *my* allure. Also good was that the vampire in the trees didn't want to kill us.

Tate came through the trees with more cracking of branches. "Hi, Cat. God, you look beautiful."

Uh oh. Why couldn't he just say, Happy Holidays?

Dave broke the loaded hostile atmosphere by coming onto the porch. "Buddy, you made it!"

Another confrontation delayed.

"Dave." Tate smiled as he received a bear hug from his friend. Juan came out next, followed by my uncle. Don's normally stoic features changed into a smile as he came forward and embraced Tate. Bones made a cynical noise and led me back inside with a parting comment to Tate.

"I'm sure you'll have no trouble finding your way to the cottage at the bottom of the hill. That's where you're staying."

Ian, ever tactless, chose that moment to sidle up to me. "You and Crispin resolved your differences, I hope?"

"Yes. Now you'll be able to sleep tonight."

Ian laughed. My mother wandered past us, and Ian eyed her with more than casual appreciation. "I say, Cat, I can see what led Max to his eventual downfall."

I gave him a black look. "Would you mind not bringing Max up in front of what's left of my family?"

Ian smiled without a touch of remorse. "Why would they be cross with me? I am owed no small amount of gratitude. If I hadn't changed Max, then there wouldn't be you."

That whipped my mother's head around. How like Ian not to have lowered his voice. I could have rammed my fist straight through his stupid mouth.

"Good one," I growled. "She didn't know you were his sire."

Bones appeared from behind him. "Mate, come with me for a moment."

He didn't wait for Ian's reply, but propelled him onto the porch. I went in the opposite direction to intercept my mother's furious beeline.

"Catherine!" she snapped as I blocked her path. "Get out of my way. I need to have a word with that thing."

Since she usually called Bones "filthy animal," I assumed "thing" meant Ian.

"Mom, I know you're upset."

She continued to shove her way past me. "Don't worry, I won't make a scene," she said with a final push by me. For her, that was the height of consideration.

"You." She marched straight up to Ian and jabbed a finger in his chest. He gave it an amused glance. "You created her father? Didn't you know what kind of filth he was? Or are you brainless, oblivious, and uncaring about the monsters you make?"

Bones let out a grim snort. "Clean up your mess, mate, but no matter how rude she gets, don't be insulting."

Ian rolled his eyes. "No, Justina, I'm not brainless, oblivious, or uncaring about those I sire. But if I'm responsible for every action my offspring does, then the same goes for you. Your daughter murdered my friend the day I met her. What do you owe me for that?"

I was nearly as taken aback as my mother was by Ian's cool turning of the tables.

"Another filthy vampire?" my mother purred when she regrouped. "One of many who tried to feast on her neck?"

"A ghoul doing his duty to defend me against a woman who tried to kill me in my own home," Ian countered. "Ask Cat. She'll tell you I never even attempted to bite her before she beheaded my friend."

I shuffled uncomfortably. How did I know Don had ulterior motives in sending me after Ian? I'd thought I was on just another job taking out the bad guys, not being the unwitting murderer of someone who'd done nothing wrong.

"I'm sorry about your friend, but I thought he was a killer, and he was sneaking up behind me to knock me out," I replied. "Besides, before that, you admitted you'd killed two people, Ian. Your employees."

"Who stole from me," was Ian's response. "Really, Crispin, what would you do to a couple of blokes who raided your home and tried to hawk your valuables on eBay?"

Bones shrugged. "The same. If you can't trust a chap with something as small as your possessions, how can you trust them not to betray you in a more serious manner?"

"Even so," Ian agreed, before giving my mother another measured look. "Then with Max we're more than even, poppet, so what else are you riled at me about?"

She appeared rattled, but then gestured at Bones. "Him. You made him, and he's the reason my parents were murdered, so we're hardly even, vampire."

A shadow flickered across Bones's face. *You weren't responsible for that,* I told him. *She's wrong.*

"Yet he also taught Cat how to fight, making her stronger, faster, and deadlier. Without that, do you think she'd still be alive? Furthermore, didn't he just save her life *and* yours recently? Are you telling me that's worth less than your parents?"

My mother stared at him in an odd way. Like she didn't know what to make of him. Ian returned her gaze, unblinking and unapologetic. Finally, after a tense silence, she turned on her heel and walked away.

"Glad we had a chance to talk," he called after her.

She didn't reply.

Ian clapped a hand across Bones's shoulders. "Shall we return inside? It's chilly out, and your wife is clearly cold." His eyes roamed over me and he laughed. "Clearly."

"Sod off," Bones snapped.

Ian walked away, whistling. I snorted. "Told you I should have worn a bra." Then I changed the subject, not wanting anything else to dampen our evening. "If you ask nicely, I'll let you open one of your presents, even though it's early."

Bones's lips curled. "What must I say? Please? Ah, Kitten, please, I implore you, beseech you—"

"Shut up." With a smirk, I pulled him into the library and retrieved a box from under the couch. A quick glance told me no one was watching, because I didn't want an audience for this. I'd been kidding when I said it was one of his real presents. It was something else. "Here."

Bones unwrapped it, and his smile grew to a dirty leer. "Aren't these lovely? Not my size, but if you'd like me to wear them, I'll be happy to oblige."

"Aren't you funny? But you know you're supposed to pick which one you want *me* to put on."

His choice was instant. "The red."

"I thought you'd like that one." My voice was wispy from the sudden flare of heat in his eyes.

Bones leaned closer until his mouth grazed mine. "Right you are."

Fifteen

THE RED NIGHTGOWN FLOWED AROUND ME, as dark as blood on my skin. Bones held me by the hips and arched underneath me, sharp noises of pleasure coming from his throat.

"Yes, Kitten. More . . . don't stop . . ."

I closed my eyes, caught up in the ecstasy. My fingers wound the sheet into handholds as I moved faster.

"Yes . . ."

The sensuality of the moment faded as a haze seemed to appear around us and the sheets began to develop a life of their own. They coiled around my wrists and ankles, as if the cotton had become an evil serpent. I tried to tell Bones to stop, but when I opened my mouth, blood poured out.

"Still trying to be brave, little girl?" a voice witheringly asked.

Horror crawled over me. I knew that voice.

The haze lifted, and I screamed in a long, piercing

wail as Bones and the bed faded, and I was somehow on the floor in front of my father. Those serpentine sheets became knives that speared me through the wrists. My gut, leg, and arms throbbed in agony.

"Know what I'm going to do to you, little girl?" Max went on. "I'm going to rip your throat out again."

He came toward me. I tried to twist away, but those knives in my wrists prevented me. Max laughed as his fangs neared my skin, my struggles as frantic as they were useless. Then I screamed as he dragged his fangs slowly across my neck.

"Stop stop stop stop—!"

Max pressed something to my mouth. I coughed, sputtered, and swallowed, but after a few moments, Max faded and I could see someone else.

"Wake up, Kitten!"

Bones focused in front of me. Before my gaze, welts and scratches on him healed, leaving only blood to show where they'd been. His wrist was pressed to my mouth, the sheets were shredded all around us, and we weren't alone in the room.

Spade was at the side of the bed grasping my shoulders. He let go and sat back with a noise of relief when I blinked at him. Dave, Rodney, and Tate hovered by the door, Denise almost hopping to see over them. Then all I saw was Bones's chest as he clutched me to him.

"Bloody hell, you're awake." He pushed me back and cupped my face. "Do you know where you are?"

In my bedroom. Stark naked and so was Bones. Spade rose to his feet and I looked away. We weren't the only ones undressed.

"Bones, what is everyone doing in here? Spade,

cover up. Frigging vampires think everyone wants to see what they've got."

Bones still had me clasped to him. At least being in his arms kept my breasts from being on display.

"Will you animals get out of my way!"

Good Lord, my *mother* was in the hallway trying to get in? She'd faint if she saw this.

"Spade, towel, bathroom," I hissed. "Save some of the mystery."

He laughed, but it sounded more like a tired wheeze. "Crispin, she's all right. I'll take myself off so she doesn't exhaust herself chiding me."

Spade had blood in drying lines on him as well. What the hell? Tate stared at me, and his presence made me squirm. He shouldn't see me like this.

Ian pushed by the other people in his way, snapping a cell phone shut.

"I told him it worked, Crispin. He said to call him later—"

"Now this is too much," I shouted. Forget Ian's businesslike manner, not even a wink or inappropriate leer. "I had a bad dream, there isn't a full-scale assault going on, so everyone, go."

Ian looked at me with pity. "More concerned with propriety than peril. We'll talk soon, Crispin."

"Right, then."

Finally, the room emptied. When the last person closed the door, I relaxed enough to tremble.

"God, that was the worst nightmare I've ever had. If I didn't know better, I'd say my neck still hurt . . ."

Which it did, actually. How was that possible?

Bones met my gaze. "Kitten, that wasn't just a dream. It was a spell to trap you in your own nightmare. Your neck hurts . . . because the spell was reenacting that day with Max, and if you hadn't have woken up, it would have finished the job and killed you."

I tensed everywhere, trying to get control. "How do you know it was a spell?"

"You started screaming in your sleep. Charles dashed in the room—that's why he was naked, he came straight from bed—and we tried to wake you. Then you became violent. Obviously, we knew it was more than a nightmare, and when I concentrated, I could read in your mind what was happening to you. No one had a bloody idea what to do. Ian rang Mencheres to tell him what was happening. He's the one who knew how to stop it."

"How long did this go on? It only seemed like a few minutes."

"It lasted round half an hour, though to me, it felt like years."

Half an hour! "You said Mencheres knew how to stop it. How'd he know?"

"Because Patra did it," Bones replied with quiet fury. "Practicing witchcraft is forbidden, but Patra studied it in secret. The spell would have been sealed with her blood, so only her blood—or the blood of her sire—could break it. Mencheres was too far away, so since he'd shared his blood and power with me, he thought it was possible mine would suffice. It did."

I shivered. Maybe the next time I went to sleep, I wouldn't wake up. Killed by my own memories. What a shitty way to go.

"So Patra can cast one of these spells anytime, anywhere?"

Bones's lips thinned into a grim line.

"Not if she's dead, she can't."

* * *

Later that afternoon, I called five delivery places. No, the humans in my house weren't that finicky, I was being practical. After all, we had several vampires to feed. The delivery people never knew that they were the real dinner, not the food they carried. They just left with a good tip and a lower iron count. Rodney made his own version of a square meal that he shared with Dave.

". . . get ahold of one of Patra's people before we plan any counterattack," Ian said during a pause in the conversation. "Or, if we're lucky, find a turncoat."

"You of all people should have the most experience in turncoats."

The spiteful remark came from Don, and I blinked. He'd hardly said a word since finding out who Patra was.

"Bollocks." Ian sighed. "Look, Max got what he asked for. He wanted to leave his job and his humanity, and I changed him because I can always use another bright, ruthless lad. End of story."

Don regarded Ian with disgust. "End of story? Do you know what Max did, when I tried to take him in after finding out he'd changed into a vampire? He murdered our parents and left their bodies on my doorstep! You enabled him to do that. You gave him the power."

This was something I hadn't heard before. After I found out Don was my uncle, I'd asked if I had any more relatives, but he'd curtly said no. Now I knew why the subject bothered him.

Ian gave Don a look. "Max was a killer before he met me, so the only power I gave him was to do it with fangs."

"You can't help your parents, but your niece is still alive, old chap," Bones said. "We could use your wits to ensure she stays that way. Right then, to the issue of—"

He stopped, staring up at the wood paneling in our ceiling. I followed suit in confusion. What, did we have termites?

"Mencheres is here," he stated.

Spade also picked his head up. "I don't sense him yet."

Bones stood. "I do. And he's not alone."

I rolled my eyes. Great. Guess we'd better call that new Italian place. Time to break in their driver's neck . . . and Denise and I could sample the chicken parm.

"Who's with him?" I asked.

Bones gave an irritated growl. "It's the bloody show hound."

That made Ian laugh. "Indeed? This should prove to be an interesting night, after all."

Unlike Ian, Spade didn't seem amused by the news. "Why would he bring him, Crispin? He knows the two of you don't care for each other."

"Not to mention I don't like him knowing where I live." Muttered as Bones began to pace. "But he loathes Patra even more than he hates me. My enemy's enemy is my friend and all that rot."

"Who?" I repeated. "Do I know him?"

Bones snorted. "You know who he is."

The sound of a helicopter approaching staved off further conversation. Minutes later, the grind of metal on concrete announced the landing of our uninvited guests.

Mencheres and another vampire stepped out of the

chopper. Bones welcomed his grandsire with a hug, but gave the other man only a cool nod.

Bones is wrong, I don't know him, I thought as I looked at the unfamiliar vampire. He was about six feet, with an angular face framed by long brown hair and a tight beard. A wide, pale forehead set off deep-set eyes. He wasn't handsome in the classic sense, but his looks were striking. I would have remembered him if we'd met before.

Scars crisscrossed the hand he extended to me. "You must be the Red Reaper."

He had an odd accent and his greeting wasn't "hello, how do you do?" typical, but I'd heard worse. "You have me at a disadvantage," I replied, shaking his hand.

Power sizzled up my arm. Whoever he was, he was a Master. And several hundred years old, at my guess.

"I rather doubt that." As he gave me the same evaluating stare I was giving him.

"Stop undressing her with your eyes," Bones snapped. "Though you weren't at the wedding, I'm certain you're aware that she's my wife."

The stranger laughed. He had unusual eyes, I noticed. Copper-colored and ringed with emerald. "My invitation must have been lost in the international mail."

Bones ignored that. "Mencheres, I hope there's a reason you brought him?"

"He has information," Mencheres said before turning to me. "Ah, Cat. Pleasure to see you again."

After all this time, you'd think I'd have known better, but *Can't say the same* was my first thought.

Bones gave me a look. I grimaced. *It just flew out!* Truth be told, I didn't know why I always had a knee-jerk reaction of dislike with Mencheres. Maybe we'd been enemies in a former life. By now, I'd believe anything.

Mencheres didn't comment on my uncouth version of "long time no see," so I tried for something polite out loud.

"Mencheres. Hi."

"Let's get this over with," Bones grumbled, turning to the other vampire. "Kitten, this is Vlad."

A bark of laughter escaped me before I could stuff it back. Jeez, someone had issues. "Not too original. You're the dozenth Vlad I've come across."

His thin lips curled. "I rather doubt they came by their names at birth as I did."

I waited for the punch line, but it didn't come. Bones still had that annoyed but serious expression on his face, and with growing awareness, I saw that none of the other vampires were laughing.

Finally I found my voice. "You're *Dracula*? You have got to be *shitting* me!"

While I was busy being flabbergasted, the other undead guests said hello. Vlad was greeted with tempered courtesy by everyone except for Annette. She gave him a kiss on the mouth that had me shaking my head at her.

Oh, Dracula as well, Annette? I guess if Frankenstein and the Wolf Man were real, they'd already have double-teamed you.

A wheeze came out of Mencheres. If I didn't know better, I'd have said it was a laugh.

Bones gave me another "watch your thoughts, for bloody sake" look. I redirected my observations about Annette's sexual history to the undead legend in front of me.

"Dracula. When I was sixteen and trying to learn anything I could about vampires, I read a lot about you. Bram Stoker almost made you sound nice, because the historical record paints you with a much nastier brush."

Bones lost his frown at once and gave me an approving grin. I rolled my eyes. *So it's okay to insult him, just not Annette? Hypocrite.*

"I don't answer to that name, and you shouldn't be so quick to believe everything you read. Recorded history's nothing if not fickle. I wonder what it will have to say of you, Catherine?"

"My name is Cat," I corrected him at once. "You remember mine and I'll get yours right."

After further introductions were made, we settled in the family room. Yes, the living room would have been nicer, but I wanted comfortable surroundings while plotting to murder one famed historical figure with another one. Vlad took the chair nearest me, situating himself as if it were a throne. He gave Bones an arch little smile that made me think he'd done it just to piss Bones off, which it had. Bones took his place beside me on the couch and clasped my hand, pointedly.

Despite the circumstances, the ten-year-old child inside me wanted to pepper Vlad with questions. *Who's buried in the church by your castle? Did you really nail turbans onto the heads of the sultan's emissaries when they refused to take them off? When did you become a vampire—before or after you supposedly drank glasses of blood on a battlefield as you dined among the men you'd impaled?*

"A peasant of similar height. Yes. After, and it was red wine I drank."

Motherfucker, I thought before slamming my mind shut. *Another one*.

"Impressive." Vlad flicked his gaze from me to Bones. "I wonder where she learned to develop such exceptional mental shields? Have you been hiding something, young man?"

"Don't come into my home and patronize me, you crusty old bat. You're a guest, so behave as one."

"Vlad . . ." There was a touch of reprimand in Mencheres's voice. More interesting was that Vlad responded to it with a conciliatory flick of his fingers.

"Yes, right. I promised to set our differences aside for the greater good and that's why I'm here. You know I don't like you, Bones, and you don't like me. In fact, if Patra had sided against you without also crossing Mencheres, I might be sitting with her now."

Bones shrugged. "And if it weren't for Mencheres, you and I would have danced a long time ago. But Mencheres holds you in high esteem and he must have a reason for it, so I'll trust his judgment that you're not the worthless sod I think you are."

I blinked. Talk about an uneasy truce.

Mencheres stood. His courtly manners made him seem harmless, but I knew looks were deceiving. In a fight, I was betting he'd be terrifying.

"Bones, I was shocked to hear Patra used magic against Cat. It's forbidden for vampires to practice magic, as you're aware. But we do have an advantage. Utilizing such a spell will weaken Patra for days, which gives us time to strike back at her, if we can find her. Vlad has information on where one of her people might be."

Bones turned a cold gaze to Vlad, who just grinned at him.

"Never thought you'd need something from me, did you?"

"You've already made up your mind whether you're going to tell me or not, so either spit it out or rack off," Bones replied shortly.

Vlad's eyes flicked to me, and then, oddly, to Tate.

"I can smell his lust for Cat. He doesn't even try to hide it. Pisses you off a great deal to have someone in your line openly lusting after your wife, doesn't it?"

"Hey, just a minute," I began, even as Bones raised a brow and snapped, "Your point?" to Vlad.

That thin-lipped grin widened. "I'm getting to it."

Sixteen

Santa looks like he's been hitting more than the eggnog, I thought as I strolled by the mix of people waiting in line to get a picture with ol' Saint Nick. Right now, a nip or two of the hard stuff sounded good to me, too.

Tate tightened his arm around me. It still felt wrong not to pull away, but I didn't. I leaned into him and smiled instead. Weren't we the perfect picture of a happy couple?

"You're so beautiful," Tate whispered, nuzzling my cheek. His mouth slid until it covered my own.

With my job, it was standard operating procedure to kiss undead targets. Hey, when playing a horny chick trying to get a guy alone, that was expected. But Tate wasn't a target, or a stranger, or someone who'd end up dead by the end of the night.

Unless, of course, Bones lost his temper and killed him before this charade was over.

Tate's mouth was cool over mine, but getting warmer

by the contact with my heated flesh. He wasn't a bad kisser, either, I couldn't help but notice, even though he'd kept things respectable by not slipping me any tongue. I tried not to dwell on the fact that I was kissing my friend. Tried to treat this like any other job, but I was failing.

I pulled away, a little too abruptly than my act as his date would have warranted.

"Um . . . I want some cotton candy," I blurted.

Tate lowered his head to whisper one word near my ear.

"Chicken."

He was right. If this was just another job, I wouldn't have thought twice about faking a little passion, French-kissing the fangs off him, or even grabbing his ass to make things appear more authentic. But this was *Tate*, so the objectivity I normally had was gone. Aside from my own lack of personal detachment, at any minute, I kept expecting Bones to leap out of a corner and rip Tate's head off.

Yeah, Vlad had a point. No one would *ever* think Bones would tolerate me wandering around a carnival making out with the man he hated.

Above us, kids screamed in delight as the Mad Hatter ride whirled them even faster. The Tilt-A-Whirl off to our left had similar squeals coming from it. Add that to the other rides, the countless conversations from people, Christmas songs blaring, metal grinding of the machines, and it made for a continuous chaos of sound around us.

Somewhere in the midst of this carnival, according to Vlad, was Anthony, one of Patra's henchmen. Anthony had a thing for Christmas carnivals. Enough not to have the good sense to stay away from them during a war. Then again, everyone thought it was someone else who'd get nabbed, sold out, followed, or killed. I was guilty of that myself. I hadn't imagined Max would be waiting for me at my mother's. So who was I to throw stones at Anthony for assuming no one would know what carnival he chose to visit tonight?

Hell, maybe Anthony wouldn't show up, and this was just Vlad's idea of a funny trick to play on Bones. To say Bones hadn't liked the idea of me playing Tate's girlfriend was to put it mildly. Bones had muttered a string of curses that raised even my brows, then said something along the lines of "Looks like Christmas came early for you, wanker" to Tate when he finally agreed it was the perfect ruse.

Of course, Vlad's intentions tonight could be more sinister, too. Mencheres didn't seem to think that Vlad would set us up. Bones must not have, either, or I wouldn't be here, but there was something to be said about trusting a vampire who openly didn't like Bones.

"Keep your eye on the prize," I muttered to Tate, avoiding his gaze.

A snort came from him. "I am."

That made me pull up short on my way to the cotton candy vendor. Tate and I were never alone anymore, so aside from our main goal, this was also the perfect time to set some things straight.

"Look, Tate, you have got to get over this . . . *thing* you have for me. It's affecting our friendship, our work, and you take your life in your hands every time you bring it up in front of Bones."

Tate came closer, lowering his voice, not that it mattered with all this background noise. Another vampire would have to be within spitting distance to focus in on our conversation.

"Do you know why I won't shut up about how I feel about you? Because I didn't say anything for years. We were friends, but I kept hoping with time, more would develop between us. I'm not making that mistake again, hesitating when I should have moved forward. I don't care if it pisses Crypt Keeper off or makes you uncomfortable, I'm done pretending that I only want to be your friend."

Tate leaned down, and I had to either let him press next to me, or cause a scene and wrest away.

"Don't tell me the thought's never crossed your mind, either," he said very softly. "I remember that night we kissed, before Bones showed back up in your life. You weren't treating me like just a friend then."

Figures he'd bring that up, I thought, frustration and annoyance competing within me. One evening of way too many drinks and loneliness had led to a kiss that should have never happened.

"You're an attractive man, and I'm not dead. Yeah, the thought crossed my mind once or twice. But that was before Bones came back. I can honestly say it hasn't happened since."

"Sometimes I hate Don," Tate spat.

I was baffled. "What does my uncle have to do with any of this?"

"Don knew what you were from the moment you were born, and I'd known him for three years before I met you. *Three years*, Cat. That fucking torments me. All Don would've had to do was look you up six months sooner than he did. Then you wouldn't have met Bones first, you would have met me. We like each other, you're attracted to me, and as a fellow vampire hunter, I would have been your perfect man. You would have fallen in love with me instead of ever loving Bones."

I was amazed by how much thought he'd put into this—and the worst part was, if I *had* met Tate before Bones, there was a good chance I might have ended up dating him. I couldn't say I'd have fallen in love with him, but there was nothing about Tate that made him unappealing as boyfriend material.

"Or I could have been killed on my first mission, that's a more likely scenario, because then Bones wouldn't have trained me first. And even if it all went like you described, it still wouidn't have worked out between us."

"Why?" Tate asked harshly.

"Bones would have been hired to kill me. He was offered the hit during the years I ran from him and the undead world didn't know of our connection. So either Bones would have killed me, or he would have been intrigued by my being a half-breed and captured me, like he did when we first met. Either way, you and I still wouldn't have made it. Sometimes two people just aren't meant to be together."

"I don't believe that," he said, stubbornness written all over him.

Refusal to quit in spite of overwhelming odds. That's what made Tate such a brave soldier, but in this regard, it also made him hold on to something he should let go of.

"Things will change," I said at last. "One day, you'll meet a woman who'll make you realize your feelings for me weren't the real deal. And when that happens, I'll be happy for you."

Tate shook his head. "Or you'll realize Bones isn't the man you thought he was, and you'll leave him. Come on, Cat, you barely even know him."

"I don't know Bones?" I repeated. "You're kidding me, right?"

"He's almost two hundred and fifty years old, and you've been around him, combined, for less than one year," Tate stated flatly.

"I know what counts," I said in a hard voice, stung.

"Or you're blinded by infatuation. Bones is a former pro, Cat. He's been romancing women for centuries. Annette's told me some things about him, and I gotta say, sometimes I don't know whether to stab Bones—or shake his hand. Someone like that doesn't just wake up one morning and change everything about their life by becoming a one-woman man."

Tate's voice became rougher, lower, and he turned until I faced him.

"But I've been by your side for almost five years. You know you can trust me. You know I'd never lie to you, or cheat on you, and baby, he will. Maybe not today, maybe not tomorrow, but it'll happen. And when it does, you'll leave him. And I'll be waiting."

This conversation was going nowhere. So much for talking sense into him about our friendship. I shot Tate an exasperated look even as I pasted a fake smile on my face and headed back to the cotton candy vendor. I couldn't swill gin here, but I could pound sugar while waiting to see if Anthony showed up.

Three cotton candies and two spins on the Ferris wheel later—hey, nothing beat the Ferris wheel for getting a good vantage point—there was still no sign of Anthony. Or any other vampires aside from Tate. It was after ten, so most of the youngest kids were gone by now. Santa was looking less jolly as the time dragged on. No doubt he was counting down the minutes until midnight, when the carnival closed.

Tate and I hadn't spoken much since our prior argu-

ment. We continued to act like a happy couple. Tate
played a marksman game, much to the dismay of the
carny behind the counter, since with Tate's military
background and new vampire status, he nailed every
target. I then had to walk around holding a huge
stuffed polar bear.

Oh yeah. *No one* looking at us would think we were
out hunting vampires.

Therefore, I was surprised when Tate abruptly spun
me around, kissing me like it was the last thing he'd
get to do before dying. My muffled protest was stilled
when he whispered, "He's here."

I dropped the polar bear to wrap my arms around
Tate, kissing him back with equal fervor and sending
my senses outward. *There.* About fifty yards away, a
tingle of inhuman power hung in the air. *How nice
of you to finally come out and play, Anthony.* Unless
this was some other vampire who'd decided on a little
Christmas cheer. That would be just our luck.

That current of power came closer. Whoever this
was, he'd felt Tate, too, because now he was heading
straight for us. I put a little more oomph into kissing Tate. He groaned, tightening his arms around
me. Between his grip and relentless kiss, there was a
reason for me to be breathless when he finally lifted
his head.

The vampire was only a dozen feet away now. Tate
didn't bother with subtlety—he stared at him and let
the barest hint of green peek out of his navy gaze.

"What do you want?"

I turned—and blinked. *This* was the person we
were supposed to take out?

Wide brown eyes stared at me from a face that appeared no older than fourteen. He had curly black hair,

a somewhat pronounced nose, and a slender build that accented his youthful appearance.

"I've never seen you before," the vampire said. His voice was more in line with his aura. He might not look old enough to see an R-rated movie, but his vibe gave him away at an easy couple hundred years old.

Tate let me step back a little, but his arm didn't leave my shoulders. "Why should you?"

The vampire smiled, showing he had dimples. God, it made him look even younger.

"Because I know a lot of people from our . . . country. But not you."

Tate gave the vampire a frosty smile. "I'm new, you could say. Name's Tate."

The vampire cocked his head. "Who do you belong to?"

"An asshole," Tate said at once. I wanted to smack him.

A dry laugh escaped the vampire, again at odds with his boyish appearance. "Don't we all? I'm Anthony."

Score! I mentally shouted. Here's hoping Anthony wasn't another mind reader, or we'd be screwed, although Bones assured me that ability was very rare.

"You never answered my question," Anthony said, that pleasant smile still dimpling his face.

Tate rolled his eyes. "Why should I? I'm not hunting, I'm just here with my girlfriend enjoying the festival."

"Let me give you some advice, sonny," Anthony said. To anyone close enough to overhear, it would be comical having someone who looked like a teenager calling Tate sonny. "When you meet one of us, you introduce yourself, and that includes who you belong to. Or one of us might get pissed and decide to teach you manners."

"Bones." Tate let the name hang in the air before muttering, "Asshole," again.

Yes, I knew it was part of the role, but I also knew he meant it, so I really wanted to smack him.

Anthony glanced around, so quickly that if I hadn't been watching his every movement, I would have missed it.

"You're *that* Tate," he murmured.

Tate folded his arms. "Isn't it your turn now?"

Anthony's smile grew challenging. "Patra," he said, waiting for Tate's reaction.

Tate flicked his gaze around in much more of a pronounced manner. I shifted, too, but in apparent confusion.

"What are you guys talking about?" I asked.

"Nothing you need to worry about, baby," Tate replied, giving my shoulders a reassuring squeeze. "Anthony here, uh, works for a competitor of my boss's and they're both fighting over the same contract. If you ask me, I wouldn't mind if his boss wins it."

Anthony raised a brow. "Really? That's a bold statement to make to a stranger about your . . . boss."

"Let's just say I had a chance to assist your boss before, but I didn't take it, and now I have buyer's remorse over what I could have gone home with instead of what I got," Tate said. His posture straightened from a relaxed stance to open defiance.

Anthony must have heard about the part Tate played back at Mencheres's house right before it went boom, because he nodded.

"What if your mistake could be remedied? I happen

to know my boss would be very interested in any information a . . . *corporate spy* could provide."

Tate smiled. "How does your boss reimburse? Because I'd want money *and* protection."

Anthony waved a hand. "You can't imagine how handsomely my employer rewards those who serve her."

I'll just bet, I thought cynically. *Unless, of course, you're talking about the people who serve Patra because she's threatened to kill their family if they don't.*

"Do you have to talk about business now?" I asked, making my voice petulant.

Anthony seemed to notice me for the first time. He gave me a thorough once-over, and there was nothing prepubescent in it. How typical that his first reaction had been to dismiss me because I had a heartbeat.

"Who's your friend, Tate?"

"Kathleen," Tate said, calling me by my middle name. "Isn't she gorgeous?"

"She is," Anthony agreed, moving closer. His eyes glittered. "But with those looks, that red hair, and her heartbeat, she reminds me a lot of someone I've heard of."

There was open challenge in his voice. I gave Anthony my most innocent "who, me?" look.

"I like to role-play," Tate replied with an edge to his tone. "So I had Kathleen change her hair color and wear contacts. You got a problem with that?"

Anthony's arm whipped out, and he yanked my jeans down over my left hip, then my right one. There was nothing on either but smooth, unmarked skin.

Tate bristled even as I hid a smile. *That's right,*

buddy. No tattoo anymore. Hurt like hell when Max slice it off, not that you would have heard about that, but now its absence is coming in handy.

"You touch her again and we quit talking," Tate growled.

Anthony seemed to relax. "Is she a good likeness of the real Reaper?"

Tate shrugged. "Close enough to count."

I'd had my hair dyed back to its normal crimson shade, all the better to smell like its color wasn't natural, and I was wearing contacts with blue flecks in them. Just enough to change my gaze from clear gray. Plus my skin was freshly darkened, all thanks to a quick rub from a self-tanner that helped hide its normal luminescence. That had been Vlad's idea. Drac was crafty indeed.

So far, the role-playing act was working. Anthony wasn't running for his life or his weapons.

"Do you have to talk about that *other* girl?"

I pouted, which would be expected, considering the topic. Tate kissed the top of my head.

"Not anymore, baby."

"Then can we go home?" With more pouting.

Tate looked down on me with an indulgent smile. "Got a little business to take care of first, then I'm all yours."

Anthony licked his lips. "Splendid. I'll take you to my supervisor, Hykso, who can finalize our transaction. Just let me bring my car around back. Less notice that way."

"I don't think so, friend," Tate said, steel underneath his genial tone. "You might change your mind and decide to involve other people in our business, and I don't want to spend the rest of my night being *dead* dead."

Anthony managed to appear offended. "It never crossed my mind."

Tate smiled intractably. "Then we leave now, together."

Anthony chewed his lower lip with normal, flat teeth. The gesture was so boyish, he could have been one of the older kids waiting in line to get a picture with Santa. He surveyed the people around us with indecision, either for the obvious leave-taking, or more sinister regrets.

I wanted a chance to nab Anthony's "supervisor." The higher up we could go on Patra's chain of command, the better this night would turn out to be.

"If we don't go with him, I still want to leave," I whispered, rubbing against Tate in a way that left nothing to the imagination as to what I was offering as incentive.

"You've got five seconds before she changes my mind," Tate told Anthony, kissing me with a hunger that was too raw to be mistaken for anything but real.

"All right, let's go," Anthony said.

Tate dragged his lips from mine. Green swirled in his eyes. My mouth was slightly swollen from the fierceness of his kiss, and I was a little out of breath.

"Let's go *tonight*," Anthony repeated with annoyance, beginning to shoulder his way through the people with the rudeness of a vampire who had somewhere else to be.

SEVENTEEN

WE FOLLOWED ANTHONY INTO THE PARKing lot. His ride was a black stretch limousine. As soon as we approached it, I squeezed Tate's hand, but he'd already sensed it.

"Who else is in there?" he demanded, halting a few feet away.

Anthony grabbed Tate just as the doors opened and two vampires streaked out. One helped Anthony hold Tate, and the other yanked me by the arm. That single gesture told me in a split second they didn't know who I was. If they had, this chump would've had me in a bear hug at knifepoint.

"Don't hurt us!" I wailed. There were only four of them, plus Anthony. Two of them were Masters, but not overly strong, so I guessed this was Anthony's guard for when he went out on the town. There were too few of them for it to be a setup.

Tate swung his gaze to me with sudden clarity, then smacked at the hands restraining him.

"I'll get into the car, no need to shove me," he barked.

Anthony didn't let go, but he nodded to the other man, who held the door open with sarcastic flourish. "After you."

Mentally I sent messages to Bones, telling him to back off and let these punks lead us straight to Hykso. It was a step of faith—I didn't how far away he was or if he could hear me. It wasn't like I could check the bars on my cell phone, after all.

I hunched my shoulders and scurried after Tate, letting fear leak out of my pores, a neat trick I'd developed over the years. To a vampire in a controlling position, it was the sweet scent of victory.

"What's going on?"

My voice trembled for effect while I measured each of the five men in the limo, gauging their strengths. They hadn't frisked me for weapons, which was just not smart. I had two throwing knives taped to my upper back, and the heels on my shoes weren't wood.

"We're being kidnapped," Tate answered coolly as the car sped off. "Don't worry, they're only interested in me."

Anthony grinned, elbowing his closest companion. "Can you believe the luck, finding one of Bones's people at the carnival? Patra will be so happy!"

The other vampire didn't share Anthony's giddiness. His gaze traveled over me in a calculated manner. *He dies first*, was my instant decision. *A thinker, didn't need one of those.*

"And his gray-eyed, red-haired friend? You haven't mentioned her."

Something was in his hand, and I made a bleat of terror as a normal person would when it pointed at me.

A gun, well, getting shot hurt less than getting burned, that was for damn sure. As long as he didn't blow a hole in my head or heart, any other area could get fixed.

Anthony giggled like a joke had been told. "Kratas, why Patra assigned you to me, I'll never know. She's a fake, of course. Tate's into role-playing. He's got a thing for the real Reaper, it's common knowledge. Maybe I'll keep the redhead for a while. She's not important, so Patra won't need her."

Kratas sent Anthony such a jaded look that the other vampires were suddenly at attention.

"None of you can think past your cocks, *that's* why Patra assigned me. Can I imagine the luck? No, I can't."

Anthony seemed a little sobered by that. He considered me more objectively. Then he shook his head.

"Her hair smells dyed, her eyes have some blue in them, and her skin . . . it doesn't have a hint of glow, and she's got no tat. Plus, you didn't see the two of them when I came into the carnival. They were all over each other. Bones wouldn't let his wife fool around with the youngest member of his line."

Kratas gave me another hard stare. "Waste of time to mesmerize her and ask," he muttered, almost more to himself. "If she's not the Reaper, she'll claim innocence, and if she *is*, she'll still claim innocence, since they say vampire powers don't work on her."

A brunette vampire shrugged. "Then kill her, it's not worth the risk."

I let out a frightened squeak for effect while I mentally readied myself for a fight. But Kratas was already shaking his head.

"And risk losing our most valuable hostage ever? I think not."

"I have an idea," one of the other vamps piped up. "Have them fuck. He wouldn't risk the death sentence if that's the Reaper, and neither would the real Reaper do it."

Tate let out a disbelieving chuckle even as my hand tightened over his.

"Come on, guys, you expect me to get it on now, when the poor girl's shaking in fear? No thanks, I'm not into rape."

Kratas, to my dismay, seemed to like the idea. He cocked his gun. "You into death? Because this gun's filled with silver bullets, and that's what you and your girlfriend are gonna get unless you do it. Here, we'll even give you some space."

With questionable helpfulness, the other vampires cleared off our seat and scrunched next to each other on the opposite one. Tate and I had their undivided attention. Great. Now what? They were all too alert for us to make a move. No, they had to be off their guard first.

Tate looked as rattled as I felt. I had to do something, fast, before he ruined it. The bottom line was, we needed them to lead us to Hykso. If we just started the mayhem now, there were too many of them for us to try and take a few alive. Sure, Bones would jump in on the fight, but what if before then, Tate or I happened to kill the only person who knew where Hykso was? We couldn't risk it.

"I don't want to die," I quavered, rustling up some crocodile tears. "We shouldn't have gone out tonight, I told you I wanted to stay home!"

Tate only took a second to fling off his unease. My act was saying to play the game—for now. Just long enough to get us a little closer to Hykso.

Tate took me in his arms. "It's all right, baby. Everything will be fine." Then he glared at them.

"You can forget about using a stopwatch, because I'm taking as long as it needs to get her in more of a mood."

"Just glare her into the mood," one of them snapped impatiently.

Tate gave a disgusted grunt. "That may be how you get chicks to want to fuck you, but I find a little something called foreplay works, too."

"Fine, do it your way," Anthony said. "As long as it's in the next twenty minutes, because we'll be at Hykso's plane by then."

Mentally I smiled. *Good, tell us how far away we are, that'll make it easier to coordinate an attack.*

Kratas waved the gun. "Get on with it."

I eyed Tate, wishing he had Bones's mind-reading skills. *Less than twenty minutes, okay, if we drag out the kissing and such, we can be almost there. Then Bones and the others will be close enough to find Hykso, if we end up killing whoever knows, we'll finish up here, and drinks will be on me. But first . . .*

Tate kissed me, brushing away my fake tears.

"It's okay, baby," he murmured. "Just pretend we're alone. Don't look at them. Think about how much you love to be touched like this."

The translation was clear—I had to act like he and I had done this before. Some of my reticence could be rationalized as fear. Not all of it.

I took a deep breath. If someone would have told me this morning that I'd spend tonight getting to second base with Tate, I would have laughed and called them a liar. But that was exactly what I was about to do, though second base was as far as I was willing to commit to this charade.

Tate gave me a deep, openmouthed kiss. I put my arms around him, letting my fingers play in his short hair as I tried to simultaneously keep an eye on the vampires through slitted lids and act like I was getting turned on by Tate's attention.

But I wasn't. Inside me, guilt was competing with the ruthlessness that said we had to get closer to our target. Right now, guilt was winning. Desire was pretty far from anything I felt.

Tate knew it, too. He broke the kiss, staring at me with mixed green and blue eyes. I knew he could tell that this wasn't doing anything for me, and so could the other vampires.

Kratas cocked the gun. Dammit all to hell. I'd have to fake this better.

I twined my arms around Tate and pulled myself onto his lap, drawing his head to my throat. The feel of his tongue and fangs grazing the sensitive skin of my neck reminded me of Bones, and there were shivers to show for that. I arched my back and sucked on his throat in return. Tate shuddered, his hands wandering up my back to my breasts.

Warning shot through me. Did Tate remember about the two knives strapped to my upper back? Or had he forgotten that in his distraction over the extremely compromising position we'd been forced into?

I reached for his hands, sliding them to the front of my jeans.

"I don't have to get all the way naked in front of them, do I?" I asked, making my voice high and vulnerable.

Tate's gaze met mine. His eyes were all green now. "No, baby. This'll do."

He helped me slide my jeans off even as, absurdly,

the night I met Bones flashed in my mind. How Bones had called my seduction bluff after I'd lured him to a deserted patch of woods. *You weren't going to shag me with all your clothes on, were you, Kitten? Guess all you'll need off is your knickers, then. Come on. Don't take all bloody night.*

I'd been embarrassed taking my pants off then and I was now, too, though for different reasons. Not because I was shy over Patra's five gawking vampires eyeing my ass in its skimpy thong—hell, I wanted them to look, it made for great distraction—but because it was Tate dragging my jeans down my legs. Tate's eyes wandering over me with a lust so raw, I almost abandoned my act right there, getting closer to Hykso be damned.

But then something changed in Tate's gaze. He glanced at the vampires leering at me, and anger tightened his jaw. I almost heaved a relieved sigh, even though Tate's being possessive was something that meant trouble later. Right now, though, it had the needed effect of getting him back on track. He kissed me again, but I could feel there was more calculation to it, even though it looked like he was being just as enthusiastic as before.

From the brief sideways glances I stole, with my mostly bare ass on display, the men were getting more into the show. Only Kratas seemed unaffected. His trigger finger didn't ease a fraction. Even through my irritation, I appreciated Patra's decision to place him with this group. Dedication in the midst of distraction was a valuable trait. I just wished it wasn't being used against me at the moment.

Of course, if he were human, I wouldn't have concerned myself with the gun pointing at me. I could dodge the bullets faster than a human could fire them, but not faster than a vampire. I knew that from painful experience.

I let Tate shift until he was on kneeling in front of me, since it completely cut off their view of my back. Much easier to go for my knives this way.

"Enough stalling."

Kratas tapped his gun for emphasis. At a guess, we were almost to the halfway point. Shit. This was going to be close.

Mentally I shouted a message to Bones, although I had no idea if he was close enough to hear me. *I'm going to count it down, Bones. School's out at zero.*

Five . . .

Tate stopped kissing me to unbutton his pants. His eyes were blazing green.

Four . . .

I clutched his shoulder while my other, hidden hand coiled around my knives.

Three . . .

Tate unzipped his jeans, and he wasn't wearing any underwear. It was all I could do not to jerk back and give the charade away. Yeah, this was way further than I'd ever anticipated things would go.

Two . . .

Three things happened at once. I whipped my arm around to send the blades sailing; Kratas fired, the bullet striking me in the side instead of the heart because of Tate's body in front of mine; and the roof ripped right off the limo.

There was a stunned second when I saw Bones before he snatched me out of the car. In the next instant, Spade and Ian descended like bats from hell onto the now-convertible limo while Tick Tock and Dave slammed into it from the highway.

The few cars on the road screeched madly around the careening vehicle. All of this I observed from my new viewpoint of fifty feet in the air, gripped in the crook of Bones's arm. I didn't have time to wonder about what we'd do with all the traffic when he abruptly swooped back down.

"Let's get this piece of rot off the road," he barked.

Bones, Spade, and Ian each grasped an edge of the limo and then propelled upward. The car lifted off the asphalt like it had grown wings. There was still scuffling going on in the interior of the limo, but it had a different sound to it now. More like muffled screams cut off before completion.

A few miles away in the distance, I saw a twin engine aircraft, propellers starting up. That had to be Hykso, and if we could see him, he could see us.

Bones growled and aimed straight for it, his emerald gaze lighting the night.

"Think they'll make it off the ground, Crispin?" Ian sang out, streamlining his body while handling his part of the limo.

"Not a bloody chance," Bones snarled back.

"We can take them on ourselves. Tend to Cat, she's been shot," Spade called out without turning his head.

"Don't even think about it," I snapped. "Flesh wound, keep going."

"We are."

I didn't need mind-reading skills to know Bones was pissed, but flying Superman style while toting an automobile and chasing a plane was not conducive for a chat.

The aircraft started to taxi, picking up speed. So did we, with a burst of nosferatu energy that crackled the air with invisible currents. I shut my eyes, not out of fear, but because the wind nearly blinded me. Through slits I saw the plane start to take off. We were still about fifty yards away.

"Now," Bones commanded, and dropped me.

A blur snatched me in midair before I hit the ground. My stupefied gaze took in the sight of bodies ejecting from the car as Bones flung it at the small plane. There was an explosion, its bright flash interrupted by the vampire setting me safely on the ground.

"Stay here," Ian muttered even as he darted away toward the wreckage. I ignored him, lurching in the same direction, but oddly shivering. Why did I feel this cold when the fire was so close?

Flaming forms crawled out of the remains of the plane and were promptly tackled. Through the wavering fire, people who were familiar to me almost appeared demonic as they hacked their way through the scrambling vampires. In minutes it was over, and somehow I was on the grass without noticing I'd fallen. That gunshot must have been more serious than I realized.

Bones came out of the orange haze. He had blood and soot on him, and his shirt was patchy in places. He knelt by me.

"This will hurt, Kitten, but it's quicker."

The warning made my eyes widen as he held me down. He took out a knife and gouged it into my side. I couldn't help but scream as his fingers followed, feeling around for the bullet. After a moment that seemed to last infinitely longer, Bones drew it out, then cut his palm and placed it over the site, healing the larger wound he'd just made. Then Bones sliced his wrist and pressed it to my mouth. I took a deep swallow of his blood, closing my eyes as the pain lost its grip.

My side tingled as it knit back together. It occurred to me that I must have been unconscious when Bones did this after Max shot me. Getting my throat torn open really had numbed me to everything else that day.

Bones drew his shirt over his head. "Bit torn in places, but it'll cover your arse," he said, handing it to me. "'Fraid your trousers are incinerated back in the car."

There were many things in his gaze, and reproach was one of them. Fumbling, I pulled his shirt on like it was a skirt. "Bones, I—"

"Later," he cut me off. "Got a few matters to settle first."

"Crispin."

Ian strode forward, dragging someone by the back of his neck. He shook the person like a rag doll and flung him near our feet.

"Here, reckoned you'd want this one alive. Charles and Tick Tock are holding Hykso, but we shouldn't linger here. Bloody coppers are on their way, I suspect."

"We don't have to worry about them. Perks of her sodding job. She flashes her badge and makes a call, and they curse and kick the stones for not being allowed to venture nearer. Almost funny, really."

Bones's tone changed to cruel in the next heartbeat. "Ah, hallo there, mate. You'll remember my wife. She's the one you shot."

Kratas wore an expression of grim resignation. "I had a feeling about you," he said to me. "Should have listened to my instinct."

"Know what I'm going to do with this bullet?"

Bones's casual tone didn't lull Kratas. His face showed he had no illusions.

"I'm going to melt it down and have a blade crafted with part of the silver. Then I'm going to run it through every part of your body except your heart."

God, sometimes Bones did scare me.

"Are you going to store him with Max?" Ian asked, not looking upset by the prospect of Kratas's pain.

"Elsewhere. We'll sort it out later. Get them set up in the truck so we can get out of here."

The two eighteen-wheelers that pulled up looked like any you'd see on the highway. Dirty on the outside, dents on the fenders, even the drivers were the quintessential trucker type. Furthermore, when the trailer back of one of them slid open, a line of crates met your eyes. Of course, those crates were a false wall that led to an interior the average shipping company had never conceived of.

"Charles, you're in this one with Hykso. Perhaps we'll get lucky and the bloke will know where Patra is. Kitten, we're in the other until we get to the airport. Ian, traveling with us or on your own?"

Ian cast a snooty glance at the trucks and shook his head. "I'll arrange for my own transportation."

"Take Tate with you."

Bones didn't make it a request. Ian shrugged.

"As you wish."

Spade led forward a heavily chained vampire. No introduction was necessary, it had to be Hykso. He certainly had an Egyptian flair to him, with straight black hair, dusky skin, and a distinctive nose. His eyes were trained on me as he approached. Then he smiled.

"Reaper. I look forward to you meeting my mistress."

I smiled back, just as coldly. "So do I, Hykso."

EighTeen

Spade led Hykso and Kratas into the trailer, where there were clamps and other such restraints attached to a reinforced wall.

Bones took my arm. "Let's go."

Bones jumped into the back of the second truck and lifted me up. As soon as I passed through the mock crate, I gaped. This interior was so vastly different from the other rig that I just stared.

Two couches were clamped in place to the floor, as were two chairs and a refrigerator. There was even a rug tacked down.

"My God," I breathed. "It's a frigging RV!"

"This is what my men will be staying in, when they're not with Hykso and Kratas," Bones replied briskly. "No need for them all to be cramped inside the one truck. We're just borrowing it to get back to the airport."

The axles made a wheeze underneath us as the truck was put into gear. There was a lurch and then intermittent jerking as we drove away.

Bones folded his arms and stared at me. I fidgeted, hating how loaded the silence was.

"You know I had no intention for things to go that far with Tate," I began. "I just wanted to get us closer to Hykso, and get them distracted before I chucked those knives . . ."

"And a brilliant toss it was, pet. Blades landed right in Kratas's eyes. He fired at you blind."

I winced at his tone. "I'm sorry," I said, and he knew I wasn't talking about blinding the other vampire.

Bones stalked around the small room. I didn't need vampire senses to feel the anger pouring off him, but I wasn't sure if it was directed at me, at Tate, or at the war that had put us in the limo in the first place.

"We should talk about this," I said, steeling myself for whatever incriminations he heaped on me. After all, I was only supposed to have kissed Tate during this charade. Not made out with him for over ten minutes while clad in only a sweater and my underwear. Yeah, if the situation were reversed, I'd be pissed, too.

Bones spun around. "I rather doubt talking will help. You did what you felt was necessary. I'm very brassed off by your methods, though I can't argue with your results."

He walked over in a measured, deliberate way that was no less predatory for its slowness. When he was only a few inches away, his hand traced down the sleeve of my shirt, and I couldn't help but flinch. There was something almost menacing in the way he touched me.

"Where did he kiss you? Touch you?"

I looked him in the eye.

"It didn't mean anything, Bones. It was nothing like how I feel with you."

"Ah." Bones's reply was soft, but his eyes went green. Whether that was anger or something else, I had no idea.

He leaned closer, his mouth almost brushing my neck. I couldn't help but shiver, wondering what he was about to do.

"He kissed you here." Bones's voice was a low growl. "I suspect he touched you here"—he touched my breasts through my shirt—"and I can smell his hands here"—while kneeling and running a hand along the outside of my thigh.

I didn't move, holding myself still the way prey does while it tries not to catch the attention of the hunter.

"I almost killed him tonight."

Bones breathed the words so close to my skin that gooseflesh broke out on me where they landed. I didn't say anything, sensing that whatever control Bones had used in not doing that before was at its breaking point now.

"I've never been jealous before I met you," Bones went on, still in that same soft, menacing tone. "It burns, luv. Like silver through my veins. Some nights, watching you with other men on your jobs, I think it will drive me mad."

His hands were still stroking my legs with a light, scary sensuality that made me want to cringe back—and edge forward at the same time. My whole body seemed to be holding its breath. Despite his outwardly calm demeanor, there was something boiling up in Bones that would break free any moment, I could feel it.

"It was just an act," I said again.

"Oh, I know that," Bones replied at once. Those glittering green eyes met mine. "Tate wouldn't be alive now if it wasn't. I know you only did this to get

Hykso, but Kitten." His voice deepened. Hardened. "No matter the cause, don't you dare, ever, let some-one handle you in such a way again."

Then, to my complete surprise, Bones yanked my underwear down.

"What are you *doing*?" I gasped.

"What does it look like I'm doing?" he muttered even as he spread my legs.

Of all the things I'd expected, this would have been last on my list. "But you're, er, still mad at me."

"Right you are," was his somewhat muted response as a deep lick made my knees weak.

I was about to say this wasn't a fair way to fight, when Bones grasped me around the waist and lifted me. Color rose to my cheeks, because my legs were around his shoulders and my head almost reached the ceiling.

"Bones," I managed to say. "Stop. Let me down."

Ruthlessly his tongue continued to tease me. "No. You're mine, and I'm taking you now."

I didn't want to respond to him. It seemed . . . wrong to do this while he was still mad, but if this was a new way to fight, I was losing the battle. A short cry wrenched from me as Bones's fangs rubbed my clitoris, not piercing it, just applying pressure. It felt incredible, inciting me to arch against him to feel it again. And again. Then repeatedly, gasping in ecstasy at the sensations bombarding me. Talking things out suddenly felt very overrated. Bones knew just what I loved, and I couldn't stop myself from getting lost in the sensations.

"Tell me you want me," he growled.

"God, yes," I managed, aching for him to be inside me.

"Say it." It was a demand even as his mouth continued to torment me. I dug my fingers into his hair and almost tore him away from my flesh.

"I want you," I rasped. "Now. Don't you dare say no to me."

A harsh laugh tickled me. "Wouldn't dream of it."

Bones set me down, dragging his mouth up my skin until my feet made contact with the floor. As soon as they did, I pushed him back toward the couch. He fell on it with me on top of him. I slid down, yanking his pants off, and then wrapped my mouth around him.

His flesh was cool, like marble come to life. I took him in until I couldn't fit any more, then began sucking with deep, rough pulls.

Bones moaned, his back arching. "Harder."

I increased the pressure. His hands tangled in my hair, then clenched into fists as I drew harder still.

"Bloody hell, that's so good," he said in a choked tone. "I can't wait."

He lifted me, ignoring my protests, and settled me on his hips while thrusting deeply into me. Filling me until it almost hurt. The jostling of the truck increased our friction as he moved with hungry, rapid strokes.

My head fell back and I moved with him, lost in blind sensation. Bones sat up, catching my nipple in his mouth. He sucked on it until it was almost numb with pleasure, then switched to my other nipple, giving it the same sweet, rough attention.

My nails raked down his sides. His mouth slid to my neck as he pressed me closer to him. I cried out at the feel of his fangs on my neck, grazing but not breaking my skin.

I held him closer to my throat. "Bite me."

He licked there instead. "No. You've lost too much blood tonight."

I didn't care. I wanted my blood inside him. It was a need almost as strong as the desperation that each new thrust within me brought.

"Do it," I moaned. "Show me I'm yours."

His arms lashed around me even as he moved faster. "You *are* mine," he ground out, sealing his mouth over my pulse.

I barely had a chance to smile at my victory when his fangs slid into my neck. A hot swell of passion flooded me, making me dizzy, but for more reasons than the single swallow Bones took before he closed the punctures.

He kissed me, the metallic taste of my blood flavoring his mouth. I clung to him while the escalating intensity seemed to make my whole body boil.

"Your turn, Kitten." His voice was rough with lust. "Show me I'm yours."

My teeth sank into his neck. Bones's hand wound in my hair, holding me closer, inciting me to bite harder, until his blood filled my mouth.

I swallowed. Bones tugged my head back to kiss me again, our mouths tasting of sex and each other's blood. There was something primal about that, his anger, and the seething urge I had to prove to him that no one else mattered.

Don't stop. Don't stop.

Maybe I said it out loud. Maybe I didn't. Either way, Bones flipped me over until he was on top of me, moving with ever-increasing intensity.

"I can't stop."

It was the best fight we'd ever had.

*   *   *

The strobe light of the control tower pierced the darkness with sweeping circular beams. It had snowed earlier. I was freezing even with my double pants, double sweaters, and jacket. Bones hadn't bothered to don anything over his clothes except his black leather coat, but that was probably more from habit than need for warmth.

The strobe light turned off. Our signal.

In the darkness, Bones circled the base in whirls of aerial speed, too fast and random for anyone with a bulky weapon to target, and if they had anything smaller, it wouldn't matter. I was clasped in his arms, closing my eyes against the dizzying dips and turns. We could have just driven up, but Bones was being extra paranoid. He didn't want to risk the chance that one of Patra's people had somehow followed us from the wreckage of Hykso's plane and was waiting near the compound with a rocket launcher like Max had.

The guard's faces on the roof were masks of carefully controlled shock as first Bones appeared out of the dark, landing, striding toward them without even a falter in his step. Right behind him was Ian, who carried Tate. Then came Tick Tock and Zero.

Don had argued about Ian knowing where the compound was, but Bones brushed him off. He didn't think Ian would betray the location to anyone, so Ian was here, letting go of Tate as soon as he touched the roof. Ian looked around with mild curiosity. His being here *was* ironic, of course, considering how Don had sent me to capture or kill Ian just a little over a year ago. How things had changed since then.

The six of us went inside. No one had been shot at and nothing had exploded. So far, so good, if you asked me, though truth be told, I didn't know why we were here in the first place. After our, um, argument in the back of the tractor trailer, Bones had said he needed to see Don. I'd asked why, of course, but he had a really effective method of distracting me. Then there had been the interesting scene at the private airport, where Bones green-eyed an unsuspecting pilot into flying us to Tennessee. So now here we were, and I still didn't know what Bones wanted to talk to my uncle about. Guess I'd find out soon enough.

I'd avoided looking at Tate since we met up with him, Ian, Tick Tock, and Zero a few miles from here. There was a big awkward factor between us now. For his part, Bones didn't act any differently, even though he would have been able to sense and hear my mental discomfort. Therefore, I was taken aback when Bones announced that he'd meet me in Don's office, saying he wanted to find Juan and have a word with him.

"Okay," I managed, torn between going with him just to keep Bones as a shield between me and Tate, and staying because of how cowardly that was. I picked staying. Whoever said I took the easy road? Not me.

Ian cast a meaningful look at Tate and then grinned. "I'll go with you, Crispin," he said.

I began walking toward Don's office. It didn't surprise me that Tate followed. I heard Bones let out a sardonic snort right before the elevator doors closed. Yeah, he wasn't surprised by Tate's actions, either.

Tick Tock and Zero kept pace behind us. I glanced back at them, once again struck by their dissimilarity in appearance. If ever there was a pair of vampires who looked less alike, it was the albino-ish Zero and the chocolate-skinned Tick Tock.

"Where did the two of you meet Bones?" I asked, struggling to fill the silence before Tate did.

"Poland," Zero replied.

"Australia," Tick Tock said.

I'd never been to either place. Tate's comment that I didn't really know Bones after spending just one year with him out of the two hundred and fifty he'd lived echoed in my mind. Then I squashed it. *I know what counts,* I reminded myself firmly.

"So, how are you and Crypt Keeper doing?" Tate asked in a casual tone.

"Fine." My voice was clipped.

Tate stopped walking and grabbed my arm. "How long are you going to pretend nothing happened, Cat?"

"Don't!" I said to Tick Tock, who'd already cleared his knife from his belt. "Back down, guys. I can handle this."

Zero's fangs slid back into his gums, and after another hard stare, Tick Tock put away his knife. Then I rounded on Tate, looking him full in the eye.

"It was a job, Tate. Things went further than they should have, but we got our targets and that's what matters. Now, before you permanently burn our friendship, would you please *stop* reading anything more into it than it was?"

"I know what I felt," Tate said roughly. "You can pretend all you want, Cat, but for a while there, you weren't acting, and you can't say you were only thinking of me as a friend."

I had a moment of warning at the power filling the air before I heard Bones's mocking laugh.

"Just as I suspected," he snorted from the other end of the hallway. "Knew it wouldn't be two minutes before you'd make that claim, but you're barking mad if you think you'll ever come between me and my wife."

Tate folded his arms. "I already have."

Bones came closer. More of that cracking power filled the air. Ian just leaned against the wall in the hallway and smiled, like he was enjoying the show. Zero and Tick Tock moved aside, until nothing stood in Bones's way to Tate except me.

"What are you about to do?" I asked low.

Bones arched a brow. "Nothing, pet. Why?"

Because you look like you're about to play soccer with Tate's head, I said to him silently. *And that's not going to happen, even if he is being an idiot.*

My uncle came out of his office, looked at the vampires lined up in the hallway and Tate's defiant stance, then coughed.

"Cat, Bones, glad you arrived safely. Won't you come sit down? I have some whiskey I was about to open up."

I couldn't remember the last time I'd seen Don drink, but I was glad for the tension dissipater. Bones smiled.

"A nip would do me just fine, old chap."

I laced my fingers in Bones's as we went inside, which was a good thing, because I almost tripped when Bones said, "You, too, mate," to Tate.

The three of us filed into Don's office. I took a seat on the couch and Bones sat next to me. Tate stood, his posture stiff and unyielding.

Don looked over each of us in turn before he sighed. "Why do I feel like I just interrupted a potentially nasty scene out there?"

"It doesn't matter, they're done now," I said to Don, glaring at Tate to let him know he'd better stick to that. "It was a vampire pissing contest, but it's over."

"Right you are, luv."

Bones leaned over to place a light kiss on my cheek. Then he dropped the bomb.

"I can read humans' minds now, Don. Therefore, I know the dilemma you're in, but the way out is right in front of you. It's commendable you haven't used your assets for monetary gain before, but desperate times call for desperate measures, don't you agree?"

"What?" I gasped, both confused by his last sentence and astounded that Bones had told Don about his new power.

My uncle didn't blink. "I won't expose the public to Brams. Synthetic vampire blood made into medicine is too experimental. In the wrong hands, it could turn the entire population into superhuman killers."

"What are you two talking about?" I demanded again.

"Don's in a bind," Bones replied. "His government's implemented deep budget cuts, and he's looking at closure in a year or two. He didn't want to tell anyone for fear of lowering morale."

My jaw dropped. Don's face confirmed it. "How could you have not said anything?" I gasped.

Bones tapped his chin and gave Don a calculating look. "Smart of you to realize how destructive Brams could be, but you don't need it. What's got the politicians in a twist today? Terrorism. Scares 'em sackless. What can you offer that no one else can? An interrogator guaranteed to get all the facts, names, places, and plots quicker than they can say full-scale retaliation."

Bones paused to let his words sink in. I was still shocked that Don had held back something as important as closing from the rest of us.

"You're offering to do that?" Don asked, openly skeptical.

Bones chuckled without humor. "Not me. Tate. Ship him to wherever their most stubborn hostage is, have him green-eye information out of the bloke, then sit back and sell him out to the highest bidder. You'll be flush inside of two months while providing an invaluable service to your country to boot. Best of all, the Geneva Convention can kiss your arse, because the hostage—and his holders—won't even remember how it happened."

"You bastard!" Tate burst, advancing on Bones in a fury.

"Sit down, soldier!" Don shouted in a tone I'd never heard him use.

Tate halted in his tracks, staring at me. "He's only doing this to get me away from Cat. He doesn't give a shit about our operation, this country, or anything else but her!"

"That's not the question, is it?" Bones asked icily. "Do *you* care about your operation, this country, or anything else but her? I seem to remember you saying your love for her wouldn't interfere with your job. Prove it."

I knew then that Bones had planned this ever since he'd ripped the roof off that limousine. *Don't get mad, get even* didn't begin to cover it.

Don stood up. "Well, Tate? What's your answer?"

Tate gave Bones a look of pure hatred. "You order me to go, Don, and I'll go."

Don sighed. "You're the finest man I know. You'll prove that everything I believed about integrity being corrupted after turning into a vampire was wrong." Don's gaze flicked to Bones. "I'll need someone to replace him. Cat's gone too much now, and Dave isn't enough."

Bones didn't flinch. "Let me have Tate 'round another week, then you can ship him off and I'll provide you with a replacement."

Don turned back to me. "Go on, Cat. I'll handle things from here."

Even though this was for the best, I felt anguished for Tate. I knew what it was like to be forced to walk away from the person you loved. I just wished that with this absence, Tate would fall in love with someone else. Maybe being away from me would wake him up to the fact that there were plenty of great women out there, instead of always having the person he thought he wanted dangled just out of his reach.

"Damn you," Tate growled to Bones.

"I hope . . ." The proper words failed me, so I just mumbled, "Take care of yourself, Tate," and walked out the door with Bones beside me.

ΠΙΠΕΤΕΕΠ

WE DIDΠ'T LEAVE RIGHT AWAY, WHICH WAS Bones's idea, not mine. I went to my office while Bones went off to talk to Juan. When the two of them came back fifteen minutes later, Juan looked paler, but he also seemed to be excited.

"What's up, buddy?" I asked him.

Juan glanced around my office. "Bones, *aqui? Ahora?*"

Bones gave him an impassive look and shut the door. "*Sí. Listos?*"

Juan's eyes met mine, and then he nodded. "*Sí.*"

I was still translating when Bones grabbed Juan and buried his fangs deeply into his neck. What the *hell*? Then what they'd been saying penetrated. *Bones, here? Now? Yes. Ready? Yes.* Oh God. Juan must be the vampire replacement Bones had just promised Don. Talk about not wasting any time.

Juan's legs buckled and his eyes fluttered closed. He lost consciousness, his body rapidly going into shock from the mass amounts of blood leaving it. Bones held him, sucking harder at his neck. Juan's face drained of color even as Bones's became pinker, almost flushed. If I touched him now, I knew he'd be warm, though his new temperature would only last as long as it took for Juan to suck his blood back out of him.

Juan's heartbeat slowed. What had been a fast, nervous beating when Bones first bit him turned into lazy, lethargic buh-booms with growing spaces in between. After a minute, Bones raised his head.

"Kitten, hand me that letter opener."

It took me a second to shake myself from seeing my friend dying in front of me, but then I passed the requested item over. Bones took it and plunged it into his own neck, blood spilling out from the unusual fullness of his jugular. He put Juan's head there, forcing his blood into Juan's mouth.

Dave came in the door, an odd expression on his face. Thin crimson lines streamed into Juan's slack mouth. The air became charged, like there was an electric storm nearby. Bones held Juan to his throat, the letter opener still piercing his skin. Juan's lips twitched. His mouth began to fasten of its own volition onto Bones's neck. The letter opener fell unneeded to the floor, because Juan was biting at him now. With single purpose, he clutched Bones, chewing into the pale neck.

Juan sucked on Bones's throat, tearing his flesh and swallowing in ravenous gulps. Bones held him, his lips in a tight line as Juan's blood was given back to him irrevocably altered. Finally he grasped Juan and tore his mouth away, wrestling him to the ground and pinning him. Juan struggled, his teeth snapping and starting to curve with the first hints of fang.

"No you don't, mate," Bones said.

Dave moved toward me, standing in the way of the now-insensible man who would kill anyone out of sheer, blind hunger.

Juan continued to thrash for another minute before he shuddered violently. Then his whole body went limp and his last few heartbeats went forever silent.

Bones grunted in weariness and rolled off him. Changing a vampire weakened him of power. Not to mention he'd just been sucked dry.

"You need a refill," I stated, and went to pass by Dave to get some plasma from our in-house blood bank.

"Don't."

Bones was on his feet before I could blink.

"Just . . . stay right here, Kitten."

Understanding dawned. The last time he'd changed someone over, I'd gone away for "just a minute" and ended up being tortured and nearly killed.

"I'll get it."

The offer came from Dave, who seemed to remember.

"No, you won't," Bones said. "You'll stay right here on the very slim chance our friend wakes up and makes a go for her throat. That way I wouldn't have to kill him. Call Ian, have him bring the blood up."

Jeez, he was being cautious. The odds of Juan rising so soon and overcoming Bones were near absolute zero, but I didn't argue. Dave made the call. The fact he also didn't argue meant he must be equally paranoid.

"Why aren't we just putting him downstairs in the secured cell? That's what it's there for."

"Because, Kitten . . ." Bones put Juan's lifeless body

on the couch and stayed close to him. "We're leaving, and we're taking him with us."

It was several hours and a dizzying free-flying jaunt from the compound back to our cars later that we rounded the last curves on our driveway in the Blue Ridge.

"Where will we put Juan?"

Three cars behind I could hear him howling, cut off the next moment by the slurping sound of him feeding from the plasma bags I'd packed. He'd just risen. Five vampires were in the car with him, and three of them were Masters. No, he wasn't going anywhere.

"The cellar," was Bones's reply. "It's reinforced, and we'll have Tick Tock, Dave, and Rattler take turns staying with him. Within a week, he'll be himself."

Until then, Juan was a danger to anyone with a pulse.

"We're not going to have enough room if everyone stays."

"Three of the couches have pull-outs and the rest will make do with blankets and the floor. Each one of them has endured worse, believe me."

"We're the ones with the urgent problems and it's our house they're staying at, we should take the floor," I noted. "It's only polite."

Bones snorted. "Right. In my own home on Christmas? I think not."

Yes, it was after two A.M. and therefore officially Christmas Day. This wasn't the romantic, private evening I had planned, but oh well. We were together.

I leaned over and kissed his neck, letting my breath tickle his ear. "Merry Christmas," I whispered.

Bones put the car in park and stopped me when I

began to draw back. His hand curled around my neck as he dipped my head back with a slow, deep kiss that made me *really* wish we were alone.

It was interrupted when Ian rapped on our side window.

"If we're supposed to wait outside in the cold while you two snog in the car, I'd just as soon have flown home."

My mouth opened in outrage when my mother trotted by and muttered, "Thank God somebody said it."

The humor of that struck me and I laughed. My mother, agreeing with the vampire who'd sired Max? Now that was a Christmas miracle if I'd ever heard one.

"I'm sorry, Ian, did I forget to ask your permission before I kissed my wife?" Bones countered. "Wanker."

"Guttersnipe."

Ian said the insult with a trace of a smile. Far from being offended, Bones chuckled, giving me a last kiss before he got out of the car and grasped Ian by the shoulders.

"I'm glad you're here, mate."

Ian had a self-deprecating smile. "Do you know why I am? Because for once, you asked for my assistance. You've never done that in all the centuries I've known you. That's why I threw in my lot with you, bloody usurping sod though you are."

Ever since I first met Ian, I hadn't understood why Bones tolerated him, but seeing the two of them like this explained a lot.

"You could have walked away, Ian. Just as you could have over two hundred and twenty years ago when I was imprisoned at the colony. I didn't thank you then and I haven't since, yet it is long overdue. Thank you, Ian, for changing me into a vampire. I am forever in your debt."

Ian's eyes flashed with emotion. Then he arched a jaded brow, recovering.

"About bleedin' time. I expect it to take another two centuries before you'll apologize for threatening to kill me over Cat?"

Bones laughed. "You'll shrivel waiting for that apology, mate."

"Let's hatch a dastardly plan, then," Ian said with amused grimness. "Or Patra will ensure that we'll *all* shrivel."

Vlad showed up at our house, remarking that he'd been in the neighborhood. I doubted that, but I wasn't about to call him a liar, especially since he'd proved to be a useful source of information. Still, part of me wondered if he'd shown up just because it irritated Bones. Vlad seemed to have a devilish sense of humor that way.

"Whatever happened to Anthony?" he asked after hearing that Hykso and Kratas were being held hostage. Unfortunately, according to Spade, so far they hadn't proved to know a wealth of information.

"I'll be shipping pieces of him back to Patra," Bones replied. "Along with pieces of the other blokes. It'll give her people something to think about."

The sick part of me wondered if Bones would cover those boxes with Christmas wrapping paper. Talk about getting an unwanted present. Here's hoping Patra didn't have something similar in the works for us. Nothing said "home for the holidays" like opening a present full of body parts.

"That's it!" I shot straight out of my seat, struck with an idea like a proverbial light bulb had gone off.

Bones arched a brow at me, not knowing what it was. My thoughts must have been whirling too fast for him to catch.

"It's Christmas. Most people are with their loved ones today," I said. "Rather than ship bits of Anthony and the other guys from flunky to flunky, hoping they got to someone high enough to pass them onto Patra, how would you like to deliver them in person?"

Ian leaned forward with interest. Bones stared at me, tapping his chin.

"You know the answer. Go on."

"We know that Patra's been on the lookout for anyone who'd give her information on us. Hell, we're doing the same thing. So what if an informant contacted Patra through one of the numbers Kratas had, offering to sell information on where she can find us? But this person wants cash up front, in person, and right away."

"Patra would assume it could be a trap," Mencheres pointed out. "So she'd expect you and Bones to be waiting for her."

I smiled. "I'm counting on that."

Bones finally caught the plan in my head. "Kitten, *no*."

"It's an acceptable risk," I argued.

Vlad must have picked the idea from my mind, too, because he started to laugh.

"Oh, Bones, maybe you should have married a docile girl who didn't stray too far from the kitchen."

"Get stuffed, don't you have more publicity stunts to pull?" Bones shot back. "How about chatting with another writer who can smear your name into greater popularity?"

"What, did Anne Rice not return your calls, *mate*?" Vlad asked scathingly. "Jealousy is such an ugly trait."

A noise escaped me before I could choke it off. Ian had no such discretion, and his laugh was clear and hearty.

"Don't glare at her, Crispin. It was funny, and that's not even counting the look on your face."

Which was far from amused, but after a beat, Bones relaxed and his lips twitched.

"Indeed it was. Right. Let us sort out this plan of yours, Kitten. It may be our best opportunity."

Bones selected the members of the vampire entourage who were going with me. When he directed Tate to be one of the five, I was speechless. Then he confounded me even more by choosing Vlad as another.

"Are you kidding?" I asked when I found my voice.

"If there's anything your bloke does better than incense me, it's watch you," Bones replied. "He'd give his life for you without the slightest hesitation. It's the one thing he's useful for."

Tate gave Bones an evil look, but didn't argue. Vlad watched their exchange with mild curiosity.

"And why do you want me with her?"

"You're a ruthless sod who never lets conscience interfere with your objectives," Bones said curtly. "It's a trait I haven't often admired in you, yet one I'm counting on now."

I grabbed his jacket. "Don't worry about me, just take care of yourself. I want you back in time for dinner."

There were two other vampires present who could hear the rest of my message, but I sent it to him anyway. *When you get back, I'm going to cover myself in whiskey and nothing else. Then I'll pour gin all over you. We're going to drink from each other, in every possible way.*

Vlad let out an amused grunt, saying, "Excellent motivator, isn't she?" as he walked away. Mencheres kept his features blank. How mannerly. Dave just muttered, "She can't cook. How's that incentive?"

Bones moved closer until his body was tight against mine. There was a distinct hardness to him as he bent me back, his mouth pillaging mine like we had all the time in the world.

When he let me go, my heart was hammering. His eyes were swirling green and he inhaled, absorbing the scent of my arousal.

"I shall scarcely be able to think about anything else."

Yeah, well, now neither would I.

"Keep those bottles close, Kitten. I'll be back before you know it."

He gave me one last kiss and walked away with Spade, Ian, and Rodney in tow. I watched them climb into the helicopter and shielded my eyes from the wind of the churning rotors. Dave stood next to me as it lifted off and then faded into the distance.

He broke the silence. "I have to get back to Juan. Rattler's staying with your mom, Denise, and Randy, and Tick Tock's going with you. He's stronger than I am, so it's better."

"I'd rather have you," I replied, still staring at the sky even though I couldn't see the chopper anymore.

Dave shifted, obviously pleased by the compliment.

"In several years maybe he won't be. I'll see you when it's over."

Tate approached, his short brown hair not even rustling in the wind, and all of a sudden, something cold slithered up my spine. *That's irrational*, I told myself. *You're being superstitious, Cat, get a grip.*

"What's wrong?"

Dave knew me too well. Enough to know it wasn't the temperature that made me shiver all over. I rubbed my hands over my arms, fixing a fake expression of confidence on my face.

"Nothing. Forgot my jacket, that's all."

Dave gave me a look, but I ignored it. Just as I ignored the paranoid little voice in my head that made me want to call Bones and insist he return.

I'll be back before you know it.

Comforting words, you would think, but not to me. Those were the last words Bones said to me before I left him all those years ago. That sentence had tormented me during the years we were apart, and now I was afraid him saying it again was prophetic.

Telling myself it was coincidence and nothing more, I went inside. I had a job to do and there was no time for groundless fears. After all, I had enough to be afraid of that wasn't imaginary.

Twenty

Many things were closed Christmas Day. Restaurants. Bars. Clubs. Malls. Of course, one establishment was notoriously busy. The movie theater.

Today's six o'clock showing of a romantic comedy starring two big-named Hollywood actors was about to get interesting. It helped that this was an upscale theater with balcony seating. More chance to show off the aerial abilities of the undead.

Vlad Tepesh rose out of his seat in the front row as if he'd been pulled by strings. His body was in stark outline against the wide screen behind him. He spread his arms and let the emerald beams in his eyes settle on the shocked faces turned toward him.

"You shouldn't have come, Reaper."

A show hound, Bones had called him. Right now I had to agree. Even his long dark hair swirled around him, blown as if by an invisible breeze. I hid my smile and stood, holding a crossbow at the ready.

"Time to die, suck head." Okay, cheesy, but if he was piling on the dramatics, so was I.

"What the fuck . . . ?"

The guy next to me barely got the words out when I fired four arrows in rapid succession. Vlad spun in midair, dodging the arrows. They landed in the screen right as there was a close-up of the actress's face.

Somebody screamed. *Finally,* I thought. Jeez, did I have to cut his throat to cause a panic? People were so jaded nowadays.

Vlad flew at me, mouth open and fangs on display. With that, one of the patrons howled out a word.

"Vampire!"

"Run for your lives," I yelled, knocking over several people as I avoided Vlad's tackle. He caught the edge of my jacket and used it as leverage, throwing me across the theater to crash into the wall. It was a spectacular toss and knocked the wind out of me, causing me to gasp even as I ducked from his fist.

"We're playing it that way, huh? Good. I like it rough."

I returned the gesture, slamming him so hard into the nearby wall that it caved inward. Insulation and concrete showered those who hadn't made it out of the theater yet. Then when Vlad sprang forward, I head-butted him hard enough to split the top of my hairline. It rocked him back, though, allowing me to ram two blades into his chest. Blood poured from my scalp, causing more screams as the houselights went up and the two of us were clearly illuminated.

Vlad ignored the knives in his chest and yanked me closer, licking the flowing red stream from my forehead.

"Doesn't hurt now," he murmured.

"Overactor," I snapped.

A gunshot went off, causing both of us to turn in amazement toward the back of the theater. Sure enough, there was a guy, popcorn all over him, sighting down a barrel at us for another shot. Tate, who was also in the theater, knocked him so hard in the head that I hoped there wouldn't be permanent damage. The shooter dropped to the floor.

"Americans," Vlad muttered over the fresh screams from the remaining patrons. "Every other person in this country's armed. Good thing that his aim was as poor as his judgment."

"Come on, let's finish this. Flashy ending, isn't that your favorite?"

"Oh, Cat, you're going to make me do something I've never done before." He laughed, kicking me hard enough to break my ankles before flinging me into the fake velvet seats. They crumpled beneath me even as I sprang to my feet, wincing but still erect. I leapt up as he charged me, causing him to crash into empty air instead of my body.

"And what is that? Be humble?"

Vlad rolled, yanking the knives from his chest like they were splinters. His eyes flicked to the last of the fleeing bystanders as they trampled one another to get to the exit.

"Nothing can force me to do that."

The empty seats around him suddenly exploded into flames. I blinked, taken aback. Tate looked shocked, too. Vlad's lips curled, and he waved his hands in the direction of the fire. Like candles being doused, the blaze subsided.

"You're pyrokinetic," I breathed. "Impressive."

"As are you." At last the theater was empty of everyone still conscious.

"Young man, the projector room?" Vlad prodded Tate.

Tate leapt onto the tiny window, jerking the camera through the opening. It served to block the view of someone dumb enough to stand there and gawk down at us.

"Here, your ankles." Vlad lost his offensive posture and walked toward me. "If you'd permit?"

He held out his hand and glanced at my knives. I knew what he meant. Refusing would be both rude and stupid, since limping after him would hardly look imposing. With a nod, I sliced a neat line in his hand, then held it to my mouth and swallowed.

Vlad watched me with that same faint smile. "You don't like the taste of blood, do you?"

"No. Well . . . no."

He must have read the rest of my response in my mind, because he let out a derisive chuckle. "Acquired a taste for Bones's, have you? Really, he has more intelligence than I'd credited him, binding himself to you. It sorely hinders his competition."

"He doesn't have any competition," I answered at once, glancing at Tate.

"That's where you're mistaken. I wasn't talking about your scorned suitor there." Vlad gave a dismissive nod to Tate, who bristled. "I meant me. That's what you're going to make me do—envy Bones, a man I have little regard for. How galling."

His self-deprecating tone made me smile. Now Tate really glowered.

"You'll get over it, Vlad. Give it two weeks, you'll be sorry you even met me."

"Perhaps. Shall we take our final bows now?"

I stamped my feet to make sure my ankles were back to normal, then gestured toward the exit.

"After you."

". . . in front of the Palace Twenty on Montrose Avenue, where terrified spectators are telling an incredible tale. Hugh, can you pan to the right to show the firefighters? . . . Witnesses report gunshots, flames, and possible occult-related activities during this otherwise quiet Christmas evening . . . You, yes, you, miss, can you tell us what occurred inside?"

"He flew!" a shaking blond girl gasped, grabbing the microphone away from the reporter. "I think he had wings or something . . . and then she shot him, and the theater started to burn, oh God, I thought I was gonna die!"

"Okay, clearly we have a distraught observer, let's see who else we can talk to."

The newswoman tried to keep it professional, but then an impromptu tug-of-war occurred over the microphone as the blonde refused to let go.

"Miss, let me have that back, I'm sure you'll want to speak to the authorities—"

"There she is," she shrieked, pointing at me. "That's her. She's the one who shot that thing. She'll tell you I'm not crazy!"

The reporter surged forward and the cameraman pointed that large black lens right at me. I gave it one full glance before hurrying into the van under heavy escort. This was live coverage, broadcast nationwide. *Hi, Patra. See? I'm on the opposite coast from where the informant is supposed to meet you, and you'd*

NEVER *expect Bones to be away from my side on a job during Christmas, would you?*

"FBI, no one's allowed past this point," Tate barked, shoving the reporter to the side. He pushed the camera down, cutting off any additional views of me or my entourage. After all, one quick look was all we needed. Any more and Patra might notice that Bones wasn't shadowing me.

Our hysterical witness kept up a steady stream of shrieking until she was dragged to the side by the local police. Either this would work or it wouldn't, we'd soon find out. Cooper, playing the informant, was supposed to be meeting Patra's contact within an hour. With luck, Patra would believe Bones and I were both here in Los Angeles.

Tate appeared in the doorway of the van and slammed it closed. Vlad was seated next to me, and Tick Tock and Zero were also inside. Tate gave the command to leave to Doc, our driver for tonight, and sat across from me.

"All right, Cat. If anyone pokes around there, they'll see the usual cleanup crew and all the brass. There'd be no reason to think Bones wasn't with you. I'll be glad to get out of here, no point in painting a target on your head."

"It went pretty well," I commented, bouncing as the van sped away. We'd change cars two times and then fly the rest of the way. Bones was adamant about that. "I hope his goes off without a hitch."

Tate compressed his mouth and said nothing.

"When will you call the Master?" Zero asked.

It always unnerved me when he called him that. Zero seldom addressed Bones otherwise, no matter how often Bones had urged him to. His milky gray eyes were trained on me expectantly.

"I won't. He'll call me when it's over, maybe in about two hours, maybe more."

My stomach twisted with worry. It was all I could do not to snatch up my cell and ruin everything with a fervent, useless plea for him to be careful.

"We'll be halfway to Mencheres's house by then." Vlad stretched his legs. "A good thing, too. I'm hungry."

"We'll all be better when we reach Mencheres in Colorado," I said. "Vlad, you'll get your dinner, Tate, you can see Annette, and I'll see Bones sometime before midnight. At least we'll have a few minutes of Christmas together. Maybe."

God, how I wanted to be at our own home with no one but Bones around. Not shoved in a van surrounded by five vampires on my way to one of Mencheres's many houses. Life. You could only make plans for it, not dictate orders to it.

"Doc." I rapped on the metal panel. "Step on it, will you?"

The sounds of a helicopter brought me bolting out of my chair with a glance at the clock. Eleven fifty-one, Colorado Mountain Time. Jeez, Bones had cut it close.

Not bothering to throw on a coat, I went outside in my thin cardigan, shivering as the helicopter landed. Snow flurries were swept away by the churning rotors that whipped hair into my face. They slowed and the side door opened, revealing Spade, Rodney, and Ian.

"Someone get me a bloody *good* set of irons, I'm

sick of sitting on this sod," Ian spat. His chestnut hair was flying almost as much as mine.

Three of Mencheres's vampires scurried to obey. The other half dozen went to assist Spade, Rodney, and Ian as they restrained a struggling, cursing figure.

"Angel, fetch your husband and have him give us a hand," Spade sang out. "Where is the lazy sod—?"

He stopped at the look on my face. Ian halted as well, giving a brutal blow to the unknown vampire they carted like so much luggage.

"Where's the other chopper? We were delayed, so Crispin should have beaten us here."

Ian had never sounded so edgy. As if in slow motion, I raised the cell phone in my hand. I'd been clutching it for the past several hours waiting for his call. Nerveless fingers punched in those ten numbers, and then I waited again for that metallic buzzing that served as a ring.

Mencheres came to stand next to me, but I didn't look at him. All I could do was stare at the helicopter rotors like I was transfixed. My heartbeat was so loud, I almost couldn't hear the phone as it rang.

One . . . two . . . three . . . four . . .

God, please. I'll do anything, please. Let him be all right. Let him be all right.

Five . . . six . . . seven . . .

He has to answer, he has to!

Eight . . . nine . . . ten . . .

There was a click and then background noise. I didn't wait for more, but screamed his name.

"Bones! Where are you?" I couldn't hear his voice, just more residual sounds. "Can you hear me?" I yelled even louder. Maybe we had a bad connection.

"Yessss . . ."

It was a hiss that drove straight through me, chilling me more than the snow falling around me. The voice wasn't masculine, and it had a distinct Middle Eastern accent.

"Who. Is. This?"

Each word was a growl coming from the center of me. I saw Spade grip my arms, but I didn't feel it.

A woman laughed, low and vicious. *Her voice is deeper than I imagined*, I found myself thinking. *What else was I wrong about? Why am I sitting on the ground?*

If she said anything else after her next four words, I didn't hear it. I knew I was screaming, that Mencheres snatched the phone from me, and Spade jerked me toward the house even as I fought to stay outside. My eyes were still fixated on the slowing helicopter rotors as if they could magically change everything. *They can't stop*, the thought streaked through my mind. *If they stop, then Bones won't come out of that chopper. Someone, turn them back on! Turn them back on!*

No one did. They halted with a last, lazy rotation even as Spade forced me inside the house. Something exploded in me then, more powerful than the word *pain* could ever encompass, and all I could hear in my mind was Patra's taunting, brutal, satisfied question.

Is this the widow?

Twenty-one

I WAS SEATED NEXT TO SPADE, ANGUISH IN MY soul gouging me like a rabid monster trying to claw its way out.

But to Spade, I simply asked, "What happened?"

Pink tears streaked his face. "Cooper waited at the train station, and about ten minutes later, we saw Anubus sneaking up on him with several Master vampires. We wanted Anubus alive, so Ian and I secured him while Rodney and Crispin fought the rest of them. Then one of the sods managed to run off, so Crispin told Rodney to fall back with us while he went on to skewer the wretch. He was supposed to meet up with us here. We reckoned he'd beat us, since he didn't have to take the long way with a hostile prisoner. I'm so sorry, angel. So damnably sorry . . ."

Mencheres strode into the room, and the rush of animosity that swept over me left a small, detached part of me curious. *Why are you mad at him? This was all* your *fault.*

"It's not safe here," he announced. "Patra may have learned our location from Bones, so we have to leave."

"Could she have lied?" I was grasping at straws, but drowning hands reached for anything.

Mencheres cast a look at me that was no less sympathetic for its briefness. "I know her well enough to know when she's lying. She was not."

We cleared out in a hurry. Randy, Denise, Annette, and my mother were on their way here when a phone call from Spade had rerouted them. He didn't say why, which I was grateful for. I could hardly bear to think the words, let alone hear them out loud again.

". . . all of my people moved at once, we are taking no chances," Mencheres snapped into his phone before throwing it to the ground and smashing it to pieces.

Another vampire hurried to hand him a fresh one. "The number is new," the lackey said, bowing to him and then, oddly, to me. I didn't acknowledge it. He could have shriveled at my feet and I wouldn't have cared. For now, I was letting myself be hustled by the current of people around me.

We left by the same helicopter Ian, Spade, Cooper, and Rodney had flown in on. My eyes were dry, staring at nothing. That's all I seemed to see no matter what I looked at. Nothing.

With a lurch we were airborne. Tate called Don and told him what happened, ending with a warning for him to evacuate. Whatever my uncle said in reply was drowned out by the sounds of the helicopter and my own apathy. What was there to care about anymore? My heart was in pieces.

"Cat," Tate sighed when he hung up, putting his arm around me, "Don said—"

He stopped and stared almost stupidly at his chest. The knife I'd pulled from my coat and jammed into him was less than an inch from his heart. I smiled, feeling my face crack like pottery that dried too quickly.

"That was a warning. The next one won't be. Did you think you could just slide into Bones's place and I wouldn't miss a beat? You lay your hands on me again and I'll finish you, Tate."

I meant every bitter word. If there was one person happier than Patra right now, it was Tate. He'd hated Bones from the moment he'd met him, and that wasn't even counting when he shot him at first glance. I'd be damned if I was going to let Tate dishonor Bones's memory by petting me like a lapdog. Whatever chance he thought he'd gained by Bones's death, he was wrong.

Tate yanked the knife from his chest without a word. He wiped the silver clean on his pants and then handed it back to me.

"I'm here when you need me," he murmured, and got up to move to the rear of the craft.

No one else spoke after that, the whole two hours north to Canada.

We landed in a frozen grass field a hundred yards from a house surrounded by thick trees. It was bitterly cold, or maybe it was just me. I couldn't seem to remember what warm felt like.

"Cat, we must talk," Mencheres stated, holding out a hand that I ignored as I hopped down from the helicopter.

"What time will Denise and my mother be here?"

He folded his arms, oblivious to the stiff wind. "Dawn. They were picking up supplies on their way."

"Whatever it is you want to talk about, can it wait until later?"

My emotional armor was on with full reinforcements, but that wouldn't last. I needed to be alone so I could break down, I didn't want to do it with an audience.

Mencheres nodded.

"Afterward, of course. I shall get you settled until then."

"Don't bother. Dawn's in less than two hours and I won't sleep. I just want to be alone. I don't have to tell you this has been the worst day of my life."

I started walking toward the tree lines.

"Where are you going?" Mencheres called out.

"It's hard to be alone with a passel of vampires scuttling around me. I assume you consider this place safe since you brought us here, so I'm taking a walk."

There were mutterings of objections behind me from varying voices. As my response, I held up my middle finger and kept walking.

The pines were thick in places. Tracks in the snow showed many different species called this frigid area home, and at this hour, it was quiet.

As I walked, I let myself remember the first time I saw Bones, bent over a table at a club with the lights reflecting off his hair. How he'd called my bluff when I drove him to a lake under the pretense of seduction. Waking up chained inside a cave, hearing him mock me with a Tweety Bird impression. His face when he first saw my eyes glow and he realized I'd told him the truth about what I was. That smug grin he gave me after I challenged him to a fight to the death. Our first kiss. The first time we'd made love. And the smile he'd given me the first time I told him I loved him . . .

My rapid pace carried me miles away. When I saw the cliffs, I started climbing them without much thought as to why. Judging from the low-hanging moon, there was still about forty minutes until dawn. Soon after that, Denise and my mother would arrive. I didn't want to see them. I didn't want to see anyone.

I'd climbed for twenty minutes before I found a wide enough ledge to sit on. A blast of wind made me rub my hands together, and the red diamond caught my eye. My engagement ring for a wedding that would never happen.

I got up and stared out over the ledge. The rocks below seemed mesmerizing, the distance to them somehow not far or frightening. After a moment, my eyes closed, and I felt myself take a step forward. And then another one.

"It must be difficult for you."

At the first syllable, my eyes snapped open. Vlad was seated on a ledge almost thirty feet below my perch, watching me.

"Yeah, it's difficult that the man I loved is dead. How brilliant of you to notice."

Vlad rose. "Oh, I didn't mean that. I meant it must be difficult for you to decide what you are. I never had to wrestle with that. When I changed into a vampire, I couldn't revert back to my humanity under any circumstances. Yet you wake up every day trapped in yours. As I said, difficult."

What the hell was he rambling on about? "I said I wanted to be alone, Vlad. Get out of here."

"That's not why you're really here, Catherine."

"Don't call me that," I said out of habit, then shook my head. Like it mattered now what he called me?

He gave me a contemptuous look. "Why not? Standing on that ledge is Catherine Crawfield, not Cat, the Red Reaper. Catherine has no obligations, no responsibilities, and she's decided to follow her husband to the grave. In the end, it appears you've chosen your human side. How interesting."

"That's not what I'm doing," I snapped, and then stilled.

Wasn't it? I'd walked out in the freezing cold, climbed a cliff, and was teetering on the edge of it with my eyes closed. Falling at this height would likely knock my head off, so there would be no chance of anyone bringing me back, as a ghoul or anything else. Who was I kidding? I'd known just what I was doing as soon as I left that helicopter, even if I'd refused to acknowledge it until now.

You could do it, the thought teased me. *Don will look after your mother, your team will be fine with two vamps and a ghoul to lead them, Denise has Randy . . . It's not like before when you left Bones and had people depending on you. You can go to him. You're ready.*

"You're ready, Catherine?" Vlad baited me, using that name again as he picked the thought from my mind.

"Fuck you, Dracula," I snapped. "No wonder Bones didn't like you. You're pissing me off as well."

"We didn't care for each other, but we did respect one another. Would Bones want you to do this? Is this what *he* would have done, if you'd been killed?"

No.

The answer came to me without needing a moment to ponder it. I knew what Bones would do if the tables were turned. If Max had murdered me, Bones would've been as shattered as I was now, but as a vampire, he wouldn't have allowed himself the option of suicide. No, not until he'd tracked down each player in my death and treated them to a horrible payback first. Only after he'd extracted his revenge would Bones have allowed himself to even think about his own death. That's how vampires were.

But Vlad was right. I had an excuse. I was half human. I could wrap that humanity around myself and leap off this cliff into Bones's arms on the other side. But vampires had no such luxury. If I were a vampire, I'd have no choice but to climb off this cliff and commit myself to a bloody retribution, broken heart or no. But if I was human, I could go ahead and jump.

Vlad gave me an assessing, unmerciful rake of the eyes as he listened to my internal struggle.

"So then, what are you?"

Since I was sixteen and my mother told me about my father, I'd wrestled with that same question. The sound of my heartbeat seemed to mock me. Each breath I took was a taunt. Yeah, I had many similarities to a human, and yes, I wanted the peace of that free fall to the other side where Bones waited for me. God, how I wanted it! But I wasn't human. I hadn't been since the day I was born, and I couldn't let myself pretend to be human now.

"Well?" Vlad asked with more emphasis.

I gave one last regretful glance at the ravine's rocky bottom before meeting Vlad's eyes.

"I am a vampire," I said, and backed away from the ledge.

Ｔwenty-two

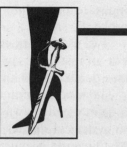

Mencheres made no comment when I appeared later with Vlad at my side. If he'd guessed at any of the drama, he kept it to himself. My mother and Denise had arrived. I'd seen their plane circling overhead while I climbed off the cliff down to solid ground.

A scream picked my head up as we approached the house. Mencheres closed his eyes and gave a shake of his head. He'd been standing outside awaiting my return.

"They've just been informed of his death," he said by way of explanation.

"You needed to speak with me?"

Mencheres blinked at my controlled tone. "I thought you wanted to see your mother first?"

"No, let's talk now."

Vlad gave a polite bow. "I'll leave you to speak privately," he said, and went inside.

Mencheres considered me with the same evaluating stare I gave him. Neither of us moved. Finally he broke the silence.

"I've used my power to try and locate Bones's body. For an instant, I saw him, shrinking into the state of true death, with a knife pierced through his chest."

The image slammed into me with more force than a cannonball. It was all I could do not to succumb to hysterical shrieks, like I could hear Annette doing. My fingernails punctured my palms as I ruthlessly squelched down my grief.

"Do you know where he is?" At least then I could bring him home. If nothing else, I could do that.

"No. I lost the image right afterward. I think Patra's using a blocking spell. She's used them before to keep me from locating her. I will try again, of course."

"Thank you."

It was the first sincere, appreciative thing I'd said to him. Mencheres didn't smile, but some of the tightness left his face.

"It is my duty and desire to give Bones the farewell he deserves."

We didn't say anything after that for a while. At last, Mencheres spoke again.

"By his order while he was yet alive, Bones bequeathed everything to you. You are now Master of his line and co-Master of mine. I swore by my blood to honor the union forged with him, so by my blood, I will swear to honor it with you, as was his wish."

A lump barreled its way up my throat, and it, too, got thrown back down with all the other emotions I couldn't allow myself to feel. Instead, I nodded.

"If that's what he wanted from me, I'll do it."

Mencheres did smile then. "He'd be proud of you, Cat."

A small, despairing smile stretched my mouth. "That's all I have to keep me going."

There was the sound of something smashing inside. I straightened. "Is there anything else? I have to see to Annette. She sounds like I feel."

"The rest can wait until later. Go on. Tend to his people."

Despite my jealousy, massive grudge for her trying to sabotage my relationship, and outright envy at the years she'd been with Bones, when I saw Annette, I wanted to comfort her. If there was anyone here who knew exactly how I felt, it was her.

"Come here, Annette."

I peeled her out of Ian and Spade's arms. Both of them had been holding her, either for comfort, or to prevent her from smashing something else. There were several broken objects around her. Pinkish tears ran in torrents from her eyes, making her look positively awful.

"Let me go," she yelled at Spade. "Don't you understand, I don't want to go on without Crispin!"

Oh, how I seconded that. Still, Vlad was right. Bones deserved his retribution, and it was my job to see that he got it.

I grasped Annette's head.

"You will go on, because you owe Bones that. Patra's hoping his death means she's off the hook, but we're going to show her that she made the biggest mistake of her life. Come on, Annette. Make Bones glad he changed you into a vampire centuries ago— and his enemies terrified of it."

Dark pink streaks continued to pour down Annette's cheeks, but her mouth tightened into a hard line. I watched as her features changed from the twisted disfigurement of sorrow to the steely, collected face of the female who'd tried her damnedest to ruin my relationship when we met.

She swiped at her cheeks and rose to her feet.

They're going down, my look promised her.

You bet they are, hers replied.

Then she startled me by kneeling, her disarrayed head bowed. "Crispin told me he'd name you Master of his line if anything happened to him, so here and now, I pledge my loyalty."

I wasn't prepared for this. Then the other members of Bones's line began to follow suit, until even Tate knelt.

Spade moved next to me, but he didn't kneel, since he was Master of his own line. Instead, he lowered his head and kissed my engagement ring.

"I'll stand by your side, Cat, for the sake of my friend who would have expected no less from me."

I wanted to say something in the face of all this, but my throat closed off. Rodney murmured similar words and also kissed that glittering red stone. Ian surprised me by following suit. I dug my nails into my palms, fighting back the tears that tried to choke me. *Don't you dare cry*, I reprimanded myself. *Don't you dare.*

After all the vampires made their pledge, I cleared my throat.

"Thank you. I swear I'll prove worthy of your trust. As Spade said, Bones would have expected no less. Mencheres?"

He tilted his head. "Yes?"

"What's next?"

"We'll hold an assembly in the near future for those

under Bones's line to formally acknowledge you. After that, the focus is the same. We are at war."

"Why in the near future? Is there a mandatory waiting period?"

Mencheres wrinkled his forehead. "No, but in light of this sudden, tragic event, you have time—"

"Bullshit. I'm not going to get any cheerier, so let's get this out of the way. Bones's people will be freaking out with him dead, and the longer they're in limbo, the stronger Patra gets. What's the soonest this thing can be arranged?"

Mencheres looked taken aback. I ignored that and tapped my foot for punctuation.

"Well?"

"Tomorrow night. I will notify the proper leaders."

"Tomorrow night, then."

The question was, what in the name of God was I supposed to do with myself until then?

After several comments that I hadn't slept, I went upstairs to one of the bedrooms just to shut everyone up. But as soon as I stretched out on the bed and felt the gaping emptiness next to me, I gave up and took a bath instead. For two hours I sat in the tub, staring at nothing.

Mencheres was in the doorway when I came out of the bathroom. "I have something for you," he said, and held out a small square box of carved antique wood.

"What is it?"

"Bones gave this to me several months ago to hold for you, in case anything happened to him."

"Set it on the bed." My voice was a rasp. I was afraid to take it, because there was a trembling in my hands that hadn't been there before. "And leave."

He did as I asked, and I was alone in the room with the box. It took me over twenty minutes before I had the courage to open it, and then I bit back a cry.

Pressed into the lining of the box's lid were pictures. The first was of the two of us last summer. Bones and I were on our swinging porch chair, his face in profile as he whispered something to me. Whatever it was, I was smiling.

The second photo was of me naked on a very tousled bed, clutching a pillow while lying on my side. My mouth was open, and I was sleeping with a sensual, lethargic expression on my face. One breast was visible while the other peeked out from the covers, as did the red curls between my legs. Somewhat embarrassed, of all things, I put it down and then noticed the writing on the back.

I took this one morning. You looked so lovely I couldn't resist. It makes me smile even now to imagine you blushing as you see it.

A strangled noise emerged from my throat at his familiar, elegant scrawl. I couldn't do this. It hurt so much I started to breathe in ragged, irregular gasps.

There was a folded note lying on top of whatever other items were in this box, with the words *My Beloved Wife* written on it.

Instantly the letters blurred, because my eyes welled with tears that almost burned to get out.

Something in me knew if I read what was in that note, my delicate emotional control would disintegrate and I'd go insane. I shut the box and slid it under the bed. Busy, I had to keep busy. With warped resolve I dressed in the first pair of pants and top I found, not even seeing if they matched, and nearly ran out of the room.

Doc picked his head up as I entered the basement. He'd been twirling his two six-shooter guns. Most vampires were into knives, swords, or other archaic weapons, but Doc had a fixation for guns. He was never without them.

"Reaper," he acknowledged me.

"How old are you?"

If he was surprised by my sudden question, he didn't show it. Although I'd been around Doc off and on for a week, we hadn't spoken at length.

"A hundred and sixty, living years included." He had a pleasant Southern drawl that made each word sound more polite. Briefly I wondered if his colors had been blue or gray.

He held out one of his guns. "Want to give her a whirl?"

I'd run as if chased about forty miles in the woods, done two hours of solitary swordplay and more thinking than could ever be good for me. Guns? Why not?

"Your guns are female?" Asked as I took the piece. It required cocking to load. Mine were semi-automatic or fully, depending on what the situation warranted.

"Because, Cat, it's the feminine persuasion that's always the deadliest."

Dark humor. Under other circumstances, I could appreciate that. I twirled the gun on my fingers, cocking and aiming it in a blur of motion. Knives might be my favorite weapon, but that didn't mean I was an amateur with firearms.

"Very good," he noted. "That wall has only dirt on the other side of it. How's your shooting?"

In reply I unloaded the barrel into the designated area in a succession of six shots that echoed like only one. Doc smiled at the triangle outlined in holes. I didn't return it, not knowing if my face could form that expression anymore.

"Give me more bullets and I'll write my name," I said without real interest. "What about you?"

He took the gun and reloaded it. Then he spun both weapons in his hands with a speed my eyes couldn't follow, bouncing them off the ground and catching them, clanging them together in midair, and whipping them around his back and through his legs. All the while they went off, making the spectacle more dramatic by the bursts of loud fire. He had them back in my hands before the noise from the shots faded away.

"How's that?"

I looked at the wall thirty yards away and got the joke. Doc had taken my triangle and turned it into an A, following up with a C and T with his fresh holes. Considering he'd done it during that dazzling display of tricks, it was very impressive.

"You'd be a hit with my team," I finally replied. "My guys would think that was the coolest thing ever."

"The law and I have a long, tangled history," he said with dry amusement. "So I'm happier far away from it."

"How did Bones come about changing you?"

Doc's features sobered. "He didn't. He's my grandsire. Annette changed me."

Oh. Now I glanced at him in an objective feminine way, noting the leanness of his frame, his attractively drawn face, hazel eyes, and slicked-back brown hair. Yeah, he looked like Annette's type.

"Figures."

"It wasn't what you're imagining. Back in the eighteen hundreds, I came upon four men cornering a woman behind a saloon. I shot two of them and the other two ran off. I didn't know I wasn't protecting the woman—I'd just denied her a hearty meal. Still, Annette didn't forget my misguided chivalry. When I was dying years later, she found me and offered me an alternative. So I took it."

It was something so like what Bones would have done, I turned away, blinking. *Never forget a kindness.* Apparently Annette believed that as well.

"You're not one of Bones's and you're a Master, so you're not under Annette's line anymore," I reasoned out loud. "So, then why are you here?"

He gave me a solemn look out of pale brown eyes. "The same reason you are. Because I don't forget my debts."

†wenty-†hree

I t was December 27, and we were assem-
bled in an opera house, of all things. I was dressed
all in black, which suited my mood. I would have been
fine wearing a garbage bag, but vampires dressed up
for occasions and I had a part to play. Black leather
boots completed the effect. The only color on me was
the thin silver chain around my waist where several
daggers of the same metal dangled. It was an unspoken threat and promise of protection combined.

Mencheres and I were center stage. Even though
everyone in the theater knew why they were there,
for formality's sake, he repeated the news of Bones's
death. I refused to let any emotion appear on my face
as those devastating words were spoken again, slicing
into me with the same pain I'd felt upon first hearing
them.

". . . and as was his decree, the Mastership of his
line passes to his wife, Cat." Mencheres held out his
hand and I accepted it. "From this night forward, all

who belong to you are mine, as all of mine are yours. To seal this alliance, blood is required. Catherine, you who are also known as the Red Reaper, do you offer your blood as proof of your word?"

I repeated the required words I never thought would be crossing my lips. Then I drew a knife across my palm in a deep cut. Mencheres took the same blade and sliced his own palm, clasping his hand over mine.

"My blood is also proof of my word. If I betray our alliance, it will be my penalty."

Our joined hands were raised for effect, mine tingling as it healed on contact with his blood, and then we let go. It was done.

Or not quite.

"I refuse to call the half-breed my leader, and I challenge for freedom from her line."

"Thomas, you insolent sod!" Spade strode forward from his place at the perimeter of the stage. "If Crispin were here, he'd rip out your spine and flog you with it. But as his best friend, I'll perform that task myself."

In truth, I wasn't surprised. At any formal gathering, a vampire could request or challenge for their independence. If the Master wanted to be benevolent or it had been agreed on beforehand, they would grant it without a fight. But if not . . .

"Don't even think of it, Spade," I said. "Bones would appreciate your intentions and so do I, but that man challenged me and I'll answer it."

"Cat." Spade gripped my shoulders, lowering his voice. "You haven't slept in days, you barely eat or drink, and all you do is train. If not me, let Mencheres answer this. He'll make such an example of this sod that anyone else considering such a thing will find it markedly less appealing."

"You're right." Spade relaxed, but Bones would have known better. "This creep does need to be made an example of, but by me. If I can't do this, then this line will be torn apart from the inside out. Thomas!"

I pushed Spade back and went to the edge of the stage. "Your challenge is accepted. If you want your freedom . . ." I cracked my knuckles and rolled my head on my shoulders. "Come and get it."

Thomas walked toward the stage, one clean jump taking him onto the elevated platform. The rest of the vampires cleared a path, Mencheres cutting Spade's further protest short with a wave of his hands. I almost smiled as I watched. This was the closest thing to therapy I could do.

"How do you want to die?" I asked, boring my gaze into his. "Because you will, you know. So pick your poison. Swords, knives, mallets, or skin on skin."

Thomas was my height, and he had blue eyes and curling, brownish-red hair. All this I noticed while measuring his aura. He had the resonating power of a strong vampire. This wasn't a teenager in undead years.

"I will kill you swiftly out of respect for my sire," he answered with an Irish accent.

I gave a sharp bark of amusement. Combined with his short height and round cheeks, Thomas reminded me of the leprechaun from the cereal I ate as a kid. *They're after me Lucky Charms!* I wanted to chant at him. Too bad he wasn't wearing green, that would have made it perfect.

"If you had any respect for Bones, you wouldn't be challenging for your freedom in the middle of a war," I hissed instead. "As he would say, *Very bad form.*"

"It was his misfortune to be enthralled by a witch

such as you," he said as he selected a knife from the display of hastily arranged weapons. I didn't bother to pick—I was wearing several on my belt. "You incited him to war based on an assault that never really happened!"

There was an eruption of curses from several of the vampires on the stage. Cold fury enveloped me. Trying to go for the low blows, was he? All right, then.

I let out a cry and hunched as if struck. Thomas sprinted forward in a flash of speed. When he was on me, his knife millimeters from a killing blow, I twisted to the side and jammed his own blade deep in his stomach. Soon more sharp silver found a home through his heart. It all happened in less than a second.

"You dumb fuck, guess you weren't paying attention when Bones told you not to fall for a bluff."

With my knife in his heart, Thomas froze like he'd been turned to ice. I leaned closer to almost whisper in his ear.

"Tell Bones hello for me," I said, then twisted the blade in his heart. "And when he gets ahold of you, you'll *really* be sorry."

I gave Thomas's slowly shriveling body a kick that sent him down into the seat where the orchestra would normally sit. Then I tucked my knife back into my belt, not even bothering to wipe the blood off.

There was commotion in the back. The sound of doors banging open. I glanced up just as Mencheres came forward and gripped my hand.

"Cat, I am very sorry, but I had no idea she would do this," he grated. "You cannot attack her at a formal gathering, it's against our laws. To do so would condemn us all."

Those words chased away my momentary confusion over who the five vampires were who entered the theater. *Late arrivals*, had been my first thought. Then that fucking laugh told me otherwise even as Mencheres was still speaking. I knew that laugh. It branded me.

"Mencheres, my husband, aren't you going to greet me?"

My fingers whitened on his, squeezing so hard, Mencheres's bones fractured as fast as they could heal. Patra had spoken to him, but her eyes were all for me as she descended the aisle with serpentine grace.

Patra didn't have the famous blunt Egyptian haircut so often shown in movies about her mother. No, she had threads of gold highlights in her long black hair. Her brows weren't as thick as Hollywood suggested, either. Actually, they were slender. So was she. In fact, she was more athletic than voluptuous. Her skin was pale, but darker than mine. Almost honey-colored. Her nose was slightly longer than fashion favored, but there was no question about it, Patra was beautiful.

"Why?"

I spat the question to Mencheres while not taking my eyes from her. Everything in me was wound to the breaking point. *Kill*, was all my mind was capable of thinking.

"It's our laws. As my wife, she can be present at any formal gathering, but she cannot attack us. Neither may we injure her, however. She seeks to provoke you to violence, but don't give her such an easy victory."

Oh, she'd provoked me to violence, all right. I wanted to rip her apart and wear her blood for clothing. My eyes flared, green rays of loathing shining on her.

"Hello, bitch."

She laughed again in an insinuating, purring way. "So you're the half-breed. Tell me." A gleam appeared in her eyes. "Have you slept well recently?"

Some part of me was amazed I hadn't combusted in rage. The other half heard me laugh in a bright, chipper tone that was so at odds with how I felt.

"That's the best you can do? Oh, Patra. How boring."

Whatever she'd been expecting, it wasn't that. Hell, I was surprised at myself.

Patra didn't like being laughed at. Her incensed expression was evidence of that.

"I'm not as stupid as you're hoping," I went on. "Now, either shut up or leave, because you're interrupting things. There's got to be a law about that as well."

"I'll go." Her smile was contemptuous. "I've seen what I wanted. You're nothing, and soon you'll be less than that. But before I leave, I thought you should know why you're in this war in the first place. I'm betting my husband hasn't told you, has he?"

"Told me what?"

She laughed again, and I found myself thinking I hated her laugh more than any sound I'd heard before it.

"Haven't you asked yourself why I turned against Mencheres in the first place? If I hadn't, then there would be no war, and no reason to kill you or Bones."

If she was waiting for me to encourage her to go on, all she got was silence. Patra sighed.

"Very well, I'll explain. When Mencheres offered to make me a vampire, I told him I wouldn't cross over unless he changed my lover Intef as well. But after I woke up from my death, Mencheres told me Intef had been killed before his people could reach him."

She paused to give Mencheres a look filled with loathing.

"Then one day Anubus, a former friend of Mencheres, broke his silence. Intef wasn't killed by the Romans. Mencheres did it. You see, little half-breed, you're in this war because I'm finally getting revenge on my lover's murderer, so who's *really* to blame for Bones's death?"

I glanced at Mencheres, who closed his eyes briefly before meeting my stare. I saw it then. That what Patra had said was true, every word of it. For a moment, I was overwhelmed with the urge to stab both of them for their ruthlessness in getting what they wanted.

Then I turned back to Patra. "I get your motivation. But you should have just gone after Mencheres. Instead, you chose to kidnap people's family members to force them to suicide bomb themselves. You chose to murder Bones, and for that, I'm going to kill you. You of all people should understand why."

Patra smiled. "Because I understand your pain, I'm going to free you of it." She raised her voice. "I offer amnesty to anyone who leaves her and joins me! Furthermore, to the man or woman who slays her, I offer a reward beyond your ability to fathom. You have the word of a god."

I gave her a stare that was harder than the diamond on my hand. "You arrogant bitch, I'll see you dead, and that's the word of a half-breed."

Patra gave me a last disparaging glance and turned her back. Her four escorts flanked her as she ascended the aisle in the same sweeping manner she'd arrived.

Only after the doors closed behind them did I let my breath out. I was so furious, I was shaking.

The silence was complete, absent of the typical human shuffling or nervous clearing of throats. I went over to the side of the stage where the weapons were and almost gently pulled out a sword. Better to deal with the repercussions of Patra's offer now than to let the idea that I was too weak to lead simmer and grow.

"All right, whoever believes that bitch and thinks they can take me, here I am."

The challenges came thick and fast, several different voices calling out. This time I didn't offer the choice of weapons—I kept my sword. And one at a time, I hacked, stabbed, or decapitated each vampire who stepped onto the stage. All my pent-up fury and grief I put into my blows, thankful that for those brief moments, I could feel something aside from pain.

When I'd finished with the eighth vampire, running my sword through his heart so deeply half my arm followed, my outfit was sliced in dozens of places and gaping indecently in some. Ironically, my own injuries had healed with the continued contact of fresh vampire blood.

I turned toward the audience. "Who else thinks they can cut me down?"

No one else called out a challenge. I drove the sword into the center of the stage like it was Excalibur into the proverbial stone. Then I wiped some blood from my cheek with the ragged remains of my sleeve and turned to Mencheres.

"Now can we leave?"

Twenty-four

WHEN I GOT BACK TO THE HOUSE, THE BED'S yawning emptiness taunted me. *See*, it mocked, *my sheets are straight. There's no dip in my mattress where a long pale form lay waiting. Bones is gone. He's never coming back.*

With impotent wrath I flipped the bed, smashing it into the wall. All it did was expose the antique box with the letter inside I couldn't stand to read and destroyed a perfectly good bed. A waste, like all my plans for a future.

I dressed in sweats and a T-shirt and went downstairs, the box wrapped in a blanket I'd yanked from the wreckage of the frame. The clock had just chimed two A.M., and no one was asleep.

Spade and Rodney were in the drawing room with Ian. Mencheres wasn't, and it didn't disappoint me. Seeing Patra had upset him, it was clear. Some part of me felt sorry for him. When he'd married Patra, he'd loved her. Not a wise judge of character on his part, but then no one was perfect. Even thousands of years later, that mistake was still haunting him.

"You did well tonight, Cat," Ian said. "Though you look like shit."

Normally I would have responded with something sarcastic, but it took too much effort. Instead I settled myself on the couch, tucking the box on the floor next to me. "Whatever."

"You need to sleep," Spade said for the hundredth time.

"If I could fall asleep, then I wouldn't be sitting here listening to you guys bitch at me. Has Anubus divulged anything interesting yet?"

Ian had been the one spending most of the time with him. Well, Ian and a few sadistic friends. Anubus no doubt wished they'd just kill him. They wouldn't, of course. No matter how much he might ask for that.

"Blasted little, as it were." Ian grunted in exasperation. "The sod doesn't even know how Crispin was taken or who else was at that train station besides the vampires we saw. It doesn't make sense why he wouldn't know more, but he's maintaining that he doesn't."

"We'll just have to try harder," Rodney grimly said. "Be more inventive."

"Even so," Spade agreed.

My fingers rubbed my temples to try and stem the migraine that had grown worse.

"Ian's right, you know," Spade said briskly. "You're in terrible shape, and you won't last much longer without rest. Shall I—?"

"You can't help her. I can."

Spade glowered at Tate as he entered the room. Ian and Rodney followed suit. If it bothered him, he gave no sign of it, and sat on the couch next to me.

"Tate," I sighed. "Maybe you should leave. They're all mentally playing catch with your skull."

He ignored that and handed me a prescription bottle. "I called Don. This is measured for your bloodline, Cat, and it'll make you sleep. That's why I've been gone for hours—I walked to the pharmacy so no one could trace a car or get plates if someone was watching."

The three other men in the room were as astonished as I was. I took the bottle.

"Thank you." The anticipation of the brief nothingness sleep would bring me made it even more sincere. For a few hours, maybe, I'd be released from grief.

He held out a glass of water. "You're welcome."

I swallowed the required dose and then lay back into the couch. The wooden box was still beside me, those words locked away inside it the closest substitute I had for Bones. After a few minutes, I felt the tension lessen in my body. The pills were strong and I had a fast metabolism.

"Well done, lad," Spade said as I started to drift off. "Perhaps you'll be of use after all."

"Bones and I agreed that we wanted what was best for her," was Tate's hushed response. "We just differed in what we thought that was."

Bones . . .

His name echoed in my mind as I slipped into the waiting unconsciousness.

Maybe I'll dream of you.

Noise woke me. Somewhere in the house, there was a scream. Then the running of footsteps. Those sounds intruded inside the restless sleep the narcotics held me in.

"What the hell—?" I heard Spade say, his voice rising in pitch.

"Bugger me dead!"

Was that Ian? Couldn't they keep it down?

There was a shriek that sounded like Annette, and in such a high octave, I pulled the pillow over my head. Even that small effort exhausted me. If I could have, I would have bitched about the commotion. They wanted me to sleep, but then they made this kind of racket? Hypocrites.

There were the unmistakable bawls of Annette in loud, unintelligible bursts. Nearby, I heard something crash to the floor. My hazy mind thought it might have been Tate. He'd been balanced on the back of his chair legs when I passed out. Maybe he'd nodded off as well and lost his equilibrium. Still, that didn't explain his mumbled sentence.

"You have got to be fucking *kid*ding me . . ."

There was now an unrestrained chorus of voices, numerous doors bashing, and so much uproar I opened one eye with difficulty. Above every other word a name finally penetrated, causing me to stumble from the couch in a heap.

"*Crispin!*"

". . . need to see my wife," was all I heard before I started to scream, staggering over the coffee table in a blind frenzy to run toward that voice. My eyes were open but unfocused, everything in a hazy double outline that made the figure striding toward me look more like a wraith than a man.

Arms seized me, pressing me against a body that collided so forcefully with mine, we fell onto the floor. My face was stuffed next to a throat vibrating with that familiar accented voice.

". . . missed you so much, Kitten, I love you . . ."

This is a dream, it occurred to me. *A dream, and I will thank Don from the bottom of my heart for this fake chance to hold Bones again. God bless modern science and tons of codeine mixed with sedatives!*

"You're dead," I slurred. "I wish you were really here . . ."

"Leave me alone with her. All of you, please, give us a moment. Charles."

Something was whispered too low for me to hear even though Spade's dark head bent until it grazed my chin. He nodded once and kissed the pale face still blinking out of clarity to me.

"Anything, my friend."

"Please don't wake me up," I begged, terrified someone would shake me out of my dream. I clutched the figure that seemed so real, squeezing my eyes shut. "Just a little longer."

"You're not dreaming, Kitten." Oh God, his mouth covered mine in a kiss that made my heart break. "I'm here."

"They saw you dead, a-and shr-shriveled, and you're not r-r-real . . ." Reality and confusion mixed, increased by the pills and doubled with shock.

He carried me to the couch. "This first, talk after," he said, breaking my water glass and slashing his palm with it. I didn't have much choice, since he clapped it over my mouth in the next moment.

With each drop I swallowed, my drugged-out haze began to lift, until I could clearly see Bones kneeling in front of me. My fingers shook as I reached out to touch him, half afraid this was another of Patra's dream spells. One that would end with his body cruelly disintegrating before my gaze.

Bones caught my hand and squeezed it.

I devoured him with my gaze. Aside from his hair, which was shockingly white, he looked the same. His skin was as incandescent as always, and his dark brown eyes bored into mine.

"Are you really here?"

I couldn't shake the terror that he was a mirage. What if I let myself believe, and then woke up to find it *was* a dream? I couldn't bear it. I'd go insane.

With sudden desperation, I took one of those jagged pieces of glass and jammed it into my leg. Bones snatched it out, aghast.

"What are you doing, Kitten?"

The instant throb of pain was the most wonderful thing I'd ever felt, because it meant I wasn't dreaming. Somehow, Bones really *was* here. The control I'd had for the past few days evaporated and I burst into tears, launching myself at him even as he tried to push me back to heal my leg.

"You're alive, you're alive . . . !"

I couldn't stop repeating it even though I was hiccupping with sobs. Feverishly I ran my hands over him, feeling the familiar hard outline of his body under his clothes. Desperate to feel his skin, I ripped his shirt open, fresh sobs coming from me at the reassuring hum of power from his bare flesh.

Bones held me tightly. He was whispering something in my ear, but I couldn't make it out. The grief and agony from the past few days poured out of me, turning into joy and shaking me with its intensity. All the emotional control I prided myself on having was shattered, but I didn't care. Everything I thought I'd lost was suddenly right here. I clung to Bones like I'd die if I let him go, which was how I felt.

It might have been several minutes; it felt like only seconds. Bones set me back enough to kiss me again and I slanted my mouth across his, hungry for his taste. He pulled me even closer, letting out a groan when I wrapped my legs around his waist. Now my hands were running over him for a different reason. It wasn't desire I felt. No, it was a need that went beyond passion or compulsion to feel him inside me.

Bones must have felt it, too, because he didn't wait. There was more tearing of clothes and then the unbelievable ecstasy of his flesh driving into mine. I was gasping through the remains of my tears, pressing myself against him like I wanted to crush him, and then kissing him until I became light-headed from lack of oxygen.

It was fast and explosive. Bones climaxed moments after I did, with a groan of pleasure that was more than primitive. My heart was thrumming in my chest, which, considering all the chemicals in my system, might have been dangerous. Not that I cared. I could die right now and I'd still count myself as the luckiest person ever.

"You don't know how much I've missed you, Kitten," Bones murmured.

"Everyone came back," I breathed with the anguish of remembrance. "Except you. I called your cell. Patra answered. She said . . ."

I stopped. That brought up the main question that my shock and joy at seeing him had delayed.

"Bones, what *happened*?"

For the sake of not repeating it multiple times, Bones called in everyone after he'd gotten some new clothes for both of us. I sat on the couch, drinking old coffee and trying to shake the last of the haziness from my brain. Bones's blood had overpowered my drug-induced sleep, but to say I still felt out of it was an understatement.

When at last Bones let everyone back in the drawing room, he was swallowed up in a mass embrace. The person who almost cleared a path to him with a gun was Annette. She threw her arms around him, kissing him full on the mouth, before he turned away with an apologetic glance to me.

"Don't begrudge her," I said, for once not jealous. "She was as miserable as I was these past couple days."

When Annette finally released him, Mencheres put his arms around Bones with an expression of amazement, fingering his new white hair.

"I have never been wrong before in my visions," he stated. "I saw you withering."

"Don't fret, you don't have a black spot on your record," Bones replied. "But we'll get to that. Thank you for honoring our accord. I won't forget it."

Ian was next, hugging Bones with a chuckle that sounded hoarse from emotion. "Bloody wanker, your wife should roast your arse for this dastardly stunt!"

Bones clapped him on the back. "You're still here, mate. Careful—you're in danger of becoming an honorable man."

The rest of the vampires in the house conveyed their gratitude at seeing him again. Some part of me thought I should be embarrassed, considering everyone would have heard both my emotional breakdown and then the physical part of our reunion, but I didn't care. My modesty could burn in hell—I wasn't regretting a moment of getting another chance to express to Bones how much I loved him, either by my tears or anything else. Life was too damn short to be concerned with the rest of it.

Finally Bones came to sit by me. I took his hand, still needing to touch him to keep reassuring myself that he was real.

"I went back to chase the last vampire, as you are aware," he started. "He dashed onto the roof of a train that was passing by. I followed, and as we jumped from car to car, I sensed the others. Patra was there, with an entire car filled with Masters. The clever bitch knew we couldn't feel her until after the train arrived. They swarmed the roof and came for me. It was a brilliant ambush. Trying to fight hand-to-hand on a moving train while dodging silver knives is tricky."

The nonchalant way Bones described such a deadly scenario made me gape at him.

"Why didn't you jump off and run for it?"

"Arrogance," he answered crisply. "Patra was so close. All I had to do was cut down her guard and this war would have ended right then. So I kept after them, and when there were only six Masters left, it happened. One of them threw a blade that went straight into my heart. The pain dropped me to my knees. The bloke went straightaway back inside the car, telling Patra that he'd killed me. I thought he had, too, yet he'd neglected to twist the knife."

I was stricken at this image, and not until something wet touched my fingers did I realize I'd been digging my nails into his hand so hard, I'd drawn blood.

"Sorry," I whispered.

"I remember thinking I was finished, and being

very brassed off about it. I managed to pull the blade out, but I was in no condition to defend myself. Then I felt the strangest kind of power even as my vision blackened and I couldn't hear. The last thing I remember, we were over a bridge, and I rolled myself off the train into the water. Then there was nothing. Until the blood."

Bones gave a soft grunt of remorse.

"I must have been carried downstream. An indigent found me, probably to check if I had anything useful in my pockets, and I woke up with his body in my arms. I'd chewed his throat open and drank him to the last drop, poor fellow. He had a mate nearby as well, and I drank him before my reason returned enough to stop. When I saw my hands . . . I was horrified."

Bones paused to stretch out his hand and examine it. I didn't see anything unusual. His lips twisted.

"My bones were visible. It was as if I were a partial skeleton. I couldn't concentrate on anything, could barely see, hear or smell, and was weak as a lamb. When the sun broke, I lost consciousness again."

"What in blazes happened to you?" Ian demanded. "I've never heard of such a thing."

"I have," Mencheres said quietly. "Let him finish."

"I awoke past sunset, and my unknown companion awakened around the same time. He tried to run but I grabbed onto his ankle. I could talk, not quite intelligibly, but enough. I told him to drag me to a phone and then I'd let him go. Chap was petrified, of course. Here a murdering half-rotted skeleton wouldn't let loose of his leg; I'm astounded he didn't fall over from a heart attack. We waited until well after midnight, so it was less unsightly for a homeless man to be seen kicking a corpse on his way to a pay phone."

The image struck me very inappropriately and I started to laugh. This had to be the weirdest thing I'd ever heard.

"We arrived at a pay phone, but the bloke didn't have any quid for the call. My mind still wasn't functioning properly—that hadn't occurred to me. All I knew was I needed to get somewhere safe. I had him ring numbers collect, but he told me all the bloody numbers were disconnected or didn't answer. I only remembered a few of them: yours, Mencheres's, Charles's . . . but all of you were in emergency mode and couldn't be reached. There was one last number I recalled, and it worked. I reached Don."

My uncle? That made me blink in surprise.

Bones gave a rueful snort. "Yes, he was taken aback as well. Don said it didn't sound like me, well, that was true. I reminded him that the day we met, I told him I wanted to peel his skin like an orange—somehow *that* I recalled—and I'd do it if he kept arguing over who I was. Don had the chap give him our location and said he'd come. So I wasn't on display in the street, I had the man throw me in a Dumpster.

"Round two hours later, Don opened the lid. When I saw him, I said, 'Took your bloody time, old chap,' and he finally believed it was me—though he did inform me that a dehydrated piece of beef such as myself should be more respectful. Don pulled me into a van and gave me bags of blood. I went through all of them, but I still wasn't back to myself. Don flew me back to the compound with him and continued to give me blood. It took me over twelve hours to fully regenerate."

"Why didn't he fucking call me!"

It burst from my mouth amid my overflowing gratitude toward my uncle. Don didn't like Bones, never had, and yet he'd saved his life. There was nothing I could do to ever repay him for that.

"For starters, he didn't know the numbers of who to call, Kitten. Not like he knew their e-mail addresses, and you hadn't been checking yours, because he did try that. Also, since I didn't heal right away, he wasn't sure if I'd recover at all. So Don didn't want to give you false hope. Round an hour after I regenerated, Tate called Don asking for a prescription for you. Don gave me the location of the pharmacy. Once I got there, I followed Tate's scent from the pharmacy back here."

There was something in Bones's voice that made me belatedly aware there was one person missing in this room. Even my mother lingered by the doorway, pretending not to care about the story as it unfolded.

"Where's Tate? And why didn't Don call him when he knew you were better? My uncle *knew* he was with me."

Bones met my eyes. There was pity in his gaze—and resolve.

"Don didn't ring Tate because I told him not to. After all, I didn't want the person who tried to kill me discovering I was still alive."

†WENTY-FIVE

BONES'S WORDS SANK IN, MADE EVEN MORE ominous by the way Spade began to squirm in his chair. When I first saw Bones, he'd murmured something to Spade I didn't catch. Then I'd been so overcome by Bones being alive, I wouldn't have noticed a stampede of elephants, let alone the noise of a struggle . . .

"Where is Tate?"

Amazing how I could be overwhelmed with joy and yet also mad at the same time.

"He's not dead," Bones answered. "He's locked up until he admits to his treachery, and then I shall kill him for it."

"You think the train station was a setup?" It made sense. That oncoming train with its host of Master vampires and one very mean Egyptian queen was too convenient.

"Only those of us in this room knew of that plot, except of course Dave and Cooper, and it doesn't add up that it would be one of them. Dave was mostly bar-ricaded in a box with Juan, and Cooper has no cause to see me dead. Tate's the only one who would risk everything to see me killed in such a manner that you weren't injured as well. His love for you has driven him to this betrayal, and I want you to hear his admit-tance from his own lips. Then I'll kill him quickly, for your sake."

No. It's not him.

Bones heard the denial in my mind and sighed. "I'm sorry, luv, I know you care for him—"

I slammed the shields in place that guarded my thoughts, not because of Bones, but for the reason that two other vampires in the room could hear them. There was no way I'd believe Tate would do such a thing. He might taunt Bones and be a dick sometimes, but he wouldn't betray him to Patra. I just couldn't believe that.

Which left someone else in the room as the real guilty party.

"Tate's not going anywhere, right?"

My calm question caused Bones to gaze at me oddly.

"No."

"Then let's not deal with him right now. If Tate does admit to doing that, you won't have to worry about killing him. I'll do it myself."

That much was true, except it didn't apply in this case. If Tate ever did try to kill Bones, he'd challenge him to a fair fight. He'd lose, of course, but being un-derhanded just wasn't his style.

"Mencheres," I went on, "you said you'd heard of something similar happening to a vampire that hap-pened to Bones? About the withering thing?"

Mencheres let his cool appraising eyes meet mine, and in that instant I knew two things. He saw through my apparent lack of distress over Tate, and he also didn't believe it was him.

Weep.

The word flashed across my mind like it was spoken in my ear. Mencheres's steel gaze didn't waver, and I jerked back in shock even as I complied. It wasn't hard. I still wasn't all the way back in control of my emotions.

I let some tears fall, big fat drops of duplicity that rolled down my cheeks. Playing weak. Sometimes it was the best offense.

"My sire Tenoch had a similar gift," Mencheres stated. "He could manipulate his body to appear withered in order to convince whoever was around that he was dead. You must have inherited more from me than I realized, Bones, when I shared my power with you. Tenoch took days to recover from its effects; you will be very lucky to have your strength back within a fortnight."

Mencheres rose, all grace and leashed authority. "We will keep the traitor secure. You will need blood and sleep. We will keep the news that you're alive undisclosed until you are completely healed. Please, take my chamber. It is soundproofed, so you will be less disturbed by the noises of the house."

Bravo! I wanted to clap, but kept my compliment suppressed under a landslide of shields. *You devious prick, I might start to like you.*

To add to the camouflage, I sniffled. "Take me to bed, Bones. I'm very tired."

He lifted himself and me up in the same fluid motion. "Mencheres, if you'll direct me?"

Bones carried me out of the study. When we passed by my mother, who still lingered by the door, Bones stopped to give her an impudent smile.

"Thought you were finally rid of me, didn't you?"

She opened her mouth, paused, and then shut it. Then she further surprised me by moving out of the way without having to be shoved aside. For her, that was the equivalent of a gushing welcome.

"Filthy animal," she called out when we were almost out of sight.

He snorted in amusement, not slowing his steps. "Nice to see you again, too, Justina."

Mencheres followed us into the large bedchamber with a vague comment about retrieving some of his things.

"Just need to get these items before I leave you to your slumber . . ." he said in a regular voice before shutting the door behind him.

"Bones, Cat is correct. It isn't Tate."

I was surprised Mencheres felt that way, too, but I didn't question it. "He wouldn't do this," I agreed.

"Why not?" Bones snarled in low, heated disagreement. "It's his only chance of ever having you. I know if I were Tate, I'd see me buried if I had to betray everyone around me to do it!"

"And you would regret it," Mencheres said.

For a second, I saw pain flash on his face, and wondered if he was thinking of the murder he'd committed all those years ago.

"Killing your rival doesn't guarantee happiness. Sometimes it ruins any chance you have of it instead. Memories of dead men hold far more power than the annoyances of living ones."

I stared at Mencheres. His face was blank again,

giving nothing away, but we all knew what he meant.

"If I had not shared power with you," Mencheres went on, "you would have been killed on that train. You must trust me, because someone under this roof is counting on your jealousy to blind you."

Bones paced in short strides. "That would mean one of the people I've loved as a brother has plotted against me. It's only logical that it's Tate."

"Maybe you're right."

Bones was so surprised by that, he quit pacing.

I came to him, brushing my fingers across his cheekbones. "If you're right," I continued, "then the traitor is locked up and can do no more harm. I'll be grieved that my friend did such a terrible thing, and I'll kill him. But if you're wrong . . . then you have a person here who's desperate not to get caught. Reeling that you're alive. Frantic over what you'll do if you find out who they are. If you're wrong, we're all in a heap of shit. So what are you willing to bet that you're right?"

Bones stared at me with a penetrating, hooded gaze.

"You know I won't take the risk. Fine, then. Whoever it is will want to report to Patra posthaste that I'm still alive, and they'll also likely try to silence Tate before he convinces me of his innocence. We'll need more than the three of us to stop this."

Mencheres nodded. "In the meantime, let that person feel secure that the blame falls on Tate. We will keep him as he is. Who do you want to include on this?"

In other words, who do you trust with everyone's lives?

"Charles, of course. If he's the rat, I'll stake myself. Rodney also."

"Annette, too," I said. "When she thought you were dead, she said she couldn't live without you."

Mencheres backed toward the door. "I can't stay any longer, it would appear suspicious. About your recovery . . . I was exaggerating. Tenoch could regenerate within an hour and be back to full power within two. You will be right in a day at most, but let them think you're weakened."

"Grandsire." Bones halted him at the now-opened door. "Once again, thank you."

Mencheres smiled. For an instant, it made him look younger than Bones, in terms of human appearance. With his sizzling aura of power, I never noticed that before.

"You're welcome."

Bones and I faced each other in the room. All at once, I didn't know what to say. Should we run through the list of possible suspects? Debate more over Tate's innocence versus guilt, for Bones still didn't look convinced. Or forget all of the above and try to sleep as suggested?

"Has anyone called Don to tell him you caught up with me?"

That won the toss, and it hadn't even been on my mental list.

"No, but he can wait a bit longer. Come lie down with me, I've longed for nothing as much as your arms these past days."

Bones pulled me with him to the bed, enfolding me under the blanket. I reached out, fingering his shock of white hair. Bones's flesh was cool against my cheek, his skin tight and sleek. It seemed impossible that not long ago, it was withered.

"Your body aged almost to the point of truly dying. That's why your hair's white, isn't it?"

"Yes. I expect so."

It hit me then, staring at his unlined, beautiful face and that stark light hair framing it, that neither of us should be alive. Bones had almost been killed by a knife in his heart, and add one more step on a rocky ledge for me, and he would have returned to find my body broken beyond revival.

Sometimes there were moments when things were perfectly clear. When the answers seemed so obvious, I wondered how I hadn't noticed them before. When I'd thought Bones was dead, nothing else had mattered for me except making sure those responsible paid. I hadn't cared that I'd need to quit my job to handle the responsibility of his line and avenge his death. No, I'd taken that as a given and had called Don to tell him I wasn't coming back.

Now, however, with Bones alive, I could return to my job. Except I didn't want to. I wasn't going to backburner Bones because his life meant less to me than his presumed death had. What do you do when you get a second chance . . . or in my case, a third or fourth?

You don't squander it, that's what.

"Things are going to change," I said.

Maybe Bones heard it in my voice. It could have been the threads forming in my mind, because his eyes widened even before I said the next words aloud.

"I'm quitting my job."

Twenty-six

S PADE GAVE A POINTED GLANCE AT THE CLOCK and then at a plate on the table. "Your breakfast is cold."

I glanced at the clock also. We should have been down an hour ago, but oh well. Some things had a higher priority than food.

I sat at the table in front of what I assumed was my plate. The Brie was waxy inside the croissant, the eggs wilted, and the julienne peppers had lost whatever brightness they'd once had. Rodney began to brew another pot of coffee, apparently thinking the previous one was a lost cause.

I smiled at Spade. "Don't worry, it's room temperature. My favorite."

I ate my food with a rush of appetite while Bones went with Spade to find a liquid breakfast. Once out of my eyesight, I heard Annette join them. Bodyguards. Since Mencheres was in the room next to the kitchen, I was covered. Besides, my money wasn't on Rodney being the turncoat. Or surprisingly, on the other vampire who glided in.

Vlad took a seat next to me, ignoring Rodney's inhospitable glare.

"With the color back in your face," Vlad observed, "Bones isn't the only one who looks resurrected."

I leaned back to sip my coffee. He considered the cup in front of me with a sardonic smile.

"Ah, a hot cup of caffeine. You must need it after yet again another night without sleep."

I felt color burn on my cheeks. Vlad chuckled, picking daintily at his fingernails.

"Really, Cat, you shouldn't be so shocked. Soundproof isn't mindproof, and telepathy travels through even the thickest walls. I could barely sleep myself with all the shouts going off in my head."

Good God, I hadn't considered that. This must be what it felt like to have someone find a sex tape of you.

"There goes your invitation to ever stay at our house," I ground out, suddenly fascinated with my coffee cup. "Here I'd been thinking I almost liked you. I'm over it now."

Vlad grinned, and it was wolfish and charming.

"And here I was lamenting the fact that the opportunity to extend our friendship had passed. I'm not a fool like the other one. You'll never leave Bones. The boy should realize that and move on with his life."

I stiffened. What his sentence told me was that Vlad, too, didn't think Tate was the traitor. If he had, Vlad would know Tate wouldn't have a future to worry about.

"I owe you."

Vlad's expression turned serious just as quickly as

the change in topic. "You would, normally. In this case, however, it's a debt of mine settled and requires no payment from you."

"Come on, Vlad, you're breaking character. Magnanimous isn't your best color."

He smiled. "Quite correct. You said before you read about my historical account? Then you know that I was married. At a battle near my home, I was struck in the head. It would have been a deathblow, but I'd been a vampire for several weeks. Dawn came, and I slept as all new vampires do, my forehead still caked with blood. My men assumed I'd been slain. A soldier ran to my house to inform my wife of my demise. You know what happened next."

Yes, I did. She jumped to her death from their castle roof, thinking to spare herself from enemy captivity or worse.

And almost six hundred years later, Vlad had stepped in to help prevent me from doing the same thing.

That scarred hand slid across the table to mine. "My wife stood alone on that roof when I should have been there. I hadn't told her what I was. Already I'd horrified her by what I'd done to keep my people safe, I was afraid that my no longer being human would drive a deeper wedge between us. I'd planned on telling her the truth in time . . . but all at once there was no more time. Since she's been gone, I've done many more things she would have been revolted over, yet on that day with you . . . I felt her smile at me. I haven't felt that in a very long time."

Abruptly he stood. "Don't squander what you have. If you do, you'll spend the rest of your days regretting it. Bones should never be afraid to show you all he is, even though he's an uppity street peasant who's been gifted far and away over what he deserves."

This last part was louder, because Bones was on his way back from the sound of the measured stride heading toward us. I smiled up at Vlad wryly.

"Petty, aren't you?"

"Of course. Along with my many other despicable qualities. But, Catherine . . ." He leaned closer until only I could hear him. "I would have never let you jump."

Vlad left right after that, taking the other exit from the kitchen to avoid running into Bones. This time I thought it was less because of their mutual dislike and more that he wanted to avoid more of his gratitude. Like it was pesky to be reminded he'd done a good deed.

Bones came in the kitchen, glancing from Vlad's retreating figure back to me. Then he rolled his eyes.

"Blimey, Kitten, don't tell me you like that conceited sod?"

A smile tugged at my mouth.

"Yeah, I kind of do."

Last night Bones had assured me Tate was being held comfortably and not subjected to any abuse. When I saw him in the tiny cell that was best described as a dungeon, I was furious.

"This is your idea of comfortable? What's a little cramped to you, the seventh ring of hell?"

Bones didn't flinch at my scalding tone. He considered the manacled and bloodied form welded to the wall in front of us.

"He's not being injured, just restrained. The blood on him is no doubt just from last night. While he might have preferred a soft bed and a nice neck to sip from, it's hardly grievous torment considering what he's done."

This was said in a clear, biting tone that would have been easily overheard by anyone eavesdropping. I resisted the urge to demand Tate be taken down. After all, there was still a real betrayer on the loose, and we didn't know who it was.

"You're the luckiest son of a bitch in the world."

It was muttered with nothing less than hatred from Tate. His eyes were pure emerald as they blazed at Bones.

Bones laughed. "You know, mate, when I woke up this morning with her sleeping in my arms, I did indeed feel very lucky."

Tate cursed him, straining against his clamps.

Ian chuckled and clapped a hand across Bones's back. He'd been the guard last night.

"Bloke's scorched you up one side and down the other since you came back, Crispin. I've had a right enjoyable time listening to it. Ah, Rodney, is it your turn now? Good, I'm knackered."

"Thank you, Ian, take your rest. I'll speak to you later."

Although Ian didn't make the top two, or even three, Bones put him high on the list of the remaining people who he didn't think tried to kill him. I thought Ian was capable of it, but Bones disagreed. Since Tate was a liability to whomever really did it, we had to have reliable guards on him.

The area cleared of everyone but Rodney, Bones, Tate, and me. We were underground in a sealed section with just one way in or out. This would be our only chance to talk, because afterward, it wouldn't seem plausible. But now, it made sense that I'd want to confront Bones's Judas.

"How could you do it, Tate?" I asked. Sound traveled well with that echoing hallway leading to this room, so whispering would have been too obvious.

"I hate him, but it wasn't me," Tate replied.

I withdrew a small notepad and pen from under my sweater. Tate watched warily. I nodded to Rodney, who unshackled one of his arms from its clamp. Letting him all the way out would have made too much noise, and Bones was still being cautious. He didn't want Tate loose around me, not trusting if he'd rather see me dead than with him. He still thought Tate was guilty no matter how I disagreed.

I quickly scrawled some words onto the paper and held it up for Tate to see.

I believe you.

Tears came to his eyes. It was all I could do not to hug him and tell him it would be okay. He jerked his head and Rodney brought him the pen, holding the pad up so he could write.

"See, I don't believe you, mate."

Bones said it with no lack of venom, and anyone overhearing would have thought it was him answering Tate's denial to me. Rodney gave a disgusted glance at the page Tate wrote on before he passed it to me.

Love you, Cat

"I don't give a shit what you believe, you sneaky English slut," is what he said to Bones.

Well, we wanted this to sound authentic, I thought ironically. *At least that's covered.*

"Want to know what I think, dickhead?" Tate went on. "I think you faked your death to send her into a spiral of grief, and then you miraculously reappeared with the guy you hate to blame it all on. You've wanted an excuse to kill me ever since you came back in her life. Got sick of waiting, didn't you?"

I blinked. Tate sure went the other way in coming up with an explanation.

Bones gave a rude snort. "Think I'd hurt her like that just to kill you? Imbecile."

This is not why we're here! I wrote and waved it in front of Bones, forgetting in my agitation that I could just think it at him.

Bones didn't even pause to look. "You're not strong enough for her by half, mate. Faith, conspiring to have me murdered is the most impressive thing you've done. Stick to your story that it wasn't you? Then you're right back in that forgotten place where she'll never notice you. So which are you, a betrayer or a pathetic loser?"

It was a trick question, of course. One answer would have him dead and the other, according to Bones's scathing analogy, emotionally dismissed. There were several points of contention I wanted to argue with him about, but that would wait until later.

Tate glowered at him with even more fury than before, which was saying something. Bones waited with a mocking curl to his lips. I was still scribbling on the notepad when Tate spoke.

"Just let's be clear about one thing—if you kill me, it won't be because I did this. I didn't rat you out to Patra, though thumbs-up to whoever did. If you kill me, it's because you're afraid that if you don't, one day you might watch her walk away with me. So right back at you, Crypt Keeper, what's it gonna be?"

Dark brown eyes that could melt me were flat and icy now.

"I gave you the chance to own up to your deeds with dignity. You refused. Right then, we'll have it your way. You'll stay chained here, no food, no companionship, until hunger and solitude soften you up. We'll see what you have to say again in a month or so. Let him be alone with his deceit and his spinelessness. In the meantime, I'll be enjoying my wife's company."

Bones took my hand. I resisted long enough to hold up the messily written page and have Tate read it as Rodney chained his arm back into place.

Promise I'll find who it is, but if anyone comes in this room but me or Bones, you scream as loud as you can.

"Don't worry, Cat," Tate said, with a touch of humor. "I'll be right here."

When Rodney closed the door behind us, I whirled on Bones. *Do you still think it's him?* I demanded.

He stared at me with competing emotions across his face, none of them pleasant. Finally, he shook his head.

No.

†WEП†Y-SEVEП

O F OUR BAKER'S DOZEN UNDEAD SUSPECTS, we had it narrowed down to four. This was an exceptionally painful process for Bones, since each of them had spent no less than a century with him, and he considered them all close friends. Caesar hadn't suspected Brutus, either, however, and look where that got him. So Bones had to be unmerciful in his evaluations.

Zero was on the list, despite his outward slavish devotion, then Tick Tock, Rattler, and Doc completed our suspects. Vlad he kept as a potential alternate.

While I'd been eating breakfast, Bones had finally called Don to tell him he'd arrived. My uncle asked about Tate, of course, and got a brusque response that he was still unshriveled "for the moment." I could just picture tiny gray hairs being yanked from Don's eyebrow during that conversation. Don loved Tate, but he was also a realist. He knew what would happen if Tate was guilty of this crime. Vampires didn't do probation.

To reinforce Mencheres's description of a slow recovery, Bones moved with notable sluggishness compared to his normal prowling strides. We spent the afternoon on the couch while Mencheres brought him up to speed on what had occurred when he was presumed dead. In brief but unsparing detail, Mencheres described how Patra had crashed the event at the opera house. My mother gave up pretending she wasn't eavesdropping and sat in a nearby chair. When Mencheres was finished, she broke the loaded silence.

"What a real bitch, Catherine. You should kill her."

Bones let out a snort. "I intend to do the honors myself."

And in the meantime, we'd see who here tried to contact Patra to let her know Bones was alive. Don had arranged for tapping of all the phones, and even interceptions of the wireless signals coming out of the house. Computers, text messaging, and anything else aside from homing pigeons were confiscated. Security purposes, Mencheres coolly stated, and no one dared argue with him. When the traitor made his move, he'd have to do it by phone, and then we'd catch him. Now we just had to wait.

"Bones, you are still pale," Mencheres said. "You should feed and get more rest."

"Right." Bones tugged my hand. "Kitten, I want to show you something."

I followed him downstairs to the basement, passing through several rooms I hadn't bothered to explore in the past few days. At least a third of this house was underground, a good vampire and ghoul analogy. What you saw on the surface was only the beginning, much like the species themselves.

Two vampires bowed at the waist before they held the wooden double doors open for us.

Several people, all human, glanced up when we entered what appeared to be an entertainment area. Some of them were on a large sofa watching the plasma TV, others played on one of the four billiard tables, and five looked to be engaged in a game of poker.

"What is this?" I whispered.

Bones's wave encompassed the room. "This is a vampire's version of a kitchen, luv. Caring for humans in exchange for their blood is how many vampire households operate. I wanted you to see it."

"Dibs on the redhead!" a freckled young man called out, coming forward with a grin. "You'll like me, I taste the best."

"You think I'm here to *feed* on you?" I gaped when he tilted his head and bared his neck.

Bones chuckled. "He does indeed. Sorry, Neal, but she's not going to bite you, and you don't taste the best," he corrected him before laying a hand on his shoulder. "You'll do, however. Though you should eat fewer onions."

I watched as Neal went to Bones, who sealed his mouth on Neal's neck and bit him like he was a walking cupcake. Less than a minute later he stopped, closing the holes and giving Neal a companionable chuck on the chin.

"Less garlic as well, mate. I've drunk Italian chefs who didn't have such a reek about them."

Neal's smile didn't slip. "Best pizza I've ever had, Whitey, and it was loaded with onions and garlic. Sorry."

Bones gave an amused snort. "Toothbrush, lad. Familiarize yourself with it or you'll never get turned.

No, don't get up," as one of the girls rose from the couch. "We're taking a quick walk and then we'll be off."

My mother would pass out if she knew this was underneath her, I thought dazedly. *Living snacks, all within biting reach*.

"Who are these kids?" I asked low. None of them looked much past their twenties.

Bones led me through another set of rooms. There was a library, computer area, even an underground Jacuzzi. And every few dozen feet there were bedrooms. Some were occupied, some were empty, and a few with closed doors had the unmistakable sounds of sex coming from them.

"Oh, they're from all sorts," he replied. "Some are college students, aspiring artists, runaways from bad homes, street children, or budding apprentices. Neal's one of those. He wants to be a vampire, so he's showing his commitment by being a meal and doing small errands. Whenever you have a group of vampires who live in a large house, you generally have one of these situations."

"Are they all tranced?"

"Blimey, no. They're aware of what keeps them and why. The runaways get homeschooled, a place to live, and an allowance they save for whenever they wish to strike out on their own. For their own safety, though, most of them don't know where they're located or the real names of who keeps them. When they leave, what they do know is wiped from their minds. It's happened this way for millennia, Kitten. A form of feudalism, as I told you before."

"Feudalism?" I stopped near one of the bedrooms with the heavy breathing. "Is that what you call it?"

"This"—Bones nodded at the doorway—"is consensual. While I can't speak for all households, as a rule it's considered very bad form to mesmerize one's food into shagging. If you're a guest and you do such a thing, it's almost cause for death. Now, if the human fancies a tumble, then who's to criticize? It's their choice."

Who's to criticize? Me. *Nice, Mencheres. Provide all-you-can-eat meals, in every possible way.* Do be sure to feed regularly, Bones, there's a good lad! *Asshole*.

"You know better, Kitten," Bones said with all seriousness. "It will never happen."

I believed him, even if irrationally I still felt threatened by the easy opportunities available. "Is that why you showed me this? So I wouldn't worry you were trying to conceal something?"

"That's one of several reasons, yes." Bones started to smile. "The main one is behind you, ogling your arse and about to get beaten for it."

"*Amigo*," a voice said in a wheedling tone. "I haven't seen it for days—"

My whirling to barrel into him cut off the rest of the sentence. Juan returned my hug, crooning in Spanish.

"*Mi querida,* your husband's back, *que bueno*."

"Yes, I'm glad he's here as well," I sniffed. "And that you are, too. How do you feel?"

Juan grinned. It was his usual lecherous grin that reminded me crossing over didn't change the essence of the person.

"I feel wonderful, and you are even more beautiful with these new eyes of mine. Look at your skin." He fingered my cheek. "*Magnifico*."

"That's all the pawing you're allowed, mate."

Bones gave him a light punch, knocking him back a pace. Juan didn't quit grinning.

"I must thank you for many things, *amigo*, but this most of all. You have made women even more appealing to me, ah, the scent of them. Their heartbeats. And how they taste . . ." He closed his eyes. "*Delicioso*."

I swung my gaze to Bones in disbelief. "You've turned him into even *worse* of a pig!"

Bones shrugged. "He's just a bit overwhelmed with all the new senses. He'll get used to them. Or get neutered if he forgets himself and even thinks of palming your arse, do you think I'm blind?" He slapped at the hand wandering with feigned innocence near my hip. "Control, *amigo*. Learn it."

"*Querida*." Juan kissed my cheek, this time with respect. "I'm not ruled by my hunger and I can once again fight. He's given me power . . . and I won't squander it."

One of the girls who were watching TV came down the hall with a flirtatious giggle, eyeing the two men. Juan went on full alert, his nose crinkling and green lights appearing in his eyes.

"Speaking of not squandering it . . ." He gave me a last quick kiss and followed after her, grinning.

"*La rubia, por favor* . . . wait. I am thirsty, and very susceptible to flattery . . . you could talk me into anything . . ."

"So much for fighting the good fight," I observed dryly. "He'll have a harem within a week."

Bones watched Juan disappear down the hall, nuzzling the blonde's neck in a manner that didn't speak only of hunger. "He's a fine bloke. He'll learn."

"Learn what?" *At least he can't get or pass diseases*

anymore, I thought. That's one advantage turning Juan into a vampire did for womankind.

Bones put an arm around me as we headed toward the exit of this flesh feast. "He'll learn that many women can satisfy for a short period of time, but when he falls in love, only one will sustain him forever."

I cast him a sideways glance "Are you trying to seduce me?"

His lips curled with promise. "Absolutely."

My fingers laced in his. Yes, there was so much wrong with our situation. Someone we trusted wanted him dead, and that was just the start of our problems. Still, life was wasted on those who didn't live in the time they had, be they human, vampire, or ghoul. Or a freaky mixture of the two, like me.

"Good."

Twenty-eight

THE WAITING WAS GETTING TO ME. UNDER other circumstances, I would have considered spending most of my time with Bones behind closed doors as a vacation. But suspiciously eyeing the people around me whenever we left the bedroom was not my idea of relaxing. It was worse for Bones, I knew. At least I didn't have emotional attachments to whoever the traitor was.

This morning at breakfast, Bones upped the ante. As I munched French toast, he casually mentioned to Zero that Reno should be a pleasant change in temperature compared to here in Whistler, British Columbia. All of our suspects were close enough to have overheard. Here I thought I'd outgrown Clue. *Will it be Zero in the kitchen with a cell phone, or Doc in the drawing room with a pistol?*

Speaking of Doc, he'd been acting strangely. Several times, we saw him lingering near the hallway where Tate was being held, wearing his guns, chewing on an unlit cigarette and watching everything around him with a surgeon's attention. He seemed to appear behind me whenever Bones wasn't there, soundless as a shadow. When Bones would appear, he'd exit in a polite but deliberate way, still staying in close proximity.

It creeped me out.

Bones didn't care for it, either, but out of necessity didn't confront Doc or show that it bothered him. Instead, he would smile and say things like, "Oh, there you are, mate," in such a breezy, unaffected tone it was all I could do not to applaud. Maybe in another couple centuries, if I lived that long, I'd have such good acting abilities as well.

Tick Tock and Rattler, the other two suspects, went about their business in such a blithe manner I mentally placed them lower on the totem pole. If anything, they seemed to sense my discomfort around Doc and tried to lead him off the few times Bones wasn't glued to my hip. I took to wearing knives under my clothes, though they didn't provide much comfort. With how blazing fast Doc was with those guns, I'd be pumped full of bullets before even getting a chance to fling one.

Soon after the Reno announcement, Bones went for his morning drink. I wandered outside on the porch. Vampires traditionally hated the freezing cold, having no internal heating system as a human did. Mencheres didn't choose to hide out in the Canadian mountains in December on a whim. He knew it was a place the undead usually avoided. At this time of year, Florida was full of pulseless visitors. You couldn't swing a cat without hitting a nonbeating heart.

It was with mild trepidation therefore that I glimpsed

a lone figure in the trees just to the left of where I was on the wraparound porch. I knew that form by now. Tall, lean, and deadly. Something glinted, and the sudden chill I felt made the outside air seem balmy in comparison. It was the reflection of sun off metal.

Without obvious rush, I turned and headed toward the door, concentrating all my willpower on not letting my pulse race. Such a sound might as well be a scream of fright to a vampire. As I walked, I wondered if I could dodge the bullets fast enough to avoid any vital organs. But it made sense that Doc would aim for my head. Why would he target anything else?

The door opened before I reached it, Vlad at my side, right in the way of any oncoming gunfire. I couldn't remember when I'd been so glad to see him.

Thank you, I sent to him without giving a last look over my shoulder like I wanted to.

"It's freezing out here," he said with a sardonic twist of his mouth. "You'll catch your death."

"Stay away from Doc, Kitten," Bones began as soon as we were in our room and I told him what happened.

"You should just grab him and find out what he knows," I muttered, irritated with myself for presenting such an open target.

"Yes, well, it would take longer to torture it out of him than to be patient and wait for him to get caught spilling it," Bones said with calculated menace. "Believe me, if it were a matter of preference, you know mine."

Yeah, I had a pretty good idea. If imagination failed me, I was sure he could arrange for a demonstration to jog my memory. Whenever we left this room, his mask of cheerful obliviousness was on with full force. Once inside, it fell from Bones like scales. He rubbed the side of his temple almost impatiently. However rough it was on me, it was certainly worse for him.

"You must go crazy wishing for a few minutes of real peace and quiet," I said. "I mean, it's never quiet for you, is it? Either you've got noise from people around you or the crap rattling off in my head."

He smiled with a trace of bitterness.

"Don't fret, luv, I had a bit of real silence not too long ago. It's highly overrated, if you ask me."

He sat on the high-backed chair near the bed. Red velvet, mahogany wood, gold threading, maybe a real Louis the Eighteenth. Bones looked compatible with it, just as beautiful and finely molded.

I sat down and rested my head on his legs. "This isn't your fault," I said, softly but out loud, so he could hear it both ways.

He sighed. "Then whose is it, Kitten?"

Whatever I might have replied cleared right out of my head. Bones yanked me down on the carpet and covered me before my heart even finished its beat. No, it wasn't from being overwhelmed by passion. It was because of the sudden eruption of gunfire.

He dragged me to the bathroom before snapping, "Stay here," and disappearing in a blur. His quickness actually made me shake myself for a second before I ignored his directive and vaulted after him. No way was I sitting it out by the tub and hoping for the best. Doc only used silver bullets. It would be just as dangerous for Bones as it was for me.

Without bothering with the stairs, I jumped the three floors down and followed the direction of the other streaking bodies, not to mention the noise.

There was another succession of bullets, too fast for me to count, and an accompanying shout that picked my feet off the ground and had me diving forward. The commotion was coming from the dungeon below, and the voice yelling out was Tate's.

I blasted past the other vampires racing down the narrow hallway and made it through the ruined door, hurtling straight at the man who raised the knife even as I crashed into him. The force of my velocity bashed both of us through the wall in an expulsion of concrete. Before I allowed myself to think, I jammed one of my silver knives into the form scrambling away. I didn't have time to wonder what part of him I'd pierced, or why the hell it wasn't Doc, because he was yanked out. Just as swiftly my legs were tugged on next, and I was plunked out of the new hole in the wall.

Above Tate's panicked cries of "Cat! Cat!" I heard Vlad's cool voice.

"You're holding the wrong man, Bones, and you owe Cat your life."

"Kitten, are you all right?"

Bones had Doc gripped in such a way that it stalled my response. Or maybe belated dizziness from the impact of my head smashing through solid concrete was to blame. I shook some of the blood off my forehead and accepted Spade's hand to help me to my feet. The small room was shoulder to shoulder with people.

"I'm fine," I managed. "He was going to stab you."

"No, Doc was going to shoot Rattler again, weren't you, mate?"

Bones asked it with caressing menace as he tightened his grip. I winced and instinctively straightened my spine. Doc couldn't; his was bent at the opposite angle. Bones had him folded like a backward sandwich.

"Bones!" He looked up from sharpness of my tone. "*Rattler* was going to stab you."

"She's right," Tate said, pulling on his restraints. "He stabbed Annette, is she okay?"

"I have her," Mencheres replied from outside the cell. "Zero, go fetch a human. She needs blood. Annette, don't move. This will hurt . . ."

Underneath the rest of the uproar her low, pained voice penetrated. It was irregularly spaced but audible, and everyone shut up as her words became clear.

". . . Crispin . . . it was Rattler—ah! Christ, that's excruciating . . . Doc shot him . . . when he stabbed me . . . is that bloody blade out yet, Mencheres, I can't bear to look . . ."

Bones released Doc. Vlad held Rattler in a punishing embrace, one hand on the silver knife I'd lodged in his chest, which was very close to his heart. Bones pushed past the people in the cramped space until he was in the hallway, kneeling by Annette's crumpled form.

"Don't move, sweet," he said with the soothing cadence one would use on a child. "There, feel my hand? It's almost over, squeeze very hard . . ."

With precision delicacy, Mencheres drew the wicked-looking silver blade from her chest. A laser beam would have been sloppier. The reason for his caution was obvious—she'd been skewered straight though the heart and any sideways motion would finish her. I held my breath as the last inch left her chest, because despite it all, I admired Annette. When it was out and she made a grunt of pain, sitting up, I let out my breath. It seemed everyone did, even those who didn't breathe.

Zero came back, holding a wide-eyed teenager under his arm. Bones moved to allow the young man to be deposited next to her, and Annette latched her mouth onto him the next moment. Her hand still was curled around Bones's and he brought it to his lips before letting her go and standing with grim purpose.

Doc stood also now, his spine having healed in the interim. He went to Annette, who just released the teenage boy with a last lick of her lips. Zero supported him as he lurched away. I hoped they had a good supply of iron pills here.

Doc stretched and his back made an audible crack. "Think the last of them settled back into place. Bones, don't try to play chiropractor with me again. After all, I'm the only certified medical professional in this room."

"You were a bleedin' dentist, and a rotten one from what I hear. Still, you are without a doubt the fastest shooter I've seen anywhere in any era, and I shall be grateful to you the rest of my days." Bones glanced at Vlad next. "Pull that knife out of Rattler once my wife is clear of his reach." To Spade, he said simply, "Let Tate loose."

The clanking of irons was the only sound now as Spade released Tate from his restraints. Once free, Tate stretched in much the same manner Doc had, only with a lot less graciousness for his rough treatment.

"Told you it wasn't me."

"I knew you suspected me," Doc said. "Sorry if I made you uncomfortable this morning, Cat, but Rattler had been skulking around the side of the house after you. He knew I saw him, and it made him desperate. I followed him down here just in time to see him stab Annette. At least my bullets kept him from finishing her."

Bones laid his hand on Doc's shoulder. "Take Annette out of here, and once again, you have my deepest gratitude."

After the two of them left, Bones turned to Vlad with a cold smile. "Let's fill that vacancy on the wall, shall we?"

There was a matching smile on the former prince's lips as the two of them strapped Rattler into the same clamps that had held Tate.

"You must be hungry," I said to Tate, who'd gone to my side as soon as he was released. "They're stocked here, believe me. Have someone show you."

Tate rubbed his arms, as if he could still feel those clamps biting into them. "It can wait. Your head's bleeding."

"I'll tend to her."

With Rattler bound, Bones came to me, pressing his lips against the wound in my crown.

"You could have cracked your skull like an egg smashing into that wall, let alone the risk of getting shot. Mule-headed woman, at least it appears your stubbornness is well protected by a thick layer of bone. Have I thanked you yet for your reckless disregard of my directive to stay upstairs?"

"No," I said with a small smile.

Bones set me back, pulling a knife from his pants. "I will. Promise."

He cut his palm and placed it over my head. The tingling sensation was almost instant as my flesh healed. With a last brush of his lips, he let me go, and turned to the vampire who was the center of attention.

"Why?"

It was asked with the threat of punishment and the pain of betrayal combined. Rattler dropped his gaze.

Spade rammed his elbow so hard into Rattler's rib cage that half his arm disappeared from sight.

"You were asked a question, Walter!"

Walter, a.k.a. Rattler, gave a gasp of pain even as Bones laid a hand on Spade.

"It's all right, mate. We'll give him a chance to confess without bloodying him first." Then to Rattler, with a much harder tone.

"You know how this will go down. No matter how brave you fancy yourself, everyone breaks eventually. So you will either detail exactly when, why, and how you threw your lot in with Patra with all your limbs and skin attached . . . or with new parts growing as fast as we can tear them off."

For once, such a grim pronouncement didn't fill me with the slightest bit of compassion. It was all I could do not to fling myself on Rattler and start ripping him to pieces just for the sheer enjoyment of it.

"Was it for money?" I hissed. "All that gold and glory she promised? Is that it, were you just greedy?"

"I don't care about money." Whether it was spoken to me or Bones was a toss-up; Rattler glanced at both of us. "I did what I had to do for love."

"For love?" I repeated. "You're in love with Patra? Then you're stupid as well as a backstabbing asshole."

"Not Patra. For Vivienne."

"Patra killed Vivienne, why would you—" Bones began, and then stopped. He shook his head with a sound that was much too callous to be laughter.

"Ah, I see. All this time, then? You told me Vivienne had been slain months ago. I grieved with you, you sod, and all the while you were waiting for your chance!"

It clicked then. I remembered the explosion at Mencheres's house caused by vampires who'd turned themselves into walking bombs all for the sake of whoever Patra had kidnapped beforehand. Seems Patra had done the same with Rattler by kidnapping someone he loved to get him to betray Bones. What a truly vile person Patra was. If possible, I hated her even more.

"How do you even know Vivienne's still alive?" Bones asked.

Rattler looked even more pained than he did right after Spade had elbowed him out the other side.

"Because every week Patra calls me . . . and lets me hear her scream."

Bones began to pace in limited, impotent strides.

"I only told her about the train," Rattler went on. "I had nothing to do with the attacks on your wife. Earlier, I was going to snatch Cat and threaten to kill her unless you slew yourself in my sight, but Doc saw me, and I knew he'd shoot me before I could grab her. So I came to where you were holding the only other person the Reaper would endanger herself for, but I failed. I know you'll punish me as an example, yet I ask one thing . . ."

"You'd dare ask me for anything?" Harshly.

"I don't plead for lenience. I know you'll put me with the other one, but before you do . . . Bones, my sire, I ask that you forgive me."

Bones quit pacing. There was a loaded silence. Then he came to stand in front of Rattler.

"In 1867, I befriended you. Five years later, I

changed you, and what did I say was the worst thing you could ever do as a vampire?"

Rattler looked away. "To betray your sire."

"Right. You have committed the worst act you could in the eyes of our people, yet you ask my forgiveness. Do you know what I have to say to that, Walter Tannenbaum?"

Bones was completely still, and that should have been my warning. Maybe it was the aftereffects of slamming my head through solid concrete that slowed me, or it could have been that he moved too fast, outdistancing even Spade and Vlad as they tried to block him.

"You have it."

The knife he'd used to cut his palm was still in his hand. It buried with a fierce twist into Rattler's heart even as he uttered those words.

There was a split second as their eyes met, me yanking futilely on Bones's arm and shouts of protest coming from the onlookers, when I would swear I saw Rattler smile. It died in the next instant along with him. His body slumped, and before my eyes, his skin started to wither.

"Bones, why?"

Now I was the one who directed that ringing question to him. He swung around to face me.

"Because I would have done the same thing if I were him, so he has my forgiveness."

In the uncomfortable moment of silence I spoke up. "He didn't have mine."

Only the pain in his voice kept me from screaming at him. Instead, in a manner very like his, I grew more still.

"I heard that bitch laugh when she told me she'd

killed you. Then saw her face when she thanked me for it being all my fault. Aren't *I* deserving of any retribution? Doesn't *my* injury measure up next to Rattler's? This might have been merciful but it was *wrong*, Bones. You taught me that. No matter how much you empathized with Rattler, you shouldn't have killed him. I let you have Max. You should have given me Rattler."

And with that, I left the small room, the other vampires clearing a path to let me pass.

Twenty-nine

Since Bones had been pretending to be weak prior to finding out who the traitor was, he hadn't spent much time with the prisoner he'd helped capture from the train ambush—Anubus, Patra's second-in-command. In fact, Anubus had almost been neglected in the furor over Bones's return, though I'm sure he didn't complain over his lack of attention. In fact, he almost seemed surprised to see someone in his cell.

This was really the first I'd seen him as well, since I didn't count that initial time when Ian, Rodney, and Spade had returned with him and without Bones. Anubus was tall for an Egyptian, well over six-three, and he had the long straight hair and pronounced features to brag of his heritage. His bearing was far from that of a prisoner awaiting a grim sentence, too. He almost appeared relaxed, even though he was welded into the steel wall he hung from.

His stygian gaze evaluated me in much the same

way I considered him. Coldly. The first flicker of real disconcertion came when I moved aside to let him view the man who followed behind me.

"Ah, hallo there, Anubus. Blimey, I think the last time I saw you was over fifty years ago. You recall, I had just met this very forward wench who took me back to her chalet and then nearly bored me to impotence with her shagging. Don't think she moved once under me the whole time, and it took hours, didn't it? Why, if the mattress would have had a hole of similar size, I wager I'd have had a grander time shoving my cock into that . . ."

A bellow of rage cut off the rest of his sentence. I managed to keep my features blank. Bones had warned me what he would use to goad Anubus, since Anubus regarded Patra as a deity, but I'd insisted on being present. Guess he wasn't kidding about it being graphic enough to piss the other vampire off.

"Shut up, filth! I can't believe you're still alive, but you won't be for long. All the flames of the netherworld are more than what you deserve."

"Oh ho," Bones chortled. "So even after all this time, she still hasn't let you sample a taste? It's for the best, mate, trust me. *Mediocre* is the most flattering description I could give to detail what lies between that woman's legs. Makes me wonder why Mencheres bound himself to such a poor excuse for a female, but then love can be utterly blind. And shagless, if that were my wife. Now here is a real woman, in every sense of the word." Bones pushed me forward. "In her sleep she's more passionate than that lump of Egyptian clay you worship. Patra knows she pales next to her. Isn't that why she's tried so hard to have her killed? Because she knew no one would be deceived by her claims of superiority once the world got a look at Cat?"

"You will all die," Anubus snarled. "Patra is the reincarnation of Isis and the goddess of this world. She has reigned for over two thousand years, and she can't be stopped by insects who are lower than locusts!"

"You need to get laid, mate," Bones kindly observed. "She hasn't even let you rub one off in all these years, has she? Wants her guards to be pure and all that rot, right? Your unspent balls have warped your brain, they have. How long has it been since you've even gazed on a naked woman, hmm? Before or after Constantine converted?"

This verbal flaying was an unusual tactic for Bones, but he'd reasoned it was worth a shot. Ian, Rodney, and Spade had already tried other means, none of them pleasant, but Anubus had proved either unknowing or disinclined to reveal anything useful. I guess Bones's continued barbs about having sex with Patra was the equivalent of some heckler boasting to the pope about how he'd nailed the Virgin Mary. Patra definitely wasn't chaste, but if she'd had affairs aside from the infamous one with Bones, she'd been discreet about it. And she was notorious about declaring herself to be of divine lineage. Many of her people literally worshipped her. Anubus fell into that category.

"Are you picturing it yet? My hands on Patra, mmmm, how many mornings have you imagined it? Lying awake, wanting to murder me for it, and then to find out that all the while I touched her, I found the whole experience quite . . . lacking."

Boy, did we sure have his full attention. Anubus's eyes were blazing green and livid. "You're not even worthy to be sacrificed to her. Patra only laid with you to sentence you to death, yet even there, Mencheres failed her. She should have just let me finish you that night as I wanted to."

Bones laughed again, but lower.

"Think she was the first female who shagged me hoping it would lead me to my doom? Not nearly. That trick had been attempted before then and repeated numerous times after it. So no, sorry, that's not why Patra was substandard in bed. It's because she's a fraud, a fake, and stripped of her lies—and her clothing—she was nothing more than a spoiled little girl with illusions of grandeur reinforced by such idiots as yourself."

"The grave is coming for you," Anubus roared, all composure gone. "She's summoned it, and it will find you and swallow you down with unending hunger—"

And then he stopped. I didn't have to see Bones's smile to feel it. He straightened, all the bantering gone from him. Anubus's face went blank, but it was too late. *You fucked up, buddy, and you know it.*

"Now, mate," Bones said as he went to Anubus and settled his finger with deceptive lightness on his face. "Whatever do you mean by *that*?"

"Should we open the champagne, or wait to hose the boys off with it?" Denise asked.

We were seated in the living room, a formal place with earth tones and gilded pieces of antique furniture. The massive table looked like it was carved from a single gigantic tree. Food adorned it, along with solid brass and silver serving pieces, but no one really ate. I'd been drumming my fingers on its polished surface before I glanced up at her question.

"Hmm? Oh, go ahead and pop the cork. They'll be a while."

The reason I was here, instead of downstairs, was twofold. One, I didn't want to leave Denise and my mother surrounded by strangers on a holiday, and two, though he didn't ask me to leave, I knew Bones didn't want me below. Since they now knew Anubus was hiding something and not just ignorant, the gloves would definitely be off. It bothered me that Bones still thought seeing him like that would change how I felt about him, but I didn't want him distracted over me. Not when lives might depend on how fast he got the information out of Anubus.

Denise poured the champagne. "This stuff is excellent," she enthused. "Man, is this place ever stocked. Did you see all the brandy? I'll need a new liver if we stay here long!"

Her cheerful mood made me smile, but with a touch of jadedness. No, she had no idea how ugly things were downstairs by now. *If you stay around vampires long, though*, I mused, *you'll learn. It's not all fun and vintage liquor.*

Instead I said, "Fill her up. There's two hours before midnight, we may as well start the party. The last report from Zero was that they were making progress, whatever that means."

While Bones, Mencheres, Spade, Vlad, Rodney, and Ian were below, Tick Tock and Zero were our guards. Hell, we wouldn't even be able to stub our toes without one of them jumping in to prevent it.

"The snow's died down," my mother commented. "At least now you can see out of these windows. I can't wait to leave this barren place—and just for the record, I won't be waiting much longer."

Uh oh, there she goes. Some New Year's wishes would never come true.

I sighed. "If you don't like being surrounded by these vampires and ghouls, imagine how much more you wouldn't like it if it were Patra's vamps and ghouls."

"I'm not a child, Catherine," she replied in her usual sharp tone. "Don't speak to me like one."

The tenseness of the past several days caught up with me, even though I of all people knew better.

"You're not a child? That is news, considering you've acted like one most of my life."

Denise's mouth dropped at my rejoinder. She gulped her champagne, settling back in her chair for a better view.

"That's it," my mother announced, furious. "I'm leaving!"

Why couldn't I just learn to keep my trap shut? With resignation, I followed her as she marched to the front door, grabbing a coat.

"Mom, be sensible. It's about six degrees outside, you'll freeze to death. Where do you think you're going, anyway?"

"I've had enough of this," she spat. "Go here, do that, stay still, silly little mortal, tricks are for kids! Well, I am through being carted around for guilt's sake."

During her tirade, she had pushed past me and marched straight out onto the lawn. I didn't stop her, partly because I didn't want to have to get physical and also so our grievances could be aired in semi-private. The living room was hardly the place for this kind of family circus.

"You're wrong, Mom," I said, trying to ignore the

biting wind. I hadn't bothered to don a coat, and the chill cut straight through my sweater and pants. "Can you be a pain in the ass? Yeah. Do I wish you weren't in my life? Of course not. Now, really, let's get back inside, it's freezing out—"

"I'll walk to the nearest house, street, town, whatever," she snapped, not mollified in the least.

We reached the trees, the fallen snow silvery in the moonlight. My breath came in plumes of smoke. "There's nothing around for at least twenty miles," I pointed out in a calm tone. "Believe me, I know. Mencheres picked this place for a reason. You can't walk it, you'd be overcome by hypothermia inside of five. We're out in the middle of nowhere, trust me, there's nothing around . . ."

And then I stopped, frozen to the spot and not from the temperature. My sudden unyielding grip on her prevented her from going another step. She rounded on me angrily before ceasing at my expression.

"What?" she whispered.

"Shhh."

It was barely audible to her, but sounded way too loud for my comfort. Then again, our bitching over the past fifty yards hadn't been quiet. Neither were the heavy footfalls in the distance, disturbing the night with how noisy they were.

I narrowed my eyes, focusing all my energy toward those sounds. No heartbeat, no breathing, but also no feeling of encroaching power. They were moving slowly. A whole hell of a lot of them. Why didn't I feel anything? Every vampire or ghoul gave off an aura of power, but there was nothing. What the fuck were they?

Without waiting to find out, I snatched her up and

ran for the house. Zero and Tick Tock were already at the door, sensing trouble from my rapid pace.

"Get everybody downstairs now," I barked, shoving my mother in that direction for emphasis. "Something's coming."

"What?" Denise began, rising from her chair.

Randy was quicker on the draw and went to her, pulling her up. Zero gestured to the stairs, ever respectful but urgent.

"Please, this way."

When my mother didn't move, I shot her a single glare. "Awake or unconscious, you're going with them."

She muttered something but went after them, her shoulders stiff.

"Tick Tock," I breathed, still straining to listen to those figures. "Get Bones and the others."

Two minutes later Bones came, Spade and Rodney close behind him. I ignored the stains on him and pointed to the window.

"Do you hear them? I can't feel anything, but there are a lot of them. Headed right this way."

Bones narrowed his gaze, staring into the darkness with green pinpoints in his eyes. After a few seconds he let out a grunt.

"Can't feel anything, either, Kitten, but they're stomping around like a herd of elephants. Whatever they are, they aren't human. Charles?"

"I have no idea, Crispin. That curls my stones in my sack."

Rodney gave Spade a grimly supportive glance. "I'm right there with you."

"All right." Bones cracked his knuckles, his eyes all green. "Let's get ready to greet them. We'll need knives, swords, crossbows, guns . . . quickly. A few of them sound like they're ahead of the pack. We'll be finding out soon what's come to call."

"Why don't we just leave?" I asked on the way to the armory.

"Because there's not enough choppers to get everyone off, and if we take cars, it could be an ambush. We'll make a stand, luv. Find out what we're up against. Now, we'll have the chopper ready just in case. If need be, you can fly your mum, Denise, and Randy to safety."

"I won't leave you," I said. "No matter what."

Bones made a soothing noise even as he began to strap on about forty pounds of silver. "Now Kitten, they're human and therefore easiest to kill. The rest of us are capable of—"

"Not a motherfucking chance." In the same reasonable tone he used. "Juan knows how to fly and I'm stronger than he is, so he'd be the best choice if their evacuation became necessary. And if you even think of pulling a fast one, like knocking me out and loading me onto that chopper, I'll return to work full-time taking on assignments that'll make your hair even whiter than it is now."

Bones gave me a quick, fierce kiss.

"Bloody woman. Learned a few mind-reading tricks of your own, have you? Right then, suit up and change clothes. Your sweater's too bulky, it'll restrain your movements."

I just pulled it off, left in my bra, sweatpants, and sneakers. There was no time to go upstairs and find a more flexible shirt. I began to strap on silver knives, lashing them to my legs, waist, and arms with the enhanced speed of long practice.

"Just not going to listen to a word I say, are you?" Bones asked as he handed me a sword. "Keep one of these, we don't know what we're trying to kill and silver might not work. You're going to freeze like that, Kitten."

"Isn't that the least of our concerns?" With a laugh that was more strained than amused. "Now I've got full range of motion, and that's what's most important."

"Right you are." Bones drew off his own sweater and threw it to the ground next to mine. Most of the vampires and ghouls followed suit. Bare chests gleamed in the reflection of the light of the chandelier as everyone strapped on weapons. Even as we did so, those footsteps outside came closer.

Mencheres came downstairs. I hadn't seen him before this, but he'd obviously heard what was going on, because he had more weapons covering him than skin.

"To the lawn, we'll start with an exterior perimeter and fall back inside if necessary," Bones said. "Zero, you gather the humans and put them in the holding cells below, since they're the most reinforced. Feel free to use physical means to make any reluctant ones obey, especially her mother."

I would have replied with something rude, but this wasn't the time. We filed outdoors in a precise manner, setting up formation around the house. Hand signals were used once we were outside, the vampires and ghouls moving with a speed any military leader would love to command. Of course, they predated most military leaders. Practice did make perfect.

The frigid wind made me shiver. Yes, it was extremely cold, but it wouldn't kill me and hypothermia was something I didn't have to worry about. I was half vampire, after all, so my blood wouldn't know how to freeze. It didn't stop me from wishing I could be as impervious to it as my companions, though. Vampires and ghouls might not like the cold, but I was the only one whose teeth were chattering.

"All right, luv?"

Bones asked it while not taking his gaze off the trees in front of him. We were dead center in front of the house, and hopefully that wasn't prophetic.

I gritted my jaw to still it. "It'll go away when the action starts."

There was movement at my side. Tate slid next to me without a word, shouldering Spade aside.

"Leave him," Bones interjected when Spade was about to shove him back. "It's what he's good for."

Tate might have replied with something, I won't ever know. His mouth opened . . . but then the first of the mysterious figures cleared the trees and stopped his rejoinder. Bones stiffened, turning as cold and hard as any of the icicles on the roof. Spade let out a low hiss, and someone muttered something that sounded like a prayer.

"Sweet Christ," I whispered, a new freeze settling in me. "What is that?"

It was Mencheres who answered, coming up behind us and raising his voice to be heard above the thing's sudden snarl as it began to run, its mouth snapping obscenely from half-rotted lips.

"That," he replied, "is the grave."

Thirty

In older movies, zombies looked almost comical. The newer films pegged them better— the insanity of eyes bulging out and flesh hanging in rancid layers over a frame hunched from hunger. Some were more decomposed than others, bones visible in places as they staggered forward. But all of them had one thing in common; they were ravenous, and we were food.

When the first one was visible, Mencheres appeared as stunned as the rest of us were. After his cryptic statement, however, he began to curse in a manner so unlike him that it broke my attention from the oncoming horde.

"Never in all my foulest imaginings did I believe she would do such a thing," he finished with. "There will be payback for this, perhaps not by me or anyone here, but one day she will account for such a deed."

That didn't sound good. In fact, it sounded like an epitaph.

Bones shook Mencheres's shoulder with a hard tug. "We don't have time to ponder Patra's capacity for evil. These things"—a short nod to the ones only about two dozen yards away. "Can they be killed?"

Mencheres lost his glazed expression and his features hardened. He placed his hand over Bones's.

"No."

The single word was delivered without emotion. Mencheres seemed to steel himself even as he squeezed Bones's hand before dropping his own.

"They cannot be killed," he continued, unsheathing his sword with a slicing noise. "Nor do they feel any pain or even need eyes to see us. They are drawn to us by her will alone."

He strode forward with a command for everyone else to stay back. The things were only a few feet from him, moving at a loping run now. They seemed to grow more crazed by his nearness. Horrible grunts came from them.

"They have been pulled from the ground," Mencheres continued, sidestepping one with a speed it didn't have, "and they will not return to it until the spell is broken. We cannot run. Every grave within a hundred miles would empty as the dead came after us, and they would kill anything in their path."

His sword moved so fast I couldn't follow it with my gaze. In disbelief I saw the things leap at him with almost equal speed. Where the fuck did their shuffling go? Oh, *shit*!

Mencheres hacked in that same blur. Pieces of them started to fly in all directions as his blade outraced their sudden, incredible tempo. "We must hold them off and find what object she used for this spell," he went on in that same level tone. "It would have to be something of hers, perhaps carried by one of the prisoners, or planted by Rattler. If we find it and destroy it, they will die. Until then, no matter how much damage they sustain, they cannot rest."

What he meant was sickeningly illustrated as he spoke. Mother of God, even the limbs he'd severed crawled in our direction. A headless body stumbled closer, and the unattached cranium chewed with demonic intentness at Mencheres's foot until he kicked it away. Now that was scary. Still, when they were dismembered, the creatures were certainly less dangerous. Maybe there was a chance.

"Send three people back in the house to search," Mencheres called out, whirling to intercept more of the forms as they approached. "It will probably be something small, easy to disregard. Destroy it with any means possible.

"Tick Tock, Annette, Zero, go," Bones ordered with a jerk of his head, pulling out his own sword.

They darted back into the house without pause, except for Annette. I saw her stop and stare at Bones before she disappeared into the house. I stared at him as well, for the same reason. Thinking this was the last time I'd see him.

"If I thought for a moment you'd listen, it would be you going inside," he almost sighed. "Yet I know better. I love you, Kitten. There's nothing on this earth or under it that can change that."

I didn't have time to reply, but it wasn't necessary. Every fiber of me shouted it back at him even as he raised his voice and addressed the four dozen people also drawing out their swords.

"Patra unleashed death on us, mates. Let us return the gesture with our compliments!"

Bones strode forward with measured, lethal steps to meet the new wave of ghastly invaders. Four dozen against untold hundreds? I knew the odds of our survival. So did everyone who gripped a blade and advanced with him, myself included.

"We are not helpless." Bones's voice was never more controlled. If I didn't know better, I'd say it was chipper. "Many times in our lives we've been powerless, but not this night. Right now we have the power to choose the manner in which we die. If you have been a master of nothing else in all your days, you are now a master of this moment. And I for one am going to give such an answer to this insult that others will dearly regret not being by my side to see it!"

Bones finished with a roar that was taken up by every throat. We trembled in the pre-midnight air with the rage of retaliation, and suddenly I didn't feel cold. Or afraid. I'd faced death before, hell, even sought it. Now by Bones's side, I had the chance to rewrite every bad decision, each instance of cowardice, and all the years of regret. Nothing else mattered but right now. This instant, I'd become the person I'd always wanted to be. Strong. Fearless. Loyal. Someone even I could be proud of.

The first creature leapt at me and my sword flashed out to answer, my hair flying as I dodged and hacked. A green glow landed on its malformed face and I laughed, bright and savagely happy.

"See that? It's the light in my eyes, and I'm going to show you what else I've got . . ."

My first fight to the death was when I was sixteen. All I'd had was a silver cross with a thin dagger attachment, and I didn't even know if it would kill a vampire. It did, obviously, and I've been killing ever since. I'd been in hundreds of battles since that initial one, but none of them, none of them, had ever been like this.

Thank God it was dark out. The glowing green of a vampire's eyes made them distinguishable from the zombies, who continued to pour out of the woods in all directions. Ghouls were a little tougher to filter, but then there were only about ten of them here. You just didn't realize how interchangeable one figure could appear from the next when your gaze was continually splattered with blood, flesh, or flying pieces of rotted limbs. And the limbs were everywhere; disgusting parts crawling on the ground, unattached fingers squirming like leeches on your body, or whole and still adorning the monsters that kept coming from the woods.

I was in the mindless frenzy of killing, slashing out at anything that came near me. A mental numbness had set in, making me oblivious to my own injuries. My arms, shoulders, legs—every part of me had been chewed on. I wasn't even sure if I was still clothed; all I saw was red from both the rage and the blood in my eyes. That's why the matching emerald lights from my comrades was so helpful. At least when I saw them, I knew I wasn't alone. I certainly felt alone, with nothing but maddened zombies surrounding me, screams blending into a continuous white noise, and the ceaseless cleaving of my sword into the inviolable force of walking dead.

Vlad had an advantage. With enough time, he could grab hold of a zombie and burn them to pieces. They ran around like macabre torches, what was left of them, anyway. Still, it seemed he needed a solid minute of holding them to burn them into a less harmful state, which meant it wasn't the most productive method of dealing with them.

Every now and then, though, I'd catch an orange glow from the corner of my eye, hear indescribable screams, and know Vlad was still alive. Even more important was that periodically, I'd hear an English accent cresting over the sounds of death and pain, urging everyone on, taunting the creatures with gleeful scorn. Bones was still alive, too. Aside from that, I had no idea who was around me.

"Fall back, fall back!" the shout came. The thing in front of me was suddenly cleaved straight down the center into two halves. Between the falling forms there was Bones, almost unrecognizable in appearance, and I stopped my sword in midarc to avoid slashing his head off.

"Come with me," he growled. He tugged on my arm and then dropped it with a savage curse.

"Bloody fucking hell, why didn't you call for help?"

I didn't know what he meant, and arguing wasn't an option, since he yanked me to his chest with one arm and began a deranged hacking at anything near us with the other. My feet barely brushed the ground, swinging with his gait while I began to feel nauseous. Some of the haze lifted from my vision and when we entered the house and went at once down the stairs, I could see with clarity again.

Every item in the house had been smashed. I was confused, because the main fight was outside, but then it made sense. Not knowing what the mysterious object was, Annette, Tick Tock and Zero had been obliterating anything they could. There wasn't even a solid stick of furniture left, and the remaining vampires and ghouls streaked through the wreckage while holding off the hideous intruders that kept coming. This house had three underground levels and just two entrances to them. That was on the plus side. In the negative column, it also meant we had no way out.

Bones deposited me into the arms of Tate, who appeared out of the spattered forms. "Take her to the lowest level," he barked and turned away. "I have to cover our retreat."

"Bones, no!" I protested, ignored by both of them as Tate whirled and ran down the stairs. He shoved past people, muttering something that sounded like, "Your arm, your arm," as he went.

We went through a door where inside, several frightened faces stared at us. *The kids*, I realized. *They're scared. Maybe this wasn't outlined in the Be a Vampire Snack brochure.*

"Clear some space," he snapped to them, and fear from either his appearance or his tone made them quick to respond. They huddled together as Tate lowered me to the floor and withdrew a knife.

"Get off me, I have to get back out there—" I started, and then shut up. *Oh*. No wonder the two of them had given me such a look.

"Give me a little blood by mouth, if you can spare it," was what I said instead as I considered my arm. Well, what was left of it. *Always the left arm*, the dispassionate part of me mused darkly. *First burned by Max, now this. If it could talk, it would never stop bitching at me.*

It was hanging by a few stubborn ligaments, but most of it was chewed off to the bone. *Now I resemble the zombies*, it occurred to me. Some of their limbs were a dead ringer for this one.

"It'll hurt when it heals," Tate rasped, pressing a knife and my mouth to his throat. "Drink deep. I'll refill."

Normally I wouldn't have drunk from him, deeply or not, but these weren't normal circumstances. Bottom line was, I'd have to be back in fighting condition and fast, because the things outside weren't calling a time-out. With that in mind, I clamped my teeth over the puncture Tate made in his neck and sucked hard, biting to keep the wound open.

He made a noise I refused to diagnose, because I knew better. Cool blood filled my mouth and I swallowed, pulling harder, feeling shards of shooting pain erupt in my arm. His grip tightened until my upper body was glued to him, tilting his head back as I applied stronger suction. By the fourth pull my arm was in agony, but by the sixth, it had settled into a harsh tingling. At the ninth I was able to shove him back using two hands, panting as cravings for more awoke in me.

Tate's eyes were green when I looked at him, and it made me scramble back further, because his expression said they weren't lit up from battle.

I jumped to my feet, watching in amazement as the skin regrew on my limb, knitting back together like a scene from a science fiction movie.

The new blood coursing in me made me feel wilder, less human. Considering the amounts I'd no doubt lost, I was probably running on a sixty-forty mixture favoring the undead cells.

"Come on, soldier," I said. "We have things to kill."

Without a backward glance I ran up the stairs and back toward the fierce sounds of battle.

The vampires were clustered around the hall in front of the landing like an undead gauntlet. Every shrieking, unholy thing that tried to gnaw their way through them was set upon by all sides. It was holding so far, but one look told me the grim truth. This barricade wouldn't last long enough. More and more creatures kept coming.

I sprinted forward to join the fray when I collided with Annette. She was wide-eyed and frantic, almost not seeing me as she rushed to smash a figurine against the wall. When nothing happened but broken glass, she gave a raw cry of despair and turned to seek out more objects.

"Annette!" I had to shake her to get her to focus on me. "Where are Tick Tock and Zero?"

She gestured in no general direction. "Tick Tock is on the other side of the house, Zero went to Anubus to attempt to beat the answer out of him, but I saw six of those . . . things follow after him, they've broken in! I heard Zero scream, and then I went this way. Oh, Cat, I can't find it, I can't find it!"

What *it* was didn't require asking. This place was coming apart at the seams.

"Just keep at it, Annette, we'll find whatever it is. We'll hold them off—"

She shoved me. "You don't understand. It's on the news! Graves emptying, rumors of things crawling from them . . . all headed in this direction. We're in an isolated area, but not that isolated. Don't you see? Patra doesn't need all of them to kill us; very soon she'll know exactly where we are, because all the zombies are a sign pointing the way!"

Shit! Didn't it ever stop? So our situation had upgraded from awful to doomed. Surprisingly, I was more angry than anything else. That bitch didn't deserve to win. We might not be innocents, but she was far worse on many levels.

There was noise behind me, coming from the basement. Screams, God, more screams. And the sounds of crumbling structure. *This is it*, the realization came to me. *The end*. No, I couldn't stop it, but I could choose how to meet it.

With renewed determination, I held out my sword. "You keep looking, Annette, no matter what. I'll keep killing. If that bitch wants us, she can come and get us."

"To the lower rooms, mates, move!" a shout ordered. Two dozen members of what was left of our forces began to fall back. I fought my way forward, seeing Bones and Mencheres at the end of the retreating line covering the exit. Both of them spun and slashed in a dizzying display of violence that made them seem like they'd been transformed into machines. I'd always guessed that Mencheres, once stripped of his polite manners, would be frighteningly lethal. I wasn't wrong. He looked like a living nightmare.

Vlad grabbed me, forcing me backward. His hands felt hot, not cold like they should have from the freezing outside temperatures.

"Come along, they'll join us soon," he barked, propelling me with his body.

"No, I'm going up there!" I yelled, trying to wrest away.

"He's the co-leader of his line so he's where he should be," was his reply. "But you're coming with me."

His fist landed a solid whack to the top of my head. Amid the wash of sudden stars, I ducked under his arm and lurched forward, brought up short by his hold on my hair.

All at once, everything seemed to move in slow motion. Vlad pulled me back, my feet slid out from under me, and faintly, above all the other noise, I heard a vindictive, satisfied laugh.

I saw six of those things follow after him, they've broken in! Annette had said. *And I heard him scream . . .*

She'd been talking about Zero, who was on his way to Anubus's cell. But while no one had seen or heard from Zero since, it was Anubus who was chuckling maliciously now. Anubus. Unharmed though he was chained to a wall with half a dozen ravenous creatures within chomping distance. How was that possible? Only one way I could think of.

"Vlad, do you have to be touching someone to burn them?"

The question startled him so much he quit manhandling me. "I have to have touched them before, and it takes longer, since it's difficult to burn someone I'm not holding."

"Difficult," I breathed. "But not impossible?"

"No, not impossible, why?"

"It's Anubus." I raised my voice because the adrenaline began to surge. "Patra's object isn't an object at all. Don't you get it? He's the ultimate Trojan horse, and Bones nearly got killed delivering him! She meant to finish Bones off in the ambush—and then the rest of us later, since we carted Anubus back home with us. Patra knew we wouldn't kill him, who offs their most valuable hostage?"

Vlad started to smile. He released me and spread out his hands, holding them over his head. All around us chaos reigned.

"He's too far away for me to reach him before I'd be cut down, but let's see if I can save the day."

"Go on," I replied, whirling to clear the area around him. "Impress me."

His hands began to glow, not red, but blue. They lit the hall with an eerie navy-violet light. Sparks flew off his hands, showering my hair as I continued to slash at the oncoming zombies.

Someone screamed, high-pitched and agonizing. I threw a heartless grin at Vlad as I recognized the voice.

"You've got his attention, Drac."

"He's strong," Vlad replied in a strained tone. His hands were now completely engulfed in flames. "And must I remind you once more what my name is?"

"You arrogant . . ." thrust though the stomach of a snapping zombie, twisting and using all my strength to cleave him in half ". . . overpublicized . . ." wasn't going to work, it clawed at the blade, and my God, these things were tough, ". . . showy old bat . . ." Crack! There went my head into the wall. If I didn't have a split skull, I'd be amazed. "What are you waiting for? Aren't you the king of all bogeymen? The legend children fear will devour them if they don't behave?"

Two more zombies slipped past Bones and Mencheres, who were now almost back-to-back trying to stave them off.

"Come on, Vlad, live up to your reputation! If you can't burn to death *one* Egyptian vampire chained to a wall, how did you ever drive the Turks from Romania?"

There was a loud reverberating snap, like an electric transformer had blown, and then in midleap, the charging zombies fell to the floor. Out of the suddenly still forms, dirt began to appear, covering them, eroding over the creature's bodies, until nothing but piles of earth remained. *Out of the ground they were called*, I thought, *and back they went.*

"You did it," I panted, dropping my sword and running not in his direction, but the opposite one.

"Of course," I heard him reply as strong arms lifted me up and crushed me against a chest covered with gore. "I'm Vlad Tepesh, what did you expect?"

Thirty-one

For about thirty seconds I held Bones, feeling his mouth pressed to my hair, his hands gripping my back, and I was truly happy. Then there was the sound, a muffled moan, one I heard even above the other vampires' cries of exultation. One that seemed to come from my very cells, which made sense, in a weird way.

"Mom."

I dashed straight down the hall toward the back like I was being pulled by a string. Bones was close behind, but not as fast as I was, not this time. I fell to my knees when I saw her, draped across Denise's lap, my friend's hands compressing her stomach. Next to them lay a zombie, now only a pile of dirt, and my mother was as still and pale as death.

"No!"

It tore out of me even as I acted without thinking, taking one of my knives and slashing it across my wrist, tilting her head up, forcing my blood in her mouth. The blade cut right through to the bone and red liquid overflowed her lips.

She gagged once and weakly swallowed, bubbles trailing out of her mouth. I worked her jaw, forcing her to swallow again.

Denise was crying and praying at the same time. Bones pushed her to the side to crouch over my mother. He took the same knife I'd used and sliced his own wrist, holding it over her mouth, instructing me to begin chest compressions to force his blood through her body.

Blinded by tears I did, bearing down on her chest. Her heart had stopped beating right as Bones gave her his blood. Over and over I pressed on her chest while Bones blew into her mouth.

"That thing came in the room," Denise choked, several injuries on her as well. "And it just jumped on her! I tried to pull it off, but it was so strong . . . Come on, Justina, don't give up!"

Denise's shout was so loud, it took me a second to hear the soft internal thumping below my hands. Then I sat back, tears flooding my eyes, as my mother coughed.

"Filthy . . . animal . . . get away . . . from me," she rasped to Bones.

I laughed even as Bones snorted and sat back as well, pausing only to cut his palm and slap it over the slash in my wrist.

"Hallo, Justina. It appears we're still stuck with each other."

Denise laughed also, and then she wiped at her eyes and looked around.

"Where's Randy? Isn't he with you?"

My smile faded. Belatedly I realized that Randy

wasn't in the room with everyone else. Seeing my mother bleeding to death had distracted me from noticing that before. I flicked a glance at Bones, who was frowning and getting to his feet.

"Why would he be with us?" he asked Denise in a sharp tone. "Randy was supposed to stay *here*."

Denise got up now, too, her face pale. "He wanted to help find whatever it was Patra was using. He said he wouldn't leave the house. He's been gone about twenty minutes . . ."

Bones turned and strode out of the room. I went to Denise and took her hands. Even with all the blood loss I'd suffered, mine were warmer.

"You stay here," I told her. "We'll find him."

Denise's hazel eyes met mine, and the vehemence in them made me actually back up a step.

"No fucking way," she said, and shoved me to the side.

I let her go, feeling a bit woozy now that the battle adrenaline was leaving me. My mother sat up, staring at the blood and torn clothes around her abdomen where that mortal wound had been.

"Mom," I began.

"Don't worry about me," she cut me off. "Go after Denise."

I gave her a grateful look and left, moving through the ruins of the house far slower than I had before. It wasn't a minute later when I heard Denise scream, loud and piercing. That brought me to a run, despite the spots starting to dance in my vision.

Bones was kneeling on the floor of the kitchen with Denise in his arms. There was a pile of something red and dirty right next to them . . .

"Oh, Jesus," I whispered.

"Fix him!" Denise screamed, pounding on Bones's back. "Fix him, fix him, *FIX HIM!*"

But that was impossible. My mother had still been clinging to life when Bones and I gave her blood, so its healing properties had had a chance to work. Randy's body lay in pieces, parts covered by the dirt that had once been the zombie, or zombies, who'd torn him apart.

"He's gone, luv," Bones said to Denise, forcing her away from the gruesome sight of her husband. "I'm so very sorry."

I don't think Denise even heard him. She kept screaming and sobbing while her fists pummeled Bones. I went to her, uselessly trying to comfort her, even though nothing I could do would ease her pain.

Spade came in the kitchen, grim-faced, and knelt down next to us.

"Crispin, I'll take Denise out of here. You need to get Cat and the others to safety. We don't have much time."

Wordless, Bones nodded. Spade gently pried Denise from Bones's arms and carried her out of the kitchen.

Everyone still left standing was in emergency mode, rounding up the dead and the living for a speedy exit. We all had to get as far away from here as possible, before Patra came to finish us off.

Bones picked me up, and I didn't even bother to argue that I could walk. Frankly, I wasn't sure if I could. As he maneuvered through the broken items in the house, I was surprised to see one of the televisions were still on.

". . . three . . . two . . . one . . . Happy New Year!" Dick Clark announced, followed by the usual noise of partymakers, firecrackers, and the beginning of "Auld Lang Syne." It seemed impossible that so much had happened in only two hours.

My vision began to get hazy, which might have been the blood loss catching up to me, because when I blinked next, we were out on the lawn. Strewn amid the odd-colored snow and heaps of dirt were bodies. What once had been vampires and ghouls were now shriveling remains. I felt a surge of gladness to see Tate milling around, and prayed that Juan and Dave had also made it.

Ian knelt on the ground, his chestnut hair making him easily distinguishable even from behind. His shoulders shook.

Bones set me down and then took rapid steps forward. Mencheres seized him, his face grim.

"How many?" Bones asked hoarsely.

Mencheres's gaze slid to several of the piles of shriveling limbs.

"We don't know yet."

Bones knelt beside Ian. "Ian, mate, we must take them and go. None of them would care for us being slaughtered over their bodies because we didn't have the strength to leave. Patra's already taken too much tonight. We shan't let her get another thing."

Through rapidly graying vision, I saw the three of them begin to collect the remains of what used to be their friends.

Thirty-two

DAVE'S FACE WAS THE FIRST THING I SAW when my eyes opened. He smiled.

"Hello, Cat. Are you hungry? Thirsty?"

"Thirsty," I rasped, downing the water he handed me. "Where are we?"

He took the glass back. "We're in South Dakota now, while everyone regroups."

A glance to my left showed bright light peeking through the heavy drapes.

"My God, what time is it?"

"About three o'clock. You lost a shitload of blood and had to be given two transfusions. Then Bones didn't want you to wake up and start to exhaust yourself, so he gave you some of those sleeping pills Don cooked up for you. You don't remember arguing with him about it and trying to spit them out?"

Not at all. I sat up, noticing I was no longer bloody and I was also wearing a clean T-shirt.

"Don's had a hell of a time these past several hours,"

Dave went on. "He's been pulling every string he has to confiscate footage of empty graves and shuffling dead people, and overall calming the media circus this thing has generated. Thankfully, the Canadian government doesn't want its people believing in zombies, either, so they're cooperating."

I groaned. I could just imagine how Don must be going nuts trying to cover this up.

"What's his angle?"

"They're using a cover story of a small earthquake and an avalanche that emptied some of the graves, but the tabloids are still going to have a field day. At least we were in a remote area—if this had happened in a big city, there'd be no lid Don could find that would be big enough to seal this nightmare up."

"An earthquake and an avalanche? *That's* what he's saying?"

Dave shrugged. "It's the best he could do on short notice, I guess. It explains the torn-up cemeteries somewhat. Then he's also saying some of the 'zombies' were shell-shocked survivors wearing filthy clothes and wandering around in a daze. You know how it is. People don't want to think what they saw was real. The average person goes through life much happier believing nothing supernatural exists."

"Where's Denise?" Poor Randy. He wouldn't have been involved in any of this if not for me.

"She's sleeping. Spade gave her a lesser version of your tranquilizer. Right now, sleep's the best thing for her."

"Dave . . . who else didn't make it?"

His face clouded. "You know about Randy. Zero's also gone, as well as Tick Tock . . ."

He went on, and every new name slammed into me. Some of them I knew, some of them I didn't. Still, they were each an irreplaceable loss. By the time Dave was finished, more than eighteen vampires and ghouls had been listed, a staggering loss. Four more humans had also been killed, in addition to Randy. Bones must be devastated.

"Where's Bones?" I asked, swinging my legs out of bed.

"Downstairs. But first, you might want to put on a pair of pants."

I looked down, seeing what I hadn't noticed while under the covers. "Oh. Sorry, I didn't realize . . ."

He smiled faintly. "You're like my sister, don't worry about it. And because I'm your friend, I don't mind telling you . . . brush your teeth. Your breath is scary."

Taking Dave's advice, I'd brushed my teeth, washed my face, and put on more clothes. My feet were bare, since I didn't bother looking for shoes. Dave escorted me to the closed doors of the drawing room and then left.

Bones came to me and I held him for a long time. Saying "I'm sorry" was so useless a comfort that I didn't even bother.

Ian was there, too. He hadn't showered or changed clothes since the battle, and he was shirtless with dirt and other things smeared over him.

"Would have been good of you to figure out the puzzle earlier, Reaper," he bitterly stated. "Not much help getting a bright idea after half our numbers are cut down."

I blinked, unprepared for his hostility. Bones didn't have any hesitation, and he had Ian by the throat before I could even formulate a response.

"Don't you say another accusing word to her or I'll lose the very thin hold I have on my temper," he growled. "If not for her, we'd all be dead right now, or did you forget that?"

Ian's turquoise gaze was blazing emerald.

"What I haven't forgotten is why we were all dragged into this war in the first place. It was all because of her! Her injury was repairable, Crispin, but you can't do anything about our friends lying in the other room, can you? How many more lives will be needed to avenge one woman's injured pride—"

"Bones, no!"

Mencheres appeared out of nowhere, and not a moment too soon. There was a wrenching sound, a blur, and then Bones was thrown backward missing an arm. The scream I made drowned out Spade's shout as he arrived just in time to witness it.

Ian stared with stupefied amazement at the hand still clutched to his throat, the limb beginning to wither. I went to Bones, but he sidestepped me and strode right to Mencheres.

"Did you have a reason for preventing me from silencing that insult, Grandsire?"

Now my whole body tensed. If Bones and Mencheres went at it, all hell would break loose.

"You were going to tear Ian's head off," Mencheres answered. "You would have regretted it afterward, for many reasons, and I think we have already given Patra enough cause to celebrate without further reducing our numbers."

Ian appeared mildly dazed by recent events. He

shook his head as if to clear it, then stared at me and Bones with a look of vague disbelief.

"By Christ, Crispin, I don't know what got into me," he breathed. "I had no cause to rail at you like that. Forgive me, both of you."

Bones started to run a hand through his hair, stopped when he saw his limb was only half grown back, and snorted incredulously.

"Two hundred and forty-seven years I've had that arm. Didn't think to lose it while trying to rip your head off. Bugger, I have to pull myself together."

"Now more than ever we all have to pull ourselves together," Mencheres agreed.

"Yes," Bones said, eyeing him in a way that made the hairs on the back of my neck stand up. "Especially you, Grandsire, because this *must* end."

Vlad entered the room. He looked around, saw the staring contest between Bones and Mencheres, and took a seat.

"I know what you're thinking," Mencheres said with bleakness. "And I tell you, I cannot do it."

Bones was next to him in a flash. "The reality is that either you or she will be dead very soon. Whatever Patra meant to you, whatever secret dreams you've harbored of fate intervening at the last moment to make things right—you of all people know better. You told me never to doubt your visions, yet here you've lingered with the hope that you could be wrong. But you're not, so you must end this, because that is the responsibility you have to the people under your line and now also under mine."

I was confused. Mencheres didn't have Patra stuffed in a back room, to my knowledge, so how could he have the power to end this, as Bones was implying?

Vlad leaned forward, picking up on my thought. "Don't you see, Cat? When Patra had you trapped in a lethal nightmare, who knew how to break it? Last night when the zombies attacked, who knew the only way to destroy them was to destroy their homing beacon? Mencheres. So if he knows these spells well enough to know what counters them . . . then he also has the knowledge to cast one himself."

One look at Mencheres's ashen face confirmed it, and then I was right in front of him as well.

"You *have* to. She's not going to stop! Do you want to see everyone around you dead? Because that's what will happen if you don't do something."

"And could you?" Mencheres flung at me. "If this were Bones we were talking about, could you mete out death to him? Could you sentence him so easily to the grave?"

He stopped, showing more naked feeling than I'd ever seen from him, and it hit me. *He's still in love with her, even after everything she's done. Poor bastard.*

I chose my words with care. "I don't pretend to know how hard this is on you, Mencheres, and if this were Bones, it would rip me apart inside, too. But"—I paused to look straight at the man I loved—"if you ever went so far off the deep end that you'd try— and succeed—in killing those I loved, and you made it very clear through countless examples that you wouldn't stop until I and everyone I cared about were dead, then yes. I'd kill you."

Bones stared back at me and a small smile touched his mouth. "That's my girl."

Then he fixed his gaze back on Mencheres. "I can't offer you any comfort in this but one, single thing: a quick death for Patra. She doesn't deserve it, and I'd promised to treat whoever plotted against my wife to a much more prolonged, gruesome experience, but for your sake I'll amend that. If you do what you must now."

Green blazed from Mencheres's eyes, and so much power crackled off him that I flinched. "Are you threatening me?"

Bones didn't even twitch. "I'm the co-ruler of your line and I'm stating my intentions toward an enemy who has butchered our people. You need to remember whose side you're on. Can't you see Patra has been betting her life on the notion that you're incapable of that?"

Mencheres didn't say anything. Every set of eyes in the room were trained on him. Then at last he stood, reining in that angry flash of power like a bird folding up its wings.

"So be it. Last night Patra unleashed the contents of the grave on us. Tonight, we will give her back its vengeance."

Thirty-three

THE STARS WERE WINKING FROM THEIR NEW backdrop of ever-deepening navy. Mencheres was in the center of the lawn. We'd cleared the snow off the ground so the large tablecloth placed on it didn't get wet. Mencheres sat cross-legged in front of it, and I couldn't help but think that with his center positioning, the dozen or so vampires in the background behind him . . . and the bones lined up on the white linen, this looked like hell's version of the Last Supper.

None of us knew what was about to happen. After making that cryptic statement, Mencheres had simply said to be dressed for battle at sunset and then he went up to his room. I half wondered if he'd make a break for it via an upstairs window, but Bones seemed satisfied that Mencheres would keep to his promise, and here he was.

Earlier I made a call to Don to tell him something was going down tonight. Maybe with a heads-up, he'd be able to come up with a better cover story than ava-lanches and mini-earthquakes. Problem was, I couldn't tell him where this event would take place. Or what time. Or what it would consist of. Or any other help-ful details that would allow him to minimize human interaction and prevent a full-scale media fallout, he scathingly told me.

Well, I didn't have those details, so I could only relay what I knew. Don's frustration was understand-able. Here I'd warned him that for the second night in a row, the undead were going all-out with a black magic attack, but I didn't know if bodies would be crawling from their graves—or raining from the sky. Don had cause to freak, sure. Me, I had other con-cerns aside from keeping the existence of vampires a secret. I had to stay alive. So I was dressed for battle, wearing over my traditional black spandex various knives, a sword, several silver bullet–filled guns, and even some grenades.

"I don't want any of you to speak," Mencheres said in the first words he spoke himself since sitting down in front of the bones. "Not until I am finished."

And how are we supposed to know that? I thought. *When you take a bow? When the ground opens up and things crawl out from it?* A memory of those hor-rible rotting creatures flashed in my mind and I shud-dered. Ugh, if I never saw one of them again, it would be too soon.

Something prickled in the air, centering my atten-tion back on the Egyptian vampire. His head was bent, long hair hiding his expression, but through gaps in the black strands I saw his eyes were glowing green. Next to me, Bones shivered, and I darted a glance at him. He seemed fixated by Mencheres. I took his hand—and almost dropped it from the electric sizzle that met my flesh. Whatever Mencheres was doing, it was also affecting Bones. Apparently that exchange of power between the two of them still had a thread of connection left. That disturbed me, though I couldn't say why.

All at once, the bones of the people who'd been killed last night rose from the tablecloth. They hovered in the air, forming a circle around Mencheres, and the bones began swirling around him.

At first they rotated slowly, hanging as if by invisible strings, but then their speed began to pick up. They circled Mencheres, moving faster and faster, until soon it was hard to distinguish any of their pieces except the skulls, grinning morbidly with their jaws swinging in the tornadolike wind. Mencheres's hair blew all around him, and my flesh crawled with a sensation of a million invisible ants. The power pouring off him intensified to incredible degrees, until I wouldn't have been surprised to see lightning strike where he sat.

With a crack, the whirling bones imploded around him, showering Mencheres in a fine cloud of white. I gripped Bones's hand, not caring about the sear of voltage that seemed to shoot up my arm, and stared in disbelief at the powdery remains of his friends. *Dust to dust*, I thought numbly. Mencheres just blasted away all that was left of those brave men. Why? Why would he do that?

Without raising his head, Mencheres pulled a knife from his lap. Then he stabbed it straight into his heart.

I did gasp then, in openmouthed incredulity as he twisted the blade. *Must be steel, not silver*, I found myself thinking. Or he'd be as dead as the grainy remains of those men spackling him like grayish snow.

Dark blood poured from the wound, flowing as steadily as if his heart still beat. It covered the knife, his hands, and his clothes with a murky crimson liquid. Soon I wasn't even staring at that, however. I was staring with growing incomprehension as the red-smeared powdery substance that was the bones of the men who'd died began to separate, expand . . . and then form into figures.

"*Madre de Dios*," I heard Juan mutter, breaking Mencheres's edict of silence.

My own thought was less religiously charitable: *What the hell is going on?*

Before my gaze, it looked like ghosts formed, shrouding Mencheres. He was muttering something in a language I couldn't even begin to recognize, and those hazy forms kept increasing. They grew until they looked like shadows come to life, because I could still see through them, but they were three-dimensional, all right. Three-dimensional figures of opaque, naked men. One of them turned, and Bones let out a soft groan. *Randy*, I thought in shock. *That's Randy!*

More of them formed from the bone dust that coated Mencheres. He kept the knife in his chest, the wound continuing to bleed, until I wondered how he still had any juice left in him. But the more he bled, the less hazy the figures looked, until I could pick out every wraithlike person. There was Tick Tock, just a little to the side of Zero, oh God, Randy . . .

Only when all twenty-three people who'd been killed the night before stood around him did Mencheres pull the knife out and speak.

"These are not our friends. They don't recognize

any of you, and they have no memory of their former lives. They are the mindless rage that lingers in the remains of all murdered people, and I have yanked that rage from their bones and given it form. They will be drawn to their murderer with the single-minded purpose of revenge. All we have to do once I release them . . . is follow them. They will lead us right to Patra no matter where she hides."

I'd barely wrapped my mind around that before Mencheres said an unknown word and the wraiths shot up into the night like they'd been fired from ghostly cannons. Wow, were they fast. How were we supposed to follow them?

Mencheres stood, raising his arms—and I screamed. The ground was twenty feet away . . . thirty . . . fifty . . . more . . .

"We need to hurry," I heard him say amid my whipping my head around to see that every person who'd been standing on the lawn was now airborne and being hurtled through the night as if by invisible jet streams. "They will find her soon."

Patra was holed up in an abandoned hotel about eighty miles away as the crow flies. Or in this case, the undead. Bones had me grasped to him, but it wasn't out of need, since Mencheres was still pushing all of us along with an amount of power that was truly mind-boggling. In my wildest imaginings, I hadn't known it was possible for a vampire to do these things, but here we were, following on the magic carpet of Mencheres's power behind the vengeance-filled wraiths he'd raised. Later I'd ponder the significance of that. Like when I wrote my report to Don and watched him faint while reading it.

The hotel was in the middle of a city slum. From the sounds, not many people lived here. In fact, this area was probably going to be razed for new construction soon, because I caught glimpses of bulldozers and other such equipment scattered around. Mencheres brought us down about a hundred yards from the hotel. How did he know it was where Patra was? Because the wraiths flew right into it, moving through the walls like they weren't even there. Neat trick. Sure beat taking the stairs.

"You must cut through her people," he rasped to Bones, gesturing to the building. "I can't go with you. If I am killed, the wraiths will fade, and they are the only things stopping Patra from fighting against you."

They were sure doing something, I knew that. Moments after they'd disappeared into the hotel, there were the most horrible ear-splitting screams.

"Why don't you just kill her yourself?" I blurted. "If you can raise vengeful spirits and levitate two dozen people almost eighty miles, she should be a piece of cake."

Mencheres seemed to fall onto the sidewalk. "I can't," he whispered. "Even now, I can't."

A brief surge of pity filled me before I squelched it. He might still love Patra, but she didn't return the sentiment, and we'd all be dead unless that woman was in the ground.

Bones gave him a cold, quick glance. "I'll keep my promise. We'll get you when it's over. Juan, Dave, you stay with him. Make sure no one comes near."

Juan started to protest being left behind, but a warning glare cut him off. Then Bones cracked his knuckles and faced the hotel.

"All right, mates. Let's end this."

Patra might have had several guards around the perimeter of the hotel. She might have had some in windows, on the roof, in the basement, and manning the entrance. But if nothing else, having twenty-three pissed-off wraiths suddenly swarm the hotel made for a hell of a distraction. In addition to Patra's ceaseless screaming—what were they *doing* to her?—there were the scrambling sounds of multiple people running up the stairs, new shouts, an eruption of gunfire, and several odd popping noises. I cast a look at Bones and thought, *Huh?* The rage-wrought specters weren't even solid, what could they be doing that would make it sound like World War Three in there?

Bones shrugged. "One way to find out."

Once we reached the building's entrance, whatever guards had been stationed there were gone. Spade frowned, shaking his head. *Trap*, he was saying. I took four grenades from my belt, pulled the pins, and then chucked them inside. Second later, glass shattered and the building shook as they detonated. Whoever might have been waiting for us wasn't there now.

We rushed in, the vampires fanning out to the sides. Bones and I kept low but raced forward. Those screams and awful noises from several floors up got louder. Finally we saw about a dozen vampires burst through an entryway under what I supposed was the grand staircase. They went down in a hail of silver before they even had a chance to back up.

"Where is everyone?" I said low to Bones. Aside from that paltry dozen, the downstairs seemed shockingly vacant.

Bones cocked his head. "There are more upstairs that I can hear. Something's got them in shambles. It must be the wraiths, but I can't imagine how."

I agreed it sounded like a Chinese fire drill upstairs. People were screaming, footsteps were thundering up and back, and there were more of those popping noises that were like nothing I'd heard before them. Whatever was going on, Patra was still alive. She was the one screaming the loudest.

Bones held out three fingers, indicating the group was to split up. Eight of us would take the stairs, another eight would climb the exterior of the building, and the remaining eight would go up the elevator shafts. It sounded like the most activity was about nine floors up, near the top of the building, so that's where we were headed.

We were on the third floor when a small group of vampires came darting down the stairs. They had blood covering them, their clothes were ripped—and they barely even looked in our direction. But that didn't stop me from unloading my M-16 with silver-bullet ammunition into them. They collapsed, their hearts shredded from the barrage of silver from my gun and the men unleashing their own weapons by my side. Sure, knives were my favorite, but this was easier when it came to distance killing.

There was more scrambling on the floor above us. Something was causing an all-out panic. Surely it couldn't just be the sight of the wraiths? I mean, yeah, they were scary-looking, but this wasn't a kids' slumber party they were crashing. This was the stronghold of a Master vampire who'd been around when Jesus walked the earth. You'd think the undead would be a little harder to rattle.

"This is almost too easy," Ian whispered, echoing my thoughts.

Vlad shot him a sardonic glance. "Never underestimate Patra's ability to make a grand entrance."

"Stay sharp," Bones said. "Whatever's going on, the shank of it is taking place up there. Let's join the party."

There were two more sets of vampires on our way up the stairs. They were each running as if from hell itself, which made it more of a slaughter than a fight to take them down. The closer we got, the more frenzied the commotion sounded above us. Finally we reached the floor where the noise was the loudest, and followed those horrible screams to the room they were coming from.

There was no guard at the door, and it was open. Vlad sent a ball of flame ahead of us, but it didn't prove to be necessary. We entered the room without anyone jumping out at us, and once inside, I stopped and stared.

Patra, far from the elegant, imposing figure I'd seen before, was writhing on the ground. Blood came from her nose, mouth, eyes, and various parts of her body. All around her—God, all *through* her—the wraiths converged. They coiled around her body like gray snakes, whipping her about, diving straight into her only to come out the other side and do it all over again. She kept screaming for help, in a number of languages, it sounded like.

Even as we watched, a wild-eyed vampire, who couldn't have been older than fifteen when he was changed, was flung away from her with both arms missing. The wraith nearest to him—was that Zero?—dove into his chest until it disappeared entirely. The vampire screamed, and then there was a pop and he came apart. His head, legs, and torso went in different directions. The wraith appeared out of the wreckage of his body, hovered for a second, and then returned to Patra until he was indistinguishable from the other blurring gray forms encasing her.

All around us were the bodies of her fallen guards. There were scores of them, and they looked like they'd been similarly blasted from the inside out. Pieces of them, their clothing and weapons were scattered everywhere. Those lethal shadows who'd done this amazing amount of carnage ignored us and continued to pitilessly torment Patra.

She was contorted in agony, her skin bubbling up each time one of them drove in and out of her. I was certain her insides had to be pureed from this. Seeing what they'd done to her guards let me know they could have killed her if they'd wanted to. The fact that she was still alive said their idea of vengeance was much more sinister than mere death.

Bones held his hand out. "Everyone stay back," he said, and gripped his knife.

I cast a frantic look at the decimated guards. "If you go near her, those wraiths will rip you to pieces!"

He brushed my face. "Not me. Don't you see? Mencheres knew it would come to this. He saw it. That's why he chose me to share his power with. It still connects us, so I'm the only person they won't harm. I can feel them . . . and as they can't hurt him, they can't hurt me."

He dropped his hand and walked toward Patra. I don't think she was even aware of him. She didn't seem to be aware of anything even though her eyes were open. Blood continued to streak from her as she was besieged by the merciless, tireless remains of the men she'd murdered from her spell last night.

One of the grayish figures rose from her and streaked to Bones when he came within a dozen feet. I started forward, but the whiplash of his voice stopped me.

"Stay back!"

I wasn't the only one who paused. So did the thing, who I saw with pained recognition was Tick Tock. Or it used to be. All that was left of him now was a rage-filled shadow. But he froze, hovering where he was even though he was quivering with what I guessed to be a conflicting desire to attack.

Bones kept coming forward. I alternately gripped my knives and let them go in frustration—not much good they could do against pissed-off phantoms! The other wraiths soon slowed their assault on Patra to glare in Bones's direction. He held out a hand to them in much the same way he'd done moments ago to us.

"Stay. Back."

Bones growled the words, and I felt the power roll off him with each syllable. The wraiths responded by retreating with each forward step he took. Soon they weren't touching Patra, but were poised in crouching threat on the ground just beyond where she lay.

After a few seconds, Patra quit her frenzied thrashing, and the countless welts on her began to heal. Her eyes, those big, lovely dark orbs, lost some of their mindless panic—and then widened as she saw who was now standing over her.

"You're dead!" Patra exclaimed, as if saying it would make it real. She began to edge away from him, stopped when she saw that she was inching closer to the silently snarling wraiths with that motion, and then looked around for help.

"No, luv," Bones said with quiet grimness. "You are."

I saw realization grow on her face as her gaze took in the bodies of her fallen guards, the rest of us standing in the doorway with numerous weapons at the ready, and the wraiths forming an impenetrable barrier behind her. If ever a person was trapped, it was her, and she knew it. Patra threw her head back and let out a cry of rage.

"Damn you, Mencheres! Do you have no mercy?"

I marveled at her nerve. After all she'd done, she truly expected Mencheres to step in and save her? Knowing full well she'd just try to kill him as soon as he did?

Bones caught her when she attempted to scramble away. She yanked back, trying to wrestle the knife from his hand . . . and that's when Mencheres shouldered past Spade.

For a split second, Patra froze. Her gaze—pleading, desperate—met his. A glance showed his face was streaked with colored tears. I tensed, wondering if we'd have to jump on him en masse to prevent him from interfering, when he bowed his head.

"Forgive me," he whispered.

Bones rammed his knife through Patra's chest, giving it a sharp twist that stilled her. Her eyes were still fixed on Mencheres, an expression of pained disbelief stamped on her face. Then, as inevitable as time itself, her features began to tighten. Her skin lost that lustrous honey shine, and when Bones dropped her to the floor, she was already starting to wither.

Behind her body, an invisible wind blew. The twenty-three wraiths slowly disintegrated into the breeze until there was nothing left of them but a faint gray dusting on the ground. Bones let out a long sigh.

"Perhaps now you can rest in peace, my friends. Someday, I shall see you again."

Epilogue

WE BURIED RANDY A WEEK LATER. DON falsified documents to make it appear that Randy had been the victim of a tragic car accident. One that had necessitated a closed coffin. Denise was staying with Bones and me, at my insistence. She blamed herself for not forcing Randy to stay with her instead of leaving that room to help us. I tried to comfort her, but in reality, I was helpless. There was nothing I could do but be there for her. I couldn't do much, but I could do that.

Mencheres buried Patra himself. Where, I didn't know. Bones didn't, either, and he didn't care. She was dead, that was enough for him.

It was enough for the remainder of her people as well. Some sought refuge under other Masters' lines. Some struck out on their own, and some even contacted Bones to throw themselves on his mercy. Depending on their place in her hierarchy, he granted it.

After all, Patra had been around for a long time, and killing every remaining person under her line would have been mass murder on an epic scale.

A few were underlings who'd followed her with no choice, so for them, Bones negotiated truces. They gave him the details on her fortune, and he gave them the right to live without looking over their shoulders. Those higher in Patra's rule, however, Bones didn't negotiate with. No, he used some of Patra's staggering wealth to offer bounties on them. Mercenaries were crawling out of the proverbial woodwork to hunt them down with the prices they had on their heads.

We hadn't seen Mencheres since the night he'd gathered Patra's body and left. That had been over two months ago. He kept in touch by phone, but he was holed up somewhere. Bones didn't press him, though he told me he couldn't understand what on earth had made Mencheres love Patra to begin with, let alone after everything she'd done. I didn't understand, either, but love had no sense sometimes. Pondering the why of it was futile.

So far there had been no repercussions for the forbidden magic Mencheres unleashed. Some notable Master vampires had grumbled, but since Patra had pulled two no-nos to our one, there weren't many who wanted to do anything about it. Or they were afraid of Mencheres, since he was one of the few people who was both old enough to know those spells—and strong enough to work them. Maybe they were concerned they'd be next. I knew I was pretty glad to be on Mencheres's good side, after seeing all I had. The idea that one day Bones might be able to wield similar power bothered me. Some things shouldn't be possible, and it was scary to know they were.

But for now, I wasn't going to worry about it. I had the man I loved by my side, and my best friend to help through her grief. The future would have to worry about itself.

Acknowledgments

I have to thank God first. No one else has the patience to listen to so many of my fears, gripes, or countless ideas—at least, not without charging me therapy bills.

Next, sincerest thanks to my editor, Erika Tsang, for keeping me on track with my stories, and going above and beyond with her support and enthusiasm.

The saying, "it takes a village," should apply to books as well, because many thanks are due to Thomas Egner, for yet another gorgeous cover; Buzzy Porter, for helping get the word out on my books; Carrie Feron, Liate Stehlik, Esi Sogah, Karen Davy, and the rest of the dedicated team at Avon Books/HarperCollins, for more things than I'm probably even aware of.

Thanks to Melissa Marr, Ilona Andrews, and Tage Shokker, for your invaluable early feedback on how to make this story better. Also many thanks are due to Tage Shokker, Erin Horn, and Marcy Funderburk, for all your hard work on my fan site. You ladies are awesome!

To the Night Huntress fans, your support and excitement for this series have been unbelievable. Thank you all so much! I couldn't do any of this without you.

Thanks to my husband, parents, and family. You keep me sane enough to write and crazy enough to come up with new things to write about. (Just kidding! Maybe.) Thanks also again to Melissa Marr, because winding roads are best traveled with friends.

Jeaniene Frost lives with her husband and their very spoiled dog in Florida. Although not a vampire herself, she confesses to having pale skin, wearing a lot of black, and sleeping in late whenever possible. And while she can't see ghosts, she loves to walk through old cemeteries. Jeaniene also loves poetry and animals, but fears children and hates to cook. She is currently at work on her next Urban Fantasy novel.

To learn more about Jeaniene, please visit her website at www.jeanienefrost.com